BEFORE I KNEW

THE FINGER LAKES SERIES

LAURIE GIFFORD ADAMS

Before I Knew

Copyright © 2016, Laurie Gifford Adams
First Edition

ISBN: 978-0-9904647-2-3 (print version)
ISBN: 978-0-9904647-3-0 (e-book)

This is a work of fiction. All of the characters, names, incidents, organizations, and dialogue in this novel are either the products of the author's imagination or are used fictitiously. Because of the dynamic nature of the Internet, any Web addresses or links contained in this book may have changed since publication and may no longer be valid. The views expressed in this work are solely those of the author and do not necessarily reflect the views of the publisher, and the publisher hereby disclaims any responsibility for them.

Windswept Publishing
4590 State Route 247
Stanley, New York 14561
windsweptpublishing@gmail.com

Printed in the United States of America
Windswept Publishing 6
12/10/2016

Cover Design and Interior format by The Killion Group
http://thekilliongroupinc.com

OTHER BOOKS BY
LAURIE GIFFORD ADAMS

FINDING ATTICUS

OVER THE EDGE

www.RUinDanger.net
(co-written with Scott Driscoll - An Internet and technology
safety guide)

DEDICATION

To all veterans and active duty servicemen and women who have put their lives on the line to preserve the freedoms citizens of the United States of America enjoy.

AND

To all dogs - service, assistant, working, or family pets - for changing and brightening our lives.

Mollie

Jax

Atticus

Finnegan

Some Non-profit groups that pair veterans with service dogs:

K9s For Warriors: www.k9sforwarriors.org/
Pets for Patriots: petsforpatriots.org
TADSAW (Train a Dog, Save a Warrior): Tadsaw.org
America's Vetdogs: vetdogs.org

To learn more about PTSD that affects veterans, visit:
http://www.ptsd.va.gov/apps/AboutFace/Index.html

For more information about the non-profit organization that helps with renovations and building homes for veterans who have earned Purple Hearts, visit:
Purple Heart Homes: https://www.purplehearthomesusa.org/

Thank you to the following people who contributed in some way to the completion of this book:
Jim Adams, Carrie Beth and Nick Adams
Laurie Herman Angel, Mary Buckham, Joan Burr, Dorothy Callahan (Critique Partner), Pat Coglianese, Sharlene Colton, John Frink, Holly Gustafson, Lorraine Lander (Critique Partner), Judy Lewis-Meyers, Purple Heart Homes, Liz Reeve, Emily Robbins - Cover Model, Chris Tolbert and the "Vet", Amanda Wright,
K.C. Alumna, Class of '64

Please stop by and leave me a message:

www.lauriegiffordadams.com
Facebook: Laurie Gifford Adams – Author
Twitter: Laurie G Adams

PROLOGUE

Melissa shoved the gun cartridges as far down behind the couch cushions as she could. Her fingers shook as the tips hit a matchbox car and some other plastic toy she couldn't identify. Even if Drew yanked the cushions from the couch, he probably wouldn't search down into the seams. Besides, if this was like the last few times, it was bombs he was looking for, not bullets.

Then something shattered in the den, and she jerked her head up. Was that the glass of the locked gun case? She shuddered and yanked her hands out of the couch, using her knees to jam the cushions back into place. In her heart she knew he'd never hurt her or their kids – at least not on purpose.

The house went eerily silent. She froze and angled her head to listen for him. Was she overreacting?

No. Not when it came to keeping their children safe. This was one of the times when he became a stranger in their home. When he was lost in a flashback to the war zone in Iraq, she never knew what or who he really saw through his glazed eyes. They weren't the kind, loving, warm eyes she'd fallen in love with six years before. They were the war-hardened eyes that had seen more atrocity than anyone should ever have to experience.

It was Drew's first Fourth of July since he'd come home from the military hospital. Their neighbors all knew what he'd been through, how sudden loud noises could affect him. One time it had been a lawn mower backfiring that had set him off. Compared to this, that episode was minor. That time he'd grabbed her at the waist and dropped them both to the kitchen floor, his body covering hers.

But another time, when a transformer down the street had blown, he'd nearly destroyed everything in their backyard shed because he was convinced it had been a bomb and that there were more planted in the neighborhood.

This time was the worst. The continuous celebratory explosions were coming from a nearby neighborhood, leaving Drew's mind no chance to recover and snap out of the flashback.

She crouched next to the couch, using what little light shone into their dark house from the streetlight to help her maneuver around the coffee table, lamp, and chair on her way to the babies' bedrooms. The muted light sliced a narrow path partway down the hall. Once she hit the dark area, she ran her hands along the wall to guide her. Her fingers skated across the door of each room along the way. First, on the right, the master bedroom. Next was the bathroom. A quick angle to the left and she was at Alex's open bedroom door.

She scurried across the few feet of plush carpet to the crib and reached in, lifting out the almost two-year-old, blanket and all. Alex whimpered and stretched, then curled his warm, pliable body against Melissa's chest, his head resting on his mother's shoulder. His thumb slid from inside the blanket, and he slipped it into his mouth. The gentle suckling sounds contrasted with the pounding of Melissa's heart.

She glanced toward the door and swallowed against the thickness of her tongue. Now to get down the hall to Savannah's room. The four-year-old would be harder to move, because she typically woke up talking.

A large firework exploded somewhere down the street. Seconds later, the den door slammed on the other side of their ranch-style home. Melissa lunged behind Alex's bedroom door and flattened herself against the wall. Holding her breath, she strained to hear some hint of Drew's location. His Marine Corps training had taught him stealth, so moving around silently in the dark was second nature.

Pow! Pow! Pow!

Another round of firecrackers shattered the silence.

Melissa squeezed Alex tighter, fear filling every fiber of her being. Would Drew snap, mistake them for the enemy, if he discovered them hiding?

A soft thud against the wooden floor down the hall sent panic careening through her. Was that Drew? What was he doing? The skin at the back of her neck prickled.

Peering through the crack in the door, at first she saw only the same finger-like stream of silver light she'd used to help guide her partway down the hall minutes before. Then, she caught a glimpse of Drew crawling on his belly toward their bedroom. A few feet away, then suddenly he rolled to his side.

And, she lost sight and sound of him.

She stiffened. Saliva filled her mouth, but she fought the urge to swallow. The slightest noise could give away their location. Pressing Alex's cheek into her shoulder, she hoped to muffle the soft thumb-sucking sound.

The tap of metal against wood caught her attention. Drew was getting closer. She pressed her lips to her son's hair and prayed. Her throat muscles tightened, making it hard to catch her breath.

And, the tapping stopped. The master bedroom door let out a low groan, indicating it was being opened very slowly. If he went in there, maybe she could get down the hall and into Savannah's room. Then, they could escape. Not forever, but until Drew was back to himself again.

Although it was only a matter of a few seconds, the wait seemed like hours. The only clues to his whereabouts and activity was an occasional scraping of metal against wood. Melissa squeezed her eyes closed in order to make her hearing acute. Every sound mattered.

Then, without warning, all hell broke loose. Drew let out a war cry and slammed the bedroom door open the rest of the way. Melissa pictured him on his feet as the door banged, and he began swearing and shouting at an unseen enemy. The bedroom door banged, and when he yelled again, she realized he had closed himself inside.

She took advantage of that moment of pandemonium and dashed out of Alex's room and down the hall to Savannah's. Once inside, she pushed the door closed, afraid the yelling from the other room would frighten the children. She laid Alex on the end of Savannah's bed, and he rolled to his side and curled into the fetal position, still sucking his thumb. Contentment in the midst of chaos. What she wouldn't give to feel that secure and be so oblivious.

Glancing around the room, she looked for a way to protect them if it became necessary. The night light provided enough illumination for Melissa to scan the room and form a quick plan. She pressed her shoulder to her daughter's dresser, used the rush of adrenaline to her advantage, and pushed the dresser along the carpet and against the door. As strong as Drew was, it would only keep him out for so long. She prayed it would be long enough.

"Savannah," she whispered against the child's ear as she shook her shoulder. "Come on, honey, wake up."

Savannah rolled toward her, clutching her Winnie-the-Pooh bear against her chest.

"Mama?" She blinked several times, then rubbed her fist against her eyes.

"Savannah, we have to go visit Auntie Nicole. I need you to get out of bed."

"I'm sleepy." She started to roll away from Melissa.

Glass broke in the bedroom down the hall. Drew's yelling intensified.

Fear drove her, and she yanked the four-year-old from the bed, immediately ashamed of her forcefulness.

"Savannah, we have to hurry. Come on." The child stumbled and wobbled, but Melissa urged her toward the window, opened it and the screen. "I'm going to help you climb out the window; then I'll come with Alex."

She lifted Savannah, but the child squirmed and kicked her legs against the sill.

"No! I don't wanna go out the window."

There was no time to argue or try to reason with a child. Melissa grabbed hold of Savannah's flailing legs and pushed her, feet first, through the opening. Once through, she let Savannah slide through her arms until she only held her by her wrists. It pulled every muscle in her hips and back to bend over and hold her until she was safely on the ground, but finally she landed.

"Stay right there," Melissa ordered in a raspy voice. She scooped Alex from the bed and struggled to work her way through the window without banging the baby's head.

"It's nighttime," Savannah protested as Melissa fell from the window and onto her knees.

"That's okay. It's an adventure, and we're going to surprise Auntie. Come on." She took hold of the child's hand and nearly dragged her along next to the house, thankful to hear less of Drew's chaos. At the side of the garage, she let go of Savannah's hand and shifted Alex to her hip so she could get her keys out of her bathrobe pocket. They jangled in her shaking hands, but thanks to the little rubber piece identifying the key to the garage, she was able to unlock the door so they could slip inside.

She went to the back, passenger side of the car and worked quickly to secure Alex in his car seat while Savannah climbed past her and into her own. After checking to make sure she'd secured all of his buckles, Melissa quietly closed the back door and returned to the driver's side, opened the door and slid into her seat.

"Savannah, are you all buckled?"

"Uh-huh."

With her eyes fixed on the door leading into the house from the garage, Melissa fumbled with the car key, jabbing at the ignition. Finally she found her mark and started the car at the same time that she pressed the button to open the big garage door. She put the car in reverse, ready to move as soon as the door was clear.

The steering wheel was hot under her tight grip as she alternated between watching the house door in front of her and the rising garage door through her rearview mirror. The garage door was almost up when the door to the house flew open, and Drew leaped through the opening, a rifle dangling from his hand.

"Oh, God, please help us!" Melissa screamed.

She slammed her foot onto the accelerator. The tires squealed as the car lurched out, the garage door scraping the car's roof. Alex suddenly came to life in the back seat and screeched in terror. Once the car was in the street, Melissa threw it in drive and again stomped on the accelerator. She kept her eyes straight ahead as she fumbled in her housecoat pocket for her cell phone. Her entire body shook so hard that she had trouble keeping a grip on the steering wheel or the phone.

Finally, she held the phone up to glance at the lighted keypad. She pressed the speed dial number for Nicole, and then the speaker key.

Her sister sounded groggy when she answered. "Hello."

"Nic, Drew's having another flashback. I think the fireworks set him off." Melissa tried to keep the panic from her voice, but there was no hiding the truth. This was the worst episode Drew had ever had, and she was terrified. "Can the kids and I stay there tonight?"

Her composure crumbled under the tension, and she gasped before sobs exploded from her. Tears clouded her vision. She blinked fast, trying to clear it.

"Lis, of course you can come here. Are you okay? No one's hurt?"

Melissa continued, her foot still heavy on the gas pedal. "He'd never hurt us, Nicki. I kn-know tomorrow this-this will all be better. Drew wi-will be himself again. I love him, Nic. He-he loves us. He doesn't kn-know what he's doing. This stupid war ruined him." Melissa slammed her hand against the steering wheel, helplessness washing through her.

"Melissa," Nicole said louder, "this has to stop."

"Nicole, I de-deserted Drew tonight when he needed me most. I r-ran instead of st-staying by his side."

"This isn't your fault, Lis. You shouldn't have to live in fear like this."

"But it's not always like this. I should g-go back. H-help him." There was little traffic to worry about, so she *could* do a U-turn in the intersection right now. Maybe if he saw them come back, he'd snap out of his hallucination.

Nicole's voice overrode Melissa's thoughts. "No! Your children are your first priority. Bring them here. They can stay with us. We'll call an ambulance for Drew. Then, you can go back to help him when there are others there. Max will go with you. Okay?"

"I don't want this to be —"

"Mommy," Savannah interrupted, "Alex is gettin' outta his carseat, again."

"What?" Melissa dropped the phone in her lap and shoved the rearview mirror over so she could see Alex, but it was too dark.

She jabbed at the control button for the overhead light, and the car's interior brightened. She shifted to look over her shoulder. Alex had somehow managed to unlatch one of the buckles of his harness and squirm part way out of his seat.

"Alex, no!"

Melissa held the steering wheel with her left hand and reached across to the back seat to take hold of Alex's leg to pull him back down into his seat. He pulled against her, and Melissa twisted more to get a firmer grip. The car jerked to the right, and she looked up in time to see the vehicle heading straight for a utility pole.

She gasped, released Alex's leg, and threw both hands back on the steering wheel as she slammed her foot onto the brake. Despite her best efforts to regain control, the car skidded sideways, across the road, and into a tree, crumpling the front driver's side of the car.

Her body was pinned by the steering wheel and the underside of the dash board. She couldn't move her head. Her eyes drifted shut. No matter how hard she tried, she couldn't open them. She couldn't check on her babies, but their cries told her they were alive.

A haze slid like a veil across her mind, and Savannah and Alex's cries started to fade — like they were going down a tunnel. She tried to call out for them, but only gurgling came from her throat.

Then there was silence, and the haze turned black.

CHAPTER 1

OMG I think I found him

My fingers shook so much I was surprised I hadn't hit the wrong letters on the keypad and texted something obscene to my best friend.

bout time she texted back.

I set the phone down and leaned back in my chair to stare at the newspaper story and picture I'd pulled up on my laptop. Yeah, about time!

Drew McAuliffe.

More than a year of Google searches had convinced me that it wasn't as unique a name as I thought. But finally, this time, I'd come up with a credible hit. I used the magnifier feature to expand the photo. Add twenty-some years to my fourteen-year old brother, Alex, and I could imagine he'd look exactly like this guy sitting on the back of a Keuka Shores firetruck. A pair of metal crutches leaned against the bumper next to him. A headline over the picture read: *Child Safe Thanks to Hero.*

Finding our father had been my goal for over a year, and my heart fluttered at the possibility of my success. The practical side of me wanted to click out of the story. Pretend I hadn't found it. Make sure the status quo wasn't shaken. Unlike my younger brother, risk-taking had never been my thing. But, I couldn't deny the twinge of curiosity that danced in my mind. Could this Drew McAuliffe be our father?

Leaning back in my chair, I let my mind wander. Savannah Nicole McAuliffe. That would have been my name before our aunt and uncle adopted us when I was four and Alex, two.

What would our life have been like if our mother hadn't died in that car accident? I'd never know. That was way in the past.

My attention slid to the strings of ribbons along the wall next to the door. I'd counted 128 one night when I sat at my desk trying to write a paper for history class. I shifted my gaze to the shelves holding nine trophies. All prizes I'd won in horse shows over the last three years.

This was my present. My plan to buy Lacey to take to college with me for the equestrian team - that was my future.

Would finding our father change life as we knew it now? Would it affect my plans for the future?

My mind wandered to the ninth grade science project that had started my quest to find our father. Because we had been adopted by our mother's sister, it was easy to gather information about my maternal side of the family. But, it was also my aunt's overreaction to my questions about our biological father that had piqued my curiosity to the point of obsession. What was it that she didn't want us to know?

A shudder rippled through me, and I was drawn back to the picture on the screen. Maybe I was so eager to find our father that I was exaggerating what I thought I saw. I needed Alex's opinion.

Even though I knew he was somewhere in the house, I texted him to avoid making Mom and Dad suspicious if they were home.

my room pronto

busy he responded.

I could envision his "busy". Some kind of video game. Probably Minecraft.

pause it!!! I jammed my thumb on the exclamation point, even though the intensity wouldn't translate to the text.

While I waited for him to show up — if he showed up — I put my hand against the screen to look at different sections of Drew McAuliffe's face. His expression was serious, but the shape of his mouth matched Alex's. His eyes were the same shape. The hair. Yup, even the same cowlick.

The door banged open behind me, and I threw my hand over my heart and whirled my chair around.

"You're gonna give me a heart attack. Close the door," I ordered.

He frowned, but did as I said, even though the way he shoved the door closed screamed bratty little brother.

"This better be good," he growled.

The tone didn't surprise me. When he played a video game, he got lost in it. I'm sure he didn't like me pulling him back to the real world.

"Depends on what you think of something I'm going to show you." I swiveled back toward the computer and maximized the screen. The news story and picture showed again. I pointed toward the picture. "Look at this."

"So? What about it?" he asked.

I tapped on the man in the picture. "Look really close at the face. Anything look *familiar*?" I drew out the word to emphasize the importance.

Alex leaned over my shoulder to get closer to the screen. I knew when he saw what I was talking about, because he straightened like someone had punched him under his chin.

"Holy shi-"

I backhanded him in the stomach to stop him from completing the swear. We didn't need to draw Mom's attention, and lately it was like she had antenna that picked up on Alex's exploration with openly swearing. Not only was he a risk-taker, he was also the rule-breaker kid.

My opposite.

He stepped around me and leaned onto his knuckles on my desk. "You think that's him, don't you?"

"Who?" I played dumb. I wanted to hear Alex say it out loud.

He glanced over his shoulder toward the door then whispered, "You think that's our father?"

I nodded.

"I look like him, don't I?" He fixed his attention on the screen. "Holy-" He broke off and pushed his fingers through his hair as he pivoted.

"Kind of spooky, isn't it?" I snagged a pad of note paper and a pen from the top drawer of my desk, then used the magnifier button to make the picture bigger.

It was no secret that our father was alive — at least as far as anyone knew, but we'd always been told that he had left us here with our mother's only sister and gone to Texas. Was it possible he had been in Keuka Shores, less than an hour away from us, our entire lives?

"What are you looking for?"

"Looking for clues in the article. If he's our father, I want to know about him." I reached for the mouse and started clicking on icons. "I want to contact him."

Alex laughed. "You're going to call up some stranger dude and say, 'Hey, I think you're my father. Wanna hang out?'"

"You're being a jerk." I didn't raise my voice, didn't even look at him. "Of course not. I'm going to try to find out where he lives."

Alex sat on the edge of my desk and folded his arms across his chest like he was a Mr. Know-it-all. "And then what? You'll ask Mom and Dad to take you to meet him? They'll freak."

I tapped on my wallet. "How convenient. My license showed up in the mail yesterday. So, I'll go over to Keuka Shores and check things out without anyone knowing about it."

He pushed away from the edge of the desk. "Now you're talkin'. Let's go."

I held up my hand to stop him. "Hold on, I'm not going now. Besides, you know Mom's rule — no one can ride alone with me for three months."

"He could move before then."

Tipping my head, I gave him my best 'get real' look. "That's highly unlikely." I thought for a moment, then had an idea. "I don't have Equestrian Team practice on Saturday, but I'll see if I can borrow the van, and say I want to go and groom Lacey. At least Keuka Shores is in the same direction as the barn."

"Look, if you're going to lie about where you're going —"

"I'm not lying," I interrupted. "I *will* go and groom Lacey. I'll just take a little detour."

"But I want to go with–"

I cut him off.

"No, I go alone." I leaned back in my chair and gripped the hard plastic curved arms. "Let me check it out first. Then, and only then, we'll decide if we want to have actual contact with him." I leaned forward in my chair and lowered my voice more. "We don't know anything about him. He could be a total creep."

Alex quirked an eyebrow. "Or, he could be the coolest guy on earth."

"Well, I'll try to find out. Don't say anything to Mom and Dad. They'd be pretty ticked to know I've even been looking for him."

He held up his fingers like he was giving the scout's honor pledge. "I'll do a search for a phone number or address."

I shrugged. "Don't need it. I'll go right to the Keuka Shores firehouse. Maybe he'll be there. And, if not, they'll know where this guy lives. "

Alex fist pumped the air. "You're brilliant!"

I shrugged. "Glad you finally admit it."

He dropped his shoulders, and groaned, "Oh, man." He started for the door then turned back toward me. "If after you see him, you think it's him, then I want to meet him, too."

"I'm not planning to meet him." I hesitated, then added, "At least not yet. The newspaper might call him a hero, but if he was responsible for our mother's death, who knows what he's really like."

Alex nodded. "But, you know, it's kind of hard to believe that someone who would run into a fire and save a kid is really as dangerous as Mom has always said."

"That was twelve years ago. Maybe he's changed," I said. And I realized deep down I didn't want that part of our family's history to be true.

"Maybe," Alex responded. "I'm on pause. See ya."

"Remember, you don't spill the beans to anyone. If Mom knew I'd even been searching — well, if this is him — "I chewed my lower lip as I considered her reaction. It wouldn't be pretty.

He scowled. "Savannah, I'm not five."

"I know. Sorry. This all makes me jumpy."

When he left, he shut the door gently as if even his leaving had to be kept a secret. I picked up my cell phone to return the text to my friend.

i'm gonna go find the guy

I set the phone next to the keyboard and hit print on the article. The whir of the printer as it spit out the evidence hummed along every nerve in my body. I snatched the paper from the tray and cut out the picture. I folded it before opening my wallet to hide it behind the part holding my license.

Guilt sent a razor sharp pain through my chest. I never imagined my first taste of real freedom with my license would take me down this road.

And the worst part was, I had no way of knowing if what I would find at the end of the road was even worth the risk.

It hadn't taken much to convince Mom and Dad to let me borrow the mini-van. After four years of driving me to Breezy Acres Stables a few times a week, they were happy they didn't have to be the "taxi driver".

There were no highways between our town and Keuka Shores. I followed Route 14 north along Seneca Lake because there was something calming about the view. The morning sun hung slightly above the hills, casting a sparkling glow across the rippling water. My nerves were jittery, and I couldn't shake the feeling that this was a mistake. I didn't plan on doing anything more than maybe getting a look at this guy, maybe ask some questions at the firehouse and then that would be it. No face-to-face meeting. Nothing like that.

Our aunt had always implied that our father had been responsible for our mother's death, and then he had abandoned Alex and me. I didn't remember him or our life as a family. I didn't remember our mom, which sometimes made me sad. We had photos, but they were of only her with us, posing. Nothing to trigger any kind of memory. And that hazy veil of our past life haunted me.

I was so caught up in my daydream that I almost missed the road that branched off to take me to the town. At the last second, I tromped on the brake and slammed up the lever for the signal light. Focus. I needed to focus.

Trees lined both sides of the street as I came into town. Keuka Shores was actually on the shore of Keuka Lake, right smack in the middle of all of the Finger Lakes of New York. The town itself was quiet when the out-of-town cottage owners weren't around, but in the summer it became a crazy busy place thanks to tourists enjoying the lake, The Windmill farmer's market, and the local wineries and breweries. But that craziness would commence in June. There was still another month before the locals had to deal with that temporary lifestyle change.

There were only a couple of families in the park in the center of the village, some type of Little League baseball game going on across the street, kids riding bikes and people strolling along the sidewalk going in and out of some specialty shops.

The firehouse was easy to find since it was right across from the park. The big bay doors were wide open, and one truck was pulled out on the ramp. A couple of firefighters leaned into an open side compartment of the truck. An older man, waving at passing cars, sat on a metal bench in between two of the bay doors. A middle-aged woman came out a side door, a cell phone to her ear.

I pulled into the driveway on the far side of the front ramps and drove to the parking spaces next to the building. Every person turned to stare at me. To make it seem less weird as I passed them, I gave a quick wave like I knew someone. Every vehicle in the parking lot, most of them pick-up trucks, had some kind of emergency-type light on top of it. Our mini-van definitely looked out of place among the rest.

After I parked, I sat in the van for a minute. My immediate plan was to see if this Drew McAuliffe was here, but I'd only look from a distance, then drive away. And if not, I planned to approach someone and ask where he lived, so I could drive to his house and see him from a distance. It would be that simple.

I opened my wallet and pulled out the article that I had printed from the internet. Even though Drew McAuliffe looked a lot like Alex, I needed to look at his picture one more time so I knew who I was looking for.

I didn't see him among the handful of men and women who were here, which meant I should ask for directions on where I would find him.

Why would they just hand over that information?

I worked my hands along the steering wheel while I concocted a plan. Here's where the improvisation activities in drama club could come in handy. I'd have to think fast on my feet. Finally, I formulated an idea. I tossed the article onto the passenger seat and got out of the van. Despite the fact that it was a typical spring day with temperatures in the sixties, heat streaked up my face and neck. I hoped they weren't as red as they felt.

As I walked up the sidewalk next to the fire station, a couple of the teenaged boys who were using big cloths to wipe down the side of the fire engine stopped and stared at me, not even attempting to be discreet.

The old guy was the first person I came to. Based on the way he was instructing the workers at the side of the truck, I figured at some point he'd probably had a big role in the department. When he noticed me approaching, he shifted on the bench and gave me a wide, warm smile.

"Howdy. I don't s'pose a pretty thing like you is lookin' to join the department are ya?"

I stopped short, surprised by his question. "Uh, no." I shoved my hands into the back pockets of my jeans, ready to give him my story.

"I'm supposed to deliver something to my father's friend, but on the way here the directions to his house flew out when I opened the car window. I wondered if maybe you could tell me how to find him."

"Who ya lookin' for?"

Guilt sliced through my stomach. The old guy seemed so nice and trusting. Dishonesty was not my strong suit.

"Drew McAuliffe." I swallowed the small lump in my throat. I wasn't sure if it was from deceiving this guy or because I was actually going through with finding the man in the picture. Asking for him made it all real.

"You're close." He gave me directions that sounded pretty simple, but then he suddenly pointed toward the other side of the park. "But, if'n you look across the park, you see that silver truck?"

I turned to look where he pointed and nodded.

"That's Drew's truck, and that's him standin' talkin' to that woman and young man. Mebbe you can catch 'im 'fore he takes off."

Although I could see the truck and the people, I couldn't really see Drew McAuliffe from here. I figured if I drove around the park I could at least get a good look at him as I passed.

Besides, I'd look like a liar if I didn't make it look like I was trying to catch him.

"Thanks, I appreciate the help."

The old gentleman tossed his hand in the air, and the greasy rag he held flopped back over to cover his hand and wrist. "You have a great day, missy."

"Thanks. You, too." I jogged to the van and turned to see that Drew McAuliffe was getting in his truck. "Shoot!"

I yanked open the door and climbed in fast. As soon as I turned the key, the engine came to life, and I threw it in reverse. I noticed the young guy with Drew was getting into the passenger side of his truck, but I couldn't really see what he looked like.

For the first time, I realized there was one aspect that Alex and I hadn't considered in this scenario.

Drew McAuliffe could have another family.

A twinge of jealousy pinged my chest. It didn't matter. We were his family first.

Or, were we?

I mentally kicked myself. This wasn't a competition. This was a fact-finding mission. As I rounded the first corner by the park, I redirected my thoughts to catching up to them.

When the truck pulled out of the parking space in front of the stores, I was still on the far side of the park. I stepped on the gas at the traffic light so I wouldn't lose sight of him, causing my tires to squeal as I took the corner. A few people whipped their heads around to stare at me. I shrank a little into the seat, glad I wasn't from this town. They wouldn't recognize me, and probably, they would never see me again, either.

The directions the man at the firehouse had given me were committed to my memory, but Drew McAuliffe didn't take those streets. Instead, he snaked through a neighborhood with several little streets intersecting it. I tried not to follow too close, but now I was lost and had no choice but to stay with him and hope he'd end up at his house. At one intersection he pulled up to the stop sign and sat, despite the fact that no traffic was coming in either direction.

I saw him glance in his rearview mirror. The kid with him turned part way to look in my direction. I considered putting the car in reverse to put distance between us. My heartbeat accelerated and my mouth went dry. Why wasn't he moving?

Finally, he put his signal light on to turn left. My blood was pumping so fast that I decided the only way for me to calm down was to get away from him, make him believe that I wasn't following him. I clicked my signal light on to turn right.

I recognized the main street area by the park, so at least I wasn't lost – not that I'd have much chance of getting lost in such a small town, anyway. I'd give it a few minutes, let the pace of my heart return to normal, and then follow the old guy's directions to McAuliffe's house.

I circled the park, taking deep breaths to settle my nerves. This was crazy stuff. I'd definitely never make it as an undercover cop.

When I came back around the park past the firehouse, the truck had been put back in the fire station, but the old guy was still sitting on the bench. He threw his hand in the air and waved at me like we were old friends. He was probably laughing inside, thinking I was lost.

I followed the directions he'd given me. It was three easy turns, and then I was on Pratt Street. The numbers at this end were low, and I needed to get to 222 Pratt. I was in the 100 block when the silver truck pulled out of a side street.

I jammed my foot toward the brake, threw my right blinker on, and pulled off to the side of the street behind a blue compact car. His truck continued for another half minute before his left blinker came on and he pulled past the driveway then backed in. I watched him and the teenaged guy get out of the truck. Drew walked toward the house, but the kid walked down the street and was quickly out of my sight.

Now my curiosity was heightened. For some reason I was compelled to see more of Drew McAuliffe's immediate neighborhood.

I drove slowly up the street until I was close enough to see the front of his house from what seemed a safe distance. I pulled off to the side and parked the van.

The street was lined with older houses with well-kept yards. I was scanning the row of houses when something caught my attention behind a brown one almost across the street from the one Drew had gone in. I leaned forward to see better around a row of trimmed shrubs, and that's when I saw it. A tan tree house with purple shutters perched among the biggest branch of a massive maple tree. The wooden ladder leading to the opening in the bottom was gone, but my mind could picture it there, as well as the wooden benches, table and shelves inside where the big girl who lived there took all of her friends. And, one day, she took me. I couldn't recall her name, but guessed she was ten or eleven years old at that time.

The memory was as clear as if it had happened last week. A "Dora the Explorer" coloring book, the animal puppets on the shelf that the girl had used to put on shows with me, and the pretend plastic stove that had all kinds of dishes to play with. I could hear my little four-year-old voice going home and pleading to have one, too.

And then it happened — a memory — a glimpse of my mother stretching her arms out to give me a hug. But the memory faded as my eyes misted over. My heart swelled. Maybe I hadn't totally forgotten my mother, after all.

Swiping the back of my hand across my eyes, I turned my attention back to the house that Drew McAuliffe had entered. I assumed this was where Alex and I had lived with him and our mother.

I felt weird staring at some stranger's house, but I justified it by telling myself that at least I'd have something to report to Alex. I rolled up the windows and turned on the air conditioning, figuring the windows rolled up would give me a little more anonymity.

He lived in a small, simple gray house. There were two floors, but it looked like the ceilings of the second story rooms probably sloped. Cape-style. My best friend lived in a house like that. I'd hit my head on the lower part of the ceiling in her room more than once. The lawn of this house was trimmed and the bushes in front were almost sculpted. A small white picket fence surrounded the house. In front, small, neatly trimmed shrubs lined the fence.

Perfect. Everything looked perfect. Not at all what I'd imagined for someone whose life had supposedly fallen apart more than a decade before.

I was lost in imagining the inside being as neat and tidy as the outside when there was a knock on the passenger side window. I almost jumped out of my skin as I whipped my head toward the sound. Then, my heart almost exploded.

Drew McAuliffe stared back at me.

CHAPTER 2

Without taking my eyes off the man staring in the van window, I fumbled frantically for the lock button and jabbed it. Hard! The locking mechanisms for all four doors snapped at once, and I startled even though I was the one who had caused it.

Drew McAuliffe leaned forward on his metal crutches and rapped his knuckles on the window again. His lips were moving but the whir of the air conditioning fan muffled his voice.

I wanted to throw the car in drive and race away, but he was leaning against the door, eliminating that option.

"Open the window," he yelled, this time loud enough for me to hear.

My blood pounded in my ears. What had I gotten myself into? I knew by his intense stare that refusing wasn't an option. Okay, I'd open it just enough so I could hear him, and then I'd take off. My finger hovered over the button. Finally, I tapped it three times, and it jerked open three notches.

"I couldn't hear you. I have the air conditioner on."

"Mind telling me why you were tailing me?"

"Tailing you?" My right knee started shaking, so I pressed my palm down to stop it. "What do you mean?"

"Following me." He tipped his head toward the truck in his driveway. "You were pretty obvious. What're you after?"

My mouth went desert dry. "Nothing. I was lost and thought you were someone I knew."

"You'd make a lousy detective."

"I don't know what —"

"What's with that?" He cut me off and pointed down at the passenger seat.

The desert in my mouth suddenly flooded, and I swallowed the pool of saliva drowning my tongue. I'd forgotten I'd tossed the article about him onto the seat. I'd kept it there so I could compare the picture in the paper with the living person if I got close enough.

And now I was too close.

He narrowed his eyes. "You looking for me?"

I slammed my hand over it and wadded it into a ball.

"No. My brother must have left that here. He's into firetrucks." I tossed the paper under the dash.

He hooked the fingers of his left hand over the top of the open window. "Quite the coincidence then, isn't it?"

I glanced into the rearview mirror. Why did I feel so isolated? Now both knees shook.

"Look, I'm sorry if I bothered you. I'll just go now." I reached for the gearshift.

"What's your name?"

"What?" His question totally threw me off, and I froze with my fingers on the handle. Sweat beaded on my palms. I felt like a trapped animal.

"Sandy," I blurted. I didn't know where that name came from, but there was no way I was giving him my real one.

McAuliffe arched one brow and ran his tongue along his lower lip. "Short for Savannah, by any chance?"

I swore I heard every beat of my heart echoing inside the van. How did he get Savannah out of Sandy? Did he know who I was?

"Sandy. My name is Sandy," I repeated, the lie burning the back of my throat.

"Right." His eyes narrowed. "Well, *Sandy*," he said, clearly not believing me, "you're not from Keuka Shores, right?"

I shook my head. And he wouldn't find out where I was from, either.

He shifted the crutch in his left hand to his right hand, and the two crutches clanged together. "Here's what I suggest. Put this van in drive and get out of here. You're treading in dangerous waters. You don't want this trouble."

"What? No, you've got it all wrong." Now I was annoyed that he was making assumptions when he didn't even know me. Or did he?

He glanced toward the floorboard where I'd tossed the crumpled picture.

"No, *they* got it all wrong. I'm not a hero. Never was. Never will be. Don't know what you're after, but I guarantee I'm not the person you're looking for."

He was right and wrong. For more than a year I'd had a fantasy going on about finding him and how happy he would be to see me. But if he had guessed who I was, then this reunion was anything but warm and fuzzy. His reaction turned my thoughts negative. If he really was my father, I knew the truth about his past, and "hero" didn't fit what he'd done to our family. Something deep inside me suddenly wanted to tear him down and expose him for lying, too.

"You must have told the reporter she could write the story," I challenged.

Some kind of emotion flashed in his eyes, and I was positive that, contrary to my usual way, I'd pushed an adult too hard.

"Not that I owe you an explanation, but the last thing I wanted was attention. The reporter told me the paper wanted to help the family raise money to get back on their feet since they lost everything in the fire. The focus was supposed to be on them. The reporter took the story in a different direction."

He sounded genuinely unhappy that he'd been portrayed in a positive way. A pang of remorse that I'd brought it up hit my nerves.

"Look, young lady, I'm not sure what you're after by coming here, but I'm going to say it again. Leave this alone."

"Leave what alone?"

"Me. Forget you ever saw me," he growled.

And that was the end of the conversation. He straightened, maneuvered the crutches under his arms and went through the opening between my van and the car parked in front of me. After checking for traffic, he crossed the street back toward the house where he'd parked.

When he reached the driveway, the teenaged boy who'd ridden with him was walking up the sidewalk toward his truck.

The kid wore a green and white lacrosse uniform with the number 18 just above his heart. He carried a duffel bag that I assumed had equipment in it. He was tall and looked very athletic. His dark brown hair was close cut, but just long enough so some of it stuck out in the wrong direction. It was tough to tell how old he was – except that he was close to my age.

A smile lit up his face as he approached the truck. Whatever he was saying, he looked animated, not brooding. Brooding, trouble-maker guys had never been appealing to me. This guy looked like he loved life. My kind of guy. And so cute, too.

As soon as that thought crossed my mind, I mentally kicked myself, repulsed. The reality was, I didn't know his relationship to Drew McAuliffe, and for all I knew, he could be my stepbrother, or worse, my half-brother.

I wished I could hear what he was saying, but with the windows closed, I couldn't hear anything. He didn't look in my direction, so I assumed the conversation had nothing to do with me. I stared at him, intrigued. Whatever his connection to Drew McAuliffe was, he appeared very comfortable with him.

He tossed his equipment bag into the truck bed, then climbed in the passenger side while McAuliffe opened the driver's door and the half cab door so he could toss the crutches on the back seat. With an awkward hop and twist of his long body, he managed to maneuver onto the seat. The cast on his left leg came to just below his knee, so bringing the injured leg into the cab wasn't difficult.

At that point I should have pulled the van away from the curb and driven away. Instead, it was like I was hypnotized, watching the scene unfold. Tentacles of jealousy curled around in my belly, poking at every nerve. The idea that my father might have another family hit me the wrong way.

After a moment, the truck pulled into the street and drove away.

I stared at the back window and their silhouettes. His focus was straight ahead. There didn't appear to be any attempt to look in either rearview mirror.

The center of my chest burned with the realization of what had just happened.

Drew McAuliffe never looked back. And that totally pissed me off.

Maybe that explained why our uncle and aunt had adopted Alex and me almost twelve years ago. If Drew McAuliffe *was* our father, chances were his M.O. had always been the same. Never look back.

I slammed the gearshift into drive and squealed the tires as I pulled away from the curb. Not a good idea with a brand new license in my wallet, but it helped release some of my frustration.

Who did he think he was? His directive to "leave him alone" had hit a nerve. Despite our family's history, I'd always known where I belonged. I'd been adopted by an aunt and uncle who had raised and loved Alex and me as if we were their own. We'd never wanted for anything. And, until that science project a year ago, I'd been satisfied to leave our biological father in the past.

But now, because he hadn't glanced back for one more look at me, for the first time in my life, I felt abandoned.

As quickly as the thought came into my mind, I pushed it out. I was old enough now to find out all of the facts about what had happened the night my mother died. I pressed harder on the gas. It wasn't what I had planned, but now I could guarantee this guy one thing.

He hadn't seen the last of me.

I turned the van down our street, still fuming because Drew McAuliffe had driven away from me. He'd acted like he knew who I was and why I had gone to Keuka Shores. Yet, he didn't care to learn anything more. That frustration brought up the one question that I had always left alone.

Did he ever regret losing contact with Alex and me?

The question chewed at my conscience, and there was an unexpected churn in my stomach. I wanted to believe that we had mattered to him at *one* time, even if he didn't want us in his life now.

I glanced at the clock on the van's dash as I pulled into the driveway at home. Two-thirty. I'd been gone a little more than three hours. I'd stopped by the stables and checked on Lacey, picked up papers with information about upcoming shows but hadn't spent much time at the barn since I'd used so much going to Keuka Shores. Three hours was a believable amount of time for driving to the stable, grooming Lacey, even riding and getting back.

I parked next to Dad's Jeep Wrangler. Of course, at a time when I wanted to be alone, everyone was home. Weather-wise, it was a perfect early May Saturday. The top branches of two huge maple trees in our front lawn swayed in the light breeze.

I snatched the show registration papers off the passenger seat and opened the van door. Across the street, the neighbor girls sat on their front steps, giggling and looking at a magazine. It made me think of how simple my life had been when the past was the last thing on my mind.

Then, one photo on the internet had stripped away all of that.

I started across the lawn toward the side door, completely lost in my thoughts, when Mom's voice came out of nowhere, "Did you have fun?"

I whirled toward her, grabbing my chest like I needed to stop my heart from jumping out.

"Jeez, are you trying to give me a heart attack?"

She was kneeling next to the garage, surrounded by tiny plants in plastic pots.

"Sorry. I thought you saw me here." She smiled and rubbed her wrist across her forehead. Fresh dirt covered her gardening gloves so a small amount left a smear above her eye. "So, how'd it go?"

My mind buzzed for a second as Drew McAuliffe's image swirled in my thoughts. Did Alex tell her what I'd really gone to do? But, then I realized that was doubtful. Her expression was warm, not angry. I mentally shook myself. My guilty conscience was clouding my reasoning. She wouldn't know where I'd been. Obviously her question was about what I'd done at the barn.

I held up the papers. "Good. These are a couple of apps for shows that I picked up, but most of the shows have them on-line. I'm going to go and fill them out now."

"Always good to get those things in early," she said.

When she smiled, I saw a hint of my biological mother in her expression. Even though I didn't remember my mother in real life, there had always been a photo collage for me and one for Alex on our bedroom walls - pictures of our mother with us.

Before today, because I couldn't remember her, she didn't seem real. But today's flash of memory when I spotted the tree house had stirred an emotion in my heart that left a little hole like something was missing.

She went back to digging in the dirt, and I continued into the house, taking the side door. As I started through the kitchen, I glanced out the window toward the back yard. Dad was trimming the evergreen hedges that lined the back part of our property. Everything looked and seemed so normal.

Except for me. Meeting Drew McAuliffe had changed me.

With the show applications in hand, I hung the van keys on one of the hooks next to the refrigerator and headed for my bedroom. Alex's bedroom door was closed, and his iPod was blaring. I hurried past, figuring he didn't even know I was home yet. Once I was in my room, I closed the door, tossed the applications onto my bed, and went straight to my laptop.

I tried to fool myself into believing that all I wanted was to fill out the show applications. It only took a few seconds to pull one up, and I started filling in the blanks. I'd just finished when my door burst open, then slammed shut. I swung around in my chair, not surprised to see Alex.

"Dude! Why didn't you tell me you were back? Did you see him?" he asked. His back was still pressed against the door, and his left hand gripped the knob.

"Ssh! Talk quieter." I glanced out my window. Mom was still on her knees in her garden, and I could hear the buzz of the hedge trimmers coming from the back yard.

"Yeah, I saw him." I wondered how much to tell him. Probably, like me, in his mind our father would be excited to see us and would welcome us with open arms.

Alex moved away from the door and crossed the room toward me, his eyes wide. "What was he like? Did he look like a hero? Did you talk to him? Can I go and meet him?"

Now he had come into my personal space. I couldn't think with him that close.

"Whoa! Whoa! Whoa!" I threw up my hands to force him to stay back, and he jerked to a halt. "Chill, Alex. You ask too many questions."

He backed up a couple of feet and dropped onto the side of my bed. "Sorry. I just can't believe this is happening," he said. He cracked his knuckles as if he had to do something to release energy.

I cringed. "Alex! Don't do that. You'll get arthritis when you're older."

"There's no scientific proof of that," he countered, cracking the knuckles on the other hand. "So, did you talk to him?"

I rested my arm on the back of my desk chair and shrugged. "It was more like he talked *at* me."

"Really?" He leaned forward with a wide grin. "What'd he say?"

"Alex, I —" I hated to disappoint him, but I had to come out with the truth. "He told me to leave him alone."

His smile dropped. "What? Why?"

"I don't know. I think he might have a new family There was some guy around my age with him."

"We might have a brother?"

I sucked in my lower lip. Should I tell Alex what bothered me most about that? "Alex, hello! If that kid is his son, you know what that means?"

His eyes darkened. Oh, yeah, he knew. "He cheated on our mother."

Nodding, I said, "I mean, maybe they're not related, but they looked comfortable with each other. And he acted like it was his kid."

There was no mistaking the disappointment that clouded Alex's normally bright eyes. "I wanna see him." His voice was choked like his throat was closing. Was my tough-as-nails brother going to cry? "Even if it's only one time," he said, "I have to see him."

"We know where to find him if we ever have to, you know, for medical reasons or something. And, that's really all I wanted, but —" I tapped my finger on the top of the computer mouse while I thought — "maybe he feels guilty, maybe if he knows we don't hold him responsible for what happened, then he'll be friendlier. I'm not ready to give up on him. "

Alex stood and paced. "If he has another kid, then contrary to what Mom has always told us, he can't be dangerous."

"I don't know that it was *his* kid," I said. "I just said he may have a new family." I shifted in my chair so I was facing the screen again, clicked on Google, and began typing.

Alex stopped pacing and stepped next to my desk. "What are you looking for?"

"We have more clues now that I've been there," I said. "I'm putting in more specific criteria."

Like my searches over the last year, a list of matches with Drew McAuliffe's name popped up. A long list. But the pictures that went with the top suggestions didn't look anything like him. I pushed Alex's fingers off the mouse.

"Let's see. Drew McAuliffe, Pratt Street, Keuka Shores," I typed.

Then some matches started coming up. The first three or four linked to the recent article about him saving the kids from the fire.

"Click on the last one," Alex suggested. "It looks like it's an actual news story from a newspaper about him rescuing those kids from the fire."

I did, and the full article with a photo of the house fire popped up.

He leaned so close to me that I could tell he'd had peanut butter for lunch.

Leaning against the arm of my chair, I said, "Alex, back off a little. You're breathing on me."

He shifted to the side a little, but he was still close enough to read the screen.

I started to skim, looking for what seemed like the most important facts in the article and read them aloud. "Member of Keuka Shores Fire Department for nine years. Found four-year-old boy hiding under a bed. Fire burned stairway. McAuliffe carried the boy onto porch roof. Rescuers put ladder up to porch. Halfway down while carrying the child McAuliffe slipped on a wet rung on the ladder and fell, shielding the child with his body. Child okay. McAuliffe broke his leg and ribs in the fall."

Alex rested his hands on my desk and leaned closer to the screen. "Wow! He *is* a hero. Let's see what else it says." Alex picked up reading, and I leaned back since he was once again crowding my personal space. I couldn't see the monitor without leaning way off to the side anyway.

"Not the first time McAuliffe has been recognized as a hero." Alex's voice rose as he read the next part of a sentence. "Although McAuliffe wouldn't share details, he did verify that he had been awarded the Bronze Star and Purple Heart while serving with the Marine Corps in Iraq."

I snapped up straighter in the chair and pushed Alex back with my shoulder so I could see the screen, too. Goose bumps erupted on my arms.

"What did that say?" I scanned the article, looking for what he had just read.

"He was in Iraq, and he got a couple of medals." Alex turned to look at me. "You don't get medals for nothing. Why wouldn't Mom and Dad tell us that?" His forehead wrinkled, and the skin around his eyes creased as he grappled with his thoughts. "Why didn't they tell us any of this?"

My throat thickened, and I struggled to get a full breath. "Alex, even if Drew McAuliffe really is our father, and I'm not saying he is," I added quickly, "and even if he did get that medal, it doesn't change the fact that Mom blames him for our mother's death. I'm sure that's why they didn't tell us any of this."

The truth was, we'd both asked at different times when we were younger. Every time Mom would burst into tears and leave the room, and Dad would say, "There was a car accident. The rest doesn't matter. We love you, and we'll always take care of you. That's all you need to know."

So, finally, we stopped asking in order to avoid hurting her more.

I gasped as a realization hit me. "Alex! Oh my gosh! We've been such idiots."

His brows furrowed. "About what?"

"When we tried to find out information about the accident before, we always searched using our mother's maiden name since that's what Mom and Dad had put on the gravestone."

Alex pushed his hands through the hair above his forehead. He stared at the ceiling. "But, we never searched using McAuliffe as her last name," he said, finishing my thought.

Since our aunt and uncle had adopted us shortly after our mother's death, our last names had been changed to theirs and all references to our mother had been with her maiden name.

"Now I'm wondering if the reason her name was changed was because Mom didn't want our mother's memory associated with our father." I slapped the butt of my hand against my forehead. "I can't believe I didn't connect the dots when I found my original birth certificate showing our real last name."

My fingers flew across the keyboard to input Drew and Melissa McAuliffe and the date our mother had died. Like the search before, at first nothing that made sense came up. I tried several combinations of searches, including names of local newspapers and surrounding towns, until suddenly what we were looking for popped up.

Toddlers Survive Crash That Claims Mother

I gasped, and Alex pointed at the headline. "Click on it."

I clicked on the *read more* link. Neither one of us read out loud this time. The details were spelled out clearly in front of us. Our biological mother had called her sister, Nicole, our aunt who had adopted us, and whom we now called Mom, and told her that Drew was having a violent flashback and that she was leaving the house with the children. Two miles from home, she lost control of the car and crashed, hitting a telephone pole on the driver's side. She was killed instantly.

The deeper we read into the article, the more details that were provided. I knew Alex and I were reading at the same speed, because I heard him read under his breath, "...McAuliffe has battled post traumatic stress disorder since returning from the Middle East." Alex glanced at me. "PTSD." Then he went back to reading silently again. I was the one to read out loud the next time.

"According to McAuliffe's sister-in-law, Nicole Cartright, the veteran has suffered disturbing flashbacks on other occasions which have put the family in danger."

Alex and I looked at each other at the same time. Although neither of us spoke, I figured we were probably thinking the same thing: this story and the story we'd been told our whole lives were very different. Our father hadn't killed our mother. And he really wasn't responsible for her death, either. She'd made a mistake, and she had crashed. It was just a horrible accident, and Alex and I were lucky to be alive.

Alex sagged onto the edge of my bed. "Wow!"

I leaned back in my chair, trying to absorb everything we'd learned in the last few minutes. All it took was finding out our father's name, and the door to our whole past was unlocked.

"Now what do we do?" Alex asked.

There wasn't time to answer because my bedroom door burst open. Mom stood in the doorway, her face bright red with tear streaks through the dirt stains. Her arm was stretched out in front of her, and she clutched something in her trembling fingers. Dad stepped behind her and put his hands on her shoulders.

"Calm down, Nic," he said.

She was focused on me, and her voice shook when she asked, "Where did you get this?"

I glanced at Alex, who looked horrified, then got up from my chair and approached Mom without saying anything.

When I was a few feet from her, she threw a wadded piece of paper toward me.

Even in mid-air, I knew what she'd found. I caught it and squeezed it in my palm.

Her lips trembled. "This was on the floor of the van."

The rough edges of the crumpled computer paper jabbed into my skin. The picture of Drew McAuliffe was hurting me just like it hurt her.

There was no way this could end well.

CHAPTER 3

I took a step toward Mom, but she moved back at the same time as if our moves had been choreographed. Tears streamed down her cheeks, and my heart ached for the pain shimmering in her eyes. Dad moved in behind her in the doorway, his forehead furrowed as he tried to figure it all out, but he stayed silent.

"We're not trying to hurt you," I offered to Mom. I held up the crumpled paper with Drew McAuliffe's picture. "I just wanted to see."

"See what?" Spit flew from her lips as her hurt turned to anger.

Dad spoke up. "What's going on here?"

Mom pointed at my hand, her finger shaking."She has a picture of *him*."

Dad glanced toward my hand that held the crumpled article about Drew McAuliffe being a hero. "May I see it?" His voice was steady and smooth, his demeanor the exact opposite of Mom's.

I swallowed the lump in my throat and lifted my leaden arm to give it to him.

He took his time un-crumpling it. He'd always been the more rational of the two when it came to the subject of our biological father, but I didn't know if this would push him too far.

Behind me, Alex cracked his knuckles, sending a chill up my spine.

Dad stared at the article and picture for a minute before he cleared his throat and looked up at me. "Well, it's only an article off the internet." He put his arm around Mom's shoulders. "They're curious, that's all, Hon. No harm done."

My neck tensed, because I realized they must think I'd only found the picture. They didn't know I'd gone looking for Drew McAuliffe. Since we'd gone this far, I figured openness and honesty were the only options.

"I did more than just print off the article," I said, fighting the cringe that would have made me look guilty. "I went to Keuka Shores to see what I could find out about him, and —" I hesitated, hating to admit that I'd lied to them earlier when I asked to borrow the van to go to the stable — "I found where he lives."

Mom gasped and her eyes widened bigger than I'd ever seen. She threw off Dad's arm and shook her finger at me. "Stay. Away. From. Him." The pitch of her voice rose on each word. "He'll ruin your life."

I didn't have a chance to respond, because Alex pushed past me and stepped in front of her, his feet spread in a challenging stance.

"He's a hero." He pointed at the paper in Dad's hand. "It says right there that he saved a little boy's life. And we found another story about the car accident. That one said he was a war hero, too. And we know how our mother died. We know she was driving, and it was only her, Savannah and me in the car when she had the accident. You can't blame him."

As he tossed out the jumbled mess of information that we'd learned through our search, Mom flinched with each fact.

"Stop!" she shouted, throwing her hands up to cover her ears. "I don't want to hear this."

She backed up, stumbling when her feet tangled with Dad's because he was still right behind her. When his hands shot out to steady her, he dropped the paper on the floor. From his angle, he couldn't see that Mom looked like she was about to collapse. Her face contorted as she shook her head, mumbling "No! No! No! Why is this happening?"

Dad put his cheek against her hair. "Nic, it's okay."

"No." She pressed her hands to her face and turned into Dad's chest, muffling her voice. "I promised my sister if anything ever happened to her that I would keep her babies safe. I promised."

Dad hugged her tight and looked over her head at us, but I couldn't read his expression. Unlike her, he didn't look angry or hurt. Only worried.

"We're not babies," Alex hissed under his breath so that only I heard.

I hit him with my elbow. We didn't need to upset her more.

Dad lifted his chin and mouthed, *I'll be right back. Stay here.*

I nodded.

"Come on, Nic," he said. He wrapped an arm around her shoulders and guided her out of the room.

Her heel dug into Drew McAuliffe's face as she stepped on the paper Dad had dropped. She hadn't done it on purpose, but it probably would have satisfied her to know she had.

As soon as they were down the hall, I stepped to the door and closed it, making sure to turn the handle to avoid the clicking sound of the latch. When I turned back toward Alex, I let out a slow breath.

"Wow!" I picked up the article from the floor, noticing the rip that cut across Drew's torso. "That went well."

Alex snatched the creased paper from my hand. "I wanna meet him."

"Just a heads up, little brother, Drew McAuliffe doesn't want anything to do with us." I pushed away from the door and went back to the chair at my desk. "He made that crystal clear."

"I'm his son." Alex jutted his jaw forward and hooked his thumbs in the pockets of his jeans. Uncompromising. Determined.

Looking a lot like a younger version of the man I'd met hours earlier.

I shook my head, trying to make sense of all of it. "This is such a mess. Maybe we should leave it alone, Alex. Maybe it's too complicated."

"No, I want to know." He puffed out his chest and jabbed his thumb toward himself. "I want him to tell me to my face that I don't matter to him."

I pushed my hands into my hair and squeezed my scalp. All I could think of was the myth we'd read in English about Pandora's box. What had we opened and let loose because we were curious? Was there anything good that could come out of this box?

Alex interrupted my thoughts. "Would you be able to find his house again?"

"Yeah. It's a small town."

The image of Drew McAuliffe's house, his silver truck parked in the driveway, and him and the kid in the sports uniform getting into the truck, played like a movie in my mind. Every little detail about that five minute period was crystal clear.

I stared past him, my mind back on the street. "You want to know what was weird about going there?"

"What?"

"I think I recognized it."

"The house?"

"No, not *his* house, but the house across the street." I shifted my attention back to Alex. "Actually, not the house itself, but a tree house in the back yard. I know I've been there."

"No way!" He dropped on the edge of my bed, a grin so big it was like he'd received the best present ever. "Then you must have found the house where we lived." He leaned forward. "It must be him. Let's go back. That would be awesome."

Goose bumps sprang up on my arms. Alex hadn't heard the growl in Drew McAuliffe's voice when he told me to leave him alone. Alex's enthusiasm made me nervous. I understood his desire to meet our father, but the idea of going back to that neighborhood right away made my body tense. And I didn't know why. I couldn't go back under these circumstances. Not even for Alex.

"Maybe we should wait." My mind spun with ways to give Alex the chance to see our father, but from a safe distance. "You know, I have a better idea of a way to see him without it looking like we're stalking him at his house." I tried to make my tone sound like I was convinced this was the way to go. Hopefully, he'd buy it.

"Okay, let's hear it."

"The guy with Drew was wearing a lacrosse uniform. The only spring lacrosse teams I know of are the club teams."

He frowned. "Yeah, so?"

"Well, we can check to see if there's a schedule online for a club team from Keuka Shores, then go to a game. I'm betting there's a good chance our fa—" I hesitated, shocked that I had almost taken that crazy step of actually calling Drew McAuliffe *our father* — "Maybe Drew McAuliffe would be there."

"Let's do it." Alex leaned forward and pointed to the computer. "See what you can find."

I clicked onto a search engine and started typing in key words to see if any lacrosse schedules would come up. There wasn't a team for Keuka Shores, but there was one associated with Canandaigua, the much bigger town to its north. I clicked on the link, and a photo of the spring team popped up.

"This is it," I said, sitting back in my chair. The uniforms were green and white, just like the one the kid was wearing when he came back to the truck.

Alex stood and leaned closer to the screen. "Is the guy you saw in this picture?"

I clicked on the photograph to enlarge it and looked at the three rows of guys. I hadn't seen him for long enough to pick him out in a picture. I looked for the uniform with the number 18 on it, but because some of the guys were turned sideways, I couldn't see all of the numbers.

I shook my head. "Nope, I can't pick him out."

Pointing to a small green box below the picture, Alex said, "Click here for the link to the schedule."

This scenario reminded me of a spy movie. Each clue led to a new clue, and I felt like we were being tested to see if we were smart enough to pick up on the next one. I clicked on the link, and the schedule popped up.

Alex read the list, but not in chronological order. "Auburn. Victor. Corning. Canandaigua." He stopped and turned to me. "That's it. Canandaigua 7:00 on Wednesday. They must play on a field with lights. Let's go."

I leaned back in my chair, shaking my head. "I'm such an idiot."

"Why?"

"How would we get there?"

He tossed the article onto my bed and shoved his hands in his pockets. "You have your license. Let's use it."

I raised my eyebrows and stared at him. "Seriously? After what I did today, I'll be lucky if Mom lets me touch keys before I'm twenty-five."

He dropped his chin and scuffed his sneaker heel against the floor like he was trying to contain his agitation. "True."

"I know!" Alex pulled his cell phone from his pocket. "I'll text Josh to see if one of his parents will take us. Bet they will." While he tapped the message into his phone, he continued. "Josh's mom thinks it would be great if we found our father. She asks me if we have any news every time I go over there."

All of a sudden I realized how important finding our father was to Alex. I thought it had just been my obsession, but if he was talking about it to his friend's mother, then it meant more to him, too. I wondered if it was a guy thing – the need to bond with his real father. As the only boy in the family, he'd had plenty of guy things with Dad his whole life, so he hadn't missed out on the male role model thing. But we'd always known he wasn't our real dad.

Without warning, a quick stab of jealousy hit my chest. Although it was going to be a long shot, there was a remote possibility Alex would be able to develop the whole male bonding thing with our father. For a second I felt cheated. I'd never have the opportunity for the female bonding with our mother.

I shook it off. Any kind of relationship was such a long-shot, that for now I'd just humor him. "I can't miss work at the stable Wednesday after school, so they'd have to take us after that."

I glanced at my work schedule posted on the cork board behind the computer. I'd been working as a stable hand at Breezy Acres horse farm since I was fourteen. As soon as I turned sixteen, I went onto regular employee status with higher pay and more hours. The job was perfect: I got paid for doing something I loved, working with horses, and I was finally able to start saving serious money.

And that money was targeted for one thing: buying Cinnamon Lace, the Appaloosa Quarter Horse I'd been riding and showing on the equestrian team for the last two and a half years. Every penny I'd earned or gift of money I'd been given had gone into the bank account I'd set up for this one goal. I didn't have much more time to save the last $1400 or Lacey, as she was called at the barn, would be offered on the open market.

I couldn't lose her.

"I work until 6:30 Wednesday," I said.

"Okay." He stared at his screen like he expected an immediate response from Josh.

A knock on the door made us both jump.

"Okay to come in?" Dad asked.

Alex and I exchanged quick glances like we weren't sure who should answer. We'd never felt this kind of awkwardness with Mom and Dad before. It was another clue that something about our lives, our relationships, was already altered.

"Of course. Come in," I called.

The door opened just enough for Dad to be fully visible. He shoved his hands into his pants pockets and shrugged.

"I don't know what to say," he said.

"Is Mom okay?" I asked.

He shrugged again. "She'll be okay. Give her time."

For the next half minute, the room was filled with a silence so big that the ticking pendulum of the grandfather clock in the hallway echoed even in my room. Every muscle fiber in my body felt tighter than an overstretched rubber band. Would something snap?

Alex, in his typical directness, broke the silence. "Did Savannah find our father?"

Dad drew in a full breath that made his shoulders heave up. Then, he let it out slowly and nodded.

"Did you know he was living in Keuka Shores?" Alex pressed.

"No." Dad shifted his weight from one foot to the other. "You have to know this is what he wanted, too. He felt you were better off with us. The support money was deposited in a bank account he'd set up, so we didn't know where he was."

I jumped up from my chair. "Support money?"

"Support for what?" Alex added.

In three steps, Alex and I were side by side. A united front.

"For the two of you," Dad said. "Child support. But we don't use it. Instead, we set up college funds for each of you, and the money goes there each month."

A lump clogged my throat. Everything we'd always believed, always been told about our father, was imploding. It was hard to breathe.

I swallowed over the lump so I could talk. "He didn't abandon us? You didn't adopt us?"

"Yes," Dad said quickly. "I mean, financially, no, he didn't abandon you. But, yes, we formally adopted you. He agreed to it. We all wanted what was best for you."

I glanced at Alex. His jaw flexed, and his eyelids twitched. I recognized the signs. Eruption was imminent. Overreaction would get us nowhere.

I stood straighter, protectiveness for my sibling stronger than common sense. "It's our turn to decide what's best for us. Alex and I want to meet him, and we're going Wednesday."

Dad stepped into my room, looking back and forth between us. "You two apparently know more than we do about where he is. We haven't seen him since your mother's funeral. We were told he was out West somewhere."

"Well, now we know he's not." Emboldened, I said, "I'd like permission to take Alex to see him. Just from a distance," I quickly added to make it sound safer.

Dad closed the door, giving it an extra tap to make sure it had closed snugly. He turned so he could lean his back against the jamb, worry creasing his forehead.

"No."

"No?" Alex and I asked the same one-word question.

"I'll take you." When he spoke, his voice was so quiet I could barely make out what he said.

Disbelief flooded me. "But, you hate him."

"No," he responded, shaking his head. "I've always supported your moth—" he hesitated, clearly grappling with the wording of his response — "my wife. Your mother's death changed her. After that, it was support her or lose her." He splayed his fingers and pushed them through the thinning hair at his temples, leaving his palm spread across the sides of his head. "And you two were the only things she had of her sister, of her family, because it was only the two of them left in the world."

"This is bullcrap!" Alex blurted, his hands balled into fists. "We were cheated."

"Alex," Dad said, "your father was fighting demons after he came back from the war. He had bad flashbacks. Your mother — and even he — feared for your safety. We all did what we thought was the best for you. We weren't trying to cheat you. We were only thinking of your safety."

"What about the safety of his other kid?"

Dad's brow wrinkled, and he tipped his head. "What other kid?"

I stepped in. "When I saw him today, he was taking a teenaged boy somewhere. We didn't know if maybe it was another son."

The wrinkles in Dad's brow multiplied and overtook his forehead. "How old?"

Shrugging, I said, "My age, I'm guessing. Maybe even a year or two older."

Dad shook his head. "No, there's no way he had another child before you. You two were the light of his world. He would have done anything for you. That's why he allowed us to adopt you. He was thinking about what was best for you, not him."

"Why didn't we ever know this?" I asked. "We grew up thinking we were nothing to him. That he'd walked away and never looked back."

Dad sighed. "We figured it was best to wait until you were grown-up for you to know the truth." He dropped his chin and shrugged. "We always knew this time would come. I guess we were in denial that you would be grown-up so soon."

"Well, we are," Alex interjected. "We can handle it."

Grown-up. I wanted to remind Alex that I was only 16 and he, 14. We weren't as grown-up as he always liked to think, but maybe he was right. We were old enough to decide this for ourselves. In order to get us all focused, I intervened.

"Okay, Alex, Dad has offered to take us." I turned toward Dad. "We actually had something specific in mind. We think the kid who was with him is going to have a lacrosse game on Wednesday in Canandaigua. We thought if we went to that game, then maybe Drew McAuliffe would be there and, and, even if we don't formally meet him, Alex could at least see him."

"Then what?" Dad asked.

Alex and I turned and looked at each other. That was a great question. What would be our next move?

The long gray stable barns loomed ahead of me. My grip on the steering wheel loosened, and I could feel the tension in my shoulders lessening. Out here with the horses was one place where, regardless of what else was going on in my life, I always felt better. A place where I belonged.

Dad hadn't even hesitated when I asked if I could come out to Breezy Acres Stables to ride Lacey. I'd waited an hour, and when Mom never came out of the bedroom, I couldn't take the silence anymore. Alex had retreated to his room, probably doing more research on Drew McAuliffe.

I needed something that was for me.

I turned off the paved road onto the rutted driveway that led to the two barns. The longest one had all of the stalls. The other contained a few stalls and a massive, sandy indoor riding ring where Phoebe Reynolds, the riding stable's owner, often hosted inter-barn competitions. Beyond the barns were the pastures.

Three other cars took up the first spaces, so I pulled in pasat them. There were always lessons at 4:00 on a Saturday afternoon. Usually it was the ten to fourteen-year old riders. It was a time slot I'd attended almost every Saturday for several years. Without even seeing the ring, I had a good idea of what the riders were being taught.

I inhaled a long breath as I climbed from the van. Someone had recently mowed the lawn, and the fresh smell of cut grass relaxed me, leaving me with no doubt that coming to ride had been the best decision for feeling more normal again.

The large sliding end door was open all the way, allowing the sunlight to wash over the center aisle between the stalls. Soft nickers and impatient snorts greeted me as soon as the horses that were in the barn heard the crunching of the rocks under my riding boots. The aroma of the mixture of odors every horse person cherished — hay, wood shavings, horse flesh and leather — relaxed me even more.

Rocket, the bay gelding on the right, pressed his chest into the rubber-covered chain that restrained him in his stall. He stretched his neck so his nose tapped my shoulder. It was a simple gesture that lifted my mood.

I turned and stroked the white blaze that ran down the front of his dark brown face.

"Hey, Rocky, you goofy boy. You trying to give me a kiss?"

He continued to nudge me with his nose. No doubt, he hoped I'd magically pull a treat from my pocket. I held my hands up, palms facing him, to show him they were empty.

"Sorry, pal. That's up to Tess to decide when you deserve treats."

I continued down the aisle, giving a quick pat to the other three horses in stalls. They were all looking for the same thing and were disappointed when I showed them I was empty-handed.

Beyond the stalls was the area where most of us groomed and saddled the horses. There was an open area on both sides of the aisle for this purpose. Sasha, a golden Palomino that reminded me of Roy Rogers' horse, Trigger, was cross-tied in one of the side aisles. Her ears were perked forward and she stared toward the tack room, so I assumed Jamie Reston, a fellow equestrian teammate, was probably inside.

Just before I reached the tack room, the door swung open. Jamie emerged pulling the rolling tack cart that held her western saddle and bridle. A basket on a shelf below the saddle held all of her grooming equipment.

"Hey, Savannah," she said, steering wide into the aisle, "you come to ride?"

I grabbed hold of the door and pulled it open the rest of the way to make it easier for her to pull the cart out. Atticus, her Golden Retriever, trotted out behind her. When Atticus saw me, his tail whipped the air and he came over to be petted.

Kneeling in front of the dog, I pressed my forehead to his and rubbed his ears while I answered.

"Yeah. It's been a crazy day. I need horsey time to help clear my head."

"Atticus and I are taking Sasha for a trail ride. Wanna come?"

My first thought was to refuse, but then I decided the company, and the opportunity for girl talk, would probably be a good idea. I gave Atticus a final pat then stood.

"Sounds perfect. Let me get Lacey."

Jamie continued pulling the rattling cart toward Sasha, and Atticus followed. I slipped into the tack room to get Lacey's halter and lead rope.

"I'll be ready in ten minutes," I called over my shoulder as I headed out of the barn toward the pastures. A warm breeze filtered through my hair when I started down the tree-lined lane. Chickens clucked and scratched at the thin grass in a large wired coop under an oak tree past the biggest barn. One chicken raced toward me, flapping her wings in warning. I didn't envy whoever had the chore of collecting the eggs from the henhouse.

I continued on, my taut muscles relaxing with each step. This was my world, where I felt I belonged more than anywhere else. The first pasture I passed held seven horses, all of them boarders and owned or leased by my fellow riders on the equestrian team. A pasture to the far right held eight more lesson horses that had once been shown but had earned a quieter lifestyle at the stables.

The last pasture was smaller and had the five horses owned by Phoebe. Technically, Lacey was one of hers, but Phoebe had selected me to be Lacey's primary rider when I was thirteen, and Lacey and I had been partners ever since. I couldn't imagine my life without this special horse in it — a threat all too real if I didn't earn the rest of the money I needed to buy her. But, I had enough on my mind without thinking about that now, too.

The horses grazed at the far end of the pasture. I pulled the latch on the wooden gate and stepped inside. A couple of the horses noticed me and lifted their heads to stare. Lacey wasn't one of them. But, there was one sure way to get her attention. I tightened my lips, kept my teeth together, and let out a shrill whistle.

As usual, her head popped up from behind the first two horses, her ears flicked forward. I whistled once more, and she swung her head in my direction. Like a bulldozer, she pushed past Penny and Apache and trotted toward me.

I whistled once more, and her trot turned into a gallop. Behind her, Penny and Apache were joined by Spirit and Sadie who had moved so they could watch. I smiled at the line-up of horses who were all probably wondering if they were missing out on something. I reached into my jeans pocket and pulled out a peppermint flavored treat. Within fifteen seconds, Lacey was less than thirty feet from me, still coming full speed.

I held up my empty palm toward her and took a step back. "Whoa, Lace!"

She skidded on the grass as she attempted an abrupt stop. As a Quarter Horse, the ability to halt suddenly was innate, but the few hops she used to come to a full stand-still brought her thousand pound body precariously close to me and the fence.

I jumped a couple of feet back. "Easy, girl." Lacey dropped her head and nosed around my pockets. I opened my palm to show her the treat. "You're not spoiled at all, right?"

Her upper lip wiggled against it, then she nibbled it from my hand. I shrugged the halter and lead rope off my shoulder and slipped the halter over her nose and ears. After snapping on the lead rope, I swung the gate wide so we could go through side-by-side. After re-latching it, I led Lacey back down the worn path toward the barn.

Jamie was saddling Sasha when we entered from the paddocks, so I trotted Lacey to the other grooming area and tied her.

"I'll be ready in a minute," I said as I hurried to the tack room to get my equipment.

"That's okay," Jamie said. "Sasha and I can do a few rounds in the outdoor ring while we're waiting." She snatched her helmet from the top of the wooden grain bin, secured it and walked Sasha from the barn. Atticus, his tail wagging, padded behind.

I worked quickly to brush Lacey and get her saddled. Within minutes, we were outside and ready to go.

A leg of the Finger Lakes Trail system ran through the woods behind Phoebe's property. The equestrian team had spent many hours clearing low branches and brush to make the section where we rode more accessible to horse traffic. The result was a great nature walk where we could imagine the rest of the world didn't exist.

The trail wasn't far from the stables. We trotted along the edge of a green field — Jamie and Sasha in the lead. Lacey pulled at the reins once, hoping to steal a bite of alfalfa, but I pulled her in.

"Keep going, girl," I said, nudging her with my heel. We trotted until we reached the entrance to the trail, then slowed to a walk. Just after entering the woods, Jamie twisted in her saddle to talk to me.

"Hey, I hear Phoebe is selling Lacey."

"Yeah, I'm trying to save the money to buy her. I want to take her to college with me and join the equestrian team. I was hoping to have more time to save the money, but there's someone who wants to buy Lacey for their daughter for *this* show season, and they offered more money."

"You know how much she wants for her?"

I squeezed my legs to encourage Lacey to walk faster so we could move next to Jamie. "All I know is she was offered ten thousand, but Phoebe said if I give her eight, she's willing to forfeit the extra two thousand so Lacey and I can stay together."

"Eight thousand?" Jamie whistled under her breath. "How much do you have saved?"

"Almost seven."

"Thousand?"

"Yeah. I babysit a lot, and I've also been saving what I earn here. I only have about another month, or I'm going to lose her."

Jamie swatted at a horse fly that landed on Sasha's neck. "I can't believe Phoebe would do that to you."

"It wasn't planned," I said, "but at the last show we were at, Lacey and I did so well that the guy found Phoebe and offered her cash on the spot for Lacey." I threaded my fingers through Lacey's mane next to the rein. "I get it. The stable is Phoebe's business. I think her offer to me is pretty amazing."

I inhaled deeply to keep calm, not wanting the prospect to ruin my ride. I'd already lost countless hours of sleep considering that possibility. It made me determined to work more to earn enough money.

"Man, you could buy a used car for that amount," Jamie pointed out.

I shrugged. "Yeah, but owning her is more important to me. We're like best friends. I can't imagine not having this horse in my life. A lot of people say, 'Just get another horse', but she and I have a bond. I don't want some other horse."

Jamie smiled and nodded toward Atticus, who was sniffing the base of a nearby tree. "That's like me with Atticus."

"When I was twelve my father went out to California to help fight a wildfire, and he was killed when the wind suddenly shifted and trapped him and a couple of other guys. Somehow the others got out. He didn't."

"Oh, my gosh. I'm sorry," I blurted.

There was a moment of awkward silence. The horses' hooves crunched through a pile of leaves that covered the trail, punctuating the momentary stall in the conversation.

"It was rough," Jamie acknowledged. "Having Atticus was the only thing that held me together." She tipped her head and smiled. "I hope it works out that you can save enough money to buy Lacey."

I laced the reins through my fingers and straightened in the saddle. "It has to work out. This is my dream."

A squirrel darted across the trail in front of us, and Atticus lunged after it. I was happy for the distraction. I couldn't imagine losing Lacey, but it was a possibility.

Jamie laughed. "Go get 'em, Atty."

The squirrel weaved around a few trees before it finally raced up the trunk of a big maple. Atticus circled it, jumped against the tree, and circled some more, but the squirrel sat on an upper branch and chattered, teasing the dog.

"So," Jamie said, "back at the barn you said you needed to go for a ride to clear your head. Anything you want to talk about?"

I pushed my helmet off my forehead and scratched the itchy part along my hairline. This was all so fresh that I didn't know if I even knew where to begin. I considered keeping it all to myself, but then I realized talking it out with Jamie might actually help.

"It's complicated," I said.

"That's okay. Lay it on me. Maybe telling me about it will make it all clearer in your mind."

Atticus barked and scratched at the tree. Lacey stopped and swung her head in his direction, seemingly interested in his game. After stopping Sasha next to us, Jamie shifted in the saddle to give me her full attention.

When I hesitated, she smiled. "I'm a good listener."

"I'm just not sure where to begin," I said.

Atticus gave up on the squirrel, and we started walking the horses along the trail again while I shared. I gave Jamie the quick synopsis, which included glossing over how Alex and I ended up being adopted by our aunt and uncle, to my obsession over the last year with finding our father, to the newspaper article and picture I'd found on-line, to my face-to-face with the guy who was our father, and finally, to the blow up this afternoon at the house when Mom found out.

I was well into the details when Lacey stumbled on a rock and almost fell onto her knee. I tightened my legs and moved with her until she steadied herself and got her foot back under her. Leaning forward, I patted her neck. We were such a good team.

"It's a crazy mess," I said. "I don't even know what to think or do."

"Why was this guy's picture in the paper?" Jamie asked.

"He saved a little kid from a house fire, and he broke his leg doing it. He got some heroism award."

Jamie reined in Sasha and turned to look at me. "Wait a minute. Is this guy from Keuka Shores, by any chance?"

I halted Lacey next to Sasha. "Yeah."

Jamie's forehead furrowed below the brow of her riding helmet. "Okay," she said, drawing out the word as if it were three syllables. "Is his name Drew McAuliffe?"

"How'd you know?" My heart rate accelerated to the point that I could feel it.

Lacey sensed my tension. She pulled at the reins and stamped her foot, wanting to walk again. I had to turn her in a circle to get her to face Jamie and Sasha.

"Did you read the story, too?" I asked.

Jamie shook her head, but the expression on her face told me something was up.

"Savannah," she said, her voice low and serious, "I know Drew McAuliffe."

CHAPTER 4

Disbelief stole my breath. I wasn't sure who was more shocked — Jamie or me.

"What? You know Drew McAuliffe? How?"

She shifted in the saddle. "I don't really *know* him, only who he is. Kyle, my boyfriend, plays lacrosse, and Drew comes to watch the games because Chase is on the team."

"Is Chase Drew's son?"

An image of the teenaged guy climbing into McAuliffe's truck earlier flashed in my mind.

Lacey must have sensed my confusion, because she shuffled and tossed her head.

"Easy, girl," I said, absently pulling back on the reins. She took a few steps back before settling down.

"No, he's not his son. Drew's just a close family friend. I used to think he was dating Chase's mom because I see them together a lot, but Kyle said no."

Still holding the reins taut, I wrapped my hands around the saddle horn and squeezed, hoping to release some of the tension in my body. In some weird way, it was a relief to find out that Drew McAuliffe didn't have more kids.

"Wow! So you think Drew might be your father?" Jamie asked.

I shrugged. "I know he is. Our dad —" I hesitated and shook my head. Could I still call our uncle *Dad* if I now knew who our father really was? "Our adopted dad, my uncle, confirmed it. He even offered to go to Chase's lacrosse game with us on Wednesday in case Drew McAuliffe is there."

Jamie rested her forearm on the saddle horn. "And what if he is?"

"That's the million dollar question. I think Alex and I have to sort out in our heads what we want from all of this. Right now Alex just wants a chance to see him in the flesh."

Atticus bounded up the path ahead of us, so Jamie turned her horse in that direction and made a clicking sound in her cheek to urge Sasha to walk. At the cue, Lacey also picked up her head and started to walk next to them.

"If our father wanted us back in his life, he's known all these years where we were. I found out today he's even been sending money to support us."

"Then he must still love you," Jamie said.

"Or feel obligated," I shot back. I felt guilty for my sharp tone, so I quickly added, "I'm worried about Alex being crushed."

Jamie twirled the end of one of her leather reins next to her leg. "Maybe you're concerned about being crushed yourself."

I settled back in the saddle. "Maybe. As much as we'd like to know more about him, maybe this is all wrong. Maybe it has to be enough that we found him and know what happened."

Jamie's brows lifted. "But *do* you know what happened?"

"Not from him, but I think we've probably put enough of the pieces together now to realize we might be chasing after a dream that could end as a nightmare. I don't know, and in some ways having more knowledge is more intimidating than having none."

I nudged Lacey with my heel so we could move ahead of Jamie and Sasha, a kind of implied hint that I was ready to put this conversation behind me. When Jamie didn't push, I knew she understood.

The snap of twigs and crunch of dried leaves under the horses' hooves filled the awkward silence. Atticus darted over logs. Squirrels scurried up trees. Birds in far off branches happily tweeted. It was the normalcy of life magnified while chaos swirled in my head.

My life had been safe and predictable up until now. One side of me felt that if I hadn't really mattered to him up to this point, then maybe I didn't need Drew McAuliffe in my life. And, based on the way he'd turned his back, climbed into his truck, and driven away earlier today, he clearly didn't feel he needed me in his.

Confusion and mixed up emotions made my brain hurt. The real test as to whether there was any chance of rekindling this relationship would come if Drew McAuliffe showed up at that game. I hoped Jamie was wrong. I hoped neither Alex nor I would end up crushed.

Four days had given me plenty of time to agonize over the possible outcomes. True to his word, as soon as I got home from working at the barn Wednesday, Dad drove us to the lacrosse game.

The lights over the field lit our way as we crossed the parking lot. Alex, who had been all big talk and confident about the possibility of getting a look at our father, was suddenly quiet when we got out of the car. As we walked, we flanked Dad the same way we always had when we were younger and fearful of something we were approaching. It still made us feel safer to have the big protector in the middle.

The subtle hesitancy in our gait conveyed our true feelings. This was something Alex was determined he wanted. I was no longer really sure what I wanted, other than for Alex to no longer feel like there was a big void in his life that our biological father should fill. And Dad, in true supportive fashion, stood by us, whether he agreed with this decision or not.

Mom had softened her stance, but she wasn't willing to come with us. I knew she feared losing us, but I would never let that happen. We owed her and Dad too much for what they'd done for Alex and me when we could have ended up in the foster care system.

The obnoxious blare of a time clock buzzer bounced off the brick of the nearby high school and echoed across the hills that rose above Canandaigua Lake.

Alex picked up his pace, not to mention, apparently his confidence. "Come on. We're going to miss the whole game."

"Chill, Alex. There are four quarters." I looked toward the field and the scoreboard. "Third quarter. It's not like we're here to see the game, anyway," I chided.

We had one purpose for being here, and the weight of that had squelched most conversation in the car during the forty-five minute ride.

We followed a family of five down the sidewalk toward one set of metal bleachers. All three of us were like gawking tourists, scanning the spectator stands on both sides of the field. I didn't know if I'd recognize Drew McAuliffe again, and I wondered if, after all these years, Dad would even know him. Alex probably had the best chance because he'd printed another copy of the newspaper article and picture from the internet and had taped it next to his computer. I'd found him staring at it several times over the last few days when I'd passed his bedroom.

The field lights illuminated the spectators as well as the field, so I was able to see when Jamie stood and waved from one of the higher rows of the bleachers.

"Up there," I said, moving in front of Dad and Alex. "We can sit with Jamie. She knows Drew McAuliffe, so she'll know if he's here."

We climbed the bleachers, weaving around groups of people clumped together. Despite the warmer than usual weather for the beginning of May, there was a group of high school girls huddled under a big blanket.

"Hey, you made it," Jamie said, when we reached her row. She slid sideways along the seat so there was room for the three of us.

"Yeah, I had to work after school," I said, sitting next to her. A shiver shook me as the coolness of the metal bleacher seeped through the fabric of my jeans.

Dad and Alex sat next to me, and I leaned back so I could introduce them to Jamie. I'd explained to them on the way here how Jamie knew Drew McAuliffe. Immediately after the introductions, Alex bent forward to talk to Jamie.

"Have you seen him?" he asked.

Him. Like the bleachers weren't full of men. But, I'm sure Alex didn't say his name because Drew McAuliffe had been the huge elephant in the room, so to speak, since Saturday. Alex had been consumed with the countdown to tonight. To him, this was important to everyone, not just us, and needed no explanation.

Jamie shook her head. "No. But I don't know if he comes to all of the games."

The excitement in Alex's expression morphed into disbelief, and he turned to me. He suddenly looked eight rather than fourteen. "What if he's not here?"

There was a tug in my chest. Less than a week ago, our lives were so much less complicated. So much safer from hurt.

"There are other games," I said. Then, with a shrug I added, "And, I know where he lives."

Alex continued to stare at me for a few seconds, almost like he was assessing whether I'd really pursue this anymore. He had to know I'd never let him down. Even in the times when he totally annoyed me, I'd always been the one he could count on most. Finally, he turned toward the field, but I could tell he was searching the bleachers and sidelines instead of watching the game.

I focused on the players to see if I could pick out Chase. But that was dumb. With their helmets on, the guys all looked exactly the same, but I had seen his number on the back of his jersey on Saturday when he got in Drew's truck.

I turned to Jamie. "Chase is number eighteen, right?"

She scanned the field, then pointed toward the far corner. "Yeah. He's a defender."

I squinted and finally found him. "Alex, number eighteen is the kid who was with Drew McAuliffe the other day."

Alex and Dad turned and looked in that direction while I sat back and considered what I'd said. Calling our father by his full name felt weird in some ways, but the fact that we had no connection with him, calling him by his name gave the relationship the appropriate distance.

Jamie pointed to the opposing team's goal. "My boyfriend, Kyle, is an attackman. He's number forty-four."

I followed where she was pointing just in time to see the ball passed to Kyle, and then he spun and hurled the ball past the goalie and into the net. The bleachers rattled as fans jumped to their feet and cheered, Jamie included. We remained seated, staring at backs.

The people around us sat down in waves, but Jamie remained standing. She reached down and grabbed my coat sleeve to encourage me to stand up.

"I don't want to point," she said quietly, as if she was concerned someone else might hear, "but look down at the front row of the bleacher on the other side of the sidewalk. See the guy sitting on this end? Tall. Wearing jeans. He has his feet stretched out in front of him? Cast on the left leg."

"Tan Carhartt jacket and baseball cap?" I asked.

Jamie nodded. "Crutches leaning next to him."

"Yeah, that's him." I couldn't get a good look at him from the side, but everything else added up.

"The lady with the long brown hair next to him is Chase's mother."

The woman was mostly behind Drew McAuliffe, so I didn't have a good view.

Fortunately since there was no one sitting in the next couple of rows behind us, it didn't matter that we were still standing.

Alex must have figured out what we were doing, because he popped up next to me and pushed his hoodie off his head.

"Is he here? Do you see him?"

"Yeah." I gave him the same description that Jamie had given me, including pointing out Chase's mother. Dad didn't stand, but he stretched so he could look in the same direction we were.

Alex stared like he was memorizing everything he saw. Spectators yelled to the players and refs, but it was all background noise that I hardly registered.

"Looks like he's tall," Alex said.

"He is." I'd had an up-close and personal chance to learn that. But then, considering the fact that Alex was taller than most of his friends his age, I wasn't surprised. He had to get the height gene from somewhere, and it didn't appear to come from our mother's side of the family.

"Be right back. I'm going to the bathroom," he said. Before anyone could respond, he was stepping down the bleacher rows, making his way through tiny gaps between people.

"Alex —" I called, but he kept going.

I jumped to follow, but Dad grabbed my hand and held me in place. "Let him go, Savannah."

"But, what if he —"

"Let him do what he has to do," Dad interrupted.

Every muscle in me tensed. Even though Alex was a little bigger than me, despite being two years younger, my instinct to protect him was the same as when he was a little boy.

Dad slowly let loose of my hand as we watched.

Once Alex reached the bottom, he walked directly toward the bleachers across the sidewalk where Drew sat. I sucked in my breath and held it. Less than fifteen feet separated them, and he was still moving in that direction.

Something happened on the field, and the people in front of us jumped to their feet, yelling. I stretched to see over them, but I wasn't tall enough. I tried to look over shoulders and between the rows of heads, but there was no clear view.

Dad stood, too. Despite his claim to let Alex be, the way Dad's lip was drawn in a tight line showed that taking the "hands-off" approach was easier said than done. I finally stepped up onto the row behind us so I was higher and had a better view.

And Alex was gone.

I glanced toward Drew and Chase's mom. Drew was gone, too.

My mind whirled. How could they disappear so fast?

"They're gone!" I yelled to Dad. I stepped back into our row. "I'm going down."

Dad put his arm around me. "Savannah, relax. Alex turned down the sidewalk before he got to Drew, and Drew got up and went toward the concession stands."

I turned to Dad. "How can you be so nonchalant? Alex could be setting himself up for the biggest crash of his life."

An emotion I couldn't decipher crossed Dad's face. "Drew would never hurt you two." After one more glance in the direction of where they'd both gone, Dad sank onto the bleacher and clasped his hands between his knees. I continued to stand, with my attention split between him and where I'd last seen Alex.

"That's why he allowed us to adopt you," Dad continued. "The PTSD made his moods unpredictable, but unless he's changed, the last thing in the world he wants is for either of you to be hurt. Including emotionally."

The spectators around us sat back down like they were doing the wave. I glanced toward the score board. Less than a minute remained in the third quarter. Then, as the buzzer sounded, Alex rounded the corner at the bottom of our set of bleachers and started back up. Finally I could take full breaths again without feeling every inhalation caught in my throat.

"Where did you go?" I asked as he plopped down between Dad and me.

He scowled. "I had to take a whiz, okay?"

I sucked in my lower lip to staunch my desire to snap at him.

"I got a good look at him before he got up and walked away," Alex added. "He looks like the picture in the paper."

"Did he see you?"

"I don't think so, but when the game's over, I'm going down. I want him to know that we're here."

I shoved my hands in the pockets of my nylon jacket and squeezed my arms against my sides. I wasn't sure if my sudden chills were from the cool spring air or my overactive senses. I wanted to get this over with. The fourth quarter would probably feel like the longest one in history.

I tried to concentrate on the game and my conversations with Jamie, but it was hard. I found myself looking from Chase to Drew and back to Chase more than paying attention to where the play was. In the end, Kyle, Jamie's boyfriend, had scored two of the seven goals to contribute toward a win.

I clapped and cheered with everyone else as the final seconds wound down, but the blare of the buzzer cut straight through me. The seconds ticking down had put me on edge, and not for concern over the game's outcome.

The game no longer separated us from the opportunity to come face-to-face one more time with Drew McAuliffe. And now merely seeing him from a distance wasn't enough. If I didn't take the leap and face Drew on my own terms, instead of him sneaking up on me, I'd be kicking myself all the way home. Besides, now that we'd come this far, I owed it to Alex to give him a chance to meet him, too. Then we could each decide on our own whether we wanted to carry it any further.

With Dad here to back me up, my courage — or stupidity — surged. Confrontation wasn't typical of me, but for some reason I felt Alex and I had been cheated, and now we could do something about it. I turned and leaned down to Alex who had sat down.

Talking just loud enough so only he could hear me, I said, "You know what, Alex? I know the plan was to let you see him from a distance, but that's not good enough. We deserve more. I'm going down to make him face me. You with me?"

Alex leaped to his feet and swiped his sweatshirt hood off his head. He squared his shoulders like it was him and me against the world.

"Yeah."

Jamie lightly jabbed me with her elbow. "Hey, the guys are coming off the field. I'm going down to catch them. You can meet Chase."

I hesitated, a prickle of discomfort zigzagging along my neck. "Great." The word escaped from between my clenched teeth. I hadn't prepared myself for any questions Chase might have — especially if Drew had said anything to him on Saturday when I followed them. But I couldn't think of a graceful way to decline. I could only hope that we would end up being separated in the crowd so my focus could stay on my current goal — facing our father.

The spectators surrounding us began leaving the stands, so Jamie led us through the path created as the seats cleared. We followed, all of us stepping onto the next row down as if it would collapse under us. The air was suddenly heavy and clammy. Each groan of the metal bleacher reverberated through my body, ending with a jolt to my heart. The closer we got to the bottom, and to Drew, the more second thoughts crept into my mind. I didn't want a repeat of Saturday's shunning, at least, not for Alex. I had convinced myself that I could handle it.

The unknown of how our approach would be received made my stomach roll. My feet grew heavier with each step.

Drew and Chase's mother stood, but Drew leaned on his crutches, angled away from us. When we were almost to the bottom, Dad held his hands out in front of us.

He looked pointedly at me. "I heard what you said to Alex up there. You two wait here."

"No," Alex argued. "I want to meet him."

Dad didn't take his hands down. "That's fine, but I want to talk to him first."

"But —"

Dad raised his hand to halt Alex's argument. "Alex." He pinned Alex with the *I mean business look*. "Wait here."

Dad turned to finish his descent. Alex moved like he was going to follow anyway, but I grabbed his sleeve. He shot me a look of annoyance, but fortunately, I didn't have to say anything, and he didn't resist. Dad blended in with the other people going down, but he didn't get lost in the crowd.

Jamie had been leading, so she didn't know we had stopped. When she reached the pavement at the bottom, she turned and glanced up at us. I lifted my chin to indicate for her to go ahead. Kyle and Chase were coming toward the opening in the fence. Each had taken their helmets off.

Despite the way the sweat matted his hair, I was surprised when I recognized Chase from the brief look on Saturday. Only this time I had a better view, and my "hot guy" radar zinged to life. Even with his hair a mess, he was a hunk. I blamed my nervousness when I'd seen him the first time for the reason I hadn't noticed how handsome he was. There was no doubt if our paths had crossed under normal circumstances, I would have found a way to talk with him.

Despite the fact that I knew he wasn't Drew's son, for some reason it felt weird to have this instant attraction.

I gave myself a mental shake and shifted my attention back in Dad's direction. He had crossed the sidewalk, and Drew hadn't noticed him approaching because his head was turned toward Chase's mother. The two of them, so close to one another after so many years, and we had no idea what their last interaction had been like — but I doubted it was good since he'd never come back to see any of us.

My heart hammered as Dad stepped within a couple of feet of him. We saw Dad say something, and as if he'd been punched, Drew hopped back on his uncasted foot.

The moment hung frozen in time. It seemed no one moved or breathed. Finally, Dad put out his hand to shake, but it was a few moments before Drew reciprocated. At least that was positive.

Dad gestured toward us, but Drew didn't turn around. Instead, he dropped his chin and shook his head. Dad pointed again in our direction and continued to talk.

Heat peppered my skin. Was Drew shaking his head because this was all a mistake, and he really wasn't our father, or was he refusing the opportunity to talk to us?

Although Drew didn't turn around, Chase's mother looked past him toward us, her forehead wrinkled like she was confused. I wondered if she even knew, before this moment, that we existed.

At the same time, in my peripheral vision, I saw Jamie wave. "Savannah," she called, "come and meet Kyle and Chase."

I looked back at Dad, then Alex. Standing here on display was awkward. Going down to meet the guy who, it seemed, had replaced Alex and me in our biological father's life also felt awkward. Although, typically, I was an extrovert, right now I would have given anything to be able to fold in on myself and pretend the rest of the world didn't exist.

Then, annoyance flashed through me. This wasn't me, and it wasn't how I faced life. I realized the heat was a combination of anger that Drew didn't seem interested in acknowledging us and embarrassment that we were the kids he'd tossed aside twelve years before. Now, we were attempting to force him to admit we existed.

I straightened and turned to Alex. "Come on."

He followed without question as we took the last few steps off the bleachers. When he realized I was leading him away from Dad and Drew, he halted.

He glanced toward them, then back at me. "What the heck, Savannah? They're over there."

"Yeah, but let's let Dad talk to Drew for a minute. Besides —" I grabbed his jacket sleeve and tugged on it — "Jamie is going to introduce us to the guy I saw with Drew Saturday. Let's see what he's like first."

"Who cares?" Alex shot back.

"Look, Alex, I want to meet Drew as much as you do, but right now I'm respecting Dad. Trust me, we're not leaving here without making him face us up close."

Alex glanced toward them once more, then grumbled, "Fine," and followed me to where Jamie stood a few feet away.

Jamie slipped her arm around Kyle's waist, and he draped his grass and dirt-stained arm across her shoulder.

"This is Kyle," she said, tipping her head toward him, and then with her free hand indicated Chase. "And this is Chase Warner. Guys, this is my friend Savannah from the riding stable, and her brother, Alex."

I lifted my hand in a weak wave and smiled, acknowledging each of them separately. "Nice to meet you."

Kyle lifted his hand that held the helmet dangling from his fingers and smiled at me. He acknowledged Alex with the guy chin lift thing.

"Nice to meet you, too," Chase said, holding his hand out to shake mine. I stared at his fingers for a few seconds. Touching him, feeling his warm flesh, would make all of this concrete and real. Almost surreal. Meet him. Face Drew. I couldn't have imagined any of this a week ago.

Finally, I forced my hand forward and quickly shook his.

He turned his attention to Alex and put his hand out again. "Hey, man."

Alex's expression revealed a combination of wariness and curiosity. He slowly pulled his hands from the pockets of his jeans and accepted Chase's handshake.

"Hey."

"You play lacrosse?" Chase asked.

Alex shook his head. "Soccer."

"Cool. Me, too."

Interest flickered in Alex's eyes. "That's cool."

Despite the ambient sounds around us, the silence among us that followed was deafening. Alex shoved his hands in his pockets and rocked back on his heels. Jamie and Kyle stared at each other. Chase and I tried to look anywhere but at each other.

"So, why'd you come to the game?" Chase finally asked me. "Know someone on the other team?"

"No. There's someone here watching that we came to see." I turned toward Drew and Dad, and my breath caught in my throat.

Sometime while we were meeting each other, Drew had turned toward us. His stare lasered into me. I swallowed against the tightness. His words from Saturday cut through my memory as if he was saying them again now.

Leave it alone.

But I hadn't left it alone, and he didn't look happy about it.

Dad motioned us over. My skin prickled. This was really going to happen.

"Excuse us. Our dad's calling us," I said to Chase, Jamie and Kyle as I put a hand on Alex's shoulder to turn him in that direction. "It was nice to meet you." We started to walk, then I threw over my shoulder, "And good game. Congrats on the win."

"Thanks," the guys said in unison.

The walk from where we stood and where Dad and Drew stood was less than fifty feet, but with all attention on us, it felt like the length of the lacrosse field. With each step I focused more and more on Drew. This time the meeting was intentional. My insides bucked and swirled.

"You okay?" I said to Alex under my breath.

"Yeah," he said, the tone of his voice huskier than normal. Nope. He wasn't okay. His bravado had probably gotten wrapped around a pit in his stomach — just like mine,

It was instinctual for us to step next to Dad — or at least the man we'd called Dad for the last twelve years. Subconsciously, we knew he was our safety net.

Out of the corner of my eye, I saw Chase leave Jamie and Kyle and walk in our direction. I turned to look and noticed his furrowed brows. If he thought he was confused now, wait until he found out whom we had really come to see — and why.

"There's no easy way to handle this," Dad finally said, "but your wish was to meet your father. Introductions are awkward, so I'm not even going to bother."

"Your father?" Chase said, stepping closer. "What's going on?" He scanned all of us, his eyes now narrowed.

It was like Drew was mute. He stared at us, for some reason, more at Alex, but didn't say anything. I wondered if it was because he'd had four days to think about what he'd seen when he looked in the van at me.

Chase's mother crossed behind Drew to move next to Chase. I didn't know what she usually looked like, but right now she looked like she'd seen a ghost. She hooked her hand on Chase's elbow and lightly tugged. "Chase, why don't we go to the car and wait for Drew?"

Chase resisted. "But what's going on?"

"Let's give them privacy. I'll explain on the way."

Chase stared hard at Drew. His lips parted, like he was going to say something. After a moment, he clamped his mouth closed, then turned to follow his mother.

Which left us alone.

Drew leaned on the crutches and scrubbed one palm roughly across his face before looking back at us.

"I'm not sure what you all are expecting," he said, "but I think you've wasted your time." He looked pointedly at me and Alex. "You're better off pretending I don't exist."

I stepped closer. "But you do exist. How can we pretend you don't?"

"You see a shell," Drew said, his voice low and hoarse. "What you see on the outside isn't what's on the inside. You're better off without me."

"No, you're a good person. You saved a little boy's life," Alex countered. "We read about it."

"Payback," he responded. "I'm also saving your lives by staying out of them. Don't make me into something I'm not. You don't know me. You don't know who I really am."

"But we want to know you," I said.

"Chase knows you," Alex added, a hint of defiance in his voice.

"I owe him." Drew's voice was even more gravelly. "Forget about me."

Drew's eyes glistened in the lights. And just like that, he shifted onto the crutches and turned to hobble away.

Alex balled his fists at his sides. "You owe *us*!" he shouted.

But there was no response. I saw Alex's jaw tense, and a tear slid down his cheek, but he kept his eyes on Drew's retreating back. My tough, fourteen-year old brother had been brought to tears.

Every protective fiber in my body sprang to life, and my heart raged over the disappointment and hurt I saw on Alex's face. I turned and watched our father walk away from us — again!

"Wait!" I yelled, bolting after him. "I have something to say to you."

If this was the last time we ever saw him, then I had every intention of making sure he knew that this was his loss, not ours.

When I was right behind him, I reached for his sleeve but stopped when I realized, with his crutches, I could pull him off balance. Instead, I lunged in front of him, making him stop suddenly and teeter to maintain his footing.

With a bolstering breath, I looked up to force him to look at me. And when we made eye contact, my heart lurched.

His green eyes shimmered and moisture wavered on his lids.

My head jerked back like I'd been slapped when the truth hit me.

Despite his bravado in trying to keep us away, it was obvious that somewhere deep inside of him, we still mattered.

My tongue twisted in my mouth as I tried to form the right words in response to his raw emotion. My anger dissolved into compassion. As compelled as I was to reach out and touch him, I forced myself to fold my arms across my chest instead.

When he dipped his head and swiped his sleeve across his eyes, my resolution was made in a split second.

"You might not want us in your life, but I'll promise you this. I'll never give up on you."

CHAPTER 5

"18.5 seconds," Phoebe called as Lacey and I raced across the finish line in the ring. "Good job! You keep shaving time off your runs," she yelled.

Lacey cut to the right in a tight circle, and we bounced to a halt. Her sides heaved from the exertion, but she tossed her head, ready to go again. I leaned over the saddle horn and patted her sweaty neck. A half hour of working the cloverleaf pattern on the barrels and I was ready for a few minutes' break.

"Easy, girl," I said before twisting toward Phoebe, who sat on the mounting block next to the end of the finish line. "Better, but if Lace and I are going be real competition for anyone at the shows this summer, we have to smooth ourselves out more." I pulled the rein across Lacey's neck and nudged her with my boot heel. Her ears flicked forward, and her muscles tightened.

"Walk," I commanded. She swung her head toward the middle of the ring, and I knew what she was thinking. If I asked her to run again, she'd leap into a full-out gallop without hesitation. Sometimes I wondered if she had more fun doing this than I did. I nudged again and she walked toward Phoebe.

Phoebe crossed her boots at the ankle and looked up at us. "The important thing to keep in mind is that your technique is improving all the time. Speed is important, but what you do in that saddle is just as important. You're a great team. There's no doubt about it."

She studied us for a minute, chewing on her lower lip, a sure sign there was something important she had to say. "David Collier called again last night, Savannah."

My shoulders tensed. "And?"

"He added another two grand to his offer for Lacey."

I sucked in a breath. I still had another thousand dollars to go before I had enough money to buy Lacey at Phoebe's bargain price for me. What if David Collier's offers made it too hard for her to resist?

"I told him I wouldn't make any decision before the middle of June, but I think it's only fair that you know. He wants her for his daughter for this show season."

I swallowed against the lump in my throat and nodded. "Thanks."

My focus dropped to Lacey's gray mane, and I buried my fingers in the coarse strands. Even though I didn't own her yet, in my heart she was already mine. My mind buzzed with images of the shows we'd been in, the rides we'd been on, the times I'd cried into the soft hair on her neck.

I was lost in my thoughts when the horses in the pasture next to the ring suddenly galloped over the small knoll that had hidden them before, snapping me back to the present. The trees on the hill behind them created the perfect backdrop, as if this was going to be a photo on a horse calendar. Beautiful animals. Beautiful spirits. Beautiful souls. I couldn't imagine my life without them. Lacey stomped her foot like she wanted to join them.

"You're fine," I cooed, rubbing my hand along her neck again. They were all beautiful, but they weren't Lacey. There was no other equine partner for me.

"So, about the way you rounded the third barrel," Phoebe interjected into my thoughts.

I turned my attention back to her. I had to focus on the positive. I *would* have enough money saved by the middle of next month to buy Lacey. And we would be a team when I took her to college with me a year from September.

"Yeah, I know. I was tight on her mouth."

"Right. The reins aren't there to balance you."

I smiled. That was Phoebe's mantra, and she was right. She was an amazing barrel racer, with ribbons and trophies lining the walls in the barn office to prove it.

Phoebe nodded toward the center of the ring. "Take Lacey around again but at a slower pace. Start with a trot. When you get back up here, turn her around and take her again at a gentle lope. That way you'll feel what she's trying to do. That horse has an instinct about those barrels. Utilize it."

A groan gurgled in my throat, but I suppressed it. I understood why Phoebe wanted me to do this, but having to go back to the basics from the beginner level of reining annoyed me. I was ready to protest when the crunching of stones under tires caught our attention. All three of us looked toward the dirt driveway next to the barn. Jamie's little dark blue car was in front, and a dark green SUV I didn't recognize followed. I waved, then turned Lacey toward the starting line. I collected myself and her, concentrated on the task, and asked her to trot.

After I rounded the first barrel, I looked up and saw Jamie get out of her car. I refocused on the next barrel. When I was almost ready to round it, out of the corner of my eye I saw the SUV's door open and a tall guy get out. He had his back to us as he talked with Jamie.

I finished rounding that barrel, and we trotted toward the final barrel at the end of the ring. I glanced toward Jamie and the guy again, wondering if it was her boyfriend, Kyle.

When we came around the last barrel, I felt Lacey's muscles tense. She was eager to explode into a run, but I sat back in the saddle and lightly reined her in. She listened, but I could tell it took great restraint on her part.

Phoebe shook her head as we crossed the finish line. "You were unfocused. You can't let things outside of the ring distract you."

Totally busted. "I know. I was trying to figure out if that's Kyle with Jamie."

Phoebe stood and stretched her neck to see around Lacey's face. "Nope, not Kyle," she said. I turned to look just as the guy turned around.

As soon as I saw his face, goose bumps jumped out on my skin.

Chase Warner. I hadn't seen him since the lacrosse game three days before, but there was no doubt in my mind that's who he was.

I attempted to catch my breath, and at the same time squeezed out, "What's he doing here?"

"Who is it?" Phoebe asked.

I was so stunned, I couldn't say his name out loud.

Chase pushed his truck door closed, then he and Jamie crossed the grass toward the ring. With his hands shoved into his jeans pockets, his body looked rigid and tense. He didn't look up but rather focused on the ground like he thought he'd trip over something. Or maybe walk *into* something. Jamie was looking off toward Sasha's pasture. Neither of them talked as they walked. Serious. They were way too serious.

When they reached the edge of the ring, Jamie leaned down to peer between the two top horizontal boards.

"Hey," she called. "Chase wanted to come out and see you."

My heart pounded against my ribs. After we'd left the lacrosse game, I didn't know if I'd ever see him again.

He stretched to look over the top railing and waved. "Hi."

Lacey shifted under me, eager to run the barrels, or at least move, but I held her in place.

"Hi."

"Can I talk to you when you're done?" he asked.

"About what?"

He hesitated, then said, "I only want to talk. I think there are some things you should know."

I glanced at Phoebe, hoping she'd insist I work Lacey a little more.

Instead, she stood and took hold of Lacey's reins.

"Go. I don't want you running the barrels if you aren't fully concentrating. Too dangerous for you and Lacey. I can hold her if you want to go and talk with him."

"No," I said, my attention riveted back on Chase. "I'll see if he wants to walk along and I'll ride Lacey out the lane toward the woods."

There was no way I wanted to be down on the ground, facing him at an angle where he naturally would look down on me. No, I was staying on my horse where I felt confident and safe.

I called out to Chase, "I was going to walk her for a cool down. You can walk along if you'd like."

"That works." He turned to Jamie. "Thanks for showing me how to get here."

"Sure thing. I'll see you when you get back." Jamie pivoted and headed for the barn.

Chase came around the end of the ring and met me at the gate. He unlatched the hook and swung it open so Lacey and I could exit.

"Nice horse," he said.

"Thanks." I was so tense that I couldn't imagine carrying on a whole conversation.

He waited for Phoebe to exit, too, then extended his hand to her. "Hi, I'm Chase Warner."

"Phoebe Reynolds." Phoebe returned the handshake. "Nice to meet you, Chase."

"Close the gate?" he asked her.

"Yes, please." Phoebe stepped next to Lacey and handed me my phone. I'd given it to her so she could time me. "I'll see you back at the barn." Before turning away, she waggled her eyebrows.

I tipped my head to warn her to not jump to conclusions.

"Okay," I said, shoving the phone into the pocket of my sweatshirt.

The gate clicked shut behind us. Phoebe patted Lacey's rump as she went behind her. "Good workout today, by the way."

"Thanks."

Chase stood a few feet away, looking sheepish. "I'm sure you didn't expect me to show up here."

"You're right." I tapped Lacey with my boot heel, and she stepped out.

"Can we walk and talk?" I asked, as if I'd given him any choice.

"Sure." He jogged a few steps to get next to us.

The lane divided two of the larger back pastures and led to the woods far beyond. It was wide open. And safe. A light spring breeze added a bit of chill now that I wasn't working in the ring. Ahead of us, several robins hopped along the ground, pecking at the grass that was starting to green.

While Chase took in the view of the rolling pastures, I studied him. With his shoulders back and square, his posture exuded confidence. A stark contrast to the butterflies that had taken up residence in my stomach.

His head swung toward me, and he caught me staring. "It's really nice out here."

Averting my eyes like I was appreciating it all, too, I only responded, "Uh-huh."

I slid my thumbs along the curved, soft leather of the single gaming rein. Agonizing didn't come close to describing the awkwardness that hijacked the moment. I hadn't even said goodbye to him after the lacrosse game. I'd been too flustered to see tears glistening in Drew's eyes when I confronted him. Now, I couldn't imagine what would possess Chase to come and seek me out.

We'd gone down the path a few hundred feet when the band of tension across my shoulders got the best of me.

"Okay, spill it. Why did you drive all the way out here?"

He lifted his face and the late morning sun made his blue eyes sparkle. "To see you."

A warm jolt shot through me. His low voice was smooth, like his words could caress. Did he have to work at that?

Then, what he said sunk in. There was no way it was just to see me.

"Doesn't answer my question," I shot back, trying to appear aloof.

He hooked the thumb of his right hand in the loop on his jeans and squinted at me like he was thinking hard. Before he spoke, he pulled in a big breath that lifted his shoulders. Perfect athletic shoulders.

"I think you should give Drew a chance," he said.

I looked ahead of us on the path and steeled myself. "I don't think he wants to give *us* a chance." Lacey blew air through her nose almost as if punctuating that I was done with the situation.

"He's an amazing person, Savannah. But he's afraid."

"He survived the war. What does he have to be afraid of?"

"Himself."

"What? Is that psycho-babble or something?"

Chase shook his head. "How much do you know about him?"

"Basically what I read in the newspaper." I couldn't control the sharp edge to my voice. "I think that's the whole point here. We don't know him. Alex wants to get to know him, but I'm afraid he's setting himself up for a world of hurt."

I looked away, bothered by the ping of pain in my heart. I wasn't sure what was worse, our father being a mystery to us, or this slow unraveling of a past that had shattered so many lives. When I'd first started exploring to see if I could find him, I hadn't expected all of this complication.

A couple of the horses in the pasture to our right, Sadie and Apache, strolled toward us, their ears pricked forward. The late afternoon sun caused long shadows to stretch out on the ground beside them. The outside world seemed so serene while a storm brewed inside me. Why should this stranger be the one to know the intimate details about *my* father?

"You know what," I said, looking back down on Chase and grabbing the saddle horn as if it would ground me, "here's something that's been bugging me since the first time I saw you with my – with Drew. What is your relationship with him? Is he dating your mother or something, because it looked pretty cozy at the game the other night."

He smiled at me, and I found that really annoying. "Are you jealous, Savannah?"

"No! Yes!" I shook my head, fighting the confusion that was keeping me mentally off balance. He even made my name sound exotic. What was it about him that could affect me like this? "Maybe. I don't know." I tightened my grip on the saddle horn. "Just answer my damn question."

Chase lifted an eyebrow and cocked his head. "Okay," he said slowly. "So, everyone thinks that, but no, they aren't dating. Drew's been around for us for as long as I can remember, but something holds him back. I know my mom would like their relationship to go to the next level. And I think I want them to get together in that way even more than my mom does."

"Why?"

"Because I leave for college in the fall, and I want to know that my mom has someone to take care of her while I'm away."

"Good luck with that," I scoffed. "He clearly has commitment issues."

"Actually, it's the opposite. I had no idea you and Alex existed before I met you the other night. So, when we were alone, I asked him point blank what the hell was going on." Chase shrugged. "I have no idea how much of the story I got, but this is what I now know. He and my dad both served in Iraq, which, of course, I knew. My dad died over there, and what I didn't know was that Drew came back home to his family and for my dad's funeral. He'd been injured at the same time my dad was killed by friendly fire. He said it ate at him that my mom and I were left without my father, so he started looking out for us from long distance."

"What do you mean from long distance?"

"We lived near Buffalo, so it was two hours away. But my mom said he came out almost every Saturday to help with things around the house that my dad would have done if he'd been alive."

Chase stopped and looked up at me. "Do you think we could stop and sit down and talk?" He indicated the field past the pastures. "I'm okay with sitting on the grass."

"Okay."

I reined Lacey in that direction, then got off her when we'd found a good place under a tree that hadn't fully leafed out yet.

"Does this work?"

"Sure."

"So what were you doing in the ring when we drove up?" Chase asked as I dismounted.

Switching subjects? Was that the end of the conversation about Drew McAuliffe?

"we were doing the cloverleaf barrel race. Lacey and I compete in regional shows."

I unhooked one end of Lacey's rein from her bit so I could use it as a lead rope. She didn't waste time in nuzzling the ground to find mounds of sweet spring grass. Normally I wouldn't have let her eat with her bit in, but there was nothing normal about this situation.

We settled onto the slightly damp ground with several feet separating us. Lacey grazed off to my side at the end of the line.

"Can we get back to what we were talking about before?" I asked. "I have more questions."

Chase plucked a tall piece of grass, then tossed it off to the side. "Sure."

"So, did all of this stuff with him helping you happen before or after my mother died?"

He stretched his long legs out in front of him and leaned back on his hands, meeting my gaze as if we knew each other well.

"It turns out it was both. That night after the game, I asked my mother a million questions. I couldn't believe I never knew he had kids. He never told me. My mother never told me."

"Did she know?"

"Yeah. It turns out that you, Alex, and I actually met when we were little."

A zing of inner electricity shot through me. "What? That's crazy."

"It's true. My mother showed me a bunch of pictures of all of us having a picnic. And your mom was there, too." Chase reached into the pocket of his hoodie and pulled out a couple of pictures. "I brought these of us kids together."

He leaned way over to hand them to me. "I'm the biggest one of us, obviously. But does that look like you and Alex when you were little?"

A chill ran up my spine, and I nodded. "I don't remember this."

"We were too little. Nothing looked familiar when I saw the pictures, either. My mom said it was at our old house in Orchard Park."

"Buffalo Bills country," I interjected, still studying the pictures, wondering what my parents were doing away from the camera's lens.

"You like football?" Chase asked.

"No, but anyone in western New York knows the Bills' home field is in Orchard Park."

"Yeah, I guess."

My mind swirled, trying to remember this moment in time. Trying to picture us together beyond these still shots.

I handed the photos back to Chase, then pulled my knees up toward my chest so I could wrap my arms around them. "This is too weird." I was quiet for a moment as I thought about it. Then, I said, "What did your mom think suddenly happened to us?"

"She told me about the night your mom died. She said Drew had a horrible flashback and totally lost it. Your mom was trying to keep you and Alex safe, so she took off in the middle of the night with you in the car. She was killed, and Drew has felt responsible every day since then."

Like a switch had been flipped, anger flared in me. The more I learned, the more overwhelmed I felt.

"So he abandoned *us*?" I snapped. "Yeah, that makes sense. Not!"

"Actually, it does." Chase kept his voice even. "My mom said he was afraid if you stayed with him that he'd have a flashback and hurt you. He thought it was better to let you be raised by your mother's sister so he knew you'd be safe and loved."

I picked at the dried leaves next to me, crumbling them and tossing them to the side. For a second I almost laughed out loud at the inadvertent symbolism. It's how I'd felt for the last few days, crumbling inside and tossed aside, even though I tried to convince myself that I didn't care and it didn't matter. I'd never been good at lying – even to myself.

"Look, Savannah, I know you're angry, but I came here to tell you that I've been talking with Drew all week, and I've convinced him to meet with you and Alex."

I jumped to my feet so fast that it startled Lacey, and she jerked her head up. "You had to *convince* him to see his own kids? Really, Chase?"

I'd heard my aunt use the term that something "made her blood boil", and I'd always wondered if that was something she actually felt. Now, I could confirm, that, yes, she could, because my body flushed so fast that my blood boiling was the only explanation.

Chase stood and stepped toward me. "You're twisting my words."

I clipped the end of Lacey's rein back onto her bit and whirled toward Chase. "You know what? Last week I promised him I'd never give up on him. But it hurts to know we don't mean enough to him. Maybe I was wrong. The dad who has raised me, and loved me all these years, is good enough for me."

"I don't think you really mean that," Chase challenged. "You've been searching for your father for more than a year."

"How do you know that?"

"Jamie told me."

I moved around to Lacey's side and stepped up into the stirrup. "Well, I won't let anyone hurt Alex, and if our father had to be convinced to see us, then I'm thinking I'm way off base." I swung myself into the saddle and shortened my hold on Lacey's rein. "I've always been told that I can't save the world and that my heart is too big. My emotions took over when I saw Drew was upset. I can't change him, and I can't make him want to be with us." I waved my hand dismissively. "You know, for now, we'll pass. Thanks for trying, though."

"What about Alex? I know what it's like to be a guy and not have my real father around. If I had the chance to be with him, I'd jump all over it. I think Alex would, too. He's fourteen, Savannah. He wants to know his father. By denying him that opportunity, you're hurting him just as much. Have you thought of that?"

My jaw clenched so tight that I couldn't make it move to respond. My body quivered, and I took slow breaths to get my brain back to thinking rationally. Although there were times that Alex drove me so crazy that I wanted to disown him, I'd never in a million years purposely hurt him. Lacey, apparently sensing my tension, pawed the ground.

"I have to get back to the barn." I pulled the rein across her neck and pushed my leg into her side. She turned away from Chase and toward the lane.

"Wait!" Chase jogged up next to us, and I stopped. The breeze ruffled the short strands of light brown hair above his ears. He held a piece of paper up to me. "This is my cell number. My mom, Drew and I are going to be working on one of the Purple Heart Homes house projects tomorrow. Drew said I could invite you and Alex to come and help, too. It would be a good way to spend time with him without it being really awkward since we'd be so busy."

I ignored the fact that he was trying to get me to take the paper. Instead I asked, "What's Purple Heart Homes?"

He lowered his hand.

"Purple Heart Homes is a group of volunteers who help veterans who were injured while serving. They help with different projects, usually house-related. Drew was actually one of the founders of the local chapter. The original chapter is located in North Carolina. It was started by a couple of veterans who saw the need for this kind of work."

Chase paused and looked toward the pastures. When he looked back at me, his expression was serious — bordering on intense.

"I like participating in these projects. It's a way for me to show my appreciation for the sacrifices our military men and women make every day."

"I can tell this is important to you."

"Sometimes when we're working on a house, it makes me think about my father. If he hadn't died when he did, maybe he would have been hurt later and needed this kind of help." He shrugged. "So, I do what I can, and tomorrow is personal. This veteran we're helping, Rashawn, is one of Drew's close friends. He served three tours in Iraq, and on his last tour his unit was hit by an IED. The injury was so severe that he lost a leg."

It took me a moment to find enough breath to respond. "Oh my gosh! That's awful."

"That's why we're helping him. A big group of us are going to his house to do some work. Painting, yard work, building a ramp. That kind of thing. Drew and I have worked on a few projects for them."

The pictures I'd seen of soldier homecomings flashed through my mind. Had my father been given any kind of homecoming? Had our mother taken us to an airport to welcome him home after his last tour of duty? I racked my brain for any hint of a memory. A little girl with a handful of balloons. A little boy toddling toward the father he hadn't seen in months. A wife, tears streaming down her face, wrapping her arms around the partner she could have easily lost.

But, there was nothing.

Chase must have sensed that I was conflicted. He laid his hand on the saddle's pommel next to the saddle horn. Even though he wasn't touching me, there was something electrifying about his hand being so close.

He lifted his other hand one more time, reminding me of the piece of paper he'd offered minutes before.

"Take this chance to get to see Drew in action, Savannah. Maybe you don't agree with decisions he's made, but he is one of the kindest and most caring people I've ever known."

I let my breath out slowly and stared at the rectangular piece of white notepaper in his hand. He'd folded it in half and held it between his fingers.

"You've made yourself clear, Savannah. But, this isn't just about you. This is about Alex, too. Do it for him." One eyebrow cocked up, and he added, "If you don't want to do it for Alex, do it for this veteran who could have died because he was protecting your freedom."

A breeze caught the paper, and it fluttered. I snatched it and stuffed it into the front pocket of my jeans. Under different circumstances, I would have been ecstatic to have a guy as good looking and nice as Chase handing me his phone number.

But, under different circumstances, I wouldn't feel like I'd been backed into a corner.

"I have to get back," I said.

I nudged Lacey to start walking again, and the paper crinkled in my pocket. Nothing so light and thin had ever felt so big to me. Its weight wasn't in pounds. Its weight came with my decision regarding what to do with it.

CHAPTER 6

Every pair of eyes was focused on Alex and me as we came up the sidewalk toward the volunteers gathered on the front lawn of the Purple Heart Homes project house. At least I imagined everyone was staring since we were the newcomers. In reality, it looked like only Chase and a couple of others even noticed we'd arrived, but that didn't stop my insides from knotting.

Lack of sleep didn't help. My overactive mind had me awake off and on all night — sometimes excited, sometimes nervous. Staring at my phone. Staring at my ceiling and the narrow streak of light from the nightlight in the hall that Mom had insisted we needed for safety since the day we'd moved there. Little signs that showed how much she cared about Alex and me feeling safe. And loved.

Of course, she freaked when she found out I'd been in contact with our father. For some reason, to her, he represented a threat.

By coming here today, even though Dad had given permission, would she think that meant her love and concern didn't matter? I hated how finding our father had turned our lives upside down instead of making everything feel right.

Chase raised his hand to us and started across the lawn, weaving around wheelbarrows, stacks of two by fours, piles of roof shingles and a couple of tables set up with a massive array of tools, paintbrushes and paint.

"Hey, any trouble finding us?" he called as he approached.

"Nope. Directions were perfect," I said. I glanced at the different groups of people but didn't see any familiar faces — specifically, Drew.

Chase laughed. "Yeah, Keuka Shores isn't exactly the big city."

When he reached us, he fist-bumped Alex. "Hey, man. Glad you're here."

Alex did the male chin lift in acknowledgement. "Me, too, man."

When Chase turned to me, I swore his expression softened and his voice lowered. "I'm glad you came, Savannah. I didn't know if you would."

I started to respond, but then his eyes locked on me. I was trapped, mesmerized by the blue depths. For that moment, he made me feel like I was the only other person on Earth. What was this irresistible pull that made me want to be near a guy I hardly knew?

Next to me, Alex cleared his throat. "Earth to Savannah," he mumbled.

Despite the chilly temperature, heat flared across my cheeks. My brain scrambled to recall what Chase had said that I needed to respond to. Oh, yeah, he'd commented that he hadn't been sure I would show up.

"Th-this is a nice thing to do," I stammered. "And, luckily, I found someone to cover my shift at the barn."

Chase held my gaze like he was looking into my soul. I struggled against the urge to shift my attention, but I was determined to not look away first. I didn't want him to know he had me flustered.

"So," Alex interrupted, "what are we gonna be doing?"

Chase smiled and shifted his attention to Alex. "Probably a little of everything. There's a lot of work to do. Come on." He motioned for us to follow him up the sidewalk where people had started gathering. "You'll get your job assignments from Joe Bailey. He's crew chief today." Chase pointed toward the front of the house. "He's the guy wearing the dark blue sweatshirt and the carpenter's belt."

I craned my neck to see where he was pointing. It was easy to locate Joe because, even though he looked like he was average height, he was heads above everyone else as he stood on the porch. He was talking to a couple of men and a woman who had their backs to us, each of them pointing to different areas of the house.

The front of the small ranch-style house was dotted with big patches of peeling paint, the porch sagged, and the bushes that I could see in between the workers milling around were overgrown and surrounded by piles of old, dried leaves. I couldn't imagine that this would be a one day job – even with all of these volunteers.

As we walked, Alex scanned the front lawn. "Is our dad here?"

Even though this was the main reason we were here, to spend time with Drew McAuliffe, the fact that Alex's question sounded so natural set my nerves on edge.

Chase stretched to look over the crowd. "Over there by the end of the porch. Come on." He weaved through the people, politely excusing himself when he cut in front of them. Alex was right behind, eagerness evident in each quick step he took.

I followed at more of a distance, trying to ignore how the hair on the back of my neck prickled the closer we got. Even though Chase said our father had agreed to us coming, I was sure my expectations for our interactions were different than what Alex anticipated. Based on comments he'd made in the car, Alex imagined Drew suddenly being the doting father who wanted to teach his son how to use all of the tools set out on the tables. I wished I could protect him from the inevitable letdown.

A slight breeze swirled around us and ruffled my hair, sending a shiver down my spine. I flipped up the hood on my sweatshirt and tucked my arms tighter to my sides with my hands clasped at my chest. Why did no one else seem affected by the chill? Maybe it was because so many of them had their hands wrapped around paper cups of hot drinks with steam swirling into the crisp air.

Like a snow plow clearing the way in a storm, Chase led us through the crowd and straight to our father. Straight into the storm.

Drew and two other men leaned over a table that had building plans stretched out on it. The edges curled in the breeze, but without missing a beat of their conversation, whoever was nearest that end slapped it back down and held it in place.

I recognized Chase's mother, involved in an animated conversation with two other women, standing next to Drew's truck in the driveway. She saw us before Drew did. Her glance darted toward Drew, then back toward us before her lips lifted into a small smile. She left the other women, starting to talk before she reached us.

"Hi Savannah. Alex. I'm Angela. I'm sorry we didn't formally meet at the lacrosse game. I'm Chase's mom." She held out the hand that wasn't gripping a coffee cup. "It's so nice to see you again. I'm glad you came today."

Alex extended his hand first. "Me, too," he answered. "I can't wait to get to work."

I stepped next to Alex and reached toward Angela to shake her hand after him. "Thanks for having us." I didn't know what else to say, and I cringed at how it sounded as if we were arriving for a sleepover.

"Have you ever worked on a Purple Heart Homes project before?" she asked.

We both shook our heads. I'm sure Alex couldn't help noticing the same thing I did. Even in a thick gray sweatshirt, Angela, with her long, brunette hair pulled back in a ponytail and a warm smile that lit up her face, was very pretty.

"You're in for a life-changing experience, then," she continued. Her eyes sparkled, and the cool morning air tinged her cheeks in a delicate rosy pink.

"Since this is your first time," she continued, "it's important to try a little bit of everything. Each work station assignment is different, and the people working them come with an array of skills and experience. More important, there's not one person here who won't be happy to teach you everything you need to know."

Even though I was hearing everything Angela was saying, my thoughts raced through the events and emotions since we'd met at the lacrosse game. Because of the brevity of our meeting and the surprise and confusion at that moment, there hadn't been a chance for us to see what she was like. She'd only had a chance to give us an apologetic look before she'd gone to her car.

As I listened to her, I couldn't help but hear what Mom and Dad had drilled into us from an early age - first impressions can totally affect how you feel about someone. I hadn't had time to form a first impression a few days ago, but now, my first impression of Angela stunned me. I couldn't imagine not wanting to know more about her.

Another pre-conceived notion blown out of the water. I'd come here prepared to tolerate her for the sake of being polite. In one minute she'd already made me like her. Everything about her screamed, *You can trust me.* After the turmoil of the last week, I was comforted by that kind of first impression.

"Let's step over here so Drew knows you're here," she said.

I pivoted to follow but faltered briefly when I looked up. Our father had hobbled on his cast to come away from the table. Now he stood just a few feet away. The other men, who had also been studying the plans, gave us a quick glance before turning their attention back to the papers. I was sure they had no idea how major this moment was.

As we approached, Angela said, "Savannah and Alex just got here, Drew." She moved next to him and laid her hand against his upper arm. Watching this brief interaction made one thing clear: she thought of Drew McAuliffe as more than a friend.

Drew cleared his throat, and his Adams apple bobbed above the collar of his dark blue fire department sweatshirt before he spoke. He glanced away for a second before looking back at Alex and me.

"I want to apologize for the other night."

"No," I interrupted. "You don't have to apologize. You weren't —"

Drew held up a hand to stop me. "I was rude. You didn't deserve to be treated that way."

He scratched the back of his head and grimaced. "Truth be told, I'm sure I owe you a lot of apologies, but this isn't the time or place."

My stomach fluttered when Drew turned his full attention on me. The last time we'd looked into each other's eyes, I'd made a promise that I wouldn't give up on him. I'd already flip-flopped once when talking to Chase the day before. Where did I come off making a promise that had such potential to backfire?

"Savannah, I'm willing to meet you halfway, if it's what you want."

"Forget what she wants," Alex interrupted, stepping almost in between us. "Even if she doesn't want to get to know you, I do. You're our dad. I'm not losing out because she's afraid."

Drew suddenly stiffened when Alex used the word afraid and tipped his head a bit. I had no way of knowing if it was that word that caused the reaction or the fact that Alex said *I* was afraid. I couldn't get it through Alex's head that I wasn't afraid for me. I was afraid for him. I didn't want his hopes and dreams to be squashed, and this was all so new, there was definitely a chance for that.

Angela stepped in. "Today is about having the chance to get to know a little about each other and to help out a veteran in need. Let's leave it at that without any expectations."

I jumped when Chase spoke from behind me. I'd forgotten he was there.

"Mr. Bailey is trying to get everyone's attention," he said, referring to the crew leader. Chase, Angela and Alex started to move in that direction, but Drew held eye contact with me for a few more seconds like he was trying to figure me out. Good luck with that, I thought. My emotions were so tied up in knots, I couldn't even figure myself out.

"I'm not making promises, Savannah," Drew said quietly. "I don't know what will happen come the end of the day. Let's just make it that far. We're all here to give back to someone who almost lost his life while serving our country. That should be our focus today."

I nodded, and he turned and limped toward Chase, Angela and Alex. I was left to stare at his back and mentally digest his words. According to the newspaper article Alex and I found, Drew had also risked his life while serving our country, and in fact had been injured, but instead of pointing that out, he focused on what he could do for someone else. I couldn't help but admire that.

Then, another descriptor came to mind. Complicated. He was basically a stranger with a complicated past - a life I'd been a part of at one time. No doubt, any potential rebuilding of a relationship with him would also revolve around the word complicated. I hoped I was up to the challenge.

Laughter rose from different areas of the crowd on the lawn. Someone rang a small bell like a teacher in the olden days would have on her desk, and like Pavlov's dogs, everyone quieted and turned their attention toward the porch. I pushed my hood off my head so I could hear better.

Joe Bailey was joined on the landing by a young man who looked to be in his late twenties. The first thing I noticed was the man was leaning on crutches, and he was missing the bottom half of his right leg. A black Labrador retriever stood between him and Joe.

"Good morning, workers," Joe called out. "First, thanks to everyone who has volunteered today to help our friend. And, second, I'd like to introduce this guy." Joe put his hand on the man's back. "This is Marine Corps Sergeant Rashawn Long. Rashawn gave me the okay to give you some background. He was injured by an IED when he and his fellow men were clearing a school during a firefight. And—" Joe looked down at the dog at the veteran's side — "this is Trooper, Rashawn's service dog. He's a working dog, so please don't approach or pet him without permission from Rashawn. The dog had originally been used as a therapy dog for a group of veterans, but now he's been assigned to Rashawn. Trooper is used to people, but he needs to focus on his job."

The dog's attention was fixed on Rashawn, who looked uncomfortable with all eyes on him. He raised a hand but dipped his head like he was embarrassed.

"Thanks, everyone. Really appreciate what you're doing," Rashawn murmured, barely loud enough for us to hear.

Joe raised his hand to Rashawn's shoulder and squeezed before he dropped it and lifted a clipboard he held in the other hand. "Most everyone already has their assignments. We have some last minute volunteers, so if you'll come forward when I'm done, I'll let you know where you're startin' off." Joe pointed to an area to our left. "We have refreshments under the canopy over by the garage, so help yourselves. We'll break for lunch at 1200 hours sharp. Any questions?"

We were dismissed, and it was clear that many of the volunteers were experienced with this type of project. They picked up tools and scattered to get to work. Alex and I moved forward with the other late volunteers to get our assignment, but Drew stopped us.

"Joe and I already discussed where to put you two since you're new at this. Savannah, you'll start out on the paint crew with Angela and Chase. That okay?"

I glanced at Chase, who gave a quick nod of approval. Work in close proximity to him for a few hours? I nodded and forced a serious look to cover my delight.

"Sure, I'm good with that." This was not going to be a difficult duty.

Drew looked at Alex. "You'll work with my crew building a ramp on the porch. That work for you?"

Even though I could tell Alex was also trying to be cool about his assignment, a smile tugged at his lips.

"Oh, yeah! I'll be rockin' the circular saw," he said, fist pumping the air.

The people near us burst out laughing. That's all it took to lift my spirits and relax me. Alex was happy he was here. That's what mattered most. Then again, my assignment wasn't too shabby, either.

"Let's go pick out our weapons," Chase joked as the group dispersed. I followed him and Angela to the table that had the painting supplies. He spread a half dozen paint scrapers out in front of me and began to talk like a salesman on a commercial.

"This is a limited time offer, folks. Scrapers like these are a once in a lifetime deal." He picked up one and pointed to the handle. "And look at this, it comes in a variety of colors. There's blue and black." He picked up another one that looked very similar. "Oh, and there's black and blue. You get all of this, plus, we'll throw in a house that needs painting for less than you'd pay in a hardware store." He held out a scraper. "What can I interest you in, Miss?" He pretended people were surrounding him and he was pushing them back. "Now, folks, step back and give the lady a chance to decide."

Angela stood off to the side of the table shaking her head but clearly amused. I laughed, and it felt good. I'd been tense since I'd texted Chase to tell him Alex and I were coming to the work session after all. Several scenarios had run through my mind while I'd tossed and turned all night. This light-hearted, fun scene had definitely not been one of them, and if he could snap me out of my wary mood this easily, then there was definitely something in this day for me, too. Chase's charm was irresistible.

I pointed at the blue one. "I'll take the one in your left hand, please."

"Great choice!" he crowed. "Here you go, miss. I guarantee you by the end of the day you won't be sorry that you made this choice."

He handed me the scraper and smiled. "I'll also give you a demonstration at the side of the house on how to operate this highly complex tool."

"Hey, thanks," I said. His smile was contagious, and I felt all tension seeping away as I smiled back. Here was another first impression – even though, really, it wasn't our first time meeting – that warmed me. So far, I hadn't seen anything about Chase that I didn't like.

"Savannah may be sorry she got paired up with us," Angela quipped. "Let's get going, you Billy Mays wanna-be. There's a whole house to scrape and paint today."

He dropped his act and grabbed tools. "I have no idea who Billy Mays is, but some day you'll appreciate my talents."

"Doubt it," Angela responded in a sing-songy voice.

A tiny stab of envy shot through my chest. While I had a great relationship with my aunt and uncle, it tended to be more serious. These two were clearly comfortable joking with each other.

I glanced over to see that Alex was already carrying two by fours to the area where measuring and cutting was being done. There was another kid who looked to be almost the same age working in that group, and knowing Alex, they'd be buddies before lunch.

After I was introduced to the other workers at our "station", Chase retrieved an extension ladder and carried it to the left side of the porch.

"If you want to work over here with me, I'll get the stuff up above and you can work on what's below."

I propped a hand on my hip and pretended to be shocked. "What? That doesn't even make sense. What you scrape will come down on top of me."

He leaned the ladder against the roofline above a double window. "Not if you work on one side of the ladder, and I work on the other." He shook the ladder to make sure it was stable, then turned to me. "We're a team, Savannah." He winked. "I look out for my teammates."

"Did you really just wink at me? Are you like eighty years old?" I laughed because I couldn't believe how comfortable Chase was making me feel with him already. Even though I hardly knew him, the way he and his mother bantered back and forth, made it easy for me to tease, too.

"Nope, not eighty," he said, "but you're close. Eigh*teen* pretty soon."

"Do you wink at all of your teammates?"

"Only the cute ones." And then he winked again.

I was unable to resist flirting. "Now you're hitting on me?"

"Nope. Only stating the obvious." He started up the ladder. "Let's get to work before I get in more trouble."

Giddiness crept through me. I watched him climb, staring at his athletic backside with appreciation until I realized what I was doing. I blinked and looked away. And my gaze fell on his mother, who was watching me as she approached, and probably noticed where I'd been staring.

Forcing an innocent smile, I felt compelled to explain my actions.

"I'm not much for ladders. I'm glad I can work from the ground." It sounded lame because I wasn't afraid of heights at all, but at least it seemed like a halfway decent excuse for why I was looking up as he climbed.

I pulled the hood of my sweatshirt back over my head. It would keep any paint chips from landing in my hair and maybe cover some of the pink that I felt streaking my cheeks and neck. This was not the way to make a good first impression with a cute guy's mother.

The morning flew by as I worked next to Angela. She and Chase told me more about the local support group for veterans that had helped find Rashawn this home.

Angela stopped scraping for a moment and wiped her wrist across her forehead. "Too often these vets come back from serving and are left to readjust on their own. It's not that simple for them. They don't have jobs. Many don't have homes. Drew got lucky. He had his family to come back to."

I snapped my head toward her, but the look of horror on her face told me that she regretted her last statement.

Several seconds passed before she continued.

"Believe it or not, Savannah, he has said many times that if it hadn't been for having his family to come back to, he might have wandered around aimlessly himself trying to redefine who he was. But he knew you all needed him." She tipped her head toward Chase. "He knew Chase and I needed him, too."

A pang of emptiness hit my chest. What made him think *we'd* stopped needing him?

It wasn't a question she could answer, and there was no point in me dwelling on it. Refocusing the discussion on Rashawn's story was safer, so I looked toward the porch where he was handing off cut boards from one group of workers to another. Trooper lay a couple of feet away, out of the way but clearly alert.

"So, what, exactly does Trooper do that's so special?" I was a dog lover and had always wanted one, but Mom argued a dog would tie us down too much. It was the first thing on my "have to have" list someday when I had my own place.

Chase answered as he came down the ladder. "The dog is trained to handle the situation if Rashawn has a flashback or is extremely anxious. Not sure exactly what he does if that happens."

Chase walked away toward the table set up with the tools, so Angela picked up the explanation.

"Joe explained at a recent project planning meeting that Trooper had been the working therapy dog at a small rehab facility, but he and Rashawn had developed a special bond. When Rashawn was discharged, the handlers also felt Trooper was a perfect fit for Rashawn. They reassigned the dog, and the two of them went through specialized training in order for him to become Rashawn's service dog. So, here he is."

"Have you known Rashawn for a long time?"

She shook her head. "He and his wife only moved in a couple of weeks ago. Drew knew him. Actually, Drew knows a lot of people. I think he keeps himself over-involved in order to not have time to think."

I looked in the direction where Drew and Alex were working. Alex was holding the end of a tape measure on a board while Drew pulled the tape to the desired length and marked it.

Angela continued while I watched them. "Drew's been a huge advocate for the veterans who need help. If it weren't for him, Chase and I wouldn't be where we are now."

I pressed the scraper hard into a particularly tough spot while I listened. "What has he done for you?"

"He brought us here to Keuka Shores to start over after T.J. was killed."

I stopped scraping, and before I could ask who T.J. was, Chase answered from his perch on the ladder as if he'd read my mind.

"My father. He died in Iraq."

"Right." I looked at Angela. "Chase told me that his dad was killed by friendly fire. I'm sorry."

The corners of her lips lifted slightly, and she squinted as if one part of her wanted me to know that she appreciated my concern but the other was still dealing with the pain. "Thanks." Her eyebrows shot up and back down. "Friendly fire," she scoffed. "It's such a ridiculous term for a soldier's death. There's nothing friendly about it."

She leaned against the side of the ladder and got a faraway look in her eyes. "I don't know how we would have made it if Drew hadn't been there for us all these years. We owe him a lot. He stepped in where T.J. would have been."

Angela glanced back at me and hurriedly added, "In the general sense, I mean. You know, making sure we're taken care of. If anything needs to be fixed around the house, like when the water heater broke, he takes care of it. And he's made sure Chase had a father figure in his life. He's been wonderful to us."

"That's nice," I mumbled. I couldn't lie to myself. I suddenly felt cheated knowing he had been willing to be there for some other kid and not Alex and me.

We went back to scraping, but I swallowed a lump that rose in my throat. Her description of their life reminded me of something I'd learned in my freshman history class. One unit focused on events leading up to the terrorist attacks in New York City and the aftermath. We worked in groups doing research on different aspects related to the event.

My group researched survivor's guilt and its role in the unusual phenomenon of firefighters in the New York City Fire Department leaving their families to marry the widows of firefighters killed in the rescue efforts. They had stepped in to take the place of the men who hadn't survived. Psychologists had partly attributed it to survivor's guilt.

Was that why Drew had thrown everything into Chase and Angela? Before this moment, I hadn't really considered what they had lost because Angela's husband hadn't come back from war.

Even though a part of me was jealous that they had been the benefactors of what belonged to Alex and me, I also felt sorry for them. "I'm glad he was there for you."

Angela must have sensed what I was feeling, because she stopped scraping and stepped closer to me. "Savannah, I'm sorry. This must all sound horrible to you, like he chose us over you and Alex."

I shrugged, uncomfortable with how she'd nailed what was on my mind. I turned back to the house, gritting my teeth and putting every ounce of power behind the tool as I scraped. Every fiber of my being seemed to vibrate with each movement.

"It's fine. We weren't old enough to understand what was happening at the time."

"He's never shared specific details with me, Savannah, but I know he believed he was doing the best thing for you and Alex when he allowed your aunt and uncle to adopt you. Despite how it seems, he's never put you out of his life. I found that out when I had to take him to the emergency room one time. He handed me his wallet to get his medical card out. You want to know what I found tucked in one of the little pockets?"

I shrugged but kept scraping. "I guess."

"A laminated picture of you and Alex when you were little."

My mind whirled, and the rapid staccato of my heartbeat drowned out the sounds of saws and hammers and voices. I kept scraping as I tried to process what that revelation meant.

Angela put her hand over mine and stopped me from scraping. "Even after all these years, there's a lot going on in his head that I don't know about. He keeps a safe emotional distance from us."

"What do you mean?" I pretended to start scraping again so her hand would have to move off mine.

She started scraping again, too. "Well, for example, he'll help us get a Christmas tree and put it up, but he won't help us decorate. And he never comes for a holiday meal, even though I've invited him for every one. He's very guarded with how much he'll let us into his life — the part that requires emotional attachment. I'm sure it's from being at war. We can't comprehend what our soldiers experience. They can't un-see. They can't undo."

I glanced again in the direction where Drew and Alex were working. Drew stood back a few feet away from Alex while Alex used the circular saw to cut boards. Even with the goggles covering Alex's eyes, when he looked at me before he started cutting, I could see the happiness on his face. He gave me a thumbs up then went back to cutting.

"I care very deeply for your father," Angela continued, "and I hurt for him, but I've come to realize that I have to accept the limits on what he's willing to give us and not expect more. It's like there's a disconnect with others that we've never been able to bridge."

I stilled the scraper and looked at her. "So, what are you trying to tell me?"

"Try not to judge him. Now that you've reconnected, take the time to get to know him."

I narrowed my eyes. "I want to, but you make it sound like he won't *let* anyone get to know him."

Angela shifted and looked back toward Drew and Alex. "He's put up a barrier, you're right. But give him a chance. He dropped his guard and was willing to allow today to happen. Every fiber in his body is wired to help and protect others before himself. It may be a long haul, but the channel for communication is now open." She turned back to me. "Wipe the slate clean, Savannah, and let this be a fresh start. You all deserve it."

When I glanced back to Drew and Alex, Drew was leaning over the boards, and he and Alex were almost head to head as they measured. It looked natural, like this was something they did all the time. Father and son, working together.

I was lost in the moment when a repetitive noise broke the relative quiet.

Bang! Bang! Bang! Bang! Bang!

I jumped, hitting my shoulder on the edge of the ladder at the same time I heard someone shout, "Cover! Now!"

The movement was a blur, but I realized Drew had grabbed Alex and pushed him to the ground, throwing his own body over top of him like he was protecting him.

Everyone stopped working and turned to stare.

"Damn it!" Chase ground out as he hurried down the ladder. "Drew!" he yelled as he raced across the grass. "Drew, it's okay. It's just the nail gun. It's okay."

I ran in that direction, too, concerned about Alex being under our father. Even though it was only a short distance away, it felt like a mile. "Alex! Chase! What's going on?"

A couple of the other men dropped their tools and charged toward them as well.

I dodged the people who had stopped to stare, craning my neck to see what was happening.

"No, don't touch him," Chase shouted when one of the men started to reach down toward Drew. He batted the man's hand away and stepped in between them and Drew.

"Drew, it's not gunfire," he said in a calm voice. "It's not gunfire. It was the nail gun. Everything is okay. Let Alex up."

The world stood still while we waited for movement. Out of the corner of my eye I saw Trooper, Rashawn's dog, bound across the yard and drop next to Drew, pushing his body against Drew's side.

Drew, facedown and covering Alex with his body, slowly pulled his clasped hands away from the back of his head and neck. Trooper nudged him next to his ear, making Drew turn his dirt-smudged face toward him. The dog pushed himself in the grass so his body was even tighter against Drew's.

A chilling silence hung over us, broken only by an occasional tweet of a bird.

Drew turned his head to look at Chase. "What happened?"

"New guy on the nail gun. He didn't know to give a warning before he started." Chase knelt, and his hand hovered above Drew's shoulder, but he didn't touch him. "Come on. Get up."

Like someone had given him an electrical shock, Drew catapulted to his feet, awkwardly shifting his weight from the casted leg to the uninjured one, until he'd found his balance. With his hands plastered to his head, he stared at Alex, who, wide-eyed, rolled over and quickly got to his feet. At the same time, Trooper jumped up and leaned against Drew's leg.

Drew limped a few steps back from Alex, but the dog stayed with him. "Jesu—" He stopped himself mid-word. "Are you all right?"

I was a few feet behind Drew, and I could see his shoulders shaking.

Alex nodded. "Yeah. I'm okay." He started to step toward our father, but Chase grabbed his arm.

"No, stay here."

I wanted to go and be by Alex, but I took my cue from Chase and stood where I was, a few feet away.

There was no movement from anyone else. The world had stopped.

Finally, Joe Bailey broke the tension.

"Hey, I need a couple of people to come over here with rakes," he called. It was what was needed to unfreeze the scene. Those who had been staring returned to their jobs, but the voices were subdued like everyone was afraid to make a noise.

"I — this—" Apparently unable to come up with the words he wanted, Drew dropped his hands from his head and stalked away, his shoulders rigid, the heel of his cast thumping against the ground.

Someone brushed up next to me, and I turned to see Angela.

"What just happened?" I asked.

"Flashback," she said. "Most of the crew knows to give a warning before they use the nail gun or do anything that could remotely sound like a sound from the war zone." She looked up toward the roof, and I did the same. There was a man sitting at the peak, his elbows on his knees, holding his head in his hands. A couple of other guys knelt next to him, apparently talking. Angela continued. "I feel bad for Paul. He didn't know."

"Does this happen a lot?" I asked. "I mean, does he — my father — freak out like that a lot?"

"It was instinct, Savannah. He's better than he used to be, but it's still something he deals with. Most times he's prepared. He must have been distracted so the sudden noise of the nail gun startled him this time."

On the far side of the lawn, Drew dropped to the ground under a tree. Far away from everyone. From the talk. From the noises.

I hated the helpless feeling of wanting to do something but not knowing what. "Should someone go and be with him?"

Angela shook her head. "He needs time to regroup. He'll be back."

No one approached him. Except Trooper. The dog circled once next to Drew, then laid down at his hip, resting his chin on Drew's thigh. Drew dropped one of his hands and buried his fingers in the fur at the dog's neck. At the same time, I saw his shoulders relax and then his chin drop.

I wrapped my arms around my middle, wishing I could settle my churning stomach. Right now, despite my promise to him a few days ago at the lacrosse game that I would never give up on him, I had to acknowledge the truth.

Flashbacks were scary. Were Alex and I ready for a relationship that might be affected by them?

CHAPTER 7

I heard Rashawn's uneven gait as he cut through the group of people. The tips of his crutches thumped against the ground, and he swung his only foot forward to cover double the amount of ground that a two-legged person would have. His focus was on Drew.

Behind us, hammers began to tap a rhythm, and drills joined the orchestration of business as usual. Angela folded her arms across her chest and hugged herself as she turned to rejoin the other volunteers. Only Alex, Chase and I stood rooted in place.

When Alex raised his hand to scratch his head, I saw his fingers shaking.

"You all right?" I asked. I wanted to put my arm around him, but I figured that wouldn't be cool with him because of all of these strangers around.

"Yeah, but is he okay?" Alex asked, staring in Drew's direction.

I was surprised when Rashawn tossed one of his crutches on the ground then used the other to lower himself on the other side of Trooper. I noticed he didn't say anything — only put his hand on the other side of the dog and buried his fingers in the black fur. Both men stared toward the work site, but I felt like they weren't seeing.

Chase shoved his hands in his pockets and rocked back on his heels. "He'll be okay. I've seen this happen before."

"We were talking about baseball," Alex said, not even acknowledging Chase's comment, but instead focused on his own thoughts. "It was cool. I was talking baseball with my *father*. A regular father and son conversation. Then *that* happened. I didn't know what to do."

"You don't need to be afraid of him," Chase said.

"I'm not afraid of *him*," Alex countered.

I almost spoke up to point out that I'd seen his hands shaking when Drew moved off him, but he continued before I could even open my mouth.

"I *was* afraid today would be awkward. That he wouldn't like me."

"Drew likes everybody." Chase shrugged. "And everybody likes —"

The high-pitched whine of the circular saw cut off the last word, but we knew what it was going to be.

Alex turned so he faced the house like he didn't want Drew to see he was talking. "I don't want it to be weird now that this happened."

"Doesn't have to be," Chase said. "He'll be upset that we witnessed it, that all of the workers did, too, but pick up the conversation like nothing happened if he comes back over to work."

Finally, I had the opportunity to interject in the conversation. I grabbed Alex's arm. "Speaking of that, come on. Why don't we go back to work. I'm sure he doesn't want us staring at him."

Chase nodded. "Agreed." He pivoted and started back toward the side of the house.

"I like him," Alex said.

I glanced over my shoulder. "Who? Chase?"

"No, Dad."

I squinted at Alex, trying to register his words. "Dad? Did he tell you to call him that?"

"Why wouldn't I call him that? He's our father?"

I shrugged. "I don't know. Just sounds —" I struggled to find the right word —"fake."

"It's not fake. He *is* our dad. And today, I felt like we were connecting." Alex jutted out his chin. "Maybe you don't get it because you haven't gone your whole life wondering if you were anything like your father."

"Neither have you. Twelve years is hardly your *whole* life."

Despite the sun shining directly on Alex, his face darkened. "You'd never understand."

I opened my mouth to argue, but he turned and stalked back to his work area. One of the guys in the group gave him a directive as soon as he got close enough.

Maybe it was a guy thing. Maybe I wouldn't understand. But, I did understand what it was like to look in a mirror and wonder if I was anything like our mother. Lucky for Alex, he'd found that missing piece to his DNA puzzle because he got to connect with our father. My puzzle would never be complete.

I glanced back toward Drew. He and Rashawn still sat with their backs to the tree, both of them with a hand on the dog, and neither talking. I focused on Drew. Despite having someone right there with him, something about the way his whole body sagged made him look totally alone. Lost.

My brain and heart battled. I knew almost nothing about PTSD, so I wasn't sure if there was something I could say or do to make it better. My heart took over, and my promise from a few days before echoed in my brain. *I'll never give up on you.*

My feet felt like they were made of cement blocks, but I forced my muscles to move me forward. The closer I got, the buzzing of saws, banging of hammers, and voices behind me faded to white noise as the beat of my heart pounded in my ears.

Rashawn made eye contact with me, but Drew never looked up. He stared. Somewhere past me. Past everyone.

I pursed my lips and resolved to do what I'd come to do. Without a word, I stepped around their outstretched feet and settled onto the ground less than a foot from my father.

"I made a promise to you," I whispered without looking at him.

There was no acknowledgement that he'd heard me or that he was even aware that I was there.

I glanced at his hand, pressing hard into the grass like it was grounding him. Closing my eyes, I imagined myself as a little girl skipping along a sidewalk near a busy street, a brick building towering over us, blocking some of the heat, and that big hand grasping mine to keep me safe. The unexpected tug in my chest told me this was more than my imagination. It was a spark of a memory. A moment we'd shared.

A longing to remember more wrapped around me. I turned my head enough so I could see the side of his face.

"Is there anything I can do for you?"

For the first few seconds there was no response. Then the muscles in his jaw began to flex.

Next to him, Trooper lifted his head and turned to look into Drew's face. The dog tipped his head and lifted his ears, his eyes alert.

Without a word, Drew maneuvered himself off the ground and struggled to right his crutches as he stood. At the same time, Trooper scrambled to his feet, but Rashawn held one hand on his service harness.

"Here. I'll help you." I jumped up and reached for one of Drew's crutches, but he yanked it farther away.

He twisted toward me, his eyes dark. "This is my battle. You can't help me."

He swung his long legs forward between the crutches, covering more ground in that amount of time than a person with two good feet could.

"I didn't mean to offend you," I called to his retreating back.

There was no response. I fisted my hands, jammed them into the side of my thighs and stifled a growl of frustration. One step forward, two steps back. Or was this ten back?

When I looked at Rashawn, who still sat against the tree, his eyebrows shot up in an *I don't know what to tell you* way. Trooper's ears were perked high, his eyes beaded on Drew.

I looked back in time to see the other workers focused on their work, but by the way a path was cleared as he approached, it was clear no one wanted to engage him in any way.

Alex held a long board upright next to a sawhorse, his attention fixed on our father. But Drew breezed past him and hobbled directly to Angela. He shoved his hand in the front pocket of his jeans and produced his truck keys. I couldn't hear their exchange over the buzzing and pounding of tools, but she shook her head and pushed his hand back.

The conversation lasted less than five seconds. As he moved away, Angela reached out and let her fingers drag from his shoulder to his elbow. Then he was out of her reach and headed toward his truck. Somehow, knowing he'd kind of rejected her, too, took away a little of the sting.

Next to me, Rashawn shifted to get up. At the same time, Trooper shifted, eager to serve.

"Can I help *you*, at least?" I asked. Rashawn, like Drew, was a big guy, and although I couldn't imagine how I could pull him up, I wasn't going to leave him there.

He smiled and waved me off.

"Appreciate the offer, but I have a system I learned in physical therapy. Less chance of falling and either one of us getting hurt."

I couldn't imagine how he could get up with one leg, but I respected his choice. And, when he rolled to his stomach, I also respected that he might not want an audience.

Brushing grass and dirt off the back of my jeans, I said, "Okay, then I guess I'll go back to painting." And I walked away.

Chase was back up on the ladder, but Angela had moved around to the side of the house. I picked up a brush and an opened can of paint. I dipped the brush in and wiped the excess paint on the inside lid of the gallon can before I started the rhythmic swish of the bristles against the dry wood.

Next to me, the ladder creaked and groaned when Chase twisted to look toward me, his paint brush dripping white paint as it dangled from his hand through the rungs.

"You all right?" he asked. Drops of paint splattered on a green bush next to me.

Tipping my head to look up, I said, "I'm fine, and you're making a mess with that brush."

"Oh, geez!" He slapped it back toward the house and swiped it along the clapboards a few times.

"So, where did Drew go?"

Chase shrugged. "Back into himself."

I squinted. "What does that mean?"

For a moment he stared toward the road, then returned his attention to me.

"Savannah, I'm gonna be honest. I doubt Drew will give you the kind of relationship you're looking for."

"We just want to get to know him."

He pulled in a deep breath through his nose, then exhaled through his mouth. Was that an indication that he was trying to be patient or spare me pain? I was getting ready to ask when he said, "You have to slow down. I'm sure it's exciting to finally find him — I'd give anything to see my dad again — but Drew's going to shut down if you're not careful. I've seen him do it with my mom."

My jaw dropped and my eyes spontaneously opened wider. "*He* said we could come today."

"But he didn't invite you to sit with him when he was coming down from the flashback."

"I just wanted him to know I was there for him. I promised him that the other night. How are we supposed to get to know him if we're not with him?"

"I don't know, but when he puts distance between himself and others, he doesn't come back around until he's ready."

"How long does that take?"

Chase shrugged.

Not the answer I needed.

He dipped his paintbrush in the can suspended from the ladder and returned to work. I shifted and looked back at the now empty spot under the tree. I had no idea what was going through my father's mind when the nail gun startled him or when he retreated to whatever that safety zone was in his mind. Maybe, as he said, I couldn't help him, but I could help me understand what was happening to him.

The first thing on my agenda when I got home would be to research PTSD in veterans.

I worked on auto pilot for the rest of the afternoon, engaging in conversation that didn't even come close to having the memorable impact the silence with Drew had on me. But the banter with Angela, Chase, and the others working on our mini crew served as a distraction right through to clean up.

"And, we're done," Angela proclaimed when the last paintbrush was rinsed of paint and added to the stack in the plastic bin. "I think we deserve to treat ourselves at Seneca Farms for ice cream." She used her wrist to push the curly strands of her hair off her forehead since her hands were wet. "Can you and Alex come with us?"

"Seneca Farms in Penn Yan?"

She nodded. "The one and only. Iconic."

I grabbed the lid that matched the plastic bin for paintbrushes and pressed it into place. "Sounds good. I remember going there once after we went boating with some friends who have a cottage near Keuka College."

"Did I hear Seneca Farms?" Chase asked as he walked by carrying the aluminum extension ladder he'd used.

"Yes, but we'll need to swing by the house and get my car since Drew took the truck."

"I can take you to get it," I offered, ignoring Mom and Dad's rules

My stomach growled loud enough so Angela could hear it, too. She laughed and nodded toward my middle.

"Guess we better hurry. Let's carry this bin and these paint cans to the construction trailer." She looked around at the other people cleaning up. "Ten minutes and we're done for the day."

I turned toward the house. The green shutters were no longer hanging at cockeyed angles off their hinges. Pristine white now covered the dull, peeling gray paint on the wood siding. And although it would need to be painted once the wood aged, the newly constructed ramp and porch made the house look bigger and more inviting. The transformation was unbelievable.

Rashawn leaned against the railing at the top of the ramp and chatted with several people gathered next to it. Trooper sat a few feet away, his ears perked forward as he watched Rashawn.

"It's amazing what we can accomplish in one day, isn't it?" Angela said as she stepped next to me. "We spent a couple of weekends working on the inside before Rashawn and his wife moved in. It's so rewarding to do this, because these soldiers have sacrificed so much for us."

I smiled, but inside I felt more amazed than happy. She'd lost her husband in the war. Did she ever think about *that* sacrifice?

"I definitely want to do this again."

"I'm glad, because I'll take you on my crew any time." She put her arm across my shoulders and squeezed. "I'm sorry things went the way they did with Drew at the end."

"How do you know what to do when that happens?"

"Honestly, I often don't know. But I attend a support group through the V.A. that helps me realize we're not alone." She squeezed my shoulder again. "And that he's not alone. There are a lot of veterans who go through what he does. It's not always the same, but the pain and fear and helplessness they feel is. The group helps me understand at least a little bit."

Chase and Alex were returning from putting bins in the work trailer, so we met them by the porch. "You guys ready to go?" Angela asked.

Alex wiped his hands against the side of his jeans. "Ready for some ice cream. I'm starved."

I made a fist and lightly punched his arm. "You're always hungry."

He nodded. "Yup. Pretty much."

"Come on," Angela said, chuckling. "We'll say goodbye to Rashawn and then take care of those hunger pains."

We waited at the bottom of the porch stairs until the couple that was talking with Rashawn finished and turned to leave.

"Our turn," Angela said to him as she stepped up onto the ramp. "I bet it feels like a brand new home, doesn't it?"

Rashawn smiled. "Yes, it does. I don't know what to say other than thank you. What everyone has done here for us is incredible."

"Thank you is sufficient," Angela responded. "Thank you for your service." She looked at Rashawn's dog. "And thank you for yours, Trooper. Thanks for being there for Drew earlier."

Trooper lifted his chin in the air and sniffed toward her as if saying, *you're welcome.*

"I owe my sanity to that dog," Rashawn suddenly said. "PTSD can be a living hell."

As if he sensed anxiousness in Rashawn's tone, Trooper sidled next to him and pressed his nose against the back of his master's hand. And Rashawn laid his fingers on the fur on the dog's neck above his red working-dog vest.

My mind tripped back to the episode earlier. There was no doubt that even though Rashawn was Trooper's master, the dog had calmed Drew in his worst moment. That one incident had been an unnerving glimpse into post traumatic stress disorder.

Then my thoughts flipped to a darker concern — the unpredictability of those moments. And the fact that PTSD could tear families apart.

Heat streaked from my neck up to my cheeks.

Anger. Confusion. Awareness. They all collided as I realized PTSD had broken *my* family, and if today was any indication, there was little hope we'd ever really be back together.

I rolled my shoulders to loosen the sudden tension in my neck. Maybe some things were better left alone.

One of those *things* being our biological father, even though it really wasn't what I wanted.

"So," Chase said, interrupting my thoughts, "am I the only one ready for Banana Madness ice cream?"

Relief, like a gentle rain, trickled through my body. Getting ice cream felt normal. Physically and emotionally refreshing. The muscles in my neck relaxed just thinking about it.

"I don't know about Banana Madness," I said, "but I'm in."

Rashawn looked at Chase. "Ice cream? That sounds pretty good right now."

"Come with us," Chase offered.

Rashawn smiled. "Thanks, but Jolene will be home with the kids, soon. I want to be here when they see the changes in the house. Maybe we'll take them for ice cream later."

I stepped up to Rashawn and held out my hand. "I'm happy I got to meet you and be here today."

He returned my handshake. "Thank you. I was happy to meet you, too." Then, patting the porch railing he added, "It's amazing! I appreciate what everyone did."

Angela gave him another hug. "We appreciate *you*."

Rashawn stepped back and held her at arms' length. "You are beautiful inside and out. Drew better stake his claim before someone else scoops you up."

Chase cleared his throat, and I turned in time to see a smirk directed at Angela. Was this subject one that came up between *them*?

"Well, thank you," Angela said as she stepped back.

Other workers were lining up to talk with Rashawn, so Chase and Alex moved in and took turns shaking his hand.

"See you later," Chase said.

Rashawn nodded, and we moved away to make room for the people waiting.

As we walked to our cars, I mulled over the day's events. For the most part, I felt good about the day and what I'd contributed. But the one dark cloud hanging over me was my father's declaration that there was nothing I could do to help him. However, I wasn't through.

My determination would get me my horse. And somehow, I knew if I didn't give up, it might also give me my father.

It took less than ten minutes to get to Angela's house so she could pick up her car. When I pulled along the curb and stopped, just as Alex, Angela and Chase started to open their doors, Chase spoke up.

"Okay if I ride with you, Savannah?"

I cringed as I formulated the answer and turned toward the back seat. "Law says I can only take one passenger without an adult with me."

Sixteen and a half and having a license seemed so grown up to me, but since Chase was older, he no longer had the "only one underage passenger" restriction. Now I felt like he was riding a two-wheeler and I was stuck on a tricycle.

Alex didn't miss a beat. "I'll ride with Angela."

"Works," Chase said, lifting his hand to fist bump Alex before they all climbed out.

Alex followed Angela toward her garage while Chase slipped into the front passenger seat of my van. I gripped the steering wheel, hoping to cover my shaking fingers. Why did being alone with a guy have to be so awkward?

Chase slammed the door closed and clicked his seatbelt into place. I reached for the gearshift on the steering column, hoping I wouldn't do something stupid like putting the van into reverse rather than drive.

"Guess it's my lucky day," he said

"Oh, yeah. Why?" I tried to keep my voice steady and casual, like my heart wasn't hammering almost out of my chest.

"I get to be alone with you."

I whipped my head around to look at him.

His smile was genuine, charming. The sparkle in his eyes told me that he was comfortable making that kind of comment.

I returned my attention to the road, but my mind buzzed with ways to respond. There was so much about him that I didn't know.

"Are you messing with me? You must have a girlfriend or something."

Chase laughed. "Or something? You mean *something* like a duck or a dog or some other alternative to a girlfriend?"

I tipped my head and glanced back at him, hoping my cheeks weren't flaming red. "Very funny. You know what I mean. You must have a girlfriend."

He outright smirked at me. "Why's that?"

My breath caught in my throat. I didn't have the guts to tell him that he was too good looking to be single. Or that most girls I know would be all over him because of his personality. Or that my former boyfriend had had no problem hitting on other girls while we were dating. Instead, I swallowed the sharp lump in my throat and tried to sound flip.

"Just an assumption. Silly me."

He laughed again and replied, "Yeah, silly you."

I could tell he wasn't laughing at me. He merely sounded happy.

"Fine," I shot back. "How about you give me some directions?" I loved the adult feeling of being behind the wheel with a guy next to me. Hopefully, an unattached, hot, super-nice guy.

If only my friends could see me right now.

He pointed down the street. "First stop sign, take a left."

I followed his directions until we were on a straight road that I knew led to the northern tip of Y-shaped Keuka Lake. Once on the main road, we rode in silence for several minutes. I racked my brain for a good topic for conversation. A million thoughts rolled around in my mind, but none of them formed into cohesive sentences, so I stared ahead at the road. Chase finally broke the silence.

"No," he said.

I tightened my grip on the steering wheel, but kept my focus straight ahead. "No? No, what?"

Out of the corner of my eye I saw him turn to look at me.

"No, I don't have a girlfriend."

My heart did a happy dance. There was a shred of hope that maybe Chase and I could become more than just acquaintances through my father. Every nerve ending in my body zapped into high alert. I'd never had a guy affect me like this. There was definitely something special about Chase.

I fought a smile as we came to a stop sign.

"Well, I'm glad to know I don't have to worry about a jealous girlfriend taking me down in the parking lot at Seneca Farms."

A car was coming from the left, so I couldn't pull out.

He laughed again, and I glanced over to see a tiny dimple crease his left cheek. If nothing else, Chase came across as a sincerely content and happy person. I wished that natural high would filter over to me.

There was more silence, so I changed the station on the radio again, even though I didn't have a clue what music was playing before. When I finally found a station I liked, I turned up the volume.

As soon as I pulled my hand back, Chase reached out and turned the radio back down.

My eyebrows furrowed, and I glanced at him. "Sorry, don't you like this station? I can change it."

He'd settled back in the seat, his hands folded across his stomach, looking very relaxed.

"Station is fine," he said, "but you're not taking advantage of this opportunity."

"What opportunity?" I asked, then forced myself to refocus on the road.

"I saw you watching Drew today. You're curious. I know it. So here's your chance. Ask away."

I gripped the steering wheel tighter. "I don't know what you mean."

"You've gotta have questions. I don't know everything about Drew, but I know a lot. So, shoot. Ask me a question about him."

It only took me a second to come up with the first one, because it had been on my mind all afternoon "Okay, you know the flashback he had today?"

Chase nodded. "Yeah."

"Does that kind of thing happen a lot?"

"I don't know about a lot, but I know they happen. I've heard him talking to my mom about them, so I know he struggles with them more than we see. I've only seen one major reaction."

Now the door was open, I wanted details. "What did you see?"

There was a pause, and I wondered if he was trying hard to remember or bothered by the memory.

"It was a few years ago," he explained. "I don't remember how old I was, maybe twelve or thirteen. We had gone to Syracuse for an SU lacrosse game and decided to get something to eat first. We were walking down the street when a truck backfired. Drew's reaction was kind of the same as today. He dropped to the ground like he'd been slammed from the back. People around us stopped and stared at him. One guy ran over because he thought Drew had been shot. I remember being so scared and confused that I froze."

Chase shifted in his seat and looked at me. "We never got anything to eat, and we didn't go to the game. Drew shook so bad all the way home that I was afraid we'd get in an accident."

He paused and looked out the side window, then I barely heard him say in a raspy voice, "It was one of the worst days of my life." Answering that one question drained the happiness from his mood.

"Sounds intense."

"Yeah, but the hard part was that I didn't really get what had happened. I wish he'd talk about stuff more." Chase pressed the window button and rolled it partway down. "I want to hear about his experiences in the war so I can understand. So we can help him. He tells me stories about my dad over there, and that's cool, but I always feel like there's way more that he won't tell me."

He was quiet for a minute, and when I glanced in his direction, he grinned. The worry lines that had creased his forehead a moment before were gone.

"Good trick, Savannah. How did that turn to being about me? So, any other questions?"

The next question had been preying on my mind since the first time I saw him getting into Drew's truck with his lacrosse uniform on. "Yeah, there is. Does he always go to your school activities and games?"

Chase nodded. "Most of them. I know this will sound weird, but I've been thinking about that same thing since I found out about you and Alex. I wish things had worked out different for your family, Savannah, because, despite everything else going on with him, he would have been an amazing father to you. You got robbed."

My defenses shot up. "We didn't get robbed. Our uncle has been a fantastic dad to us."

Chase's happy expression morphed into a look of embarrassment. "Sorry. That was a stupid thing for me to say."

Regret for being so sharp pinged in my chest. "No, I'm sorry. I know you didn't mean anything by that. This whole situation is incredibly confusing and has me on edge."

My fingers gripped the steering wheel tighter than necessary, and I consciously loosened them. Even though neither of us touched the dial, the music on the radio was suddenly easy to hear.

We'd been quiet for a few minutes when Chase reached across and put his hand on my arm. "What you did today, when you went and sat next to Drew, was amazing."

"I only did what I thought was right. Even though Rashawn was there, Drew looked alone. I wanted him to know he wasn't."

"Well, you were brave."

"No, I —" His compliment, his warm hand on my arm, flustered me. "Well, obviously *he* didn't appreciate my bravery. I'm not sure he's going to want to see me again."

"I can't guess what he's thinking," Chase said, "but remember what I said back at Rashawn's. Take it slow. Maybe give him some space."

"Space? He's had twelve years of space." Triggered by frustration and fear, my voice rose at the end.

My lip quivered, but I'd be damned if I'd cry in front of Chase. Glancing in the rearview mirror, I saw that Angela's car was behind us.

"They caught up to us," I said, pointing my thumb over my shoulder, needing to shift our conversation before I couldn't hold back the tears.

Chase twisted to look. "Just in the nick of time. Seneca Farms is up the road a little."

He settled back in the seat. "I know this is going to sound out of the blue, but I'd like to spend more time with you, Savannah. I really like you. You're sweet."

I gave him a sideways glance. "Thank you, I guess. I sure haven't felt very sweet lately."

"I'll cut you some slack. The last couple of weeks haven't exactly been normal. So, can we hang out again after today?" Chase pressed.

"We're both pretty busy, you know. You have lacrosse, I have the equestrian team and work, and—"

"Is that a no?" he asked, cutting me off.

I sighed and gave him a quick look. "No, I mean, not no, I don't want to hang out again. I meant no, that's not what I meant."

He chuckled, once again pulling my attention momentarily from the road. There was his adorable smirk that made me melt. I couldn't help but smile back.

"I'm rambling. Sorry." Shrugging, I added, "Yeah, I'd like to hang out again. I don't want to set up any expectations because I'm working a lot. I only have a few weeks to earn the last bit of money I need to buy Lacey."

What kind of a fool was I to answer him that way? I wouldn't choose him over Lacey, but I didn't want him to disappear either.

He squeezed my arm before dropping his hand. "I promise I won't get in your way,"

"The next month will be crazy," I added quickly. "But once I have enough money to buy Lacey, I won't have to work so many extra hours. Then I'll have more free time. I promise."

"I get it," he said. "You're revealing another layer of Savannah. If I want to hang out with you, I have to accept that you have goals and you're determined to reach them." His voice softened. "That's admirable."

I squeezed the padding on the steering wheel, happiness coursing through me. Although he barely knew me, Chase understood me. There just might be a chance for us some day. No response came to mind, so I was happy when the red and white striped building came into view.

"There's Seneca Farms," I said, pointing. I put on the signal light and slowed to turn into the driveway

"We'll take it one day at a time, okay, Savannah?"

Boy, was this guy focused.

Nodding, I said, "Good compromise. I can live with that."

I pulled into a parking spot and Angela maneuvered her car into a space next to the van. We all got out as a car pulled through the drive through lane next to us. The passenger rolled down the car window and threw her hand up.

"Hi, Ang!" the woman called. The driver leaned over once he was stopped in front of the drive up window and waved, as well. "Drew gonna play for Birkett Mills softball team again?"

Angela moved toward the car. "Hi, Donna." Then she dipped her head a little so she could see the driver. "Hi, Tim. Yes, he's planning on playing as long as his leg is healed."

"Heard about that fire," Tim responded. "Sounded bad."

"It was pretty scary." She backed away from the car. "Good seeing you both. Hopefully we'll see you in a few weeks."

Just then the door slid open at the drive through, and Tim's attention was pulled to the teenager holding two ice cream cones. We continued to the front of the building where Chase held the door so we could all file in. We'd no sooner stepped inside than someone sitting at one of the high top tables called over.

"Hey, Angela, how's Drew doing? Leg healing?"

I turned to Chase and whispered. "Does Drew know everyone?"

Chase's eyebrows shot up. "It's a small town. Even though in a lot of ways he stays to himself, I think people still admire him and think of him as a friend. "

That made me smile, and, I realized, also made me proud.

We stepped next to Alex at the ice cream counter. Behind the glass panel were huge round cartons of ice cream, some of them unusual flavors I'd never heard of. Deer tracks. Bangin' Brownie. White Mountain Raspberry.

"Gotta love this place," Alex proclaimed. Angela laughed as he checked out both sides of the glass case before coming back to join us.

"Ice cream's on me," Angela said. "Order what you want."

Alex gave her the double thumbs up. "I'm all over the Hokey Pokey sundae, then." There was no hesitation on his part as he stepped up to order.

Angela turned to me. "How about you, Savannah?"

Her tone was soft to the point that it felt like her voice hugged my name. Except for my first grade teacher, I'd never felt anything like it before, and I swallowed a lump that filled my throat. Angela had a special warmth that Mom didn't have, even though she was always attentive to our needs.

My mouth watered as soon as I started thinking about what I wanted.

"I'll have a hot fudge sundae with mint chocolate chip ice cream," I said.

Angela looked quickly at Chase, then back at me. "Are you serious?"

"Yeah." I squinted a little as I tried to figure out why that choice mattered. "Is that okay?"

She looked at Chase again and smiled. "That's pretty crazy."

"What? Is that unusual?" I looked at them. It was my favorite kind of sundae, and she had said to get whatever we wanted.

A dimple creased Chase's cheek. "No, not unusual. That's what Drew orders every time we come here."

My mind flashed to a lesson in one of my science classes when we learned about nature versus nurture. I wondered if before my mother died, when I was a small child, if that sundae was something my father and I had shared then. Had I acquired the taste for it because I wanted to be like my daddy or had nature given us similar tastes?

At first, I couldn't explain the gentle tug inside my chest, but then it hit me. Because of those lost memories, I'd never know which it was, and that made me sad.

After we ordered, we carried our desserts outside to a picnic table under the pavilion. Families with small children occupied the tables nearest a large rock that the little kids were lining up to jump from like it was a big deal, even though it was only a little more than a foot or so off the ground. Their giggles and childish chatter sprinkled the breeze with happiness.

Whether it was because of the relaxed atmosphere or the fact we were all exhausted, our conversation was easy. Discussion about the job site and the projects done. Sharing snippets of conversation we'd had with the other workers. Unanswered questions about Rashawn and his service dog.

We were almost done with our ice cream when we heard a familiar voice behind us.

"Hey, fancy meeting you guys here."

I twisted in my seat to see Jamie and Kyle coming into the covered area, too.

Chase fist-bumped Kyle."Hey, man. This must be the place to be tonight."

"We just came from the kennel," Jamie explained. "Figured we'd get our Seneca Farms fix on our way home."

"The kennel?" Alex asked.

"She has a job at a dog kennel," I explained. "She's learning to train dogs."

Alex dug into his sundae. "That's cool."

"Yeah, it is pretty cool," Jamie said. She shifted toward me.

"We're having a demo next weekend for therapists and social workers to see the different ways the dogs are used once they're trained. It's open to the public. You should come out."

I stopped mid-bite of my sundae.

"If I'm not working, maybe I will." Mint green ice cream and hot fudge started to slide off my spoon, but I caught it with my tongue before it was totally off.

"Good catch," Kyle said.

I let the treat melt in my mouth before I answered, "Too good to let it get away."

Jamie turned to Chase. "You should come, too. Kyle will be there."

Chase looked at me, then back at Jamie. "Sounds good."

"Well, we need to get our ice cream," Jamie said. "See you later." She gave a quick wave to Angela and Alex.

She'd taken only a few steps when she turned back to me. "You're riding in the barn to barn competition on Saturday, aren't you?"

"Absolutely," I answered. "Lacey and I need all of the practice we can get."

"Ha! You and Lacey will probably blow everybody else out of the water again." Jamie smiled and turning her attention to

Chase, Angela, and Alex added, "Savannah is an amazing rider. She and her horse can't be beat."

My face flushed when everyone turned and looked at me. It was true, we had won each of our classes in the last few barn to barn competitions, but it wasn't something I bragged about. My goal was to compete at the regional level in college. That's what I was working toward. And I was determined to do it with Lacey because we were a team.

"See ya at the barn," Jamie said. She took hold of Kyle's hand, and they continued across the parking lot toward the front door.

"That's pretty neat, Savannah," Angela said. She took a sip of her milkshake then asked, "Have you been riding long?"

"Since I was ten, but I've only been competing the last three years."

She swallowed the milkshake in her mouth, then smiled. "Hmm, something else you and Drew have in common."

Alex jumped in, saving me from asking. "He shows horses?"

"Well, I know he did a few rodeos," Angela said, "but I don't think he's ridden in a while."

I stared at her, wondering how many other surprises were going to be sprung on me today.

"Mind if I come and watch the competition?" Chase asked.

I shrugged and turned toward him. "Anybody can come."

"Great. I'll come after lacrosse practice."

"Okay."

It was a simple answer because my mind was whirling. I was excited that Chase wanted to spend time with me, and that made my heart sing. At the same time, I tried to wrap my head around the realization that my father and I had yet another trait in common. It made one side of me feel closer to him, but the other part of me was reminded that, despite the fact that he was my father, we were strangers.

"Oh, man!"

We all turned as Alex squeezed his eyes shut and ground his fist against his forehead.

"Brain freeze, big time," he announced.

Everyone else laughed, but I was mesmerized by the scene and barely smiled. In this one day, the dynamics among all of us had shifted and changed like some unusual multi-pointed geometric shape, with each point representing a different emerging relationship. Alex seemed comfortable with his place in all of it like none of those points were poking him, but an edginess wormed its way into my core.

Two of those relationship points were poking my skin, and they were sharp. I was always the cautious one, avoiding the chance of being hurt at all costs.

My mind reeled. I had some big decisions to make going forward. There was no telling what direction these relationships would take.

Deciding the course with Chase was easy. I'd had a couple of boyfriends before. I knew how to create a relationship with a guy. I knew the risks.

Drew was a totally different matter. There were no maps to guide us on how to proceed down the father - daughter road with all of the baggage that needed to be sifted through.

I took another spoonful of mint chocolate chip ice cream and hot fudge, comfort food, and let it slide down my throat while I considered the risks I faced. Even though I'd promised Drew I'd never give up on him, there was no reciprocal promise from him.

Then the truth hit me like ice water, and I stifled a shiver. The real risk was that maybe Drew could never break through the barriers to make that promise.

And as badly as I wanted it, the reality was maybe we never would be a family again.

CHAPTER 8

Thunder rolled across the sky when I got out of the car. I glanced up just as a bolt of lightning cut a zig zag through the thick, dark clouds. No doubt, this cemented the decision that the inter-stable competition would have to be held in the indoor ring.

I was reaching into the back seat to retrieve my helmet and riding boots when I heard Phoebe.

"Hey, Savannah. I'm glad I caught you before you went in the barn."

A surge of adrenaline shot through me. I straightened and turned at the same time, nearly hitting my head on the door. "Is something wrong with Lacey?"

Phoebe stopped by my door. "No, no. Lacey's fine, but we do have a bit of a surprise."

I relaxed. If Lacey was fine, then nothing else would be a big deal. "I hope it's a good surprise."

I reached back into the car for my helmet and boots, then used my elbow to push the door closed.

"I guess it's all in how you interpret it," she said. She wiped at the hay chaff clinging to her flannel shirt.

I tucked the boots under my arm and let the helmet swing from my fingers by the straps. It wasn't like Phoebe to be dramatic, so this behavior made me a little nervous.

"So?" I prodded.

"So, I don't want you to feel pressure, but you should know that I got a call last night from Cassie Potter –"

I stopped and whirled toward Phoebe, cutting her off. "The trainer from the equestrian team at McDonough College?"

She nodded. "Yeah. She'll be here at some point today. She's actually scouting Alyssa for next year's fall team, but she also asked about you as a prospect for the following year."

Saliva flooded my mouth, but I swallowed fast. "What did she ask?"

"She said she'd been hearing whispers on the show circuit about you and Lacey. Wanted to know what I thought of the two of you as a team."

"What did you tell her?"

Phoebe shrugged. "That if you two stay together, I think you have the potential to be unstoppable in competitions."

I bristled. "*If* Lacey and I stay together?"

Running the tip of her tongue across her upper lip, Phoebe broke our eye contact. "Savannah, you know I don't want to sell Lacey to anyone but you, but I have to make that tough decision at the end of June if you aren't able to come up with the money for her."

"I'll do it," I said, sounding more confident than I felt. If it were summertime, I'd have more free time to work and earn the money. Eight hundred dollars was a lot to come up with in a short time. I'd thought about asking Mom and Dad if I could borrow the money, but then a huge repair on the house roof this spring required them to take out a loan. A roof took precedence over my horse.

"You know, I'm sure you will, so let's not talk about the *ifs*. You need to be able to concentrate with Cassie in the stands."

Another roll of thunder preceded the fat drops of rain that hit my face. Just what I needed was to get soaked, too.

I glanced toward the barn. "So she's here, now?"

"Not yet." Phoebe started walking, but I almost had to jog to keep up with her. "Don't worry about it, though. Get in that ring and do what you and Lacey do best, Savannah. Just like with Alyssa, if Cassie likes what she sees, she'll be following you in shows."

I blew out a big puff of air that fluffed my bangs for a second. "What did you say about no pressure?"

First a reminder that there was a chance that I could lose Lacey. Then an equestrian team scout here. Yeah, no pressure!

My boots slipped under my arm, and when I moved to readjust them, the helmet in my hand swung and smacked my funny bone.

"Ow!" I groaned and laughed as I used my elbow to squeeze the boots against my side. "Sheesh! My day can only go up from here, right?"

Phoebe laughed, threw her arm over my shoulder and squeezed. "You've got this, kid."

I made a conscious effort to tune out the chatter and laughter of the other riders as we groomed and tacked our horses. For most of them, this was just fun and games, but for me, having the trainer of an equestrian team here took today's competition to a whole new level. If I wanted to compete at a college, Lacey and I had to be strong and precise.

When I pulled the girth tighter, Lacey sucked in a deep breath. It was when I realized I actually *heard* her take the breath that I became aware of the sudden stillness in the barn. It was like birds in trees that stop singing when danger is near. All chatter from the other riders ceased.

With my hands still on the leather strap, I twisted toward the aisle. Every girl in the barn who was within my sight was looking toward the wide double doors. Because I was around the corner, I couldn't see what had caught their attention.

Except for a pawing hoof and another horse nickering from a stall, it was silent, so I stayed quiet, too. The fine hairs on the back of my neck prickled. What was probably only seconds seemed like minutes. Like a slow wave moving through the barn, the talking and horse sounds resumed, but the girls still seemed to be curious about something.

Then I heard a familiar voice.

"I'm looking for Savannah."

My heart had a mind of its own, and it raced through several beats.

Katie, the girl grooming her horse three stalls down from me, pointed in my direction. "Down there."

"Hey, thanks," Chase said, and rounded the corner at the same time. He carried a small white box in one hand and a reusable zippered frozen food grocery bag dangled from the other. As soon as he spotted me, his face lit up with a smile.

"Hi. I hope it's okay that I came to watch you compete," he said as he approached.

"Sure." I tried not to look at what he was carrying, but he must have seen my attention dart toward the box and bag.

He held up the bag. "Drew asked me to give you this."

My father was giving me something? I reached for it like it was going to give me an electrical shock. "What is it?"

Chase shrugged one shoulder. "Didn't ask. Mom told him I was coming to watch your competition, and as I was getting in my car, he came over and handed it to me."

I grabbed the handles, surprised when the weight caused my arm to jerk down. "What the heck? It's so heavy."

The temptation to unzip it and look inside was strong, but since I had no idea what was in it, I wanted to wait until I was alone. I couldn't even imagine what Drew wanted me to have. Especially after the way he'd left us at the work site Saturday.

I ducked under Lacey's neck to get to my wooden trunk where I stored all of my grooming tools. "I have to finish prepping Lacey, so I'll put it in my tack trunk for now."

The rectangular trunk had been a gift from Mom and Dad for my fourteenth birthday. They'd even had my name engraved on the top. My plan was to have Lacey's name engraved below mine once I owned her.

The fear that I wouldn't be able to save enough money before summer to buy her squeezed my heart, but I tamped it down and forced it out of my thoughts. Stay positive. Envision the outcome. Those were my mantras.

I lifted the trunk's lid and set the bag on the far right where there was the most space. I pressed down on it, not so much to fit it in but to get a quick idea of the shape. I hit something flat. Maybe it was the top to a box?

I closed the lid and ducked under Lacey's neck again so I was standing in front of Chase. Even though I hadn't seen him since the work day at the veteran's house, he and I had been texting a few times a day and we had video chatted twice. While we talked about his lacrosse games and practices and what was happening at our respective schools, we'd kept conversation about my father out of it. Somehow, with Chase here with me, bringing up the subject now felt safer.

"Have you seen my father this week?"

"Yeah."

That was it? He was going to make me drag information out of him?

"Is he okay?" I needed something to do with my hands, so even though I had already groomed her, I grabbed the mane comb and started working the snarls out of Lacey's mane. "You know —" I glanced at him — "after the episode with the flashback?"

"Yeah, he's okay. We didn't see him for a couple of days, but then he was fine when we saw him."

I paused with the comb in Lacey's mane. "I wish there were something I could do to help. I feel like there's this wall that he's put up, and if we try to get over it, he builds it higher. But he's let you and your mother on the other side of it. Why you guys and no one else?"

He shook his head. "I don't know why us, and just to be clear, he's allowed us to look *over*, but we've never been on the other side of the wall, either."

That revelation startled me, as did his furrowed brows that hinted at a hidden hurt. It was easy to make assumptions based on very little actual knowledge. Would I ever really know?

I returned to working the comb through Lacey's mane as Chase and I fell into an awkward silence. I hoped I hadn't offended him.

While I worked on her mane and tail, he turned to watch the other riders preparing for the competition. He cleared his throat a couple of times, and I wondered if he was also a little nervous when we were together. I totally empathized — if he was.

After a few minutes, I put the comb down and finished the tacking process. While I tightened the girth more, I looked at Chase. He still faced away from me, so I could study him. His dark blue lacrosse team jacket fit snugly across his shoulders, accenting his athletic build. My fingers itched to touch the dark hair at the nape of his neck, to feel the warmth of his skin against my fingertips.

Lost in my musings, I was startled when he suddenly turned around and blurted out, "I forgot to tell you that Drew got off his crutches this week."

My breath hitched in my throat before I swallowed against the little lump there. All he had to do was look at me and I was flustered. "Wow! That was fast."

Heat flashed across my cheeks like I'd been caught doing something I shouldn't have been doing. Could he tell I'd been staring?

"Yeah. Doctor said he healed faster than expected." Chase stepped closer and stroked Lacey's gray face above her nose. "He's still limping a little, but for the most part he's doing great. I'm sure that will help his mood, too. He's not much for being slowed down."

"I bet." Two words was the best I could do in my tongue-tied state. Why couldn't I feel as casual as Chase sounded right now?

I checked the straps for the girth on both sides one more time, then yanked on the stirrups to make sure they were secure.

"Have you ever been to anything like this?" I asked.

"Nope. How many riders compete?"

"Oh, usually around six or seven from each stable." I gave one more strong pull on the cinch strap then hooked the pin into place. "Did you see Jamie? She's one of our team members today."

He shifted and looked behind him. "No, I didn't. I'll go find her in a minute."

When he turned back around, he stepped away from Lacey and toward me. He extended the hand with the small square box in it. I'd forgotten that I'd seen it in his hand when he first arrived.

His face lit up with a warm smile. "I got you something."

"Me? Why?" I tipped my head in puzzlement and slowly took it.

"I saw it and wanted you to have it."

The box wasn't wrapped, so I lifted the top off, and then nestled the two halves, putting the lid underneath. My fingers trembled with excitement. Why would Chase give me a gift?

A strip of cottony material covered the contents. I peeled that back to reveal a round, silver charm about the size of a quarter.

In the middle was an etching of two puzzle pieces nearly interlocking. The words "Perfect Together" were inscribed along the top curve above the puzzle pieces.

My breath caught in my lungs. I lifted my head to stare at Chase and gulped against the pressure in my throat, trying to form words, but nothing came out.

"I saw it in Longs' Cards and Books in Penn Yan and had to buy it," Chase said. "Jamie told me that you're hoping to buy Lacey and that you two make an amazing team. It's for good luck."

The breath I'd held escaped. Had my initial reaction in my head really been that Chase thought he and I would be perfect together? What a dope! I shook that off.

"Aww, that's so thoughtful, Chase. Thanks." Every fiber of my being was tempted to kiss him on the cheek, but I didn't want him to get the wrong idea, so I didn't.

I replaced the cotton on top of the small charm and reached for the lid, but Chase took hold of my hand to prevent it. His fingers were warm, big and strong.

"Don't put it away. It's to keep in your pocket."

When I looked up and met his gaze, my nerves tingled. This was movie scene material. This kind of thing didn't happen to me.

But it was happening, and it felt fantastic.

Although I didn't want to break the touch, I slipped my hand from his grip and took the charm from the box. The metal was cool against my hot fingers. I smoothed the pad of my thumb across the engraving of the puzzle pieces then along the etching. It was so simple, but it felt like he'd given me gold.

I looked back at Chase. "It's perfect. Thank you."

I slipped it into my pocket, and let it drop.

He pressed his palm against the side of my face and leaned toward me. Every movement was magnified in my mind. His lips came within inches of mine. His breath felt like a feather against my skin, making my cheeks ignite with heat.

His voice was low, barely more than a whisper when he asked, "Can I give you a good luck kiss?"

My mind blocked out everything around me. Before I could catch myself, I ran the tip of my tongue across my upper lip and nodded. When he closed the few inches between us, my eyes fluttered closed, and I lifted my face toward him.

He slid his hand around to the back of my neck and leaned into me. A hint of a spicy scent swirled between us. In the midst of a barn full of animals and hay, that was all I could smell. When he pressed his lips to mine, my stomach flip-flopped. Somehow I knew this was more than a good luck kiss. This was a promise of something more to come.

The kiss lasted only a couple of seconds. Definitely not long enough. I didn't want to open my eyes for fear that I would find out it was all in my imagination. I was frozen in place until Chase kissed my forehead.

My eyes slowly opened, and he stepped back, his hand still lingering on the nape of my neck. When he looked into my eyes, my heart tripled in speed.

"You and Lacey knock 'em dead out there, Savannah." He moved away, but let his hand drift along my neck, across my shoulder and down my arm until his fingers intertwined with mine. "I'll be the one cheering the loudest."

"Thanks." My voice was almost a squeak.

"See ya later." He pivoted and walked back down the aisle toward the exit. His shoulders were squared, and his back tapered down to a perfect waist. Confidence radiated from his saunter.

And he'd just kissed me. The reality of it was hard to grasp.

When he rounded the corner, he turned back and looked at me one last time before he was out of sight. How had we gone from 'Hey, I'd like to get to know you' to this feeling of 'We're supposed to be together'?

I shook my head and tried to refocus. It didn't matter. Whatever this was with Chase, it felt good. I pushed my hand into my pocket and pressed my fingers against the token, tracing the raised outline of the words. If this was any indication of how the rest of my day was going to go, there was no way Lacey and I could lose.

Since there were parents and friends of the girls here that I didn't know, I had no idea if Cassie Porter was already sitting in the viewing area. Maybe she really wasn't going to be here after all. And, it didn't matter. I was going to ride the same way whether she was or not.

Chase leaned against the pinewood wall a few feet away. As hard as I worked to focus on what I had to do, there was still a part of me that was very aware that he was there as I competed.

I finished with the highest times in the first three events: cloverleaf, the obstacle course and the keyhole. Lacey and I couldn't have been any more in sync. We were going into the next event, pole bending, with the lead in our division. I hoped my success wouldn't affect Alyssa's chances of being recruited.

While the other riders moved their horses into place outside the ring, I scanned the spectators again — just as I had before every event. When I spotted someone new sitting up in the viewing area in a folding chair at the far end, I sat up straighter like that would help me see better. With a clipboard resting against her crossed knee, she looked official.

Cassie Porter. It had to be.

I rubbed my fingers across Lacey's withers. Her head drooped like she was ready to take a nap. I was okay with her being relaxed. It would help me stay calm and focused, too.

"All we have to do is keep doing what we've been doing, Lace."

I watched the ring stewards set up the poles in a straight line. Phoebe carried the tape measure and marked the 21 foot distance required between each pole as the stewards set them in place. The exact measurement was important, because a well-trained horse weaving its way through the poles expected precision in placement. A misplaced pole could have a major effect on the horse's ability to gauge the angle of its turn.

Lacey and I stood at the edge of the ring. I relaxed in the saddle with one leg hooked over the horn as we watched the first four competitors. Alyssa was up next, then it was me. Everyone knew Alyssa was my strongest competition in this event. I glanced toward the loft. Cassie Potter was focused on Alyssa's every movement. Nothing would make me happier than Alyssa and me both being recruited by McDonough College.

Alyssa maneuvered her Quarter horse, Jack, through the gate to the ring, angled him in front of the starting line, then waited for the signal to go from the steward. And when he pointed, she loosened her hold on the reins, bent forward in the saddle and urged Jack to jump into a gallop. Her long braid slapped against her back from underneath her helmet.

The sand under the horse's hooves flew as Alyssa moved smoothly with Jack. He raced around the poles like a slalom racer on a ski slope. The crowd was quiet, the sound of the squeaking saddle and Jack's rhythmic hard breaths loud.

I looked toward the McDonough equestrian coach one more time. She had her phone in the air, and I realized she was taking a video. Like a little kid, I crossed my fingers for luck for Alyssa. McDonough College was the first choice for both of us.

Alyssa made a kissing sound to her horse to urge him beyond the last pole, and it drew my attention back to them. She wheeled Jack around the end and started back through to finish the pattern when she miscalculated a move. She reined Jack in too tight at the third pole and her boot and stirrup caught the edge, toppling the PCV pole into the sand.

A collective "Oh" rose from the crowd, but despite the fault that would cause her to have seconds added to her time, Alyssa pressed Jack on, undaunted by the mistake. They moved through the last three poles flawlessly. When she leaned forward and urged Jack to give one more burst of speed to cross the finish line, the horse responded and the crowd erupted in cheers. It was still a good run.

Alyssa reined Jack in, but because he was still hyped from the run, he was prancing when they passed us entering the ring. I held my hand up to high five her.

"It was a great run, Lys," I said. "Great recovery."

She responded with a tight smile, giving a hint of the frustration she was trying to hide. "Thanks."

I trotted Lacey to the far edge of the ring while I waited for one of the stewards to reset the pole. Phoebe held up the tape measure, but the steward waved her off.

"I'm good. I can see where it was," the steward called.

I patted Lacey as I watched and waited. It took four slow, deep breaths for my heart to slow. Once the pole was in place, the steward jogged to his usual place at the side of the ring.

Lacey's sides heaved and quivered under me. She was ready to go whenever the signal was given. Since the timing judge was still recording notes about Alyssa's run, I swung Lacey away from the starting line. As hard as I tried, I couldn't resist looking up toward the loft. Cassie Potter had her phone extended toward the ring.

She was going to record us, too.

My automatic response was to pat Lacey's neck again. I wondered if through my touch I could convey to her how important this run was. Out of the corner of my eye I noticed Chase move closer to the white fence railing. Someone next to him spoke to him, and I saw Chase answer without taking his attention from me. Me. I was his focus, and the realization sent a little shiver through me. He raised his hand to acknowledge our eye contact.

"Ready?" the timing judge called.

My mind popped back to the task at hand. How could I get so easily distracted at such a crucial time? I reined Lacey back toward the starting line, drew in one more calming breath, and raised my hand in acknowledgement. "Ready."

He lifted the stopwatch, then dropped his hand to signal me to go.

Simultaneously, I leaned forward, loosened the reins and tightened my legs to cue Lacey. "Hee-yah!"

She burst across the start line toward the line of poles. My focus was back, and so was Lacey's. With perfect precision she cut through the first four poles, but as soon as she moved toward the next one, I knew it was all wrong. The cadence we used to maneuver around the first poles was broken as I realized the next pole was set too close.

I tried to negotiate by pulling the rein across Lacey's neck a little early, but she over-compensated. In an instant, her massive body jerked. Before I could respond, she twisted to get around the pole, but it was too close for the rhythm we'd established. Her front legs lifted off the ground. She struggled to maintain her balance on her hind legs. I looked past her neck and could see her front hooves pawing the air as if she could get traction from nothing, but she was already rearing up and falling backwards.

There wasn't time to be scared, because there was nothing I could do to prevent the inevitable. This twelve hundred pound horse was falling over backwards, and she was going to land on me. I grabbed hold of the saddle horn in hopes of preventing it from slamming into my stomach.

Then there was a loud thud and a cloud of gritty particles blew up around us. My shoulder and hip hit first, smashing into the thick sand of the ring's floor. My last breath of air whooshed out of my lungs, and my helmet bounced against the ground. Lacey landed on her side with my left leg trapped underneath her.

I barely registered the gasps from the crowd.

And neither of us moved.

Terror ripped through me. Why wasn't she moving?

The arena went deathly silent. I opened my mouth to pull in air, but it was as if my lungs were frozen. I'd had falls before, but none compared to this impact. I was terrified to move.

Terrified that some part of my body was broken, and I couldn't feel it because it was so bad.

Terrified that Lacey was badly injured, and it was my fault for pushing her so hard.

A wave of panic washed over me. What had I done to my horse? What if she'd broken a leg? Adrenaline surged through me, and I shifted, pushing against the saddle for leverage so I could pull myself from under her.

It was like that movement was what she'd been waiting for. Her head popped up off the ground, and she scrambled for traction. Throwing my arms over my face, I tucked the best I could, preparing for her metal horse shoes to grind into my body. Her tail swatted my helmet as she struggled to get her rear feet under her.

As soon as she was off my leg, I gasped for my first full breath of air and rolled away to avoid her hooves. Even though I was wearing my helmet, I kept my forearms across my face for protection. It didn't feel like I'd broken any bones, but one misplaced hoof could cause massive internal injuries.

I was slightly aware of people running toward me, but all I cared about was Lacey. When I could tell she wasn't moving anymore, I uncovered my face. She stood squarely on all four legs, not appearing to favor any, and had her head lowered toward me as if she was worried about me.

Relief enveloped me, and I rolled over so I could get to my feet. A twinge of pain in my shoulder and arm were the only hints of what could have been a disaster.

Phoebe reached us first. She planted her hands on my shoulders and held me down in the sand.

"Savannah, are you okay? Don't get up until the E.M.T.s can evaluate you."

Air finally completely refilled my lungs, and I could talk. I shook off her hands and sat up. "I'm okay. What about Lacey?"

Two of the stewards were conducting a body survey on her. They ran their hands down her legs to her hooves, across her withers and along her neck. Nothing made her react.

"Do you think she's okay?" I asked again.

Phoebe stood. She took hold of the reins and encouraged Lacey to step forward. The horse swung her head to look at me, but when Phoebe asked her to move again, she followed the instruction. All eyes were on her, watching for any sign of lameness or pain.

With the attention on her, I stood and walked a few feet from her so I could see, too.

"I think she's okay," Phoebe declared, "but it would be wise to not use her any more today. We'll have the vet come in and evaluate, but I'm pretty confident that it was a scare for everyone. And what are you doing standing up?"

I stepped next to Lacey and wrapped my arms around her neck.

"I'm fine. I was more scared for her." My eyes welled up, not from pain, but from relief. I swore she leaned into me, too. We were both lucky.

When the people outside the ring started to clap, I waved to acknowledge their support. I glanced toward the loft where Cassie Potter sat.

She had put her phone away. I wondered if she had also just made a decision about my future on McDonough College's equestrian team.

I sighed and took hold of Lacey's reins to lead her from the ring. I hoped Cassie would realize the accident had occurred because of the misplaced pole not my error. Regardless, the important thing right now was that neither Lacey nor I appeared injured. I shuddered when the fleeting thought of what could have been zipped through my mind but shook it off. For now, I'd focus on our good fortune.

Chase was waiting at the gate to the ring when we reached it. His eyebrows were pulled together in obvious worry.

"Are you guys okay?" he asked as he moved up next to us.

"I think we're fine, but we won't run again today. We can't take the chance. I'm going to take Lacey back to her stall."

"You looked like you were limping," he said. "You're sure you're okay?"

I laid my hand against my hip and winced when I realized I'd probably have a nasty bruise there later. "My pride's hurt more than anything else. There's a scout here, and she was looking at Alyssa and me for the McDonough Equestrian Team."

Chase fell into step next to us as we walked. "Geez, I'm sorry about the scout."

I unlatched the clip on the throatlatch of my helmet and let it dangle under my chin. "I'll have to hope she comes another time. This has never happened before."

He nodded, but didn't say anything. The walk back to Lacey's stall was monopolized by other riders offering good wishes and condolences for the unfortunate fall.

Once back at our end of the barn, I slipped Lacey's bridle off and put her halter on so I could hook her to the cross ties.

"Is there anything I can do to help?" Chase offered.

I ran my hands along Lacey's legs, checking for any hidden injuries. "No, thanks. Just keeping me company is help enough."

He plucked a piece of hay from the bale next to Lacey's stall, then leaned against the wall and broke the hay into pieces.

"I'm impressed," he said. "I don't really know anything about this horse stuff, but you seem like a great rider. I think you'll go far."

"Thanks," I responded. "I don't know much about your lacrosse stuff, but I think you'll go far, too."

He laughed. "I guess we understand each other, then." He grabbed another piece of hay and started tearing that one apart piece by piece, too.

My shoulder was starting to ache, but it was more of a nuisance than a concern. From here, I could hear the crowd cheering on the other riders. I fought the nagging disappointment. For today, Chase would have to be the consolation prize – and I had to admit, at least he was a good one.

"Do you want to learn how to groom a horse?" I asked.

Chase pushed away from the wall. "Sure."

"I'll grab the brushes. You can start at her neck while I'm taking off her saddle." I turned toward my equipment trunk and lifted the lid.

And my heart lurched.

There sat the zippered bag that Drew had asked Chase to give me. Somehow I'd pushed that out of my mind. Since I had set it on the carrier that held all of my grooming equipment, I had to pick it up and was surprised, again, by its weight. With my free hand, I took out a soft brush and handed it to Chase and grabbed a curry comb for me to use.

"Aren't you curious about what's in that bag?" Chase asked when I started to set it back inside the trunk.

I hesitated. Yeah, I was curious, but something about it also made me uneasy. Without looking at him, I pulled it back out and eased down the top of the trunk. I didn't know if the slight tremble of my hands was an after effect of the adrenaline rush in the ring or the uncertainty of the contents of this bag.

Chase laid his hand on my arm. "Wait! I didn't mean you had to look now. It's not my business."

"No. I *am* curious." Whatever was in the bag thudded when I set it on the trunk. "And, it's okay that you're here to see whatever it is. I mean, as sad as it is, you know my father better than I do."

He winced. "Not my fault."

My shoulders sagged, and I dropped my chin, sucking in a breath before letting it out on a sigh. "I know. I'm so sorry. I don't know why I said that."

Lacey shifted next to us, but to Chase's credit, he didn't flinch, even though being around horses wasn't routine for him.

"Hey." Chase lifted my chin so I had to look into his eyes, then he rested his hands on my shoulders. "The situation sucks. I'm sure I'd be ticked if roles were reversed."

I shook my head. "No, it was a mean dig. That's not what good friendships are built on."

Chase leaned down to press his forehead against mine. I loved his warmth against my skin. "I'm past it," he said.

I closed my eyes and savored the same spicy scent I'd noticed when he kissed me earlier. "Good. I promise I won't be jealous of your relationship with my father. It's not fair."

He smiled, then brushed a kiss against my forehead before stepping back. "So, about that bag."

"Yeah. The bag." I grabbed the zipper and pulled it around the three sides to open it. As if spiders would jump out of it, I gingerly pulled back the top.

Chase hooked his thumbs on the sides of his pockets and rocked back in what seemed an effort to give me space.

There was some kind of soft, thin pink, blue and yellow material covering whatever was underneath. I reached in to pull it out, and as soon as I touched it, an eerie sense of familiarity washed over me.

A baby blanket. I squeezed a handful of the soft fabric between my fingers and pressed it against my chin. Was this mine?

I set it aside and returned my attention to the bag. When I saw what was inside, my breath caught in my throat and a chill shot up my spine.

CHAPTER 9

Our Baby Girl.

I stared at the off-white photo album. On the front was a raised plastic frame area that contained a photo of an infant in a white gown and matching bonnet being held by a young woman and man.

Me. That infant had to be me. And the parents: my real mother and father.

A shiver shot through me.

Chase leaned in closer. "What is it?"

"Photo albums." I lifted the top one out, and underneath was what appeared to be another. "He gave me photo albums." I was so stunned that I couldn't say anything more than that. My aunt and uncle had a few photos of Alex and me as babies, but this looked like a whole album.

I angled so Chase could see, too, and flipped open the top. The first page had all of the statistics of my birth. My weight, height, time – all of the specifics my aunt couldn't recall but I had thought about every time someone we knew had a baby. I ran my finger across each one as if they were written in Braille, and by touching the old ink, I could commit the information to memory.

The next page held a collage of photos obviously taken right after I was born, some where they were snuggling me. Warmth filled my core. They looked in love with me. With each other.

I gulped against a swell in my throat. These were photos of a time in my life that had been totally lost to me. I'd been so young when my mother died and we'd been adopted by my aunt and uncle, that I hadn't realized how much I didn't know about me as a baby.

Chase interrupted my thoughts. "Wow! Must be crazy seeing yourself with your real parents."

Words eluded me, so I nodded and flipped to the next page. The first picture on the page was a photo of Drew holding me close to him, his eyes closed, his lips resting against my forehead. Love jumped off the page from a man who I didn't even remember.

I lifted my chin and gasped for a full breath of air. Unprepared for the conflicting emotions surging through me, I battled tears that stung my eyes and blurred the pictures.

Chase squatted next to me and laid his hand on my forearm. He used his other hand to raise my chin so he could look into my eyes. "Savannah, are you okay?"

His touch on my face was light but electrifying. There was something so intimate about his callused fingers touching my face. Had he learned that gentleness from my father who had cuddled me so tenderly when I was a newborn?

I cleared my throat. "Um, yeah." I slowly closed the photo album. "I think I want to wait and look at these with Alex. Is that okay?"

He stood and held his palms up before taking a half of a step away from me. "This is a personal thing. I get it."

"Hey, Savannah, here to make sure you're okay."

Courtney, one of the emergency medical technicians who Phoebe always hired to be on standby at competitions, arrived with a huge, red medical bag. The timing was perfect. I wanted to think about anything other than those albums right now. My initial reaction had been too overwhelming, and I needed time to let it sink in.

"Oh, hey, Courtney." I scrubbed the back of my hand across my eyes in case there was any moisture lingering on my lids.

She set her medical bag on the trunk next to me.

"Hi, Savannah. I know you told the others you were fine, but I wanted to check in with you. That was a pretty nasty fall you took."

Lacey stretched her neck and dipped her nose toward the medical bag. I set the album on top of my trunk so I could intervene. She didn't need a horse's nose and lips wiped all over something she needed to keep clean.

Courtney stepped next to Lacey and rubbed her neck. "Nothing in there for you, pal," she said. And as if she understood, Lacey pulled back and swung her head toward me.

"No, there are no treats in there for you," I reiterated.

"So," Courtney said, turning her attention back to me, "any problems? Headache? Dizziness? Stiffness in your neck or shoulders?"

She took a small bottle of hand sanitizer from one of the side pockets of her medical pants and squirted the liquid into her palm.

"Nope. The sand in the ring makes it softer when you fall," I said. "And, wearing the helmet helps. I'm sure something will probably be sore tomorrow, but really, I feel fine."

Courtney reached into the other side pocket of her blue cargo pants and pulled out a pair of clear latex gloves and put them on. Next she removed a thin, white flashlight.

"Mind if I check the reaction of your pupils?"

I shrugged. "No, that's fine." I stepped closer to make it easier for her. Lacey nudged me, but I used the back of my hand to push her away.

Courtney flashed the light into each of my eyes a couple of times and asked me to follow her finger. I was starting to feel a bit of a headache, but I didn't mention it because I couldn't rule out a physical reaction to seeing the pictures in the album.

"That checks out fine," Courtney said. "Make sure if anything suddenly changes that you call your doctor."

"Will do. Thanks."

Courtney shoved the flashlight back into the pocket in her pants, peeled the plastic gloves from her hands, and picked up her medical bag. "Okay, take it easy, and no more scaring the heck out of people. Okay?"

I smiled. Yeah, like I had done that on purpose. I held up my fingers in a Girl Scout salute, something I'd learned in the one and only meeting I'd attended before we found out they met on a day when I had riding lessons. Riding lessons trumped Girl Scouts.

"Scout's honor."

Courtney glanced at Chase. "Make sure she takes it easy."

"Absolutely," he said, nodding.

Courtney walked back down the barn aisle, and I turned back to Lacey to remove her tack. I'd taken off the bridle earlier so I could put her in the cross ties, so I stepped to her side and began loosening the cinch strap on the saddle.

"Will a veterinarian come and check Lacey?" Chase asked.

"Yeah, although she looked completely sound when I walked her out of the ring. Probably, like me, she was just shaken up a bit. We'll both be fine."

Chase let out a low whistle. "And people think lacrosse can be rough. I've never had to worry about something over a thousand pounds coming down on me."

The image of that possibility in a lacrosse game made me laugh out loud. "Yeah, that would have to be some massive defenseman."

The girth dropped away from Lacey's belly and I looped the cinch strap back up onto the metal ring on the saddle. When I reached up to take the saddle off, Chase stepped in.

"Here, let me grab that," he said, correctly grasping each end of the saddle. He lifted it off Lacey's back, then turned toward me. "Where do you want it?"

I pointed to the metal rolling rack on the other side of the aisle. "You can put it on there. I'll take it up to the tack room later."

After he set it on the rack, he turned back toward me, wiping his palms against his jeans. "Now what?"

I shrugged. "We groom Lacey, and I let her rest in her stall. Then, I go back and watch everyone else compete. And, I pray that the coach from the McDonough equestrian team didn't write off Lacey and me."

"Is it okay with you if I stay and watch with you?"

I smiled. "You won't be bored out of your mind?"

He stepped next to me and brushed his arm against mine. "I'll be with you. That would never be boring."

A burst of warmth shot through me. Tipping my head up toward him, I batted my eyelashes. "Oh, you're such a charm —"

I stopped mid-sentence and looked past his shoulder. Mom was hurrying down the aisle past the stalls toward us. She'd probably have no idea who Chase was, but I couldn't imagine what her reaction would be if, or when, she figured it out. In an attempt to slow the inevitable, I brushed past him, feeling like I'd been caught doing something bad.

"Mom, hi. If you came to watch me compete, I'm done for today." I took a few steps in front of Lacey, a weak attempt to put distance between her and Chase.

"I know," she said, "I'm here to make sure you're okay." She stopped in front of me and her eyes did a quick scan of my body. "Phoebe called and said that you and Lacey had taken a tumble."

Laughing, I said, "Tumble is a pretty tame word. Two of the poles were too close together, and it threw off our rhythm. Lacey ended up flipping over on top of me."

Mom winced and reached toward me like she was going to touch me, but stopped short. "Ouch. But you're both okay?"

"It seems like it. The E.M.T. checked me over. The vet will be out to check on Lacey, but we're going to play it safe and not compete any more today, which is a bummer. Did Phoebe tell you the trainer from McDonough College equestrian team is here?"

"No, she only told me about the fall, so I wanted to make sure you were okay, especially since your dad and I will be going to the show in Rochester later."

Her attention darted toward Chase. There was no avoiding what had to be done. My heartbeat accelerated, and I stepped aside to give a clear path to him.

"Mom, this is Chase Warner."

They moved toward each other with hands outstretched to shake.

"Hi, Chase. Do you go to school with Savannah?"

"No, ma'am," he said, taking her hand. "I live in Keuka Shores. I met Savannah through Dr—"

I panicked and cut him off. I wanted this detail to come from me. "He and his mother are friends with my father."

Her eyes narrowed slightly, and her smile faded as her lips rolled in and clamped shut. She slipped her hand from Chase's grip. "I see."

"It's nice to meet you, Mrs. Cartwright." Either Chase was oblivious to her distrustful expression, or he was determined to not let it affect him, because his smile didn't waver.

She took a step back and clasped her hands in front of her. "Well, this is a bit of a surprise. She glanced away like she was trying to orient herself. Her gaze slid beyond Chase to the trunk behind him.

And she zeroed in on the baby album I'd set on top of the trunk. Now my heartbeat tripled in speed, and I thought at any second my heart would jump into my throat. Mom wet her lips with the tip of her tongue, then reached toward it like it would burn her. Finally she laid her finger on the photo on the cover, and her hand started to shake.

"Where did you get this?" Her voice was tight.

"Drew asked Chase to bring it to me." I hadn't removed all of the albums, but at a quick glance, it had appeared that there were at least four others.

She lifted her trembling fingers to her cheeks, and I could barely discern her shaking her head *no*. "I, um, I'm going to go home since you're all right. Would you like me to take those with me?"

"No!" My response was more powerful than necessary, but given her previous reactions to anything having to do with my biological father, I feared she would destroy the albums in some way. The image of flames devouring each precious memory in those books pushed any reasoning ability from my brain. I stepped between her and the trunk. "I'll bring them home with me. I want to look at them with Alex."

I braced myself for an outburst, but instead, she nodded. That was an improvement over her reaction when she'd found the internet picture I had of our father, but then she'd been eerily calm after that initial crazed reaction. I had to assume that Dad had found the key to calming her.

"Will you be home for dinner?" she asked.

My mind whirled. That was such a normal question in the midst of a very abnormal moment. "Yes, I will."

When she looked at me, her eyes appeared glazed, like someone who was overwhelmed. "Good," she said. "I'll make chicken and stuffing casserole for you and Alex to have since Dad and I will be seeing *Jersey Boys* in Rochester."

Chicken and stuffing casserole. My favorite meal. Was that on purpose?

I wanted to reach out and touch her, make sure she was okay, but something held me back. Instead I said, "Thanks for coming to check on me. I'm sorry if you were worried."

"I love you," she responded.

"I know." I had never doubted that — even when her love over the years was smothering.

"We're going to dinner with the Crowleys. Maybe we'll see you before we leave."

"Okay. I'm not sure what time the competition will get over."

She nodded, then walked between Chase and Lacey, ducked under the cross tie holding Lacey in place and continued down the aisle. After a moment, she disappeared around the corner to head out of the barn.

Chase stepped closer and put his arm around my shoulders. "I'm sorry if my being here made it awkward between you and your mom."

I leaned into him, glad to have his warm strength supporting me. "No, you were fine. She hasn't come out and said it, but she's made it pretty clear that she blames my father for my mother's death. Us finding him seems to have opened up old wounds."

"But you deserve to know your father and to learn about your past. It's not fair of her to hold you back." Chase pulled me in even closer, almost like he could protect me. "When I saw he'd given you your baby album, I was trying to figure out why he'd do that. I think, knowing Drew, I've figured it out."

"What?"

"This is only a guess, but I think Drew gave you those albums because, as much as he's keeping you and Alex at a safe distance, he's trying to connect with you. For the first time in a long time, he's allowing someone into his private world."

I looked up at him. "But it's our world, too. We just don't remember it. I just hope this isn't his way of saying this is as close as we can get."

The vet wasn't coming until later in the afternoon, so I decided to go home and take a shower. My neck, shoulder and hip had tightened, so I hoped a hot shower would loosen the muscles.

When I pulled the van into the driveway, Dad's SUV wasn't in the garage, so I knew he was still out since.

My fingers hurt from the weight of the bag with the albums. I shifted it to the other hand. That pulled on my sore shoulder, so I switched it back again. As eager as I was to share these photos with Alex and to see more myself, I couldn't ignore the butterflies in my stomach. These pictures might be more reminder than Mom could handle.

After kicking off my riding boots in the mudroom, I came through the back door into the kitchen listening for clues as to where Mom and Alex were.

The television was on in the living room, and because it sounded like some sort of comedy, I figured that's where I'd find Alex. I passed through the dining room and glanced down the hallway toward the den. Most likely, Mom was on the computer.

When I stepped into the living room, the scenario was exactly as I'd imagined. Alex was stretched across the couch. He was so tall now that he covered it lengthwise. As was typical, he was totally oblivious to me coming into the room because he was so focused on the show.

I moved to the end of the couch and whacked his sneakered feet. "Hey, shoes off the couch."

He kicked at my hand but didn't take his attention from the television. "You're not my boss."

This time I leaned over and grabbed his ankle and shoved his feet off. "I'm not bossing you around. Let me sit. I have to show you something."

He gave me a withered *you're a pain in my butt* look, but he moved. "Why can't it wait. This show is almost over."

"Trust me. You'll care more about this." I held up the bag. "It's from our father. Chase brought it to me today."

He sat straighter and tipped his head in confusion. "What is it?"

I sat next to him, putting the bag on the floor between us. "Photo albums. From when we were babies."

He started to reach for the bag, then stopped, and twisted to look toward the den. He lowered the volume of his voice and said, "Shouldn't we take them upstairs? What if Mom —"

"She already knows about them. She saw one when she came to the barn."

His eyes got wide. "She didn't freak?"

"No. She was actually calm."

I unzipped the bag, and he leaned in closer. I pulled out the first album, the one I'd already started to look at. "This one is all about when I was born." I set it next to me and reached in to take out the next one. I hadn't looked at the others beyond glancing in and seeing that there were a few albums.

The next one was larger. I set it on my knees and flipped open the cover. Just like my baby album, someone had taken the time to label these pictures, as well. This one was clearly still all about me and our parents based on the dates.

"Are there any that have me in them?" Alex asked. He reached into the bag and withdrew the next one.

Although it wasn't clearly marked as a baby album like mine was, as soon as he opened the cover, there was a picture of a newborn baby with special blue paper outlining it with his full name, date of birth and other statistics written in neat calligraphy.

"That's me," he said, sounding like a little kid. When he flipped the page, the next photo was of him being held by our mother. The one below that included Drew.

Alex moved the album so it rested on top of the one I had out. "Look at that. He looks so young."

"He looks like you," I pointed out. The resemblance was eerie, right down to the same cowlick in his hair.

"I can't believe he gave you these. This is cool."

We were in the middle of the last album when I heard the wood floor creak behind us. Alex froze, and I turned to look. Mom stopped at the entrance to the room.

"What are you two up to?" she asked.

Out of the corner of my eye, I saw Alex lean forward like he was trying to cover the album with his body.

"I'm showing Alex the photo albums." Then my heart fluttered and a crazy idea filled my head. "Do you want to see them?"

Alex kicked my foot with his like I'd made some mistake and he was trying to secretly correct me under a table. I ignored him. We shouldn't have to hide our past.

To my surprise, Mom moved into the room. She didn't look confident in the decision, but she was still calm. "Thank you, but I have to get ready to go out."

When she stopped at the side of the couch, Alex slowly closed the album we'd been looking at.

"You don't have to do that, Alex," she said. "I understand your curiosity."

She looked away toward the fireplace on the other side of the room. I wondered if she was looking at the photos of Alex and me that she hung and updated every year after school pictures were taken. The photos went in chronological order, hung like steps going down each side of the mantel. They started with photos of me when I went to kindergarten and Alex was three, because those were the first formal photos taken after our biological mother died. When she looked back, her lower lip was trembling.

"We love you both so much." Her voice shook along with her lip. "You're all we have. The four of us are a family, now." She pressed her fingertips to her lips, then added, "I've always been afraid of losing you."

I pushed the albums aside, stood and went to Mom to hug her. She wrapped her arms around me so tight that for a second my breath caught in my lungs.

I couldn't really understand her fear, but I could at least acknowledge it. "You won't lose us," I reassured her.

She unfolded her arms from around me, stepped back and smiled. "I need you two." And with that, she turned and walked from the room.

My heart ached for her, but when I turned back toward Alex, I could see that he wasn't feeling any empathy or sympathy.

"I don't think she understands what *we* need," Alex said.

I returned to my place on the couch. "What do you mean? What do *we* need?"

His jaw was set, and his eyes hard. "We need the chance to get to know our father. They've kept us from him all of this time."

"Alex, he knew where we were. He didn't come to us, either. And, it looks like he's not so sure about all of this now."

"He gave you these albums. That must mean something," he countered.

Sighing, I dropped back against the couch. "I have no idea what that means. Chase said we have to slow down."

"No!" Alex slapped his hand on the cover of the album on his lap. "Look how much time we've already lost. We're almost grown up, and we don't know him, and he doesn't know us."

"We're getting to know him, Alex."

"Yeah, well, spending a few hours with him isn't enough." Alex opened the photo album again and flipped through the pages until he came to a particular one.

"Right there, Savannah. See that picture?"

I leaned over to look closer. It was our father in his firefighting gear and toddler Alex perched on his shoulder in tiny matching gear.

"And look at this." He pointed at a photo of Drew playing basketball with some other guys. "We both play basketball. I want to play a game with him. That's what I want, Savannah. He's cool. According to that newspaper article and what people have said, he's done cool things. I want to be like him."

"What?" I shifted to face him. "You don't know him. How can you even say you want to be like him?"

Alex flipped the album shut and stood. "I'll never get to know him if he's there and I'm here."

Our conversation had taken a weird twist. "That's the reality, Alex. Our father lives almost an hour away. Who even knows when we'll see him again? He's pretty much calling the shots."

Alex scooped up the albums that were primarily photos of him. "Not anymore." He turned and stalked from the room.

"What's that supposed to mean?" I called to his retreating back.

He didn't answer. His feet clomped on the wood of the stairs as he retreated to his room.

I glanced around at the familiarity of the living room. In one way, I knew this was where we belonged. Where we'd been raised. Where we'd enjoyed all the love any children could want or need.

I glanced at the albums. And then there was our first home. Clearly, by looking at the photos, there was no love lacking there, either. So, where did that leave us now? Like Alex, I wanted to know more about our father. I wanted to know if we could again have a place in his life. I wanted to not feel like there was suddenly a gaping hole in my life.

Sighing, I picked up the remaining albums to take to my room. I wanted the simplicity of my life back.

I laid the albums on my dresser while I changed out of my riding clothes. As was my habit, I reached into both front pockets of my jeans to make sure I hadn't left anything in them before I put them in the wash. As soon as my fingers hit the bottom of a pocket, I felt the token Chase had given me before the competition. I pulled it out, smiling and shaking my head at the memory.

'For good luck' Chase had said. It hadn't brought us good luck - well, at least not the kind I had hoped for. Maybe it had brought us good luck because Lacey nor I had been badly hurt, which very well could have happened. The few seconds of the fall played through my mind. Actually, we were both very lucky.

I figured a shower and fresh clothes would cleanse my body and clear my mind. After grabbing what I needed, I headed down the hall to the bathroom. When I passed Alex's room I heard the hard bass drum of a heavy metal song. Our music tastes were very different. I preferred pop or the new country songs. Something I could sing along with and understand what the artist was singing.

When I returned to my room after my shower, there was a text from Phoebe on my phone.

Finishing chores No sign of injuries with Lacey. Doc Rovic here around 5

I was relieved by her text, but since it had been a couple of hours since I'd left the stable, I wanted to see for myself that Lacey was really doing fine. Maybe I could catch the vet there. It only took a few minutes to throw on clean jeans and a t-shirt, then I was headed down the stairs.

Dad stood in front of the mirror in the hallway straightening his shirt collar.

"I know you're getting ready to leave for the show, but would it be okay to borrow the van to go out to check on Lacey before dinner? Phoebe said she seems fine, but she's having the vet stop by just in case."

Dad nodded. "That's fine as long as it's okay with your mother."

His ordinary comment, one I'd heard hundreds of times over the years, sounded wrong this time. Was it because now I knew what I looked like in my biological mother's arms, so now calling my aunt *my mother* sounded like a lie?

I must have been thinking and staring longer than I realized, because Dad turned toward me as he smoothed the front of his shirt. "You okay, Vannie?"

It was his pet name for me, and he was the only one who called me that. The familiarity and caring sound of it touched me. I'd never doubted that he loved me as if I were his biological daughter. He was a great father.

"Yeah. I was just — just thinking about Lacey." I stepped forward and gave him a quick hug. "I'll check with Mom."

At the same time, Mom came out of the bathroom down the hall. "Check with Mom about what?"

"Borrowing the van to go out to the stable. The vet is stopping by, so I'm hoping to catch her, even though Phoebe is there."

"That's fine. Where's Alex?"

Like she had willed him to appear, Alex bounded down the stairs, seeming to be in a hurry.

"What's up?" Dad asked.

Alex breezed past us on his way toward the kitchen. "I'm going for a bike ride. Checking to see if any of the guys want to hit the trails behind the school."

Mom glanced at the clock on the fireplace mantel in the living room. "Be home by six. That'll give you almost two hours. Savannah will have dinner ready."

Alex didn't acknowledge the curfew, and instead hurried out the back door, letting it slam behind him — one of Mom's pet peeves, but she didn't react.

"Well, Babe," Dad said, a smirk playing at his lips as he wrapped an arm around her waist, "are you ready for our hot date?"

She patted his cheek. "I'm not so sure about the heat level, but I'm ready to go."

Mom lifted her eye brows as she turned back to me. "The casserole and yams need to go back in the oven at 5:30 at 350 degrees. Cover on. It shouldn't take long to reheat them."

I gave her a hug. "Thanks for making my favorite meal. It's a great way to end a kind of stressful day. I appreciate the thoughtfulness."

She nodded, sucked in her lower lip and bit down on it. It was what she always did when she was trying to keep her emotions in check. Probably knowing that I had more contact with my father, even in an indirect way, was difficult for her, but she was handling it better than I expected. Maybe she'd decided to give up the fight. I didn't know, but I was okay with letting things ride for now.

I backed away. "Well, I better get going so I'm back here in time. Have fun at the show. Don't worry about anything here." With a little wave, I turned, grabbed the van key off the hook on the rack and scooted out the back door.

Even though Dad had tried to be playful with her, there was still a sizzle of tension in the air. I missed the easygoing relationship that had always been our family's typical interaction. As I got in the van and turned on the ignition, I couldn't help but wonder if we'd ever be like that again.

I pulled the van into the garage a little after 5:30, and right away noticed that Alex's bike wasn't where he stored it. I wasn't surprised. He'd never been good at following the rules. No doubt he'd come zipping in a few minutes after six with some excuse as to why he was late.

While I waited for the oven to preheat, I texted Chase, Jamie and Alyssa to let all of them know the vet had declared Lacey perfectly fine. Once the oven was hot, I put the food in, set the timer for 6:15, then went up to my room to look at the photo albums again. Images of several of the photos had been popping into my mind ever since seeing them earlier. It was like piecing together a puzzle of my life without having the cover picture on the box to help me see what it was supposed to look like.

A while later I was sliding one of the photos back into its pocket when the timer on the stove went off. It was then that I realized I hadn't heard Alex come home. He could have slipped in without me noticing, but he rarely went through that back door without letting it slam — which then echoed throughout the house.

"Alex?" I yelled, setting the album aside. "You here?"

Other than the ticking of the clock in the hall and the beeping of the stove timer, there was no sound. I glanced at my phone to make sure he hadn't texted.

Nothing.

I pulled the casserole and yams from the oven and set them on the stovetop. I dished some out on a plate and took it upstairs. No doubt he'd decided a curfew didn't matter if Mom and Dad weren't home.

Whatever. At fourteen years old, he didn't need me to be his babysitter.

Since he wasn't home, I decided to get the photo albums from his room. Two were on the chair next to his bed. I grabbed those, but I left the one that was open on his bed so he wouldn't know I'd been in there. Back in my room, I set my plate of food on the nightstand next to my bed and spread the albums out on the comforter to compare his baby pictures to mine.

I wasn't sure how long I'd been looking at them when the grandfather clock in the hallway downstairs chimed, bringing me back to the present. What time was it?

Like I'd been wrapped up in a dream world, I glanced around my room, trying to orient myself. It wasn't dark out, but it was clear the sun had dropped behind the hill outside of town.

I closed the albums, picked up my empty dinner plate and fork and went out into the hall. Had I been so absorbed in looking at the pictures that I hadn't even heard Alex come home? I went toward his room.

"Alex?"

There was no response. His door wasn't latched shut, so I pushed it open a little. Maybe he had on headphones.

"Alex, you in here?" I poked my head in, but the room was empty. The photo album he had taken was still laying open on his bed.

Moving down the hall toward the stairs, I strained to hear if the television was on. Or maybe he was out in the kitchen finally eating dinner.

"Hey, Alex, you home?"

As I went downstairs, I reasoned with myself that he and his friends were probably having so much fun biking that they'd lost track of time. He was probably being his typical self and pushing the limits.

I slipped my phone from my pocket and dialed his number. While it rang, I started toward the kitchen. The faint sound of a phone ringing upstairs made me stop and wheel around. How could I have missed him when I looked in his room? And why didn't he answer me when I called his name?

I ran back to the stairs and took them two at a time. The sound of the ringing led me back to his bedroom.

"Alex, why didn't you answer me?"

I slammed open his door and hurried into his room. No Alex. But his phone rang and vibrated on the bed under the photo album.

"What the heck?" My voice was barely a whisper as I pushed the end button to stop the ringing.

His phone was never far away from him. Why wouldn't he have taken it with him, especially if he was going into the woods?

Heading back downstairs, I went to the kitchen where Mom had the phone numbers for all of our closest friends neatly typed and posted on the inside door of the spice cupboard. Running my finger down the list, I found the names I was looking for.

I called Josh and Tim since they were the ones who usually biked with him. Both answered their phones. Neither had seen him. I tried Pete, the kid who lived down the street and also hung out with Alex, but he hadn't seen him either.

The other friends listed didn't live nearby and weren't his biking buddies. I glanced at the clock on the stove. He was an hour late. My heart hammered in my chest. He'd gone biking alone, and without his cell phone. What if he'd gone on a trail and had fallen and was hurt?

I paced between the front window in the dining room and the side door in the kitchen. He'd stretched his curfew many times, but never by this much. Something had to have happened. Even my knees started feeling rubbery the more my imagination took over.

Panic was starting to creep through my body when my phone rang. I prayed it was Alex, then mentally kicked myself. His phone was upstairs.

I was surprised when Chase's name showed up on the caller I.D. I figured he was calling to see how I was feeling. I'd have to make it a quick call, because my next plan was to take the van and see if I could find Alex. I pressed the button on my phone to answer.

I didn't even have time to say hello before Chase blurted out, "Savannah, we have a problem."

CHAPTER 10

"We have a problem?" I echoed Chase's statement.

He cleared his throat. "Yeah, do you know where Alex is?"

I whirled around like I would see him standing behind me, which was ridiculous because I hadn't heard any doors open.

"No. He hasn't come back from his bike ride."

"That's because he's here," Chase said.

"What? Where?" I darted to the front windows in the dining room to look outside.

"In Keuka Shores."

I turned away from the windows and hurried toward the kitchen. "Keuka Shores? Is he with you?"

"Not exactly. He's on Drew's front steps. I'm hoping he doesn't trip Drew's alarm."

"Great!" I growled. "Just what we need is the police involved."

"The police would only be involved if Drew called them. His alarm system alerts only him."

I ran my free hand through my hair and pushed the heavy strands off my neck like that was going to help me think clearer. "Do you know how Alex got there?"

"Rode his bike."

"He rode his bike forty miles?" Now I was in the kitchen walking circles around the island. My mind buzzed. This was crazy.

"I have the van. Mom and Dad are at a show in Rochester. I'll come to pick him up."

"That's fine, but just so you know, he already said he's not going home tonight."

"What did Drew say about that?"

"He's at a fire call on mutual aid the next town over. I have no idea when he'll be back."

"This is insane. If I don't get Alex back before Mom and Dad get home, he's going to be so grounded. I can't believe he'd be this impulsive."

My stomach rumbled, nervousness threatening to sour the food there. I opened the refrigerator door and looked in, wondering if eating something else would help.

"Do you know his motivation?" Chase asked.

"I'm assuming it's because he's convinced he can have a relationship with our father. I'm not sure it's a reality."

I grabbed a couple of slices of cheese from the drawer, then bumped the refrigerator door closed with my hip before heading for the back door.

"Can you put him on the phone, please?"

"Yeah, okay, hold on. I'm out by the street. I'll take it to him."

Hinges squeaked in the background, and I pictured Chase going through the front gate at Drew's house. "Hey, Alex, Savannah wants to talk with you."

Alex's response was choppy, so I couldn't make out what he said. I was almost to the van and wouldn't be able to have my phone on when I drove, so I hoped this would be quick.

"Come on, man," Chase said, his voice a little farther away, so I guessed he was holding the phone toward Alex. "Savannah's on her way."

"Doesn't matter." The phone was close enough to Alex that now I could hear. "She can come if she wants, but I'm staying here."

I climbed into the van, buckled my seat belt, and put the key in the ignition, thankful we weren't a one car family. At the same time Chase came back on.

"No dice, Savannah. Drive safely. There's no hurry."

I put my phone on speaker so I could buckle the seat belt. "Uh, yeah, there is a hurry. If I don't get back with him before Mom and Dad get home, we'll both be in deep you-know-what."

"Still not worth getting in an accident. I'll wait here. Maybe Drew will be back from the fire by the time you get here."

"I'm not sure whether that would be a good or bad thing. Based on our last interaction, I'm guessing he won't appreciate a surprise visit." I turned the key in the ignition and the engine came to life. "Well, I'll be there in a little while, so I guess we'll find out then, won't we?"

"Yep. See ya soon."

"Bye."

I pressed the end call button and set the cell phone in the cup holder. I couldn't lie to myself. As stupid as this stunt was that Alex pulled, knowing I would get to see Chase for the second time today made me eager to get there. He was the first guy who'd caught my attention since I'd broken up with Matt Stephens before Christmas. Since then, I hadn't been ready to trust someone else. Chase was making me change my mind.

The drive to Keuka Shores was an easy one. I would have enjoyed the rural scenery with the dairy farms, the cows dotting the pastures and huge tractors pulling heavy equipment through fields if I hadn't been so aware of the clock ticking away the precious minutes. Alex would owe me big time for saving his butt. That was if I could get him back home before Mom and Dad got home.

True to his word, Chase was waiting with Alex when I arrived. I pulled the van in front of the house on the opposite side of the street and climbed out.

The porch held a two person swing that was suspended from big hooks in the ceiling, and past that was a small round wrought iron table with four matching chairs where Chase and Alex sat. As I climbed the porch stairs, I kept my head down, bolstering myself to deal with Alex's pig-headedness. At the top step I looked up. Alex was leaned over sideways in the chair with his elbow resting on the armrest.

I glanced at Chase. "Is the alarm off?"

"No, but in the front it would only be triggered by someone messing with the door or windows."

"Let's go, Alex," I said as I crossed the wooden porch. "We can't screw around here. We have to get back home before Mom and Dad."

He jutted out his chin and looked up defiantly. "Nope."

That was it. His sole response. I'd never been a bossy older sister, so in some ways I wasn't surprised that he was resisting me now.

"I'm putting my neck on the line for you just by coming out here. If we leave now, Mom and Dad will never have to know this happened."

Alex crossed his arms over his chest and shook his head. "You can go back home and tell them I'm here. I don't care. It's the weekend, and I decided tonight that unless we spend time with our real dad, he's never going to get to know us. This has always been out of our control. Right now, I'm taking control of my life back."

I looked at Chase, but his expression was unreadable. "How do you think Drew is going to react to Alex's plan?" I asked.

He shifted and tapped his heel against the wooden floor. "I have no idea."

I turned back to Alex. "Forcing yourself on him isn't going to make him love you if he doesn't. This stuff takes time."

"Well, I'm making time. Right now."

"Uhhh!" I whirled away and balled my fists by my hips, squeezing my fingers so tight, my fingernails dug into my palms

In an effort to control my impatience, I stared out at Drew's lawn, at the immaculately mowed lines in the grass, the perfectly shaped shrubs, the rose bushes with leaves and buds but no flowers because it was still too early in the season. Everything looked perfect.

Nothing felt perfect in our world, though. I started to turn back toward Alex and Chase when the screeching of fighting cats pierced the quiet.

Alex launched from his chair. "They're going to kill each other."

He raced off the porch and toward the back of the house where the sound was coming from. For a macho teenaged guy, his one unexpected weakness had always been animals in distress. And these cats sounded like they were going at it.

"Stay away from the back porch," Chase yelled as we followed at a run. I went behind Chase, not the least bit interested in getting between cats in the middle of a major hissy fit.

Alex had no qualms about it, though. Ignoring Chase's order, Alex leapt past the three steps and up onto the porch. An orange tabby cat was hunched, with its tail wrapped part way around its back leg. It's adversary, a black and white cat with fur sticking straight out all over, slapped the end of its tail in the air as a warning. Their angry yowls raised in a crescendo, then eased into more reserved growls before their feline voices rose again in an ear-splitting pitch.

"Knock it off!" Alex yelled at them, but they maintained their warning stances, oblivious to him. The black and white cat slowly put one paw forward like it was going to advance. The orange cat hunched more. In a quick sweeping motion with his foot, Alex pushed a large, empty flowerpot between them. It was enough to break the tension.

The orange cat jumped in the air and at the same time twisted its body so that when it landed it could run in the opposite direction, off the porch. The black and white cat slowly unpuffed like a deflating balloon, then, clearly wary, slinked into what looked like a small dog house that sat in the far corner of the porch. I bent to peer through the square, upright railing posts. The cat disappeared into the darkness of the interior.

Alex took a couple of steps toward the shelter, but Chase startled us both when he blurted out, "The cat's feral. Leave it alone."

Alex turned to Chase. "It's wild? Will it attack? Is that why you wanted me to stay off the porch?"

"I don't know what it would do if it felt cornered, but I didn't want you to go up on the porch because Drew has an alarm system with a motion sensor directed at that door. Hopefully you managed to stay out of its range."

Alex whirled in a circle, scanning the porch ceiling. "Where is it?"

"It's concealed."

Alex's eyes widened. "Are the cops going to come?"

"Not unless Drew calls them. This is a system set up to alert him on his phone."

I turned to Chase. "Don't the cats set it off?"

He shook his head. "Drew installed an animal immune system. It only goes off when it detects movement from something over one hundred pounds."

Scanning the porch, Alex said, "So, if I just set off the alarm, then Drew knows right now that we're here?"

"Yes, unless he doesn't have his phone on him," Chase answered.

Alex stepped back toward the railing and slid himself along it to stay as far away from the door as possible. He jumped from the top step to the ground, bypassing the two steps in between.

"And, this text is probably from him," Chase said, reaching into his pocket for his phone. He pulled it out and glanced at it. "Bingo." His fingers flew over the keypad. "I'll call him in a minute."

"Is this a high crime neighborhood or something?" Alex asked. "Why does he have an alarm?"

"No, it's because of his PTSD. He's afraid if someone comes and accidentally startles him that it could cause him to react without thinking. He calls it hypervigilence. His mind never turns off to possible threats."

"Man, that's intense," Alex said.

"Sometimes." Chase turned and started back around the side of the house toward the front, and we both followed.

"I can't imagine having to live like that," I said.

Drew's reaction to the nail guns going off popped into my mind. Everyday things that might merely startle most of us sent his mind back to Iraq.

We walked single file along the sidewalk, Chase, me, then Alex. We were halfway to the front when Alex said, "Hey, are those feral cat houses over there, too?"

Chase and I stopped and turned to look where Alex pointed. Three more small houses were tucked on the far side of the lawn near a big shed. One could barely be seen under a bush that hung over it, another was under a big maple tree and a third was in the far corner of the yard tucked into the ninety degree angle of the fence.

Chase nodded. "Yeah. All cat houses. Drew builds them."

I squinted, trying to see if there were any cats in them. Two looked empty, but the one in the corner by the fence appeared to have a lighter-colored cat in it.

Alex turned toward Chase and frowned. "What the heck? Is he trying to be like a crazy cat lady or something? Why does he have all of these cat houses?"

"It's therapy," Chase responded as he started to walk again. "He said after all of the horrible stuff he's experienced, it makes him feel better to do something positive to help another living thing. He and a vet friend make them."

"A veterinarian?" I asked.

"No. Veteran. An Iraq war vet. She got out last year."

Alex jogged up next to Chase. "She? Did you say the veteran is a woman?"

We reached the front of the house, and Chase stopped on the sidewalk. "Yes, *she*. There are women in the service, too, you know."

"I know. I guess I didn't picture my father hanging out and building things with some woman." Alex shoved his hands in his back pockets. I could tell by the expression on his face that he was trying to make sense of this new insight.

I turned and looked back toward the cat houses. There was obviously a very nurturing side to our father that didn't mesh with the image of a man who would give his children away to his sister-in-law because their mother died. The complexity of Drew McAuliffe was mind-boggling. I wondered if there was really any way for us to get through all of the layers to know him — if he'd even allow it. But the more I saw, the more intrigued and interested I became in getting to know him. Lost in thought, I looked at Alex. Maybe he and I weren't so different in that regard, after all.

Alex walked to the porch stairs and stood on the bottom step. "So, wild cats just come here to live?"

"Kind of," Chase answered. "There's a local rescue group that he deals with to find them homes if they're adoptable." His phone rang and he reached into his pocket to get it. "I don't really know how it works. I just know he does it." He glanced at the face of his phone. "It's Drew. Excuse me."

Tension shot across my shoulders and up my neck. At the same time, Alex straightened, his eyes bright and curious.

Chase turned away to talk, so all we heard was, "Hey," when he answered.

"Come on, Alex," I said. "If we go now, we'll get home before Mom and Dad."

He shook his head. "Go home, Savannah. I'm staying. I'm not messing around anymore. He's okay with Chase being around, so I would think he'd be okay with his own son being here."

"Chase told you about the PTSD, Alex."

He jutted out his chin like a defiant child. "Not good enough. There's gotta be therapy or something."

"How do you know he's not in therapy?" I countered.

"I don't. Those are the answers I'm looking for. Maybe now that we're grown-up —"

"What?" I interrupted. "Grown-up? That again? Alex, you're fourteen."

"I'm not a little kid. I want to know my father. It's only going to happen if I make it happen."

I drew in a breath to argue, but let it out on a sigh. I knew better than to try to change Alex's mind. It was that kind of unwavering determination that made him excel at so many things — school, sports and hobbies.

Chase had moved down the sidewalk so he was next to the street. I was sure he was filling Drew in on what was happening here, but I could only catch part of a word here and there. Maybe Alex hearing what Drew had to say about him riding his bike here would satisfy him for tonight. When Chase turned toward the house he was shaking his head. Then he ended his conversation.

"You tripped the alarm," he called.

For the first time, Alex looked concerned. "Is he mad?"

"Well, let's just say he's not thrilled. Be right back."

"Where are you going?" I pulled my phone out of my pocket to check the time. It was almost 8:00. We had to leave. There was no way I was taking a chance on losing my license when I'd only had it a few weeks. Driving after curfew or speeding home could be the end of it.

"Mom has a key for his house in the safe."

"In the safe?" I said..

"Yeah, I know, kind of strange. Drew gave us a key, and taught us how to disarm the alarm, but otherwise, his house is pretty much off-limits. This is only the second time he's asked me to reset it. Be right back."

Chase was back in minutes.

Alex stood. "Do you know when my father will be home?"

Chase passed him and went up the steps to the porch and front door. "They're almost back to town with the trucks, now, but he usually helps get them back in service." He unlocked the door and started in. "Give me a sec, and I'll be back out." He left the front door open a bit and disappeared down a hallway.

Alex watched him. Once Chase was out of sight, he bounded up the steps.

I ran up the stairs after him. "What are you doing?"

"Going in."

That was obvious, but he was inside before I could stop him. I halted at the doorway, feeling like a trespasser even coming this far. I leaned in to see if I could spot Alex or Chase. I could see what I assumed was Chase's shadow against a cabinet straight ahead down the hall, but I didn't see Alex.

"Alex!" I called.

"What?"

His voice sounded like it was coming from the room behind the door. I hated the feeling that I was violating Drew's privacy, but I also wanted to make sure that Alex wasn't violating it even more, so I stepped inside to look beyond the door.

A sense of déjà vu swept over me like a tidal wave. My whole body heated and tingled like mini sparklers going off all over inside me. I swallowed against the mass of air that caught in my throat.

I'd been here. I *knew* this place.

Alex stood in the middle of the room, turning slowly like he was trying to take it all in and memorize it. But I didn't need to. I already knew in my head what this house looked like. It was as if nothing had been moved or changed in the twelve years since we'd lived here.

I pictured myself jumping on the light brown couch cushions. In my mind, I could actually feel the springiness, and the way the couch felt when I flopped down on my back like it was a trampoline. And suddenly, I heard my mother's voice telling me to stop. I squeezed my eyes tight, picturing the face that I knew from the photos to go along with the voice in my head.

When I opened my eyes again, I glanced down the hall to the left — where I knew the bedrooms were. My heart pounded and sweat popped out on my palms. The compulsion to walk down the hall toward those rooms was stronger than anything I'd ever felt. Even though in my heart I knew this was wrong, I moved in that direction.

"Where're you going?" Alex asked.

But, I couldn't answer. It was like I had time-traveled and nothing around me was real. His voice was a weird echo in my head as I pictured myself as a four-year-old walking down this hall.

The farther I went, the heavier my legs felt, like the emerging memories weighed me down. All of the doors along the hall were closed. I remembered the first one on the right was my parents' bedroom. How many nights had I woken up from a bad dream and scurried down the hall to climb into their bed? They'd cocoon me between them, making me feel safe and loved. The memory was so strong and vivid, I swore I could smell the fresh scent of my mother's shampoo. It was tempting to stop and look in, but I tamped down the urge. This invasion of Drew's privacy was bad enough.

I passed the first room on the left, Alex's old room, because I wanted to get to the one at the end of the hall. Mine.

"Savannah? What are you doing?" It was Chase's voice this time, but my mind was far away, far back in another time in my life. I was aware of the footsteps as he and Alex came down the hall behind me, but I kept going. "We have to get out of here," he said. "Drew would be ticked off if he knew you were in here."

I reached for the door handle, expecting it to be as hot as fire because I was going somewhere I felt I shouldn't. But the metal was cold in contrast to my sweaty palm. I turned it slowly, preparing for the ghosts of the past to swoop out at me as soon as I cracked open the door.

When nothing happened, I pushed it wider so I could see everything at once. Light from the setting sun streamed in through the window, the rays and shadows of the tree leaves danced on the twin bed that was perfectly made up. Instinct, or memory, I wasn't sure which, made me reach for the light switch just inside the room, even though it wasn't dark. My eyes were drawn to the Dora the Explorer bedspread. My favorite childhood show.

"This was my room," I whispered like I thought my breath would disturb something if I talked louder. "I remember this."

A shiver shot through me. It appeared nothing had changed in this room. My mind swung between being touched by the seeming preservation of a happy time to being creeped out. Why had Drew left it exactly as it had been when we lived here? It went against everything my mind wanted to believe about his desire to wipe us out of his life and memory.

My life as a four-year old was frozen in time in this room.

I took a step inside and made a visual sweep. My bookcase was against the same wall as my bed. Even from here I could see the perfectly aligned copies of Dr. Seuss books, as well as the other classic children's books I remembered my parents reading to me before bed. I looked toward the rocking chair where I had cuddled in their laps while they read to me or my father told me stories he made up about a scared little bear cub.

Cubby. The name had been in my head all of these years, and I hadn't understood until now. Every time I saw a picture of a bear cub or saw a cub in the zoo, the name Cubby came to mind, and I never understood why.

Now, I remembered. That was my special time with my father. I remembered feeling so loved. Daddy's little girl.

A sense of contentment, of being deeply loved, then betrayed, skittered through me, momentarily throwing me off balance. How was he able to give his little girl away?

My eyes welled up, and I brushed the back of my hand across them. This was private. Between me and my younger self. I didn't want Alex and Chase to see how deeply I was affected.

To collect myself, I refocused on my surroundings. The toy box. The stuffed animals lined up on top of the dresser. My name in multi-colored wooden letters above my bed.

Then I looked at the window, and a whole different memory flooded back.

My mother pushing me through the window, over the sill, and dropping me into the darkness of night. Confusion and fear so strong that they overwhelmed me then, and made me a bit queasy now. This felt like a time warp. The moment surreal.

I whirled toward Chase and Alex who stood in the doorway. "Oh my gosh. Nothing has changed. This room is exactly as I remember it. It's like time stopped the night our mother died." I stepped closer to Chase. "Have you ever been in here?"

He shrugged and nodded. "I wasn't supposed to. Drew got pretty mad the day I did it. I was going with him to something at the firehouse, and he had to stop at his house first. He told me to stay in the truck, but I had to go to the bathroom, so I got out and went in without him knowing. I was young, maybe seven or eight. I was looking for the bathroom and found the bedrooms first."

"What did he do?"

"Slammed the door shut and told me I was never to go in those rooms. I remember asking whose rooms they were."

"What did he tell you?" Alex asked.

"He told me they'd belonged to a little girl and boy who were gone. Of course I asked where they were." He leaned against the door frame and shrugged again. "He didn't answer. Instead, he told me I had to go home. And that night my mother told me to never ask about the boy and girl again, because it made Drew too sad. So, I didn't."

"Where's my room?" Alex asked.

It was hard to pull myself away, but I moved to the door and pointed down the hall. If it's still the same, then your room is that one down on the right."

Alex pivoted, and in a few long strides he was at his old bedroom door, swinging it open. He must have found the light switch right away, too, because light washed out into the hall.

"Wow!" he said as he stepped inside. "He never forgot us."

Chase and I followed him into the room. It was decorated with everything a person would expect in a themed room for a little boy — trucks of all kinds were stenciled onto the walls, and unused sports equipment lined the top of his dresser. The crib that had been his was still nestled against the wall, with little blue blankets laid neatly on the mattress.

Alex moved around the room, touching the things that had once been his, except, unlike me, he was too young to have memories of them. "This is crazy! I can't believe this was *my* room."

Chase laid his hand on my arm, and I dragged my attention away from Alex and looked up at him. "We shouldn't be in here," he said. "We need to leave."

"I know. I'm sorry. I was so shocked to realize I remembered this house."

"You're lucky," Alex interjected. "I wish I did."

"Come on," I said, grabbing Alex's elbow. "Let's go."

He shrugged off my hand and looked back at the side of the room with the crib. In some ways I felt guilty that I was the only one with the memories when he wanted so badly to feel a connection to our father.

Chase led the way, with me following a couple of steps behind him. I was curious about the bedroom down the hall where I remembered my parents sleeping, but looking in that room really felt like an invasion of Drew's privacy, and I couldn't do it.

Suddenly I couldn't get out of the room and house fast enough. This was wrong, and guilt stabbed through me. He rounded the corner to enter the hall and without warning jerked to a stop. I was in such a hurry and so close that I bumped into the back of him.

"Hey, a little warning would've —"

I cut off the last couple of words as soon as I looked up and saw why he had abruptly stopped. If shock could stop a heart, then I was perilously close to needing a defibrillator.

CHAPTER 11

"What the hell's goin' on here?"

Drew blocked the hallway — not on purpose, but because it wasn't a wide hall, and he was a tall, muscular man. At the moment, he looked gigantic. His short hair was messed up and going in every direction, probably from wearing a helmet at the fire, but that and his expression made him look wild.

My throat muscles constricted. I could barely pull in a tiny breath.

Without turning or looking, Chase reached his arm back to put his hand on my wrist. Was he trying to protect me or hold me back? The latter was unnecessary. There was no fear of me going toward Drew. I imagined he felt violated finding us snooping through his house. I felt that way when Mom went into my room to pull sheets off my bed, and that was nothing in comparison to this. Did this kind of thing set him off?

"I came in to reset the alarm," Chase said, the respect for Drew's right to be angry clear in his tone. "We weren't going to —"

Alex cut him off, stepping past Chase and me to stand in front of our father. Alex was tall for his age, but even with his shoulders squared and his feet set apart in a strong stance, he was no match for Drew's intimidating stature.

"It's my fault," Alex said. "I followed Chase in."

"Why are you in here?" Drew's expression was hard, unforgiving. He cut a glance toward me.

My knees started to tremble. It wasn't all Alex's fault, and there was no way I was letting him take the blame. I pushed Chase's hand aside and stepped next to him, but still a step off to

Alex's right. As difficult as it was, I forced myself to meet Drew's unwavering glare.

"No, it's my fault that we're in here. I came in to get Alex, but then when I realized I remembered this house, something took over and I had to see my old bedroom." I dropped my chin and gaze, embarrassed by my impulsiveness. "I'm sorry we invaded your privacy. We're way out of line."

"Yeah, you are." Drew stepped to the side and pointed down the hall toward the front door. "You need to leave, now."

Alex sidled past him, my brother's bravado apparently gone. He looked from Drew to me.

"Come on, Savannah."

When I didn't move, he stepped back toward me and grabbed my arm.

"Come on. Let's go. This was a stupid move on my part."

Even though I could see a storm brewing in our father's eyes, I wasn't backing down.

"No!" I yanked out of his grasp but never let my attention leave our father's eyes.

"I don't get it," I began. "You never changed anything in this house. It's just like I remember it. We haven't lived here for twelve years, but it's still the same. Were you pretending we were still here?"

Drew didn't react except for the muscle flexing in his jaw. I wasn't sure that he even blinked.

I stiffened my back, summoning courage I didn't know was in me. "Or were the doors closed because you were trying to forget us?"

Extra color inched up Drew's face. "There hasn't been a day since either of you were born that I haven't thought about you."

The slightest twitch of his eye hit my nerves. Any idiot could read his body language. But I railed on.

"Then, why? Why did you give us away?"

"I didn't give you away." His mouth barely moved so the words came out between his gritted teeth, making them sound almost like a growl. "I did what I had to do to keep you safe."

"Safe? From what?"

His steely gaze bore into me, and his mouth clamped shut. Seconds ticked by, counted off by the blood pulsing in my ears. We were at an impasse.

"Forget it," I said, grabbing Alex's arm. "Let's go."

But Alex was an immovable statue. His eyes didn't blink. His chest barely rose with a breath. His focus was so razor-sharp on Drew that he wasn't even aware that I was next to him.

I'd seen that look before. He was posturing for a challenge. Oh, lord, how I wished there was a way to push a button and get us out of here.

"You know what?" The tone of his voice was lower than I thought possible for a kid in the midst of adolescence. "I'll go back to your first question and tell you why I'm here."

Alex shifted his body slightly as if shoring himself up to take on whatever might come at him. "I want to know why you spend all of your time with Chase and go to his games and do things with him, but you can't spend time with Savannah and me." He hooked a thumb in the air to point over his shoulder in Chase's direction. "What makes him so damn special that *he* can have *you, my father,* in his life, but I can't have you in *mine*?"

I gulped against the lump that blocked the air in my throat. I had to admit, I'd wondered the same thing in the last few weeks, but more out of curiosity than anger or feeling slighted.

Not even a molecule of air was disturbed by any of us. I was sure I would either collapse or die at any moment.

Then suddenly Drew threw his hands up as if surrendering, and we all jumped. He lowered them, pushed his fingers through his hair and grasped his scalp tight before pivoting away from us and stalking down the hall toward the living room. His biceps bulged, revealing his outward strength, but I wondered if Alex's badgering had exposed our father's emotional weak spot. Was he internally combusting? Did we need to run?

I couldn't make my feet move, but I twisted to look at Chase who still stood behind Alex and me. My heart lurched when I saw the expression on his face. I'd been so focused on how Drew would react to Alex's verbal tirade that I hadn't even considered how deep those hurtful words could cut into Chase. Although the hall lights were dim, the tinges of red on his face made it obvious that he'd been affected by Alex's outburst.

That got my feet to move, and I whirled toward him. "Chase, Alex isn't blaming you for anything. I hope you know that."

Alex turned, too, his eyes wide. "Oh, man. No. I mean, you didn't even know we existed."

Chase's gaze swung from me to Alex and back again. "I'm not trying to compete for his attention. He was just always there. I don't even remember my own dad." His shoulders dropped, and he rubbed the back of his neck like it was tight. "I don't know what to say. Does sorry even cut it?"

I stepped in front of Chase, took his hands in mine and looked into his eyes. "No. No. You don't owe us an apology."

And that statement made my mind somersault: Did our *father* even owe us one? There were twelve lost years of a relationship, and we didn't really understand why. It was time to end the silence.

All of the hurt, confusion, and anger from the guys forced me in another direction, again emboldening me. Alex had opened the door. I was going to barge through it.

I pushed past Alex and Chase and charged into the living room. Drew had dropped into a corner chair. His elbows were perched on his knees, and his hands were clasped with his fingers steepled. His index fingers were pressed against his lips as he stared at the far wall.

There was no acknowledgement from him when I came into the room, not even a brief glance, so I slid onto the end of the adjacent couch. I folded my hands in my lap, and because I couldn't be still, twirled my thumbs around each other while I stared at the movement like it was the most interesting thing on Earth. What I wanted to ask was so simple - yet scary.

In my periphery I saw Alex and Chase enter from the hall. Chase stepped next to the still open front door, shoved his hands in his pockets and stared out toward the street. It appeared Alex wasn't leaving himself vulnerable, either. He stopped, and remained standing at the foyer. Somewhere beyond the door, I heard kids laughing and, in the distance, the hollow sound of the bass of a car radio with the volume cranked. Everyday life happening around us.

I let those sounds seep into my psyche, giving me some semblance of calm and normalcy. I rubbed my sweaty palms across my jeans, then stretched my arms to release some of the tension before letting my hands settle back onto my knees. After several deep breaths, I managed to gather my courage, then looked directly at our father.

"I'd like one question answered, and since you brought it up, you're the only one in this world who can answer it. If you can at least do that, then I'll leave."

His shoulders rose as he pulled in a deep breath, then they dropped and he slowly brought his attention to us. His forehead creased like he was in pain, but he nodded slightly to give permission.

"Why aren't we safe with you? We aren't little kids anymore."

His eyes narrowed, and he moistened his lips with the tip of his tongue. I guessed I'd hit the most sensitive question I could. Somewhere, a car door slammed, and he flinched. He immediately drew in a deep breath and slowly exhaled what seemed like twice as much air as he'd taken in. I wasn't sure he was going to answer me, but then he pointed toward the door and spoke.

"It's things like that," he said.

I scrunched my forehead as I tried to figure out what *that* was. The outdoors? The people outside? "Sorry. I don't know what you're trying to say."

"Do you know what PTSD is?" he asked.

I nodded and sat up a little straighter. I'd read an article in a magazine in the waiting room of the dentist's office a few months before about how on average twenty-two soldiers and veterans committed suicide every day because of Post Traumatic Stress Disorder caused by the horrors of war. I'd also done more research after finding him. Was he trying to tell us that he had tried or wanted to commit suicide? I opened my mouth to ask but stifled my curiosity. I wasn't sure I wanted to know the answer.

"PTSD is a demon that hides in the shadows," Drew said. "I'm a strong person." He hesitated and cleared his throat. "Sometimes the demons are stronger, and when I think I've managed to push them into a corner out of my life, they're still there, rearing their ugly heads again. All it takes is a lawn mower backfiring." He shrugged. "A nail gun suddenly going off."

That reference I understood. I remembered the way he'd dropped flat to the ground, covering Alex with his body, when the worker on the roof at the work site started using the nail gun without warning Drew to expect the noise.

Alex shoved his hands in his pockets and stiffened his arms like he was uncomfortable. "What does that have to do with us?"

"Everything," Drew said. "It's about why I couldn't risk having you live with me." He sighed and lowered his fingers from in front of his mouth. "Your mother is dead because of those demons. My problem cost the life of the most beautiful person I'd ever known. It's my fault she's de—"

His voice hitched on the last word, and his Adams apple bobbed in his throat like he was struggling to maintain control. He closed his eyes and slowly shook his head before looking back at me.

"It damn near cost you yours, too. It's only by the grace of God that you and Alex survived that crash."

"But it was a car accident," I said, trying to understand. "A horrible accident. You weren't driving the car. You weren't even in it, right? Why do you act like it was your fault?"

His face darkened, and he shot to his feet. "Because she was running from me!"

I jerked back on the couch, partly because his words were so forceful that it was almost like something hit me, and partly because I was shocked. He turned his back to us, so he was unaware of the confused looks that Alex and I exchanged.

"Running?" My voice almost squeaked. "She was afraid of you?"

He stared out the front window for a second, shaking his head, but not turning around.

"No, she was afraid *for you*. You and Alex —"

He turned around, his eyes darting around the room like he was struggling with a thought before he focused on Alex and me. "We were her world. The two of you. Even me. Even though I was different after I came back from Iraq. There were times when I didn't deserve it, but I never doubted how much she loved me. She loved her family. *We* loved our family," he said, emphasizing his feelings.

He dropped back into the chair like all of his energy was spent. His eyes glistened but no tears surfaced. My heart swelled. He was so not the man I'd imagined in those rare moments in my childhood when I'd felt abandoned. The man I imagined couldn't love.

The man sitting in front of us — a man who was practically a stranger — had bared his soul to us. I didn't know how to react, but I did know that the animosity I'd been harboring felt like wasted energy.

Alex moved to the end of the couch but remained standing. "What's any of that have to do with PTSD?"

"Sometimes I feel like a ticking bomb," Drew said. "Everything can be great, like at the work house last week, then bam, a loud noise — a door slamming, a nail gun, a car hitting a pothole —" He threw one hand in the air "—fireworks like the night your mother died. Anything like that can cause a flashback." He leaned forward in the chair and hunched his shoulders when he looked at us, looking insecure and vulnerable. "Your mother was an angel. A godsend. My rock."

His voice sounded raw. He was talking about our mother. The woman I barely remembered, and Alex didn't remember at all. He was talking about a time when we were a family. An intact family. His love for her was so obvious. His sudden despair, heart-wrenching.

My throat constricted, and I stretched my neck to breathe. I wondered if all of these feelings had been trapped inside him and the floodgate had opened. Had he shared any of this with Chase? Asking about counseling was way too personal, but with all he had going on, how did he handle it without therapy or counseling — or a loving family?

Alex slid onto the other end of the couch to sit. "None of that matters. You're our father." He glanced at me, then back at Drew. "We want to be here with you."

Drew launched from the chair again. "No. I'm unpredictable. I won't risk it."

Alex rocketed to his feet, too, yelling at Drew's back as Drew pushed past Chase and out onto the porch. "But you risk it with Chase. He's getting all of the benefits of you being there for him. Why aren't we good enough?"

The screen door slammed behind Drew, and the porch floorboards creaked as he crossed them.

Chase looked out the door toward Drew, then turned back to us, speaking for the first time since we'd moved to the living room. "It's not the way you think. Time that he spends with me and my mom is on his terms. It's always been on his terms."

I tipped my head. "What do you mean?"

Chase looked at me, but he was clearly talking to Alex. "Nothing is ever long-term. A few hours here, a few hours there. And never holidays." He lowered his voice and added, "I never understood why — until now. Or at least I *think* I understand."

"But you knew about the PTSD. You told us about it when he had that flashback at the work site. What more is there to understand?"

Chase shoved his hands in his pockets and rocked forward on his feet. "Drew is the bravest man I've ever known, and he'll do anything for anybody. Now it makes sense. As brave as he is on the outside, I think he's petrified on the inside. If he keeps everyone at a distance, my mom and me included, he thinks he can't hurt anyone."

Chase looked toward the floor, shook his head and mumbled, "Stupid. How could I not figure that out?"

We were all quiet for a minute. At the same time, Alex and I looked toward the screen door, probably each wondering if we should go out on the porch.

"Does he see some sort of counselor?" I asked.

Chase shrugged. "I have no idea. He's very private. I've never heard him express his feelings like he just did. Maybe he does to my mom when I'm not around, but I don't think so. I don't think he trusts people." He lifted his eyebrows in emphasis. "After hearing him now, I don't think he trusts himself."

We were all quiet again for a minute, then Alex rose from his end of the couch. When he started toward the door, I got up and followed, with Chase behind me.

Our father was standing in the far corner of the porch, leaning onto the horizontal railing. He didn't look toward us as we came out of the house.

"I wanna stay here tonight," Alex announced.

A jolt of internal electricity radiated through my abdomen. "Alex!" I hissed.

"No!" Drew's clipped response didn't sound mean, just decisive.

Alex took a few steps toward him until he was within a few feet. "I'll take care of myself. I'll sleep on the couch. Just for one night. Is it so wrong to want to spend one night in the same house with my father?"

There was no mistaking the sudden tensing of Drew's body, but he still stared out toward the street. "No." His voice was calm. "Nights are the worst. Sudden noises when I'm sleeping can be a trigger."

"Then I'll be here to tell you it's okay." Relentless. It could have been Alex's middle name. At the moment, I thought idiot would fit, too.

Now Drew turned only his head to look at Alex. "It's not that simple."

"You're only making it harder," Alex countered. His hands were fisted like a little kid getting ready to throw a fit.

"Come on, Alex. It's time to go." But he didn't budge.

"What do you want from me?" Drew sounded like being patient was taking every ounce of his energy.

I turned toward him, annoyed that it wasn't obvious to him.

"Just your time. He wants a chance to get to know you. So do I. Both of us like a lot of the same things that you do. We could tell that from the pictures in the photo album."

"Yeah," Alex interjected. "I'm pretty cool." He tipped his head toward me. "Even Savannah's kind of cool."

Now that surprised me. For siblings, Alex and I got along pretty well, except for the occasional disagreement that could get boisterous, as Mom would say, but I never thought he'd describe me as *cool*.

Drew peeled his hands from the railing and eased his back against the corner post. "Give me time," he said.

"You've had twelve years," Alex threw back.

There was no response from Drew — only a long, unreadable stare.

I pulled out my phone and checked the time. This was getting a little too close for comfort. I crossed the porch, grabbed Alex's arm and pulled. "Let's go. We need to get home before Mom and Dad, or we'll be grounded for months."

At first I thought he was going to argue, as usual, but then he started to walk backwards, still watching Drew.

"I'll get Alex's bike and put it in the back of the van for you," Chase offered.

I followed him down the stairs, glancing over my shoulder to make sure Alex was following me, which, thank goodness, he was.

A gray cat scurried past my legs and up onto the porch. It trotted toward Drew, and then leaped onto the railing next to him. When he didn't acknowledge it, the cat batted his wrist with its paw, and he absently reached out and stroked it between its ears. It stretched up, reveling in his attention. The same way we craved his attention.

Partway down the sidewalk, I stopped and looked back. A fresh wave of guilt washed over me as I looked through the screen and down the hallway where we'd gone. I wasn't sure how I felt about everything we'd discovered in those few minutes.

I decided I couldn't leave without apologizing one more time. "I'm sorry we went in the house. I hope you'll forgive us for being so rude."

"It's done," Drew said.

Alex stopped on the bottom stair and twisted to look back at our father. "It was my fault, but I'm not going to lie. Even though it didn't go how I thought it would, I'm glad we saw you again. We won't give up."

There was no acknowledgement from Drew.

"Chase has our phone numbers for whenever you're ready." I hoped my implication was clear but not pushy.

Drew nodded as he picked up the cat and let it snuggle its head under his chin. The gentle way he cuddled it against his chest made me melt inside. I wondered if we would ever have the chance to break through the barriers that our father hid behind.

As I watched, I realized that something had changed in me with this personal glimpse of Drew. Deep in my heart I felt a tug. More than ever, I wanted his love again.

But the biggest hurdle stood cuddling a cat on the porch. Were the walls that he'd erected around himself so strong that we could never break them down?

"Savannah, you in here?" Jamie called from around the entrance to the barn.

I wrapped my arm around Lacey's neck as I slipped her bridle off and slid the halter on.

"Yeah. By Lacey's stall." I hung the bridle on a hook, then loosened the girth on the saddle. "What's up?"

"Chase just pulled in the driveway. You expecting him?"

"Nope." But the tingle that shot through me was proof that I was happy he was here. It had been four days since I'd last seen him, although we'd either texted or talked every day since then. "Can you send him in, please?"

"Yup," Jamie called back to me. "I'm putting Sasha out in the pasture, then heading home. See you at the demonstration at CharTay Kennels on Saturday."

"Yeah. Thanks for the invitation. I think Chase is going to come with me, too."

"Cool. See you then." Her voice trailed off a bit at the end as she left the barn.

Lacey stomped her foot, impatient for me to remove her saddle so she could have her grain. I lifted it off her back and carried that and the saddle pad to the saddle rack by the wall. I'd given her enough time to cool down. All I needed now was to brush and feed her, and turn her out into the pasture. I was working the rubber curry in circles along her back and rump when I saw Chase come around the corner.

"Am I too late?" he asked as he approached.

My stomach fluttered, and I couldn't stop the smile that inched its way along my lips. "I guess that depends on what you want to see or do."

Lacey stretched her nose toward him when he got in front of her, and she nuzzled his hand, looking for a treat.

"I'd hoped to watch you ride. When you sent me the text about going to the barn, I assumed it would be after dinner."

I worked my way around Lacey, trying to groom all of the areas caked with dried sweat. "Nope. Tonight we're on our own for dinner because we're all going in different directions, so I I'll eat later."

Chase ran his hand along Lacey's neck. "That's perfect, because I haven't had dinner either. Any chance I could convince you to go into Penn Yan with me to get something to eat at Seneca Farms?"

I tossed the curry comb into my equipment trunk and pulled my phone from my pocket. "I have to check with my parents, first." My fingers flew over the keypad, and right away Dad responded. "I'm good to go," I said. "I don't have other clothes with me, so I can wash up a little in the bathroom, but you're going to have to deal with the remnants of the horse smell."

He smiled and held up his hands. "No complaints from me as long as I can be with you."

My cheeks warmed, and I stifled a sigh. The best thing to come out of this crazy situation with my father was looking at me with a look of adoration that made me feel like I was the most beautiful person on earth. No guy had ever made me feel as accepted, as comfortable in my own skin, as Chase did.

I put my hand on my hip and gave him my sassiest look. "You know, you're really good at that."

He tipped his head and his eyebrows shot up in a confused expression. "Good at what?"

"Making me feel special." I pulled the *Perfect Together* token from my pocket and held it up. "And feel special every time I look at this."

He wrapped his fingers around my fingers and the token. The warmth of his skin blended with mine. Also perfect together. I would have been content to stand that way for hours.

"Savannah, you *are* special," he said, his voice low and husky. "You're not like any other girl I know."

I met his gaze, mesmerized. "And you're not like any other guy I know."

He loosened his fingers and took the token, turning it between his fingers like a magician. "Maybe *we'd* be perfect together, too."

I swallowed against the lump in my throat. This was fast.

Because my brain couldn't wrap around the warp speed of this conversation, I resorted to one of Mom's most-used sayings.

"Time will tell."

Chase nodded and extended the token to me. "Time's on our side."

I tucked the token back into my pocket, then cleared my throat. "Well, let me finish here, then I'll wash up and be ready to go."

"Anything I can do to help?" he asked.

"Nope, but thanks for offering."

Chase settled on the bags of wood shavings stacked along the aisle, and I turned back to Lacey.

"I keep thinking about everything that happened at Drew's Saturday night," he said.

"Ha!" I ducked down and looked at Chase from under Lacey's neck. "We said a lot. Way more than we should have."

He stretched his long, jean-clad legs out, crossed his ankles, and leaned back against the stall's wall. "No, I don't agree. Sometimes guys let too much build up inside. Girls tend to let it out and say what's on their minds more. Drew needed to hear how much you want to have him in your lives."

"I'm beginning to wonder if that's really possible." I undid the cross tie from Lacey's halter and snapped on a lead rope. Lacey lowered her head so I'd rub her forehead with my knuckles. She closed her eyes and pushed against the pressure.

"But I won't give up," I continued. "Alex and I have spent every waking moment researching PTSD. We want to understand what's wrong with him."

Chase pulled his stretched out legs back and sat up straight like he'd been poked. "It's not about what's *wrong* with him, Savannah." He stood and stepped next to me. "Understanding PTSD comes from learning about what *happened* to him. The majority of us can't fathom what he's seen and experienced, and he refuses to talk about it."

"You asked?" I couldn't imagine being bold enough to ask.

"Yeah, I asked," he said, looking a little annoyed. "I'm a couple of months away from having to register with selective services. Believe me, that makes a guy curious about war."

"Selective services? You mean, like for a military draft?" My hand slid down Lacey's long face and settled on the soft spot at the top of her nose. I didn't have to think about registering, so that was the farthest thought from my mind.

"Yeah. Not that there's a draft right now, but just knowing because I'm an eighteen-year-old male, and I'd be eligible to go and fight in a war if that suddenly changed, well..." His voice trailed off.

"I'm sorry. That was stupid of me. I never considered how you might be affected."

Chase shook his head. "No, don't worry about it. This isn't about me, anyway."

I stared at him for a few seconds. "Yeah, that conversation did take kind of a strange turn, didn't it?"

He smiled, and my attention was drawn directly to his lips. A tingle raced through me with the memory of the last time he'd kissed me, and I was thankful he couldn't tell. I'd been kissed by other guys, but none left my knees weak like Chase's kiss. And I looked forward to the next one. And the next.

There was something about the silence between us that actually sounded loud from the thoughts running through my brain.

He tipped his head. "Whaddya thinking about?"

My face heated. I hoped my cheeks didn't get pink. In that split second I toyed with telling him or just reaching up on my toes and kissing him. I opted for coy.

"You really want to know?"

He took another little step closer so there was very little space between us. One of his hands slid across my waist and settled on the small of my back, bringing my body up against his.

"Sure." He lowered his lips to within inches of mine and looked into my eyes like he could read my thoughts without me uttering a word.

I ran the tip of my tongue across my lips, suddenly bolder than I'd ever been with any guy. "I was remembering how great our last kiss was."

Maybe it was my imagination, but I swore his eyes sparkled as he lowered his head even closer. "Then let's make this one an even better memory."

I dropped Lacey's lead rope, wrapped my arms around his neck and lifted my head to meet his slightly parted lips. His kiss was smooth at first, but then took on an urgency, like he couldn't get enough. If that was what he was feeling, then it was mutual. I never wanted this kiss to end.

The moment and kiss were interrupted when Lacey swung her nose into my back as if to remind me that she was there. Although Chase had his arms around me, the force still threw me a little off balance, and I jerked to the side.

We laughed, and Chase said, "Guess she's the chaperone, huh?"

"I guess so. Sorry about that."

He brought his hands up to frame my jaw. "I'm glad we met, Savannah." He stroked my cheeks with his thumbs. "You're easy to talk to. And, I trust you."

"Trust me?" That seemed like such an odd thing for him to say. I hadn't given him a reason to not trust me. "I'd never lie or do anything to hurt you."

"I'm not worried about me." He slid his hands from my face, across my shoulders and down the length of my arms until he took hold of my fingers with both hands. "I trust that you won't mess with Drew. I owe a lot to him. I'm not sure where my mom and I would be if he hadn't taken us under his wing. "

The true depth of Chase's concern for *my* father showed in his eyes. The fact that he trusted me made me adore him even more.

"Then I need you to help us navigate through this, Chase. A month ago we had no idea our father was still alive. And, now — " My thought trailed off because I didn't know what came after the now. "It seems like you know him the best. We want to know him."

"He's a great guy, and he's gotten better over the years, but he doesn't open himself up to people." He used his thumb to rub the back of my hand. "But the other night, I don't know, I sensed that he feels the void of having lost his family. I think he wants to know you. And the only way that's going to happen is if I step out of the way."

"What do you mean?" I asked.

"Saturday night after you and Alex left, I went home, too. Then Drew came over to my house and demanded to know what I've told you and Alex about him." Chase dropped my hands and took a step back, his expression serious. "I'm going to tell you exactly what I told Drew, and I hope it doesn't make you angry."

My stomach clenched. When he hesitated like he was trying to choose his words carefully, I sensed bad news.

"I don't like being caught in the middle of this thing between you and Alex and Drew. He asked me to give you the albums. You asked me about his life. He asked me what I've told you." He shoved his hands in his pockets, lifting his shoulders like he was trying to disappear into himself, a bit of insecurity that I hadn't seen before.

"I know it's not on purpose," he continued, "but it's pressure that I didn't sign up for. I want to spend time with you. I want to spend time with him. But that's where my involvement in your relationship ends. I gave him your cell number. I'm going to give you his. If you guys want to directly contact each other from now on, go for it, but I'm not playing middle man anymore. Do you have your phone on you?"

I nodded and pulled it from the front pocket of my jeans.

"Let's put Drew's number in there so I know you have it."

I opened up my contacts and added the number as he gave it to me. I saved it as Drew. I already had a number for Dad in there.

"Use it," Chase said. "If you want to see him, you'll probably have to make the first move."

"Okay." I turned and grabbed Lacey's lead rope while I mentally digested what he was saying. Somehow holding the rope made me feel in control, even if it was only in control of her. Then I looked back at him.

"I-I'm sorry. It was never my intention to use you that way or put you in the middle. It's all so new, and I figured you know him, so —" There was no need to finish my sentence.

"I understand that. I really hope it works out for you and Alex and Drew. I know I wish I could be reunited with my father, so I'm happy for you that it's a possibility with yours. But if it doesn't work out, I don't want to feel like I was responsible because I didn't do enough or the right thing. This is something the three of you have to work out on your own."

The knot in my stomach tightened. "Is this going to change us?"

He furrowed his forehead. "What do you mean?"

"We're starting to get to know each other, too. I don't want to lose that."

He leaned forward and gave me another quick kiss. "That's exactly why I don't want to be in the middle. I want whatever happens between us to be unconnected to your relationship with Drew. Like I said, I really hope it works out for you guys, but if it doesn't, I don't want it to mean it can't work out between you and me. Does that make sense?"

I nodded. "Perfect sense." Chase had put us all in our place, but kindly.

Lacey nudged me again with her nose, and I pushed back with my shoulder. "Guess she's ready to go to the pasture. Wanna walk out with us?"

"Sure."

I gave a slight tug on Lacey's lead rope and clicked my tongue. "Come on, girl."

We walked out of the barn without talking. Enough had been said, but when I thought about it, I realized it was the right kind of *enough*.

When we reached the gate, Chase swung it open and I walked Lacey into the pasture. As soon as I slipped her halter from her head, she shot off toward the other horses. The cloud of dust that she kicked up swirled around us, causing us both to turn our heads and cough away the remnants.

I waved my hand in front of Chase's face to try to clear some of it. "Sorry about that. She likes being with her herd."

He grabbed my hand and pulled it to his chest, resting my open palm against his heart. The beat was solid, steady. "I like being with you."

I smiled, dropped the lead rope and laid my other hand on top of his, creating a warm stack. "And I like being with you."

I tipped my head up to offer a silent invitation. And he accepted. His lips met mine again, and I closed my eyes in contentment. Everything inside of me pulsed like I was coming alive in a new way. It was a feeling that I wanted to hold onto forever.

When the kiss ended, Chase leaned his forehead against mine. I opened my eyes to look into the blue depths of his and smiled again.

"That was very nice, Chase Warner. Thank you."

The corners of his eyes crinkled when he smiled back. "Ooh, so formal." He kissed the tip of my nose. "You're welcome, Savannah Cartwright."

Although I feared I might, I actually *didn't* melt into the dried earth. We stood forehead to forehead for a minute before Chase said, "Well, should we head out for food before it gets too late and you can't go?"

As much as I didn't want to share him with the rest of the world at the moment, I still stepped away and bent to pick up the discarded lead rope. "Good point. I'll go and clean up in the barn. It'll only take me a minute. I'll meet you at the cars."

He backed away. "That works."

Chase crossed the grass toward the parking area, and I headed in the other direction toward the barn. Halfway there, my phone dinged with a text. I pulled it out of my pocket and glanced at it.

I miss you already

I laughed and turned toward him. He was still walking, but he was looking at me over his shoulder and sporting a silly grin. He lifted a hand and waved.

I shook my head and waved back. Something told me a relationship with Chase would be full of surprises.

When my phone dinged with another text, my smile grew wider, and I turned and looked at him before even checking it. But, this time he wasn't looking at me and was almost to his car. He was playing coy. A happy sigh escaped before I looked to see what he'd sent this time.

When I glanced at the screen, my smile dropped and my eyes locked on the message.

It was from Drew.

CHAPTER 12

will be at demo Saturday

I stared at the text message from Drew and had to fight the urge to rub my eyes and read it again to make sure that I was reading it right. Was it really from Drew? Was he really telling me that he purposely planned to go where I'd be? I wasn't sure after last Saturday's mess at his house that he would ever want us near him again.

I read it again. Checked to see if there was a message above it that I'd missed, but there wasn't. Was this his way of extending an olive branch?

I whirled around to look at Chase. He was leaning against his car checking his own phone. Had Drew sent him a message, too? I tossed Lacey's halter and lead rope onto a metal bin near the door, then jogged across the grass toward Chase. He looked up and smiled.

He pushed away from his car and reached for the door handle. "That was fast. All set?"

"No," I said, coming around the hood. "I have to show you the text I just got."

I decided not to tell him it was from Drew so I could see his reaction. I held my phone out for him to read. He cupped his hand around mine and pulled the phone in front of him. A small smile lifted the corners of his mouth.

"Well, props to Drew," he said, looking up and letting go of my hand.

As if I hadn't read it twice before, I looked at the message again. "Did you know he was going to do this?"

He leaned back against the car again. "Nope. But he and I have talked a couple of times since Saturday. I laid it on the line with him and said if he's not comfortable with you guys coming to him, then he has to go to you, because it's obvious you're not going away."

The hair at the back of my neck bristled. "He doesn't want us around?"

Chase crossed his arms and dropped his chin. "No, it's not that. I think he needs to get to know you, but on neutral territory — like it was at the house work site — where there aren't memories for him with you two."

"How did he know I was going to the demo?"

"Jamie and Kyle were over for a bonfire at our house Sunday night. Drew was sitting with my mom at the picnic table nearby when Jamie told Kyle you and I would be there. Jamie told us the owner of the kennel, who trained Trooper, asked Rashawn to be part of the demo. So, then Rashawn called Drew and asked him to be there for moral support."

"Do you think Drew will follow through?"

Chase nodded. "Drew never goes back on his word. Ever. He'll be there."

I looked back at the message, then typed a reply.

Great! See u then

I hit send, then pulled in a deep breath. Progress. This definitely felt like progress.

"I'll be a couple of minutes," I told Chase, and I turned to go back to the barn to clean up before going to eat. Whether Chase could see it or not, I felt the lightness of my steps, and I couldn't fight the smile that tugged at the corners of my mouth. My heart felt full. Knowing Drew was willing to take this step and be there made me happy.

I prayed he wouldn't back out.

Alex was disappointed that he couldn't go to the demonstration, too, but Mom and Dad were insistent that his commitment to his soccer team had to take precedence. The look of longing in his eyes when I left was etched in my mind, and it kept popping in as I scoured the vehicles that lined the road and driveway leading to Char-Tay Kennels. Despite   purposely taking slow, deep breaths, my heart rate increased when I didn't see Drew's truck or Chase's car. Had they both backed out of coming to the demonstration?

The van's steering wheel slipped under my sweaty palms as I maneuvered into a tight space between two cars on the grass. As soon as I opened the door, I heard dogs barking. It sounded like most of it was coming from the kennel, not the big grassy field where everyone gathered.

Kyle spotted me from across the lawn and waved as I walked toward him. We met not too far from the demonstration area.

"You're just in time. They're starting in a couple of minutes. Jamie's participating in the demo, but we have chairs set up over on the end if you guys want to sit with me."

"Sounds great," I said. Once again I scanned all of the cars parked in the area. "Have you seen Chase or Drew?"

Kyle shook his head. "Not yet."

At the same time, my cell phone dinged with a message. I hoped it wasn't Drew texting to cancel. Relief washed through me when I saw the message was from Chase.

Be there in 5

I poised my fingers over the keypad to ask the burning question, but before I could type, he sent another text.

Drew picked us up late

Relief zipped through me. Drew hadn't backed out.

"Chase says they're almost here," I told Kyle as I slid my phone into my pocket.

"Cool. Do you want to wait for them here?"

"No. I can text Chase and tell him where we are."

"Sounds good." He pointed toward the kennel. "Looks like they're bringing the dogs and handlers out now."

A parade of people and dogs stepped out from the kennel's front door. I recognized Labradors, Golden Retrievers, a German Shepherd and then other dogs that looked like ordinary mixed-breed family dogs. As they got closer, I could see they all wore vests with the words "Service Dog" in bold letters on the side. The vests varied in colors, but most were blue, red, green and orange. The dogs walked perfectly next to their handlers. Jamie walked with a Golden Retriever toward the back of the line of about ten dogs.

"Are those trainers or owners with the dogs?" I asked, dividing my attention between following Kyle and watching the teams crossing the grassy area.

"Both. They're all considered handlers. Some people who have gone through the program came back to be part of the demo."

Then I spotted Rashawn and Trooper, and I did a double take. He had a pronounced limp, but he was walking without crutches.

I grabbed Kyle's arm and stopped him as I stared.

"Oh my gosh! It's Rashawn and Trooper. Do you know them?"

Kyle nodded. "Yeah. Jamie introduced me to Rashawn when he was here for training with Trooper."

"Wow!" My eyes welled up and goose bumps jumped to my skin. "I can't believe he's walking without crutches. He must have a prosthesis?" It was a silly question, because obviously he was walking on two legs.

"Yeah. I don't know why he doesn't wear it all the time."

I wanted to wave hello, but I didn't want to distract him or Trooper if he was nervous. I watched them walk by, and smiled in case he remembered me.

When I turned my attention back to those who followed him, I noticed a young kid who looked to be eight or nine walking next to another Golden Retriever.

"That boy isn't a handler, is he?"

Kyle nodded and started walking again. "That's Erik and Scout. Erik has autism. Scout was from the same litter of puppies that the dog Jamie's handling is from. Their father is Atticus."

I took a couple of extra long steps to get next to Kyle. "Atticus? Scout? Is this like a *To Kill a Mockingbird* tribute or something?"

He laughed and shook his head. "Charlotte Taylor, who owns this kennel, loves literature. Each litter of puppies has names connected to literary classics. Atticus's pups all connect in some way. The one Jamie is handling is named Jem."

"Wow!" I said. "I had no idea there was a whole system to naming dogs."

We wound our way through the last couple of rows of people.

Kyle continued his explanation. "Atticus was Charlotte's show dog, but now he's Jamie's. Charlotte retains rights to some of his puppies. Certain pups from each litter are trained as assistance, service, or therapy dogs if they have the right temperament."

"You seem to know a lot about them," I said.

"Jamie's tried to teach me. I think I've figured out most of it."

Many of the other spectators had also turned to watch the parade of dogs making their way past the chairs and into the center of the demonstration area. As we approached our seats, I saw that there was what appeared to be an obstacle course set up in one section. Ramps, large tubes, hoops and two free standing doors and frames, that looked like they were ready to be fit into a house, were arranged haphazardly.

Jamie tipped her head to acknowledge she saw us when she and Jem passed, but otherwise, she was all business. I couldn't miss the smile specifically directed at Kyle. When I looked at him, I caught a wink.

Yeah, I wanted that kind of relationship.

Chase's face popped into my mind. I didn't know where our friendship would lead, but my lips tingled with the memory of his kiss.

Kyle pointed to a row of folding lawn chairs. "There are our seats that Jamie set up."

We crossed behind the last row of seated people to reach them.

From this vantage point, we had a perfect view of the action. The dogs and handlers lined up in a row, and a middle-aged woman stepped forward. Her curly red hair bounced in the light breeze. When she lifted a microphone to speak, I realized that there were wireless speakers on either side of the demonstration field. I hadn't expected such an organized event.

"Good morning, everyone. I'm Charlotte Taylor, owner of CharTay Kennel. I'm pleased to see so many of you have come out to learn about the valuable roles dogs play in assisting individuals to lead a more normal life." Charlotte glanced up and had to close her eyes when the sun hit her in the face. "We are certainly blessed with a perfect day. Cloudless sky, comfortable temperature. It's a great day to be outside."

There were several murmurs of agreement from the crowd, and even a few claps. Charlotte angled herself a bit toward the dogs and handlers so she could look at them, but also at the audience.

"I won't take the time to introduce each of our guests right now, but rather, as each one comes to participate, we'll tell you who they are, their role with the dog they're handling, and what skills the dog will demonstrate."

Someone tapped me on the shoulder, and I jerked around as Chase knelt next to my chair.

"Hey, sorry we're late," he whispered.

His warm breath glided across my cheek, making my skin tingle. He could whisper to me all day, if he wanted.

"Oh, hi. You haven't missed anything," I said, keeping my voice low. "Charlotte just started talking." I leaned over to acknowledge my father and Angela as they stepped up. "Good morning."

I wanted to appear nonchalant, but my insides were jittery. I wondered if there would ever be a time when it would feel natural for my father and me to be together.

"Good morning," Angela said, her smile as bright as always. "I'm excited to see the dogs in action." She laid her hand on my shoulder. "And, it's nice to see you again."

Drew smiled. "Morning."

"I'm so glad you came today," I said to him.

"Me, too," he responded. "Thanks for asking me."

I smiled. "You're welcome. It'll mean a lot to Rashawn to have you here."

"Maybe, but I didn't want to disappoint you. *That's* why I'm here."

Warmth shot through my core. "Thank you. I appreciate it."

Kyle raised his hand and pointed to the empty chairs, indicating the ones closest to me. "Have a seat," he offered.

Chase came around and sat in the chair next to me. That was followed by an awkward moment when Drew looked at the other empty seats. I wondered if he was trying to decide how close he should sit to me. Kyle saved the moment.

"Here, Drew and Angela, you can take the two seats by Chase, and I'll sit at the end."

They all moved at once, creating what looked like a moment of musical chairs as everyone shifted and settled. Out of the corner of my eye, I couldn't help but notice how stiff we all looked. It was awkward enough wading my way through getting to know Chase, let alone throwing my father into the mix. I hoped awkward wasn't our new normal.

After everyone settled, I focused on Charlotte, who was in the midst of describing the process of dog selection and the training regimen.

"The cost to train a service dog can vary drastically. Depending on the situation and the extent of the training, the amount could be as low as five thousand dollars or as high as fifty thousand."

Gasps and whispers mingled as the people in the crowd reacted.

Charlotte smiled and nodded. "That's a typical reaction. Most dogs require one to two years of training to gain the skills needed to be effective for use in public. The length of training depends on the dog's temperament and focus, but the new handler also has to be dedicated to forging the bond." She swept her hand to indicate the dogs and handlers lined up behind her. "But, in the end, this is what you get."

Charlotte pivoted to walk in front of each of the dogs and handlers.

"There are three types of working dogs that we train at CharTay Kennel: service, assistance and therapy. We don't have a therapy dog for today's demonstration, because we wanted to focus on dogs with specific training for specific needs. Matching the dog and its person is the most important part of the process. If they don't click, the partnership could fail, which could be devastating to both the human and animal."

She stopped in front of the young boy, his dog, and a woman who had come from the crowd to stand with them. I assumed it was the boy's mother.

"Each of our handlers will give a brief demo, and we'll start here with Erik, his mother, and Erik's service dog, Scout."

Kyle bent his head toward me and said, "She's one of the local veterinarians. Moved here from New York City about a year ago."

Erik's mother took the microphone and shared Erik's story.

"My son, Erik, has autism," she began. "I can't even begin to tell you how having a service dog has changed the dynamics of our family for the better. Life isn't perfect, but we can all breathe again, thanks to this dog. Scout is our hero."

Charlotte directed Erik and Scout to step forward.

"Erik and Scout will demonstrate how Scout finds Eric if they're separated, and how she redirects and protects him if he bolts."

As if on cue, Erik dropped Scout's leash and darted across the field. In only a few long leaps, Scout was in front of him, thwarting his effort to get around and continue running.

Next Erik's mother took hold of Scout's leash and instructed Erik to hide in the large, long tube on the course. While she led Scout away, the dog kept pulling to go back to Erik, but she forced Scout to go through the crowd and far enough away so that Scout couldn't see the boy.

Charlotte was at the microphone again. "Now, if you, in the crowd, can cheer and make noise so Scout can't hear Erik's retreat, that will help us make this more authentic."

The crowd complied. While people yelled, cheered and whistled, I watched the other dogs that were still waiting patiently off to the side. None of them reacted. They remained focused on their handler and responding only to that person.

"Okay, Erik, go hide like we told you," Charlotte instructed.

He jogged across the field, zig zagging from obstacle to obstacle until he shimmied into the tube and was totally out of view.

"All right," Charlotte called to Erik's mother, "go ahead and release Scout and give the find command."

We all turned in our chairs to look behind us. Erik's mother gave the dog the command, and Scout immediately put her nose to the ground. We watched in awe as the dog wound her way around the chairs, and back to the demonstration field. It was clear that she was following the path that Erik took, because she ran up the same ramp that Erik had gone on. Her tail wagged even harder when she spotted him in the tube. She got down on her belly and crawled part way into the tube with him. Erik's giggle echoed so much that we could hear it from where we sat.

A shiver shot through me.. I leaned against Chase's arm and whispered, "That's amazing."

He nodded and smiled. "Yeah, it is."

Charlotte laughed as she spoke into the microphone. "That's one happy dog. Look at that tail go."

People in the crowd started to clap and cheer, but Charlotte held her hand up to interrupt. "Please hold your applause, and instead show your appreciation with big smiles so that we don't distract any of our handlers."

Her comment surprised me. She was concerned about the people losing focus, not the dogs. I glanced at the crowd and saw many people sharing over-sized smiles.

"Erik, could you, your mom and Scout come up here by me, please?"

Erik looked hesitant, but his mother encouraged him to take Scout's lead and join Charlotte.

"Of course," Charlotte continued, "we have to thank Erik for being such a good helper with this, too, because he had to pretend a lot."

"Erik, is there anything you'd like to tell our visitors?"

Erik beamed and wrapped his arm around Scout's neck. The dog, in turn, nestled against the boy.

"Thcout ith my good dog," Erik proclaimed.

A collective "aww" lifted from the crowd, and I was right there with them. Erik's little speech impediment was endearing, and the bond between the boy and dog was sweet.

The next few demonstrations showed how the dogs could help a paraplegic or someone with medical conditions such as diabetes or epilepsy.

Charlotte stepped back and indicated the vests on the dogs. "If a service or assistance dog is wearing a vest, never approach to pet it. If it isn't wearing a working vest, always ask the handler if it's okay to approach, because they could still be working."

A couple of more dogs and handlers gave demonstrations before it was Jamie's turn. She, the Golden Retriever she was handling, and Rashawn and Trooper, stepped forward together. They stopped on either side of Charlotte. I was curious to know the connection.

"I'd like to introduce Jamie Reston and Jem on my right." Charlotte swept her hand in their direction. Jamie commanded Jem to sit, and then she waved. At the same time, Jem lifted her paw like she was waving, as well.

Chuckles and murmurs rose from several of the spectators. Jem kept her paw lifted until Jamie commanded her to put it down.

"And on my left is Rashawn, a Marine Corps veteran who served three tours of duty in Iraq, and his partner, Trooper. Rashawn is affected by PTSD, and he also has a prosthetic leg. That requires Trooper to pull double duty, but he does it admirably."

I leaned back in my chair so that I could see Drew without him noticing me watching. As he stared at Rashawn, his jaw flexed repeatedly. His hands were tightly clasped across his waist, his thumbs constantly moving. To me, he looked nervous.

Angela covered one of his hands with hers, but didn't look at him or say anything. Silent support that revealed her understanding and connection.

"Rashawn," Charlotte said, "why don't you tell a little bit about yourself and how Trooper assists you on a daily basis."

Rashawn shifted as if he was uncomfortable, and I noticed Trooper leaned against his leg and looked up at his owner as if encouraging him. Rashawn reached a hand down and lightly rubbed the top of the dog's head. Within a few seconds, Rashawn looked more comfortable.

Even from this distance, I saw his lips puff out as he expelled a long breath.

"It isn't easy for me to stand up here and talk in front of people like this, but, here goes." He shrugged and looked down at Trooper. "This dog saved my life," he continued. "He also saved my marriage." Rashawn turned and smiled at someone in the audience. Everyone looked in the same direction. I recognized his wife smiling back at him.

"You see," he continued, "war can mess with your mind. As strong as I thought I was, I wasn't prepared for my inability to mentally disengage from everything I'd seen and experienced during my tours. Once I returned to civilian life, the war wasn't really over for me. More times than I'd like to admit, I'm angry, and frustrated, and even scared. Loud noises sound like explosives to me. Every person I see out in public, whether it's a man, woman, or child, is a potential threat. Three years ago, I never would have told you any of this, but therapy has helped." He looked down at Trooper. "My partner, here, has helped even more."

I looked again at his wife. The moisture balancing on her eyelids reflected the rays of the sun. My chest tightened. I started to look at Drew, again, but instead what caught my attention were the two tears trickling down Angela's cheeks. She brushed them away, but they were quickly replaced by two more. Even though they didn't live together, I wondered if she'd seen Drew go through the same things.

Without warning, a vague scene flickered through my mind. Me, as a little girl in Drew's house, crawling into a big bed and snuggling between my parents. My mother and Drew. A younger version of the man that I now knew. I pictured my father getting out of bed, carrying something long and thin. My mind snapped. Was my father sleeping with a gun after he came home from the war? Did he still?

Rashawn cleared his throat and looked back at the crowd. "So, that's where Trooper comes in. He's been trained to help me keep both feet solidly in reality. If I'm in a crowd and start feeling nervous, or feel an anxiety attack coming on, he senses it and forces me to vacate the premises, whether it's in a store or at a parade. Anywhere."

At that point Rashawn knelt next to Trooper and buried his hand in the black fur on the dog's neck. "Trooper saved my marriage because he makes our home safe for my wife and kids. He sleeps next to my side of the bed, and when he senses I'm starting to go into a flashback or nightmare, he nuzzles me and forces me to focus on him and the present, not the past."

What Rashawn said made me sit up straighter and had my brain whirling. Out of the corner of my eye, I saw Drew lean forward with his elbows on his knees as he steepled his fingers under his chin. I wondered if he had the same thought I did. Could a service dog make a difference for him?

After Rashawn finished sharing, there was complete silence except for the birds chirping in the nearby trees. Many people wiped tears from their faces. I stared at his dog, amazed by its power to improve Rashawn's life.

Rashawn and Trooper stepped back, and Jamie and Jem moved next to Charlotte. "I asked Jamie to bring Jem out with Rashawn and Trooper because Jem, too, is slated to be a service dog for a veteran. She's already gone through almost two years of intense training. The next step will be to match her with a veteran who would benefit. While I'm the primary trainer, Jamie is my apprentice and is learning, which is why I've asked her to talk about the training process."

Jamie spent several minutes putting Jem through her paces, telling us what the dog had to learn to get to this point. "And, Jem is nearly ready to graduate from our part of the program. I'm excited to see her go out and make a difference in someone's life."

The final handlers brought their dogs forward and demonstrated how the dogs could assist owners with physical disabilities. From opening doors to retrieving items the owners needed but couldn't get themselves, the dogs showed amazing skills. One dog was even able to pull a wheelchair.

I couldn't get my mind off Trooper. That dog had changed Rashawn's life. I wondered if Drew had ever considered getting a dog to help him the way Trooper helped Rashawn.

Although I watched the other dogs and handlers, what they were saying didn't completely register. My attention vacillated between Trooper and Jem. Because I was distracted by them, I was surprised when the demonstration was complete. Charlotte came to the microphone a final time.

"I'd like to invite everyone to enjoy refreshments over by the kennel. Also, some of the dogs will be unvested so that you can pet them. Those dogs will remain in this area." She indicated the grassy area behind her.

For the first time, the audience clapped, but not too loud. Small kids swarmed the dogs that were available for petting. I stood and stretched. The demonstration had lasted less than an hour, but the amount of information I'd gained was almost overwhelming.

I turned to Chase. "What did you think?"

"Incredible!" he said. He stood and turned toward Drew and Angela. "Good stuff, huh?"

"This was fantastic," Angela answered. "I'm so glad we came." She looked toward the dogs that were already surrounded by people. "Anyone else going to go over and see the dogs up close?"

By way of an answer, we all moved in that direction. Several others from the crowd approached the dogs and handlers ahead of us, but we eventually made our way closer to Jamie and Jem.

Rashawn and Trooper stood off to the side. Rashawn hadn't removed the vest, so we knew he preferred that Trooper not be approached. But without her vest, Jem was moving from person to person looking for attention.

"Come 'ere, Jem, and I'll rub your belly," Angela coaxed.

As if Jem understood what she said, the dog came right to her and dropped to the ground, turning her belly up. We laughed at her antics as we took turns rubbing her stomach or shaking her paw. It was clear that she knew how to turn off the working dog part of her personality when allowed.

"So," Jamie said, "Jem is an SDIT, service dog-in-training. She recently finished the first phase of training, and now, Charlotte and the trainers work with some of the local veterans groups to find a veteran in need, and hopefully place her. They aren't always placed locally, though."

"She's awesome," I said.

Jamie nodded and smiled. "Yup, she's one of Atticus' pups."

"Yeah. Kyle told me about that." I kneeled and rubbed the top of Jem's head. She twisted her neck so she could push against my hand when I started to pull away.

Suddenly Jem jumped up on full alert. When we followed her line of sight, we realized why. Behind Drew and Angela, a family had approached Rashawn, and he had removed Trooper's vest and was allowing the boys to throw a Frisbee for her to retrieve. The boys looked like they were younger than ten, so their throws didn't fly in a predictable path. Trooper ran in the direction he thought the Frisbee would go, but usually it went wild in a different direction. He adjusted and raced in an arc to retrieve it.

Jem's tail wagged. She paced, but she didn't try to go after the disc. Instead, her head swung back and forth to follow the action.

"Here," Jamie said, pulling a lime green tennis ball from the pocket of her hoodie. "It's a tease for her to see Trooper playing. If I asked her, she would refocus and ignore them, but she might as well play for a minute, too."

Jamie unclipped the leash. Jem pranced in front of her, eager for the ball to be thrown.

We were so focused on her execution of Jamie's commands that we were no longer paying attention to anyone else around us until suddenly, behind us, we heard a smack and then a grunt-like sound.

From the corner of my eye, I saw Drew whirl around, his arms thrown up in a defensive position. The Frisbee the boys had been throwing for Trooper had hit Drew in the back, and now lay in the grass at his feet.

And he looked ready to counter-attack.

CHAPTER 13

By the expression on everyone's faces, I guessed the intensity of Drew's reaction to being hit with the Frisbee startled all of us. My pulse whooshed softly in my ears as my heart rate jumped to panic speed. Rounding his shoulders, Drew held his hands in front of his face like a boxer ready to strike. His attention darted around the yard like he expected someone or something else to come at him.

"Drew," Chase said, taking one tentative step in Drew's direction. "It was just a Frisbee."

There was no response from Drew. He twisted, maintaining his defensive stance, but he didn't acknowledge that he heard or even saw anyone else.

No one moved, unsure of how to react or proceed.

The little boys who had been playing with the Frisbee stood twenty feet away, their eyes wide and fixed on Drew.

I heard Jamie say Jem's name and give some sort of command. Jem abandoned the ball she'd so badly wanted to retrieve and instead bounded toward Drew. When she reached him, she pressed her body against his leg. She looked up at him with soft brown eyes that seemed to say *I'm here for you*.

Drew shifted and looked at her as if trying to register what she was doing there. Then, he lowered his hands, and his shoulders dropped with the visible release of tension. Jem raised her head and pressed her muzzle into Drew's palm.

First his fingers twitched, then they moved to stroke the top of her head. She sidled even closer to him, so he leaned down. She pushed her nose under his chin, her full focus on helping Drew.

And, I breathed a silent sigh of relief when he responded. Although the whole episode only lasted a few seconds, it seemed like minutes. Is this how it would always be when we were with him? Would we always feel like we were walking on eggshells, waiting for the next trigger for Drew to lose it? Was I prepared for this kind of life?

The older of the boys who had been throwing the Frisbee jogged toward us, his eyes wide with fear, but he stopped a few feet from Drew's reach.

His eyes shifted from Drew to the Frisbee to us, then back through the same pattern again. He used his left hand to wring the thumb on his right hand as if he thought that would give him courage.

"Sorry, Mister," he said. "My little brother isn't good at throwing a Frisbee. He didn't mean to hit you."

Drew lifted his hand from petting Jem. "It's okay. Surprised me, that's all."

He grabbed the Frisbee from the grass and held it toward the boy. "Tell your brother throwing a Frisbee is all in the snap of the wrist."

The boy took a tentative step forward and smiled, obviously relieved by the kind treatment. Instead of getting too close, he leaned toward Drew and reached out as far as he could to take possession of the Frisbee.

"Thanks. See ya!" The boy pivoted and raced at a full sprint toward his family.

The knot in my stomach loosened as I exhaled slowly. My imagination had blown the situation out of proportion. The truth was, I had no idea what went through Drew's mind in those moments. His reaction wasn't his fault. He was reacting to conditioning from his war experiences. Experiences that I couldn't even fathom.

"Cute boy," Angela said from a few feet behind Drew.

Drew ruffled Jem's ears then stood. "Think I'll go over to see Rashawn."

He walked away without inviting us to join him, lifting and rolling his shoulders as if to loosen them. I looked at everyone else to see if anyone was going to follow, but like me, they watched his retreating back and didn't move.

Even Jem watched, her ears lifted and tail wagging slowly. She stared, unblinking, her tongue lolling out of her mouth.

As Drew approached, the boy holding the Frisbee shoved it behind his back and stepped closer to his mother. Rashawn reached out to shake Drew's hand, then spoke to the mother and boys. We couldn't hear the conversation, but the boys visibly relaxed and patted Rashawn's dog one more time before the three of them moved on to another dog and handler.

Chase came up next to me, and as he did, his arm brushed against mine. The touch was casual but still sent little pulses of awareness across my skin. His voice was barely above a whisper when he spoke.

"You okay?" he asked.

"Yeah, why?"

He reached up with one finger and stroked the skin between my eyebrows. "Worry creases right here." Then he winked and added, "I wouldn't suggest you become a career poker player.

"What do you mean?"

He brushed the tip of my nose as he lowered his hand. "You're as easy to read as an open book."

I looked quickly toward the others to see if anyone else was catching this interaction, but fortunately they were still watching Drew and Nate.

"Well, then what's my face saying?" I wanted to sound playful, but his nearness had every fiber of my being on alert, making my voice shaky.

He shrugged. "It's saying that you care about Drew and what's going on with him. But, it's also saying you're a little nervous about it."

My heart pounded, and I swallowed the lump in my throat. Dead on right. And that scared me, too. No one had ever been so in tune with my emotions.

"And you don't feel the same way?" I countered, not knowing what else to say.

His eyes drilled into mine. "Absolutely."

And time stood still until Angela broke into our thoughts.

"Look at how Jem is still watching Drew," she pointed out. "Or," she said, redirecting the comment to Jamie, "is Jem only interested in Rashawn's dog?"

"No," Jamie said, "I think you were probably right the first time. The way she responded to Drew when he was startled by the Frisbee makes me think that she's put a bead on him. That's good, though. If she's going to be an effective service dog, she has to have that instinct.

Jamie knelt and stroked the back of Jem's head. "Good girl, Jem. Good girl."

The dog's eyes sparkled as she met Jamie's gaze. The respect and adoration between the two warmed me. I took out my phone and took a picture of them.

"How can you give her up after investing that much time in her?" I asked as I slid my phone back in my pocket. "It's obvious that you love her and the feeling is mutual."

Jamie shrugged as she stroked Jem's golden fur. "I know how important her work will be. All of us" — she looked in the direction where Charlotte was talking to a couple — "accept that our purpose is to prepare the dogs for someone else. I feel really good about that." She pressed her cheek to the side of Jem's face. "She has the potential to save a life - physically and emotionally."

I noticed we all stared at Jem as if she were a piece of precious gold — a different kind of gem.

Looking in Drew's direction, I stepped past Jamie and Jem. Another couple had joined Drew, Rashawn, and Rashawn's wife. The three men seemed to be engaged in conversation while the two women stood off to their sides.

"I wonder if Drew knows that guy he and Rashawn are talking with," I said to Chase. Drew's social life was such a mystery in so many ways, that I didn't want to miss the opportunity to meet someone else who might be a part of it.

Chase looked in that direction, then shook his head. "I don't recognize him."

I took a couple steps in that direction. "Think it would be okay if we went over?"

Angela must have heard our conversation, because she turned toward Jamie and said, "Thanks so much for sharing Jem with us. I'm impressed with everyone who was part of the demo."

"I'm glad you came," Jamie said. "It's fun to show people what I do for my job." She put the leash back on Jem, and the dog immediately alerted to Jamie's voice.

"Wow!" I said. "She's so tuned into you. It's amazing what you've trained these dogs to do. All those times you've talked about it at the barn, I never really knew what it was about."

Jamie shrugged. "Thanks. I still have a lot to learn, but Charlotte is a pro."

Jamie reached down and picked up the ball that Jem had left in the grass. "Kyle, would you mind grabbing Jem's vest, please?"

"Sure." He scooped up the vest that had been left several feet away on the ground and handed it to her.

Before Jamie put the vest back on, we took turns giving Jem a pat before heading toward Drew, Rashawn and the other couple.

Chase turned to Kyle. "See you later, man."

As we moved past Jamie and Kyle, I was surprised when Chase laid his hand against my back and guided me next to Angela. Although it wasn't as intimate as holding my hand, it still felt like he was making a statement. I liked it, although I did feel self-conscious when we got within a few feet of Drew and Rashawn.

"Are we interrupting?" Angela asked as we approached.

Drew, whose back had been to us, turned and shook his head. "Nope." He held out his hand toward Angela, and she stepped up next to him and turned toward the man I didn't know.

"This is Angela. She tries to keep me on the straight and narrow," he joked.

The other man stepped forward to shake her hand. "Your wife?"

"Uh, no," Drew stammered. "We're not married. She's just a good friend."

There was a moment of awkwardness as the man winced and said, "Oh, I apologize." He smiled, but the red streaking up his neck gave away his embarrassment. The man stepped back and held his hand out toward the woman with him. "I'm Larry Richards. This is my wife, Claudia."

Claudia extended her hand. "It's nice to meet you."

"And you," Angela responded with a smile. She turned her attention to Larry. "And, don't worry. You're not the first to make that mistake." She glanced at Drew, who lifted his eyebrows as if apologizing with his eyes.

Drew laid his hand on Chase's shoulder. "And this is Angela's son, Chase."

The man and woman extended their hands to shake. "Chase. I think I remember seeing you with Drew at the Robbins Nest diner."

Chase nodded and laughed. "Probably. We do go there quite a bit."

Claudia turned to me and asked, "And you are?"

Every cell in my body froze. Out of the corner of my eye, I saw Drew angle his body toward me and pull his shoulders back. I wasn't sure what that body language meant, but if it was a challenge, I was accepting. My heart tripped over the next beat before it sped up like a runaway train.

"I'm Savannah," I said, locking my gaze on Drew's. "His daughter."

What I interpreted as surprise flickered in Drew eyes, but he didn't flinch.

I pulled my attention from him and turned it back to Claudia, barely aware of her grip when she shook my hand. My entire body hummed with the mixture of emotions ricocheting through me.

Larry snapped his head toward me. "Wonders never cease." He mock punched Drew in the shoulder, and added, "You must be proud of this young lady. Best kept secret?"

Drew sucked in his upper lip and worked it between his teeth for a couple of seconds while he shot a look in my direction. He hardly knew me. How could he possibly answer?

He cleared his throat, but his voice still came out raspy. "I think she's a lot like her mother, and that's a good thing."

It was my turn to be surprised. In a million years, I wouldn't have expected him to compare me to her, but it made my heart swell. He'd made it clear at his house how much he had loved her.

My breath wheezed out of my tight throat, and I blinked against the sting in my eyes. Until this moment, I hadn't realized that I actually did miss my biological mother, but more of a surprise, that I was pleased by my father's approval.

"You're a lucky man," Larry said, nodding. "And, I'm sorry to do this, but we have to pick up our kids at their grandmother's house. I hope our paths cross again sometime." The comment was directed at all of us as he gave us a sweeping look.

When Larry and Claudia walked away, our little group began to separate like magnets that repel each other.

"Wait!" I said as I pulled my cell phone from my pocket. "Can we take a picture of all of us with Trooper and with —" I hesitated, then added — "my father?"

I tried to make it sound like the term was rolling off my tongue, but in truth, uttering it was the same kind of feeling as trying to get peanut butter unstuck from the roof of my mouth. It came out, but it was work. No one else seemed to notice.

"Picture for what?" Drew asked.

"To give to Alex since he couldn't be here. I know it would mean a lot to him." The purpose sounded reasonable, but in reality, I had the urge to capture this moment in time. Almost as if having my father acknowledging me was a rebirth.

Rashawn glanced at Drew. "It's okay with me if it's okay with you."

Drew gave a slight shrug and took a step closer to Rashawn. I stepped in front of them and snapped a couple of pictures. Then, on impulse, or because of the high I felt from this unexpected acceptance as Drew's daughter, I pushed my brazenness one step further.

"Okay, now let's do a selfie with all of us." My voice was higher than usual because this felt like a cutesy move that wasn't typical of me, but deep inside I sensed a leap forward in my relationship with our father. I grabbed Chase's hand to pull him into the picture, too.

"Angela and Vickie, you, too. Make sure we can see Trooper," I said, pointing to Rashawn's service dog.

We sandwiched together into an awkward pose, arms over shoulders and backs to keep us in place. I stretched my arm out in front of us.

"Ready. 1-2-3," I counted before hitting the button twice. "Got it."

I glanced at the screen to make sure I'd captured the moment. Today, it looked awkward. I hoped there would come a time when pictures of us together would give the impression of a family that was comfortable with each other.

"Looks great!" I proclaimed, turning the screen so that everyone could look. "Alex will be sorry he missed being here."

Rashawn turned once more to all of us. "We better get going. Enjoy the afternoon." His wife started to follow, but then he pivoted toward Drew.

"Hey, man, thanks for comin'."

I waited for Drew to answer, but instead, he offered an almost imperceptible nod. The direct eye-to-eye contact between them said it all. Ultimate respect.

With a slight tug of the leash, he encouraged Trooper to heel. His wife smiled at us, then took hold of his free hand.

I clicked on the photo of all of us to send to Alex.

Angela pointed toward my phone. "I'd love of a copy of that picture. Can you send it to me?"

I lifted my phone and prepared to send. "Sure. What's your number?"

She recited it, but before I could press send, Drew stepped to where he could peer over my shoulder. "I'd like it, too."

"Really?" I asked, whirling toward him. I realized then that the term warm and fuzzy really did connect to a physical reaction, because my whole body felt it.

His lips lifted into a smirk. "Yeah, really."

I added Drew's contact to the list and pressed send.

"Okay. It's all yours."

Within seconds, Alex responded with a text that only I could see. *thats huge*

Chase wrapped his arm around my shoulder and squeezed. "So, I heard there are snacks over there. You with me?"

"Sure."

Chase guided me toward the refreshments table while Drew and Angela followed. Drew sounded surprisingly light-hearted considering the episode with the Frisbee.

At the refreshment table, we each grabbed a cookie and lemonade. We'd just finished them when Kyle returned.

"Jamie's going to be busy at the kennel for a little while." His attention slid from me to Chase and Drew. "You guys want to see Charlotte's new Gator?"

My head snapped toward him. "She has an alligator?" Was owning an alligator even legal? And what made him think only the guys would be interested in seeing it?

The guys exchanged quick looks, but I couldn't get a read on whether or not they thought Kyle was serious. Kyle shoved his hands in his pockets and rocked back on his heels.

"Yup, she got the Gator last week."

Drew and Chase scanned the property, so I figured they were also skeptical. I didn't know Kyle well enough to gauge his sense of humor.

When I looked at Angela, she shrugged and gave me an *I haven't a clue* look.

Propping my hand on my hip, I tipped my head and narrowed my eyes. I was calling his bluff. "So where does she keep it?"

Kyle pointed somewhere beyond the kennel. "In the barn out back. Follow me. I'll show you."

Drew and Chase didn't hesitate to follow. I held back, staring at Drew's retreating back, sizing him up as a possible "Crocodile Dundee". It was a father's job to protect his kids, right? Besides, he'd acknowledged me in public. I hoped he was ready to take on that responsibility.

"You coming?" Angela asked.

I nibbled on my bottom lip. "Do you think there's really an alligator back there?"

"Only one way to find out," she said as she stepped off to follow the guys.

When we rounded the corner of the kennel, Chase was stretched up on his toes, leaning in a side window of the barn. He pulled back out to let Drew look in, his exclamations of "cool" and "I'd love one of those" carrying on the light breeze.

"Hey, we're going in," Kyle said, leading Chase toward the big wooden sliding door. He pointed back toward Drew. "He'll help you look in the window first so you can decide if you want to risk going in."

From this distance, I couldn't clearly see Kyle's expression, but I swore a smirk hovered on his lips.

Part of me wanted to go in the barn with them, but I decided to heed Kyle's suggestion and check it out from the window before venturing in.

"I'll go to the window," I said. Giddiness worked its way through my body. The demonstration was cool, but this was an unexpected bit of excitement. In fact, this whole scenario was crazy.

"What do you think?" Angela asked Drew as we approached.

"It's definitely green." He stepped away from the window, which was easy for him to see in because he was over six feet tall, but it was higher up than a house window. He knelt and patted the leg that was up. "Here, use my leg as a step so you can see in, if you'd like."

I was taken aback by this sudden ease that I'd never experienced with him before. Had he had an epiphany somewhere between answering Larry's question about me and walking to the barn? It was as if someone had snapped his fingers and suddenly he was comfortable with me. For the moment, it was beyond my comprehension, but I made the split-second decision to not try to over-analyze. This is what I'd wanted. I'd accept this, even if for some reason it was a momentary fluke.

Angela turned to me. "You want to look first? I'll stand behind you and be your spotter."

"Okay," I said, excited to see Charlotte's newest acquisition. I stepped over to Drew and looked from his leg to the window, wondering how I could get up there the least awkwardly.

He must have sensed my discomfort. "Grab hold of the window sill, and then step onto my leg," he said. "I can help keep you steady."

"Sure," I said, reaching to grab the sill. I put one foot up onto his leg then used my upper body strength to pull myself upright. There was something awkward about this proximity to him, but I forced myself to react maturely to make it seem like it was no big deal. Meanwhile, my knees felt like Jell-O.

"I can't really see," I said, shifting myself so I could look in the window. "It's kind of dark inside."

"Lean in a little," Drew said.

I looked back toward the window, and for some reason my heart started to beat faster and sweat popped out on my palms. Could an alligator crawl up a wall and stand on its hind legs? Would I be face to face with it if I leaned in too far?

I swallowed the saliva that had gathered at the back of my mouth, took a deep breath, and slowly leaned forward.

My face had barely cleared the sill when BANG! Something slammed against the side of the barn under the window.

"Ahh!" I screamed, scrambling down off Drew's leg and using all of my muscle to push myself away from the barn as fast as I could.

I turned to him, my eyes so wide with fear that nothing would get past me if it was within a 180 degree angle. "Oh my gosh! What was that?"

A shiver shot up my spine. My heart was beating so fast that I thought it was going to jump from my chest. I looked up toward the window when I heard the guys burst into laughter inside the barn. Drew started to chuckle and shake his head as he glanced away and rubbed his forehead as if trying not to laugh out loud.

I whipped toward Angela to see if she was in on some kind of joke, too, but her raised eyebrows told me that she was perplexed, as well.

"Ooh, Chase! You are so getting it!" I yelled, pivoting to sprint around to the front of the barn. When I got there, the doors were wide open. I skidded to a halt before rounding the corner to go in. Instead of bursting through the door, I peered around the side.

And knew I'd been had.

Kyle and Chase stood next to a grass-green John Deere garden vehicle that had a little dump bed in the back.

"So," Chase said with a huge smirk on his face, "this is a Gator. Isn't it cool?"

I threw my hands on top of my head and started to laugh. "Jerks!" I sputtered as I went toward them. "You'll pay for this."

Drew and Angela came into the barn behind me.

"Don't feel bad, Savannah," Angela said, coming up next to me. "I had no idea what a Gator was, either."

I sucked in a deep breath so I could slow my laughter. "Rest assured, I'll get him back," I promised.

Drew came up next to me. "I can give you the opportunity, if you want."

I turned toward him, happy to have an ally. "Oh, yeah. How?"

"The fire department is having a muster next weekend. It's a picnic and fun competitions using fire equipment." He lowered his voice like we were co-conspirators. "There will be plenty of water and high pressure hoses — and opportunity, if you know what I mean."

"Yeah?" I said, wondering if he was getting at what I thought he was.

Suddenly his expression was serious. "I'd like you and Alex to come if you're interested."

It was almost unnoticeable, but I saw Angela grab hold of his hand and squeeze his fingers. She didn't look at him, but she didn't need to. Even I could read her gesture.

Was there hope for some kind of family relationship after all?

CHAPTER 14

"This looks like a blast!" Alex exclaimed as I drove along the rutted path in the field that led to the parking area. Beyond that, the firefighters had lined up all of the firetrucks like giant matchbox cars. Most were the typical red, but two were bright yellow.

Alex continued to gawk out the window. "If they have all of their firetrucks here, I wonder what happens if there's a fire in their town?"

"I'm sure they don't have all of them here," I said, braking for a family of five that wanted to cross in front of us. I waved them past, then continued on the bumpy path.

I tried to focus on safely parking, but it was too easy to be distracted by all of the activity. Except for the time when I was nine, when the Catholic church in our town burned down, I'd never seen so many firetrucks or firefighters in one place. The sight left me awestruck, too, but there was no way I was admitting that. I maneuvered the van into the next space in a line of cars parked in the field.

I'd barely put the van in park before Alex threw the door open. "Grab the duffel bag with the extra clothes from the back seat," I directed before he slammed the door. Chase had warned us that we'd probably end up wet and dirty. We were prepared.

Alex whipped open the back sliding door and reached in to snatch the bag. "I think maybe I'll become a firefighter," he said. He hooked the duffel bag over his shoulder.

"Really?" I frowned. "Since when?"

"I think it's in my DNA," he responded in total seriousness.

"Yeah, probably," I scoffed. Then I remembered the scene at Seneca Farms when I'd ordered exactly the same thing that Chase and Angela said Drew always ordered. Maybe my negativity was a little hasty.

Chase must have seen us drive in, because he weaved his way through the parked cars so he could meet us part way across the field. When I saw his worn t-shirt, shorts and old sneakers, I glanced from my clothes to Alex's. Yup. Based on what Chase wore, we'd dressed appropriately for the day.

"Good timing," he said as he approached. "Competitions are just getting started."

He put his arm around my shoulders so that I was tucked comfortably under his arm. "I'm glad you're here," he said against my ear before he kissed my hair above it.

I couldn't pinpoint when we'd gone from being tentative friends to more, but somewhere in the last couple of weeks we'd eased into a relationship. It wasn't exactly a full-blown romance, but signs pointed in that direction. We hadn't taken the step to make it official.

"The first one is Battle of the Barrel," he said.

"What's the Battle of the Barrel?" I asked.

Chase led us around firetrucks and through groups of people as he answered. "There's a barrel suspended on a cable and two teams with fire hoses. The object is to use the water to force the barrel across the other team's line."

As soon as he'd finished describing it, we came to an area where people were gathered in a wide circle watching two teams already battling it out. The enthusiastic cheers vibrated through me, making me smile. I'd been here less than five minutes and the electricity of fun in the air had zapped me and made me want to join in.

Because he was taller than most kids his age, Alex was able to stretch up on his toes to see over the heads of the spectators who were lined up behind yellow caution tape.

I poked my head up and around shoulders and other heads to see which firetrucks were poised at either end of the poles."Who's competing right now? Is that Keuka Shores on that end?"

"Yeah," Chase said.

"Where's our dad?" Alex asked.

A zing of surprise shot through me. Alex's ease with referring to Drew as our *dad* threw me every time. It still felt too surreal to me.

Chase tipped his head to our right. "He's over there getting things ready for the next event. He's not doing this competition. He wanted to wait for the ones he could do with you."

Alex smiled and nodded. I knew him well enough to know that he was again probably reading more into this than was warranted. Even though we didn't know him well, Drew had demonstrated his tendency to think of others' needs or wants before his own. We didn't know him well enough, yet, to know if this special treatment was because we were his kids.

"What do you get if you win?" Alex asked.

Chase pointed toward the small garage beyond the competition. "Points. And they're tallied on that big white board against that wall. The department with the most points at the end wins the trophy. Also, all of the money that was collected for entry fees gets donated to the charity of the winner's choice. So, not only do they get to display the trophy at their firehouse until the muster next year, they also get the satisfaction of knowing they've helped someone else."

"Do you know who their charity of choice is?" I asked.

Chase nodded. "Purple Heart Homes. A lot of the firefighters go on work sites with Drew."

"Cool!" Alex said, turning to Chase. "When was the last time Keuka Shores won?"

"Last year, so they're the defending champions and hoping to take it home again."

"Bring 'em on!" Alex growled. There was no doubt his competitive nature was already making him imagine what his contribution to the winning effort might be.

We returned our attention to watching as the barrel slid back and forth along the cable until somehow the team opposite Keuka Shores managed to get control and forced it against the far pole. Part of the crowd and the winning team erupted in cheers while the Keuka Shores supporters good-naturedly groaned. Despite how fierce the competition seemed, what I noticed was that everyone was smiling. It felt like a big family reunion.

Chase grabbed my hand and led me away from the crowd. "Let's let Drew know you're here."

Far off to the side, smoke rose from a long, rectangular steel grill, spreading the pungent aroma of barbecuing chicken and adding to the festive atmosphere. My mouth watered even though I wasn't hungry.

Alex charged ahead of us, and, as we approached, Drew met us with a big smile. There was a sparkle in his eyes that I'd never seen before.

Alex stopped next to him. "Hey! No crutches!"

Extending his arms, Drew replied, "Nope. Done with those."

"Thanks for inviting us. This is so cool."

Drew looked from Alex to me. "I'm glad you came. Are you ready for some crazy fun?"

"Sure," I responded.

"You remembered your other clothes?"

Alex patted the duffel bag.

"Good, because with all of these fire hoses around, you're guaranteed to get wet at some point," he said. "Follow me."

A voice boomed from the speaker of one of the trucks. "Potter, Rushville, Stanley and Gorham, you're first up for the Midnight Alarm."

With that announcement, a dozen or so firefighters took their fire coats and helmets and tossed them into a big pile. Then they took their fire boots connected to pants and lined them up at the starting line thirty feet away.

"What's happening here?" I asked.

Drew pointed to the pile of coats. "Each firefighter puts his coat and hat in the pile. It's a relay race. The first person has to put the bunker pants on at the starting line and —"

"Bunker pants?" I interrupted.

"Yeah, the pants connected to the boots are called bunkers. Once they have those on, they run to the pile of coats and have to find the gear assigned to them, and put it on, including the gloves in the pockets. In each pocket is a tennis ball, and they have to run back and drop the ball into the bucket. When it hits the bottom, the next person in the relay puts on the gear, runs and drops all but the bunkers in the pile, grabs a tennis ball and runs back. There are three on a team. It's all timed, and in the end, points are assigned by times."

"Who's doing it for our team?" Alex asked.

Drew rubbed his chin. "That's what we have to go and decide right now. I'll let each of you pick the competitions you want to be in."

While the first set of teams were getting ready, Drew took us to the big sign on the side of one of the firetrucks that listed the games and who had already signed up for which ones.

Drew explained the object of each. Kitten Rescue had a stuffed kitten in a tree, and the competitors used ladders or whatever was necessary to get it down. There was a separate ladder climbing race, and another competition, Victim Rescue, where someone had to be rescued and carried across the line in what he called a Stokes basket. The one that caught Alex's attention was Drown the Inferno. That game required teams to carry buckets of water from the pond to build up the water that filled a tube that eventually pushed a ping pong ball out of the top. I was interested in that one as well as Kitten Rescue, and Chase and I decided we'd make a good team for Victim Rescue. I had to admit, the required physical closeness was the most appealing aspect.

While we were signing up for our events, Jamie joined us, this time flanked by Atticus and Jem, who wore her vest that said Service Dog in Training.

"Hey, there," she said, stopping the dogs short of us. "Kyle said you'd be here. That's so awesome. Ever been to a muster?"

"No," Alex and I answered in unison.

"It's a ton of fun." Atticus nudged her hand and she reached down to rub the top of his head while she continued. "I've been coming since I was little. My mom and sister are somewhere around here. And now Kyle is a junior member, so we come as a family, too."

Family. The word buzzed through my head. She said they come as a family, *too*. Were others already categorizing us as a family? I was uncomfortable with the perception and the encouragement it would give Alex. I wanted him to be happy — but I wanted it to be long-term. At this point, we had no way to predict the longevity or depth of any relationship with our father.

When he'd stalked off at the work site, he'd made it pretty clear that he preferred dealing with life on his own.

Drew cleared his throat, and I turned my attention to him. Was he having the same thoughts?

He took a couple of steps back. "Better get going if we're going to do the Midnight Alarm. See you later, Jamie."

"Sounds good," I said to her, as I turned to go with the guys.

During the events, if the other people wondered what Alex's and my connection was to Drew, they didn't ask, and, in fact, didn't even seem interested, which made it easier for me to relax and get into the spirit of the competitions. We scored good times on some, and not such good times on others.

Drown the Inferno was the last competition of the day, and all of us, including Angela, were able to participate because the water bucket relay could include as many team members as each department wanted.

Chase, Alex and I picked the end spots closest to the pond because that required getting into the water to fill the bucket. We'd gotten so warm in the previous competition, we were okay with getting wet. Drew and Angela were next in line, but firmly on the ground and out of the water.

There were three departments whose points from previous competitions brought them close enough to each other that this competition would definitely determine the overall winner for the day. Keuka Shores was one of them.

The spectators gathering around the perimeter reminded me of our middle school tug-of-war competitions between the classes, and it seemed like we were all as giddy as middle school kids, too.

The Keuka Shores fire chief cut through the laughing and loud talking with a piercing whistle. "K.S.F.D., let's huddle over here."

Anyone connected to the department moved into a tight circle. Chase was on one side of me, and Drew moved in on the other, with Alex on the other side of him. The chief stretched his arms to put them around the people on either side of him, and that started the wave of movement with arms going around each other. It was easy to put my arm around Chase, but when it came to my father, anticipating the physical contact froze me. Lifting my arm required every ounce of energy that I could put into it.

Drew turned toward me, his eyes locking on mine. I couldn't tell if it was an invitation or a challenge. Then I saw his shoulder lift, and his arm came around to cross Chase's arm along my back. I took a deep breath and forced my arm to move, and slowly it slid around Drew's waist. I couldn't concentrate on what the chief was saying. Instead, my mind bounced to my early childhood and wondering exactly when the last time was that my father had put his arm around me or held me? Based on the pictures in the photo album, I knew we'd once had a typical father-daughter relationship. Lost in my musings, I was a bit behind when we ended the huddle with a big cheer.

"Okay, everyone back into position," the chief called.

The chief of Keuka Shores waved an orange construction flag to signal the start, and everyone immediately erupted into cheers of encouragement.

I had five buckets at my end to start with. I filled them with water, then sent the sloshing pail along the bucket brigade toward its destination. Our team chose to have four separate runners who brought the empty buckets back to me. It didn't take long for the adrenaline to kick in, and between the laughing and racing, I was on a natural high.

Interspersed with the cheers were screams and squeals from some of the kids who were getting hit by the cold pond water splashing over the sides of the buckets. One woman on the team next to us, who looked to be in her forties or fifties, danced around in a circle when someone next to her purposely dumped half a bucket of water over her head. I was already out of breath from running back and forth with the buckets, so laughing at her forced me to stop and bend over until I could catch my breath.

"Hey, no time to stop!" Alex yelled. "Get me another bucket of water."

Snatching a bucket from his hand, I managed to straighten enough to race toward the water's edge.

We were less than a couple of minutes into the scurrying and sloshing when one excited kid threw a green bucket toward me from halfway down the line in an attempt to get it to me faster. It sailed over my head and into the high reeds several feet away.

Because the buckets were color coded and had to be used in the same order through the relay, I had no choice but to retrieve it before we could continue.

I dashed toward the tall cattails, laughing so hard my sides hurt. Near the edge of the pond, I lost my footing and fell head first into the reeds. As I scrambled to get to my feet, I lunged toward the bucket that bobbed just beyond my reach in the shallow water.

When I stretched, a large bee swooped toward my arm. I swung at it and knocked it away, but as I did, it was like the bee had multiplied in seconds. Dozens, if not hundreds, of bees surrounded me, landing on my exposed skin faster than I could swing.

"Bees!" I screamed, struggling to get myself out of the reedy area and murky water. While my feet were being sucked down into the mud, I slapped against the assault. The stings on my back and both arms felt like needles.

Panic surged through my body as I struggled to get away. I whirled and pulled against the suction of the mud, oblivious to the world around me.

"Help me!"

Then suddenly something slammed into me, forcing me back into deeper water. My calf muscles strained before my feet flew free of the mud. I flipped my head around to see that it was Drew dragging me toward the middle of the pond.

"Go under the water," he ordered, pushing on my shoulders.

"Watch ou—" My warning was cut off as I gasped for a full breath of air before being submerged. The last thing I saw before I closed my eyes and went under was a black mass of bees whirling around Drew's body.

Under the surface, I spit out a mouthful of water and instantly felt the burn from the lack of air in my lungs. The constriction of the muscles in my chest added to my panic. I pushed against Drew to force myself to the surface for another breath of air. I had barely sucked it in when he pushed me down again.

I flailed against him, fearing I'd never surface again under his strong arms. He was still pulling me deeper into the water, and I needed to take another breath.

"Stay under," I heard his muffled yell from above.

Then, I felt the water next to me splash, and I knew he had come under the water, too. All I wanted was air. One breath, but I was afraid to resurface. The cold water eased the pain of the stings.

I concentrated on holding my breath and moving farther from shore.

Away from the bees.

I stretched my toes toward the bottom of the pond and felt something solid under me. A moment of relief swept through me. I could still touch bottom. The surface, and fresh air, couldn't be too far away.

Using my free hand, I pulled up against the water to assist Drew in keeping me submerged. It was a struggle because my body naturally wanted to go up. I concentrated, wanting to open my eyes to see if the sun's rays were still visible through the water. But I sensed our frantic splashing had stirred up mud, so I squeezed my eyes even tighter.

To my surprise, Drew's arms dropped away from me, and I started to ascend. I reached for him, wanting his strength to be there to protect me, and to let me know when it was safe. But when I grabbed hold of his arm, it was unusually rigid, then gone.

Still under water, I swept both hands out toward him. My fingertips brushed across his shirt, but it felt like he was floating away from me. I thrashed around to try to get to him. My lungs burned. I needed air. I needed to know if it was safe to surface.

Why did he suddenly abandon me?

Time was up. I swore my lungs were clawing their way up my throat in search of air. Water flew everywhere as I exploded to the surface at an angle.

I didn't see or hear bees, so I swam only a couple of yards before I had to let my legs drop for rest. My feet touched the bottom, but the water was as high as my neck. I whipped around, my wet hair flinging slapping my face and getting into my eyes. I swiped at it, fighting against the hold the water had on me, looking for my father, watching for the bees that thankfully did not come back out over the pond.

I heard Drew before I saw him. Short choking breaths between tight coughs. Almost gagging. Using my arms like paddles, I turned myself around toward him.

His eyes were wide with panic. He slapped at the water, trying to stay upright. His mouth was contorted as he gasped for air. The pink had left his lips. I saw at least four puffy red welts on his neck and the side of his face.

"Ca-can't —" His words wouldn't come out. His head rolled like he was losing control of the muscles in his neck.

"Drew!" I screamed, pushing myself to go the few feet to him. "Drew, what's wrong?"

He looked at me, but his eyes glazed over, like he wasn't seeing me. His head dropped back and splashed against the surface.

"What's happening?" I screamed. But, he didn't respond.

As his head dropped back even farther, the top part of his chest lifted above the surface. His soaked t-shirt clung to his chest, but I grabbed a handful of it to keep him from falling backwards into the water.

"Get up!" I yelled yanking on the shirt. But it only made his body roll more toward the water. "What are you doing? Stand up!"

He glided toward me until his shoulder pressed against mine. That's when I saw his eyes were rolled back.

Adrenaline surged through me, and I angled my arm under his back to keep him above the water.

"Help!" I yelled toward shore. His weight took my breath away. "Suh-someone help h-him. Suh-something's wrong!"

His shoulders heaved high as he tried to draw in a raspy breath. His head rolled one more time before he went limp and started to slip under water.

"No!" I yelled. I sidestepped through the water to get behind him the best I could and wrapped my arms around his chest to keep him from going completely under water. "No! No! W-wake up!"

From behind me, I heard others yelling to hold on. I struggled to keep his head out of the water, but his weight forced me to bend backwards until I worried that either I would lose my footing or my back would snap.

Loud splashes told me that someone else, or maybe multiple people, had entered the water opposite of where Drew and I had gone in.

"Hang on!" a deep voice called.

I put my face against the side of Drew's so the back of his head rested on my shoulder in an attempt to stabilize both of us. My heart pounded with the combination of exertion and fear. I pressed my ear against his skin, hoping and praying that I would feel or hear him breathe. But what I heard could barely even be categorized as a wheeze. He was getting almost no air. My cheeks felt hot against his cold skin.

There was some kind of movement on the other side of Drew. I lifted my chin so I could see over his chest and was surprised when Jem's head bobbed along the water's surface, the tips of her ears trailing in the water. She paddled directly toward us. When she reached Drew, she dipped her head under water, then used her nose to push his hand up. But it slipped from her muzzle and dropped under water. She repeated the action, obviously trying to get him to respond.

"Breathe!" I yelled as I tightened my arms around Drew's chest. "D-damn you! You can't die. B-breathe." My voice was shrill. I tried shaking him, like that would make a difference, but it only made it harder to keep my footing on the slippery bottom.

Then there was a flurry of activity. Someone grabbed my arms and yanked them away from Drew at the same time a burly man moved in and shoved his arms where mine had been.

"Got him!" the man said. "Let's get outta here."

The person holding me let go and moved toward Drew while someone moved in to take his place to hold me.

Jem paddled in a circle, trying to get close to Drew again, but the man was positioned between them.

"I've got ya, Savannah."

Chase. I almost melted into his chest as he dragged me backwards through the murky water. My arms and legs were like lead. I had no strength left. I turned my head to see the other man dragging Drew the same way. Jem paddled off to the side, her head swinging between watching what was happening to Drew and Jamie who was calling her from shore. When we were close to land, I scrambled to get a foothold, cringing as I swiveled, searching the air.

"The bees," I gasped.

Chase wrapped his arm around me and helped me onto dry land. "They're in the weeds way over on the other side. That's what took us so long to get to you."

"Dr-Drew?" I couldn't even utter half a syllable without needing a breath of air.

Chase guided me to the right as two other men pulled Drew up onto the grass.

Just like the bees, several people swarmed around him until I couldn't see what was happening. I turned to look for Jem. She had exited the water, stopped to shake the excess water from her fur, and then immediately responded to Jamie's command to return to her.

From that distance, the dog's attention was still trained on Drew, her head lifted, every inch of her alert. She was looking as worried as I felt.

My stomach rolled, and I grabbed my abdomen to keep the contents from coming up, struggling against a realization that made me want to vomit. If Drew couldn't be saved, Alex and I would truly be orphans now.

"Hang on, Savannah," Chase said. "You're okay." He held one of my arms while he rested the other hand under the dripping hair at my neck. Goosebumps peppered my arms when the cool breeze swept across my wet skin.

I lifted my head to look toward the group of people surrounding my father. They moved fast, but my mind slogged down to slow motion. Holding my stomach, I puffed out my cheeks, trying to catch my breath, hoping I hadn't swallowed so much water that I would throw up.

"Get a medical bag over here, *now!*" the burly man called when he looked up from Drew.

"Is he —" gasp — "he go- going t-to be o-okay?" I bent at the waist to try to catch my breath.

Chase leaned over with me. His fingers shook as he pulled the wet hair off my face. "You kept him above water."

"But, wh-what ha-happened?" I wondered if I would ever be able to take a full breath again. "I th-think he's dead."

"He's allergic to bees."

"What? Then he shou-shouldn't have co-come in the wa-water."

Pressing his cheek to my temple, Chase murmured, "He'd never let anything happen to you."

Tears stung my eyes, but I didn't have the strength to brush them away. Every inch of my body trembled. Chase guided me to sit, all the while keeping his arm wrapped around me. I pulled my knees up, laid my arms across them and rested my forehead on my wrists. My tears mingled with the pond moisture clinging to my cheeks. Fatigue overwhelmed me. My mind blanked.

A gentle hand settled on my shoulder above where Chase held me. "You've been stung. Have you ever had an allergic reaction to bees?"

I didn't recognize the female voice, but it was calm and comforting. Rolling my head so I could look at her kneeling to the side of me, I shook my head. My mind was so overwhelmed with what had happened to Drew that I hadn't noticed the burn of the nasty, red and white welts popping up on my arm.

My head came up, and I stared at them. Ugly, mean-looking marks. I lost count at five.

"No, I d-don't think so." I had to stop to pull in another full breath before continuing. "I've been st-stung before. Just swelling."

"Any difficulty breathing?" she asked as she took hold of my wrist and pulled my arm out straighter.

"K-kind of. But, I th-think it's from stru-struggling to h-hold up Drew."

She tipped her head to scan my other arm. "Any tightness in your throat?"

Again, I shook my head.

She put her fingers below my jaw on both sides and lightly pressed. "We'll give you an antihistamine as a precaution. Do you feel stings anywhere else?"

I lifted my arms to look. I saw two spots on my left arm, but it appeared most stings were on the right one. "I feel something on my back, but I don't know if they're stings."

"Mind if I take a look?"

I shrugged. "That's fine." While she lifted the back of my shirt, I looked again at the group surrounding Drew, and my heart raced.

Two people were on their knees working on him. One of the female firefighters tipped his head back and was putting some kind of clear tube in his mouth. Someone else was rummaging through the big, red medical bag.

"Call in the helicopter," I heard someone say. "We need to get him to Rochester."

I whipped my head toward Chase. "The medical helicopter? No! That's bad." I swung my attention back to the woman helping me. "Why the helicopter? What's going on?"

The woman smoothed the back of my shirt down, put her hand on my shoulder, and looked directly into my eyes. "He's having a severe reaction to the bee stings. A helicopter's faster. Think of it as an air ambulance ride."

My heart hammered against my chest as I struggled to get to my feet. I had to get to him. To see him. To see what was happening.

Chase wrapped his arms around me to keep me from rushing toward my father.

I shook my head, looking back in Drew's direction. My throat tightened with fear. It took every ounce of energy I had to squeak out words past the emotion clogging my throat

"No! No, this can't be happening," I moaned as I sank against Chase's chest. "We just found him. He can't die!"

CHAPTER 15

The beating of the medical helicopter blades against the warm air reverberated off the surrounding hills above Keuka Lake. I clapped my hands over my ears and leaned into Chase as we watched it lift into the air, then swing toward the northwest. As it faded from view, I wondered if I would ever see my father alive again.

"I'm going to meet them at the hospital," Angela said. I turned in time to see her wipe moisture from under her eyes. She looked at Chase. "Are you going with me?"

"Yeah," he answered, his voice choked.

Alex pivoted toward me. "I want to go, too."

Fatigue overwhelmed me. "I can't drive to Rochester."

When he opened his mouth to argue, I flipped my hand up to stop him. I knew Alex's tactics, and I knew what would come next. No way would I let him guilt me into breaking the rules.

"I don't care if this is an emergency. Mom and Dad would take away my driving privileges for driving the van to the city without permission."

"Then call them and ask them," Alex urged. "This is an emergency."

"We have to go," Angela interjected. "I'm heading for the car." She turned away from us, but Chase took several long strides forward and grabbed her arm, stopping her.

"Mom, we rode with Drew. Do you have the keys to his truck?"

Her stunned look gave the answer. She whipped her head around. "Someone will give us a ride." She started away again, half walking, half jogging.

"Wait!" Chase said. "Rashawn. We can call Rashawn and see if he'll take us up. "

She stopped, pulling in a big breath. Her cheeks were suddenly flushed, and then I knew she was trying not to panic. She patted air, like she was trying to calm herself and us down. "Okay. Yeah."

When she took her phone out of her pocket to dial, her hands shook so much that Chase snatched it from her and completed the call. He walked away from us while he waited for Rashawn to answer.

Less than a minute later he hurried back, giving a thumbs up.

"He's on his way. I told him we'd meet him out at the road."

We all took off running toward the parking area. People milled around, many in small groups, probably talking about how the afternoon had ended. Some people were picking up the props from earlier games. As we approached, they opened a path for us to hurry through.

My mind whirled as I ran alongside Angela and Chase. Maybe Mom and Dad would understand this one time. It was worth a call.

When we reached the road, I took out my phone. I'd sealed it in a plastic bag before we'd started the games so I wouldn't have to worry about water getting on it. I held the bag up toward the sun to see if I saw any moisture. All appeared to be good.

"If our parents say it's okay to go, can we follow you?" I asked Angela.

She looked up and down the road, then turned toward me. "Yes, of course."

I started to punch the number for home when Angela said, "Rashawn has a van. Ride with us."

My nerves tingled as the phone rang. I prayed Dad would be the one to answer. He was more likely to say yes than Mom. But neither of them picked up, and then the voicemail came on.

"They're not answering the house phone. I'll call their cells."

I glanced up to make sure Rashawn wasn't here yet, then dialed each of their cell phone numbers. Again, no answer. Sometimes when they were working in the yard they left their phones inside. I wondered if that was the case this time.

"Nothing?" Alex asked.

I shook my head. Did I dare leave a message telling them we'd gone and worry about asking forgiveness later? Alex's eyes pleaded with me. This was not an ordinary situation.

I dialed the home phone number again and waited for the voicemail and the beep.

"Hi Mom and Dad, it's Savannah and Alex. I tried calling your phones." I paused. How did I explain all that had happened in a short message? "We're both okay, but Drew got stung by bees trying to protect me, and he's allergic. They took him by helicopter to Strong Memorial Hospital. I wanted to ask permission, but since you're not answering, this is to let you know that Alex and I are going up to the hospital with Chase and Angela to make sure Drew is okay."

All of a sudden my throat clogged and tears sprang to my eyes. The scene when the EMTs were working on him replayed in my mind. I had to clear my throat before I could continue.

"He was unconscious and they had to put a tube down his throat so he could breathe. We need to know if he's okay." My breath hitched, and I turned away from everyone else so they wouldn't witness me breaking down. After another deep breath, I added, "I'll keep my phone on. We love you."

I pressed end, and at the same time, Chase's arm slipped around my shoulders.

"He's going to be okay," he whispered, his voice husky.

I turned into him and buried my wet face against his shoulder as all of my pent up fear burst from my body. Although I knew it was irrational, I couldn't fight off the guilt that clawed at me. As much as Chase wanted to reassure me, and I wanted to comfort him, we couldn't deny the reality.

Drew might die.

The forty-five minute drive to Rochester seemed to take forever, even though I could see Rashawn going over the speed limit a couple of times on the Thruway. Other than sharing with Rashawn the details of what happened, we were all silent — except for an occasional sniffle. I rubbed a finger along the seam of my jeans, thankful there had been a few minutes for me to change into my dry clothes before we left.

We all looked out our respective windows, lost in our individual thoughts and fears. No one dared to break the silence or look at anyone else. Chase sat with me in the smaller middle seat. As soon as we buckled the seatbelts, he took hold of my hand and never let it go. Occasionally, when I was lost in thought, he swirled his thumb across the top of my hand. I wasn't sure if it was to soothe me or him, but his warmth and strength helped calm the tornado of fears swirling through my mind.

When Rashawn exited Route 390 to navigate the city streets, the tension in the van was palpable. On the highway, far away, it was easy to imagine we'd get there and Drew would be okay. Now, as we got closer, the reality that we might find the opposite to be true seemed to hit everyone. Angela sat up straighter in the passenger seat. At the same time, Chase squeezed my hand. When I looked at him, he stared at me, like that would give us both strength to face whatever was ahead. Behind us, Alex shared a seat with Trooper, Rashawn's dog, and the vinyl squeaked when he fidgeted, his nerves probably on edge, too.

After a few turns, Rashawn pulled up in front of the hospital's emergency entrance, and we all spilled from the van like clowns from a clown car.

"I'll be in as soon as I park and walk Trooper," Rashawn said before Angela shut the door.

We didn't run in, but it was the fastest I'd ever walked without breaking into a run. The receptionist gave us a sympathetic look when we said who we were there for, but said she had no details and would let the emergency room staff know we were there.

Heads turned when Rashawn hobbled in with Trooper. The dog was wearing his service dog vest, but it didn't keep people from staring. Without acknowledging anyone, Rashawn ordered Trooper to "tuck", and the dog maneuvered himself under Rashawn's chair and curled into a ball.

I cradled my phone in my hands, expecting it to vibrate with a call from Mom or Dad. And, now, the muted conversations of other people in the waiting area were nerve wracking. It wasn't planned, but we took turns pacing, twiddling our thumbs, checking our phones.

Mom and Dad still hadn't called over an hour later when the doctor came out looking for us.

"Drew McAllister's family?"

All but Rashawn popped up from our chairs like we were each a jack-in-the-box.

"Right here," Angela said, taking the lead as we moved toward him.

The doctor extended his hand toward her. "Dr. Loomis. And you are?"

Angela met his hand. "Angela Warner. I'm —" She hesitated, and pink streaked across the top of her cheek. "I'm a very close friend."

"Does he have family?" Dr. Loomis asked, looking past Angela toward us standing behind her.

I stepped forward, my heart fluttering from nerves. "I'm his daughter. Savannah." He reached out to shake my sweaty hand. I only met his eyes for a second because I wanted to be sure to acknowledge Alex, too. "And this is my brother, Alex."

Alex moved next to me to shake Dr. Loomis' hand. "Is my father okay?" Alex blurted out.

"He's still being treated," Dr. Loomis said.

He was alive! I'm sure the relief that flooded through me had to have been the same for everyone.

Shifting his attention to Chase, Dr. Loomis said, "And you are?"

"Chase, sir." He held his hand out to shake at the same time that he tipped his head toward Angela. "Her son."

"How is he?" Angela pressed. "Can we see him?"

Dr. Loomis scanned the four of us as if assessing his next move. "Is there anyone else?"

Angela shook her head, and in a hushed tone answered, "No. We're all he has."

That pronouncement sounded sad, and for a few seconds, I caught myself wondering again about his parents — my grandparents — and any other family on his side. Although I'd been curious, I'd never felt comfortable asking about them. Had he shut them out the same way he had us?

"Please follow me," Dr. Loomis said as he pivoted and headed toward a wide hallway. He led us to a small room with two institutional type couches, which he indicated with a sweep of his hand. "Please, have a seat."

He sat on one of the chairs and leaned forward with his hands clasped between his knees. I couldn't read his expression. My heart fluttered as I braced myself for whatever he had to tell us. If he'd brought us to a private room, maybe it was bad.

Chase sat next to me, our thighs touching. Angela sat on the other side of him, and Alex had chosen a chair adjacent to Dr. Loomis. And all of us, except for the doctor, sat straight and stiff.

"I'm not going to sugarcoat this," Dr. Loomis began, which only increased my anxiety. My blood pounded in my ears. "Drew's lucky he was surrounded by medical personnel when this happened, otherwise, it's very likely the outcome would have been more grim."

A lump swelled in my throat, and I stretched my neck to breathe around it. This was my fault. My father was fighting for his life because he tried to protect me.

Chase must have sensed my distress because while Dr. Loomis continued talking, he put his arm around me and pulled me against his side.

"He was in anaphylactic shock when he arrived, but as I said, we have him stabilized. And he has started responding appropriately, so I'm pleased."

Angela pressed the shaking fingers of one hand to her lips. Moisture teetered on her eyelids when she turned to look at Chase. I heard him swallow, like there was something in his throat, too; then he reached over and took hold of her free hand, enclosing it with a gentle squeeze.

"Our biggest concern right now," Dr. Loomis continued, "is that even though it looks like we got him over this hump, anaphylaxis can occur as two reactions. Symptoms can return as many as seventy-two hours after the initial reaction. We can do our best to help his body fight that, but there are no guarantees." He paused and looked at each of us. "Mr. McAuliffe's on the positive side of this reaction, but it's still going to be a little while."

Directing his attention to Angela, he said, "If you'd like to go in to be with him for a few minutes, I'm okay with that."

When he stood, we all got up, too. Looking around at the rest of us, he added, "I can only take one with me right now, but I promise, if he's feeling up to it, you'll all be able to see him in a while. Maybe you can take a walk or go get a drink or bite to eat."

I could tell by the look on Angela's face that she was torn about being the "chosen" one to go in.

"I'm going to go out and see if Rashawn wants to walk Trooper," Chase announced. "You guys want to go, too?"

I tucked my hands in the back pockets of my jeans and nodded. "Yeah. I could use some fresh air. Alex?"

He shook his head. "No, thanks. I'll stay in the waiting room."

Angela gave us each a quick hug. "I'll be back out soon. He's going to be fine, I can tell."

"I'll need each of you to stop at the check in desk to get the blue stickers that authorize you to come and go from this area," Dr. Loomis said. He looked at Angela, "We'll stop and take care of you first." Dr. Loomis gave an encouraging smile. "The rest of you will be able to see him soon."

Angela followed him through a set of wide swinging silver doors, and we went back toward the waiting room.

As we approached Rashawn, he glanced up from a magazine. Trooper was still curled up under the chair.

"What's the word?" Rashawn asked, closing the magazine and setting it back on the coffee table next to his chair.

"They've stabilized him," Chase answered.

Rashawn blew out a loud breath and nodded. "Angela with 'im?"

"Yeah."

"Good. He needs her." Rashawn stretched his real leg out in front of him.

"The doctor said that it will be a while before we can see him. We thought maybe we could all go for a walk."

Without hesitation, he lifted himself out of his seat and indicated for Trooper to come out from under his chair. "Great idea. We're in."

He took hold of the solid handle on Trooper's vest, ignoring the stares of the people who had come in after us and probably didn't realize his dog was under the chair.

Alex dropped into a seat. "I'm staying."

"Fresh air would do you good, buddy," Rashawn said.

He settled back into the chair. "I'm good. I'll feel better waiting here."

Rashawn and Chase turned to me, but all I did was shrug. Only a fool would think they could change Alex's mind once he got something in it. I swatted his shoulder with the back of my hand.

"We won't be gone long. If you leave here, you text me. Got it?"

"I'm not moving unless the doctor comes back."

"Okay." I stared at him for a second, wondering what fears were careening around in his head right now. Chances were good they were mirroring mine.

The sun had dropped behind the hospital, so the cool air washed over us as soon as we exited through the sliding glass doors. The warning beeps from an ambulance backing up somewhere out of our view mixed with the sigh of car tires meeting pavement in the busy street in front of us. Chase took my hand as soon as we were out of the building. His nearness was a comfort.

We walked in silence for several minutes before I decided I needed to think about something other than the vision of my father struggling to breathe.

"How long have you had Trooper?" I asked.

Rashawn glanced down at the dog as if giving the animal a chance to answer, then said, "About two years."

"It's easy to see how he's tuned in to you."

Rashawn only nodded, so I continued. "I'll never forget what you said at the demonstration about him saving your marriage and your life. That was really powerful."

"It was the truth. This dog brought me back up from rock bottom. He reads me like no one else can and keeps a situation from escalating."

"What kind of situations?"

"Anxiety, nightmares, flashbacks. I swear he senses them coming on before I even know it's happening. If it weren't for him, walking down this street right now would have me totally on edge. He keeps me grounded. In the present. These dogs do wonders."

"If only Drew wasn't so stubborn," Chase muttered. His voice was so low I almost didn't make out the words.

I looked up at him. "Stubborn? About what?"

Rashawn hurumphed and answered before Chase had a chance. "Applying for a dog. I keep telling him that he should at least try it."

"Why doesn't he?"

"I think part of it is being scared that it won't work out."

He stopped talking when he checked for traffic at a crosswalk. When it was clear, we continued walking, and he continued his explanation.

"Depending on where you get the dog, there could be a long waiting list. And if you want to buy one, if you don't have a sponsor, you've gotta have money. And then, the dog's gotta be a good match."

"But he seems to really like dogs. Remember how Trooper helped him that day at your house? And Jem, the dog Jamie is helping train. Jem helped him calm down at the demonstration when he was startled by the Frisbee hitting him in the back. It's like she knew exactly what to do when he overreacted. They both helped him."

"We can see it," Chase interjected, "but he's too independent to count on anyone for anything. He also claims there are others who are more deserving and should get the dog before him. He has a comeback for every suggestion."

Chase's tone drew my attention. It was tinged with bitterness, and I wondered why. No one was closer to Drew than Angela and Chase. In some ways, they were like family for each other. As curious as I was, that conversation was for another day.

The sidewalk ran next to a large cemetery that sloped up away from the street. I remembered passing the entrance on a cross street on our way to the hospital and seeing the sign: Mount Hope Cemetery.

It seemed ironic to have a cemetery with the word hope in it across the street from a major trauma hospital. I shuddered, needing to think about anything but death right now. Hope. I'd cling to that word and let Rashawn continue to distract Chase and me. Quiet as Chase had been on the walk, I wasn't sure where his mind actually was.

"So, where did you get Trooper?" I asked.

"I went private. Got him through CharTay Kennels. Charlotte Taylor trained him. She charges a lot less than other places. I got lucky. I also had a sponsor who paid for him. Otherwise, it would have taken me a while to save enough money."

I was getting ready to ask how much Trooper cost when the tone for a text message on my phone interrupted my thought. Panic surged through me when I saw Alex's message.

get back here now

My head shot up as I looked down the street toward the hospital. "It's Alex. He said we have to get back now."

Chase's arm stiffened. "Why? Did he say?"

I slid my hand from Chase's grip and picked up my pace. "No. Come on."

My heart and mind both raced. Had Drew taken a turn for the worse? Was he dead? My anxiety was at an all-time high. Even though I wanted to run, I didn't want to leave Rashawn behind. He tried to walk faster, but his artificial leg created an awkward gait when he hurried. Finally I heard him slow down behind us.

"You two go ahead," Rashawn called, pausing to catch his breath. "I'll be right behind you."

Chase and I stopped and pivoted toward him.

"You sure?" Chase asked.

Puffing his cheeks in an attempt to catch his breath, Rashawn nodded and waved us on. "Yeah. Go."

For the briefest moment, Chase and I glanced at each other, then, like we'd been shot out of a cannon, we sprinted down the sidewalk. When there was a break in traffic, he grabbed my hand, and we dashed across the street, racing through the hospital entrance.

We turned toward the waiting area, scanning the room for Alex. He wasn't where he'd been sitting when we left. Fear ripped through me. How could things turn so bad so fast?

"There he is," Chase said, pointing toward the far corner.

A woman stood between him and me, so at first I didn't see him. Then, she stepped to the side and turned around.

And my jaw dropped. With the air stinging my lungs, I managed to wheeze out one word.

"Mom."

CHAPTER 16

"Mom, what are you doing here?" I approached her and Alex like the floor between us was sheer ice.

A sympathetic smile lifted the corners of her mouth. "I got your message. I wanted to be here for you and Alex." She met me halfway and pulled me into a tight hug. "I truly hope he'll be okay," she whispered.

I hugged her back, grateful, but shocked, by her support. "I'm glad you're here."

When we moved apart, I turned toward Chase. "Mom, do you remember my friend, Chase Warner?"

For a second I'd considered referring to Chase as my boyfriend, but that seemed crazy. We really hadn't taken that step. Now, I hoped saying he was my friend wouldn't upset him.

"Hello, Mrs. Cartwright. It's nice to see you again."

"And you," she replied. Her eyebrows raised slightly, and I knew it was because she was trying to put the pieces together regarding just what *kind* of friend he was. She studied Chase for a moment before stepping back.

Glancing between all of us, she said, "Is there anything I can do while you wait? Get you something to drink? Eat?"

My mind reeled. This was the same woman who just weeks before had almost forbidden us from contacting our biological father. But, now, she was more herself — the loving, supportive mom who had raised us the last twelve years. Was the change because she thought our father might die?

"I'm good, thanks," I answered.

She looked at Alex and Chase, but they both shook their heads. She scanned the room like she thought someone else might need something. Behind her, Alex made eye contact with me, widening his eyes as if to say, *What the heck?*

Since I was as confused as he was, I arched my eyebrows to convey my thoughts.

"Well, okay, then," Mom said, turning halfway around to look at the chairs behind her. "I'll wait here, and if I can help, you know where I am." She settled into a chair near Alex and picked up a *Time* magazine. While she thumbed through, I sat in the seat next to her, and Chase sat on the other side of me. Despite my bewilderment, her nearness and calm demeanor actually helped me relax. It was a far cry from the eggshells we'd been walking on recently.

A minute later I looked up as Rashawn and Trooper made their way past the gawking people and joined us in our corner of the room where we had isolated ourselves. Rashawn stopped in front of a chair and pointed down.

"Trooper, tuck," he instructed. The black Labrador worked his way under the chair and curled into a ball so he fit as snugly as possible. Rashawn looked toward my mom, who had looked up from her magazine as he approached.

"Mom, this is Rashawn. He's Drew's best friend."

Rashawn extended his hand. "Nice to meet you, Ma'am. You've done a wonderful job raising these two. You should be proud."

Mom smiled and nodded. "Thank you. I am."

"Any news?" Rashawn asked Alex.

Alex shook his head. "Nothing."

After a quick glance toward the hall that led to the emergency department, Rashawn sat, folding his hands across his stomach.

While the din of chatter around us resumed, our little group sat quietly, each lost in our own thoughts. I stared at the face of my phone, watching time crawl. Five minutes turned into fifteen and fifteen into thirty. It was almost another hour later when Alex launched from his seat.

"Here comes Angela," he said.

When we all stood to face her, mom rested her hands on my shoulders like she was helping me brace for bad news. But Angela's tired smile lifted my hopes.

"It's good. It's good," she offered, her voice choked. She cleared her throat, and then continued. "They're admitting him and moving him to a room now." Her mouth twitched and moisture gathered in her eyes. "He's out of the woods. Unless something unusual happens, Dr. Loomis said he should make a full recovery. He has to be watched for a few days."

We melted together in a group hug with Angela in the center — all except for Mom. Out of the corner of my eye, I saw her study us for a moment before a pained expression darkened her features, and she turned her head to look away. I assumed she'd probably guessed Angela's role in Drew's life: a role her sister had filled before the terrible accident. I squeezed Angela even harder, realizing that when the hug was over, this would actually be the most difficult introduction of all.

Just as we'd melted together, we seemed to melt away from the hug. I made a quick decision to make the introduction but to leave any explanation to Angela, allowing her to choose whether or not to divulge the specifics of her relationship with my father.

"Angela," I said, turning toward Mom, "this is my mom, Nicole. She got my message and drove up to be with us."

Angela stepped forward and held her hand out to shake. Mom glanced at it, then back up to Angela's eyes.

My muscles tensed. I wanted to grab Mom's hand and shove it toward Angela's — force her to make peace. It was only seconds, but they seemed endless until finally Mom lifted her arm and shook Angela's hand.

"Hi," Angela said. "I've heard such nice things about you."

It was obvious that Mom was caught off guard by the statement. Her attention darted toward me, then back to Angela. She probably wondered what I had told people, but I had purposely kept any discussions positive because I knew how much Alex and I owed our aunt and uncle for loving us as if we were their biological children.

"Thank you," Mom replied. She dropped her hand and looked toward the floor for a second before returning her gaze to Angela. "Are you and Drew married?"

Angela shook her head. "No. Drew never remarried." An expression that looked like resignation crossed her face. "I honestly don't know if he'll ever marry again. He's never stopped loving your sister."

Mom's mouth dropped open, and she quickly lifted her hand to cover it as her lips quivered.

Shock waves rocked my body. The entire hospital could have exploded around me, and I don't think I would have noticed. I'm sure none of us expected that response, and the direct, right-to-the-point admission left everyone in stunned silence. It was something I'd wondered about from the moment that I learned Angela was part of my father's life. I'd come to really care for Angela and wondered if she felt like she lived in the shadow of a ghost. That part seemed unfair. She deserved better.

"Well," Angela said, breaking the tension, "who wants to go up to Drew's room?"

Alex, Chase and I moved toward her, but Rashawn remained seated, and Mom actually stepped back.

"I'll wait here," she said.

"Me, too," Rashawn added. "Family should be with him right now."

Angela swung toward him. "Rashawn, you're like family."

But he shook his head, pressing himself back against the chair as if resisting being pulled. "No, I'll go up after all of you have had time with him. I'll stay with Mrs. Cartwright."

My attention darted between the two of them. Was it a bad idea leaving them here alone together? What would they talk about? *Would* they talk?

"Okay, then," Angela said, "we probably won't be up there long. He's pretty tired and out of it because of his treatments."

"Don't worry about me," Mom said, as she picked up a different magazine and returned to her chair. "You take whatever time you need with him."

With a last glance between Rashawn and Mom, I turned and followed the rest of them down the hall toward the bank of elevators. Uneasiness prickled my core, but I couldn't pinpoint whether it was connected to the unknown of the situation I'd just left or the one I was headed for.

When we reached the floor for Drew's room, we were directed down the hall. My uneasiness skyrocketed into dread. The idea of facing him, knowing that he could have died protecting me, messed with my head. I hung back and let everyone else go in first. The natural wall worked. When I stepped in all I could see was the foot of the hospital bed and Drew's feet under the sheet.

The rhythmic beeping of one machine coordinated with another. I had never liked hospitals. Now, the sounds, the antiseptic odors and hushed voices ramped up my anxiety.

"Okay," a male nurse said as he and a female nurse moved to the end of the bed where they were within my view, "glad you're feeling better, pal. We'll leave you to your company, but I'll be back in a little while to check on you. As I said before, any tightness in your chest, your throat, your tongue, you press that call button immediately. Got it?"

There was no audible response, but I assumed Drew answered in some way because the nurse rapped his knuckles on the end of the bed and said, "Okay, see ya."

As they passed us to exit, the woman smiled, and the man nodded. The fact that they looked confident helped me to feel less stressed.

"Hey," Angela said as she stepped to the side of the bed. "You're looking even better than when I left you."

Through the gap between Alex and Chase's shoulders I saw her bend at the waist and, I assumed, gave Drew a kiss.

"Savannah?" Although the raspy voice didn't sound like Drew, he was the only other man in the room, so it had to be his. "Where's Savannah?"

"She's right here," Angela said. At the same time, Alex and Chase stepped in opposite directions to open up a space between them, leaving me a direct view of Drew. The skin tone on his hands was darker than normal, but it wasn't as horrible as my imagination had conjured. I skimmed my attention from his hands to his face. A clear, thin oxygen tube ran across his cheeks and under his nose, with the little prongs holding it in his nostrils. His focus, through swollen eyes that made it look like he was squinting, was squarely on me. When he saw my eyes connect with his, he slipped his hand from Angela's grasp and lifted it from the bed, holding it out toward me.

And I didn't know what to do.

Except for when he helped me look into the barn at Charlotte Taylor's farm to see her Gator, my father and I had never touched in any way. And now he silently asked me to take his hand.

With four slow steps forward, I was at the side of the bed. I sucked in my lower lip as I stared at his hand. My father's hand. The same hand I'm sure I'd held hundreds, or even thousands of times, when I was a little girl and had never given it a second thought.

In slow motion, I reached out and slid my hand into his, and he squeezed his fingers tight around mine. At the same time he sighed deeply, and his eyes closed.

"Thank God you're okay," he whispered.

My chest tightened. There was no mistaking the love and genuine relief in his voice.

Even though I fought them, hot tears slipped over my lower eyelids and trickled down my cheeks. My lip quivered as emotion overwhelmed me. Before I realized what I was doing, I leaned over my father's bed and hugged him the best I could, avoiding the wires and tubes. I didn't care that it was awkward. There were no words to express my gratitude.

His arms came up around my waist as he laid his hands across my back and pulled me tighter to his chest. Welcoming me. Fresh tears burned my closed eyes, and I sniffled against the crisp pillow case.

"Savannah," he whispered, his voice cracking, "forgive me?"

His question sounded like begging. But he'd kept his feelings, and his past, concealed, so I didn't know what he wanted forgiveness for. For my mother's death? For abandoning Alex and me? For resisting my attempts to reunite our family?

One of the machines at the side of the bed started beeping faster. Was something wrong? I tried to pull away, worried that I was causing the problem, but he hugged me even tighter.

"Please," he croaked. "I want to make it up to you and Alex. Forgive me."

Hope stirred in the pit of my stomach. Could something good come out of this horrible incident today?

My forehead, already hot, rubbed against the pillow as I nodded. "Done."

I'd forgive him anything if it meant he'd give us a real chance to be a family.

He slowly exhaled against my cheek, and his body relaxed. At the same time the beeping on the machine decelerated. Again, when I tried to straighten, he held me in place. Although my lower back muscles hurt from bending over in a contorted way, I didn't resist.

For this moment my father needed me. With this turn of events, I was determined to show him that I would be there for him. He'd cracked open the door of trust and was letting me get a foot over the threshold. Now, I'd work even harder to push that door wide open.

Earlier, I thought we'd lost him forever. I recognized a second chance when it was given, and there was no way I was going to waste it.

Ten minutes later, Drew was asleep again, so Angela urged us to leave.

"He'll need rest," she said, "and this has been an emotionally exhausting day for you, too. You and Alex go home with your mom. Hopefully Drew will go home tomorrow or the next day, and you can see him then." She shooed us, including Chase, from the room. "I promise if anything changes, I'll call you. Drew wouldn't want you wasting time hanging around here. Go."

I turned to Chase. "What are you going to do?"

"I'll wait with Rashawn downstairs." He draped his arm over my shoulder, and we started walking. "I'm sure my mom won't leave the hospital tonight. We'll play it all by ear."

We took the elevators down to the lobby. Rashawn and Mom still sat opposite each other, but they were talking. When they saw us, they stopped and stared while we approached.

"He's doing okay," I said. "Angela said we should go home."

Mom stood, tossing aside the magazine that was open on her lap. "Good idea. Your father's in good hands here."

The world seemed to stop as we each stared at her, processing the term she'd used. *Your father.* Yet another surprising twist in the day.

She glanced down, fidgeting with the zipper on her purse like it's what she needed to do right then. Finally, she looked back up and completely changed the subject. "We'll get you two something to eat before we leave the city."

I glanced toward the window. It was still light out, but that was fading.

Because Alex and I were exhausted, we opted to get fast food that we could eat in the car on the way home. I wasn't sure I'd have the energy or appetite to eat, let alone sit at a table in a restaurant.

After giving her the update on Drew, Mom was very quiet during most of the drive, but there were obvious signs that she had something she wanted to say. She flexed her fingers on the steering wheel, stretched and rolled her shoulders, tapped her perfectly manicured fingernails against her lip, fluffed her hair away from her face. It made me edgy wondering what was running through her mind.

The city streets of Rochester disappeared behind us as the highway took us past suburbs, shopping centers, and malls. Thousands of people were going about their lives like nothing extraordinary had happened today. They meandered in and out of stores, not knowing that today my father almost died. As hard as I tried to think about other things, the scary scene played over and over in my head. A shiver raced through me. It all could have ended so badly.

I stared straight ahead, watching as the view of the landscape faded in the twilight when Mom finally spoke again.

"Rashawn is a very nice man."

Turning to look at her, I nodded. "Yeah, he is."

Out of the corner of my eye, I could see the shadow of Alex as he leaned forward to hear better. She ran her tongue along her lower lip, then continued.

"He said some things that I'm not going to share now, but our conversation made me realize there's a lot of misunderstanding that has never been cleared up." She glanced at me, then shifted her gaze to the rearview mirror. "Alex, can you hear me?"

Alex leaned in even closer. "Yeah."

She flexed her fingers on the steering wheel again, then her shoulders lifted with a big breath. I clasped my hands tight in my lap because she was making me feel like I needed to steel myself against whatever she had to say.

"Because of what I learned from Rashawn tonight, I think it's time to tell you why I was so protective of you." Mom pursed her lips and glanced at me and then again at Alex in the mirror like she wasn't sure she really wanted any words to come out of her mouth. Finally she continued.

"The night of the accident when your mother —" she hesitated, like she didn't want to say the word — "the night she died, she called me. There were fireworks in their neighborhood and it caused Drew to have a flashback." She paused, then added, "He took out a gun."

I gasped and my hands flew up to cover my mouth. "Our mother thought he wanted to kill us?"

Mom shook her head. "No, no. Not you. The terrorists he was imagining. That's why she wanted to get you out of there."

"But then she died in an accident trying to get us away," I whispered, thinking of the article we'd found during our Google search. Pieces of the twelve-year-old puzzle started to click together for me.

She swallowed so loud I heard it from my seat. "After the funeral, I convinced him that it was too unsafe for you to be around him, that you were better off with us." She swiped at tears that had raced down her cheek. "I blamed him for taking my sister, my only family away, so in my mind, it was only fair that he should lose you."

Alex spoke up from the back seat. "And just like that he gave us up?"

I didn't miss the edge to his voice. He felt betrayed.

"No. It was a very difficult decision for him." She pursed her lips, then added, "I threatened to take him to court and tell them about the gun, about what your mother had said. He was still in such grief that he didn't fight. He believed I was right." She shook her head. "I used what my sister had said in confidence against him."

Alex flopped back against the seat.

"I can't believe he pulled out a gun," he muttered. "We could have died."

"No," Mom countered. "After the accident, investigators went to the house when I told them why Melissa was so upset. There was no proof that the gun had been loaded."

"Why are you telling us this now?"

"I already told you. I didn't want to lose you, too. I wanted you to believe that he was responsible for your mother's death so you would never want to know him. Then, sitting with Rashawn tonight, I learned things about Drew's life in the last twelve years that I couldn't fathom."

"Like what?" I asked.

She shook her head. "He's not only been dealing with the PTSD and the guilt over Melissa dying, but he's convinced himself that he isn't safe to be around. *I* convinced him he wasn't safe to be around. Rashawn thinks that's why he takes care of Angela and Chase but won't let them get too close."

We rode in silence for a couple of minutes. I assumed we were all trying to wrap our heads around all of it. Mom's motivation. Drew's motivation. All of it confusing. Intertwined.

"I was selfish," Mom suddenly blurted. "In my own hurt and anger, in my desire to hurt him like I was hurt, I didn't stop to think that this isn't what your mother would have wanted when she asked me to take care of you."

She started to sob.

I glanced over the seat at Alex. He shrugged and turned his palms up toward me as if to say, *Now what do we do?*

I looked back at Mom. Her face was scrunched up like she was in pain.

"Are you okay to drive?" I asked, assessing her speed versus traffic versus her emotional condition. "Maybe you should pull over." I fought the urge to grab onto the steering wheel to make sure someone was in control. Only my fear of crashing kept me from getting emotional, too.

She held up her hand. "I'm okay," she squeaked out. "Give me a second." She stretched her arms out straight while steering and her chest heaved with full breaths as I watched her fight to regain control of her emotions.

Grabbing a tissue from the console, Mom sniffled and wiped her nose before wadding up the tissue and setting it in the cup holder. It was then that I noticed several other balled up, used tissues stuffed there. Had she been crying on her way to the hospital? *Was she crying for our father?*

I rested my hand on her sleeve. I wished I knew exactly what was upsetting her. "It's going to be okay."

"You're our whole life, so Drew reappearing scared me." Wiping her sleeve across her face, she puffed out her cheeks, then released a slow breath. "But tonight, when I had time to think while I was driving, I realized how wrong I've been. I thought about that saying 'If you love something, let it go. If it comes back to you, it's yours. If it doesn't, then it was never meant to be.'" She looked at both of us with a weak smile before returning her attention to the road. "I've held on for too long. It's time to let you choose."

I turned and looked at Alex, wondering if he was as relieved as I was that the invisible line drawn in the sand had been wiped away. His eyebrows came together as if bewildered, but I wasn't sure it was connected to Mom's admission. He turned and looked out the window while tapping his fingers on his legs. I knew him well enough to know that there was something more on his mind.

But he didn't say anything the rest of the way home, and neither did Mom or I. I guess, for tonight, enough had been said.

Since we had to pick up the van in Keuka Shores, Mom made the detour to drop me off. The van and Drew's truck were the only vehicles left in the parking area. When she pulled up next to the van and put the car in park, Alex jumped out at the same time I did. I thought he was going to come around to the front seat.

Instead, he said before he closed the door, "I'm going to ride with Savannah."

There was no time for Mom to disagree. He was around the back of the car and to the passenger side of the van before I'd even closed my door.

I used the key fob to unlock the doors, and we slid into our seats. As I put the key into the ignition, I looked at Alex.

"Okay, spill it. What's on your mind?"

The engine purred to life while I waited. His brows furrowed with concern.

"Savannah, what if Drew still has guns?"

CHAPTER 17

Alex didn't look like a fourteen-year old on the verge of manhood. He looked like a frightened little boy.

I stared at the van's dashboard for a moment. I should have guessed that was what had sent him reeling.

"Well, I - I don't know." I grabbed my phone. "I'll text Chase. He must know."

But his answer a minute later wasn't what I'd expected.

I've never seen a gun but I don't know

I held my cell phone toward Alex in the passenger seat so he could see Chase's answer. "Chase doesn't know if Drew still has guns."

His shoulders slumped, and he sighed. "How can he not know? He sees him all the time." The force Alex used to click his seat belt into place conveyed his feelings. "He's lived down the street from him for years, for God's sake."

He had a point, but agreeing with him wouldn't help. We'd already learned our father also had the penchant for not letting others get too close. Even Chase and Angela.

I put the key in the ignition and started the van, looking toward the road where Mom waited, apparently planning on following us home. "Maybe if he still has a gun he keeps it locked up in his bedroom or somewhere so Chase has never seen it."

I put the car in drive and started toward the road. He didn't respond, so we rode in silence for a few minutes, with only the dull thump of the bass from some rock song on the radio filling the void.

When he finally spoke, the intrusion startled me, and I glanced his way.

"This changes everything, you know." In the lighting from the dash I saw his narrowed eyes, and through gritted teeth he added, "I'm not going to end up like Bobby Peck."

Just the mention of the eleven-year-old from our town who, three years earlier, had been accidentally shot by his older cousin, sent a chill up my spine. An hour before Bobby was killed, Alex and four other friends had left the Peck's house after a sleepover for Bobby's birthday.

I'd never forget that night, sitting on my bed reading, and barely registering the phone ringing. Then, the next thing I heard was Alex yelling repeatedly, "What? No! What? No!", like his brain couldn't formulate any other response.

On a scale of one to ten, with ten being the worst, witnessing my little brother suffering through that grief over the next few weeks registered a hundred and ten. For a year afterward, Alex saw a counselor. Because in the last couple of years he never talked about Bobby or the tragedy, I assumed he'd worked through his grief.

His reaction to the new knowledge that our father had brandished a gun the night our mother died, and his fear that Drew might still own one, told me the wound hadn't completely healed.

My heart hurt for him.

"Somehow I'll find out if he still has a gun," I promised, sounding more confident that I'd be successful than I felt. "If he does, then we have to let him know how we feel about it. That's all. And, hopefully we matter enough to him that he'll get rid of it."

"And if we don't matter enough?" The defeated edge to Alex's voice saddened me.

Gripping the steering wheel harder, I made sure the tone of my voice sounded as positive as possible. "We *do* matter, Alex. He risked his life to save mine today. That means something, doesn't it?"

Alex turned and looked out the window without responding.

And then a thought flashed into my head. What if Drew hadn't jumped into the water because he wanted to save his daughter? Maybe I was just another person he needed to rescue like the little boy in the fire.

Silence overtook the van again, punctuated by the occasional thud of the tires going over cracks in the pavement. We were both so lost in our thoughts that we nearly jumped out of our skin when my cell phone rang in the cup holder. I glanced toward it without picking it up but had time to see Phoebe's name light up the screen.

A rush of adrenaline kick-started my heart.

"Alex, can you grab that? It's Phoebe. I hope there's nothing wrong with Lacey."

He roused from his stupor, picked up the phone and hit the call accept button.

"Put it on speaker phone," I directed.

He punched the button and held the phone toward me.

"Hey, Phoebe."

"Hi Savannah. Sorry to bother you so late, but I figured on a Saturday night, you're probably up into the wee hours of the morning like most teens."

I looked down at the clock on the console. 9:15. For a Saturday night it was early, but my body felt like it was the middle of the night.

"No, we just started on the way home from the hospital in Rochester."

"Hospital?" Immediate alarm caused her voice to raise an octave. "What's going on?"

"It's okay now," I said, then gave her a brief summary of the day. When I finished, and before she had a chance to respond, I asked, "Is Lacey okay?"

"Yes, she's fine. But I'm sorry to hear about the scare with your father. I hope he's better soon."

"Me, too," I answered. "The doctor said he should be."

Phoebe let out a loud breath on the other end of the phone. "Whew! That's good."

We'd arrived at the end of our street, so I hit the turn signal. "What's going on? Why'd you call?"

"Well, this is actually good news." The brightness of her voice made the inside of the van seem lighter. "Cassie Potter from McDonough College called today."

My body stiffened. "Really? What for?"

"She's coming back tomorrow to talk to Alyssa and see her ride again."

"That's awesome," I said.

"I thought it might be good if you just happen to be there, too." Phoebe dragged out the word happened to emphasize this needed to look coincidental. "She can't ask you because of the NCAA rules, but I'm suggesting that tomorrow would be a great time for me to give you another lesson."

I glanced toward Alex, and he gave me a thumbs up. "What time will she be there?" I asked.

"Ten-thirty. Try to get a good night's sleep, kid. I'll see you at the barn."

So many conflicting emotions. This was one more thing to add to the day's overload of thoughts. "Yeah, see you in the morning. Good night, Phoebe. And thanks."

"You're welcome. Good night."

My fingers tingled as I gripped the steering wheel tighter than necessary. "What a crazy day."

I eyed Alex. In the dim glow of the dash lights, I caught his tired smile. His expression said he wanted to be more excited but exhaustion ruled. I could empathize.

"I feel it in my gut, Savannah. Your dream of competing with Lacey at college is going to come true."

"Thanks, bud," I said.

As I pulled up in front of our garage, I considered his comment.

The timing of the scout from McDonough coming was ironic after today. Yes, life was on the right track for that one dream to come true, but that wasn't the only one on my wish list. The other, more recent dream of having our family back together had taken a nightmarish turn when Mom told us about the gun. In my mind, even though it was a shock to hear about it, the gun was another wrinkle that needed to be smoothed out.

But I was determined that I'd bring our family together. I'd had a brainstorm during my conversations with Nate on our walk and in the waiting room. Tomorrow, as soon as I was done at the stable, I'd take the first step toward implementation. There was no doubt in my mind that Drew would resist, but after he saved my life today, I owed him.

It was payback time.

"Ye-e-ess! You did great out there," Phoebe squealed as she jogged down the aisle toward Lacey and me, her fist pumping the air. I froze with the body brush resting against Lacey's neck, forcing a smile. Despite my inner turmoil about the future, Lacey and I had given it all we had so the recruiter from McDonough would see us at our best.

"Guess it's good news," I said.

Phoebe did a little dance as she approached and nearly sang her response. "Cassie Potter is signing on Alyssa for this fall, and she wants to come back and talk to you as soon as the college rules allow."

I let the brush slide down and hang in my hand at my side. "Wow!"

"Yeah, wow!" She stopped in front of me and threw her hand in the air for a high five.

I responded, but the conflict surging through me tempered my enthusiasm. This should have been an exciting announcement, but after a restless night of trying to process all that had happened since I found my father and now trying to figure out my role in his life, this only added to my turmoil.

When she'd called last night, I was positive of where my immediate future was headed if Lacey and I performed well today. But then when I was thinking with a rational head, not my emotional head, I thought of my father, what he'd done for me, and the options Rashawn had suggested for ways to get our family back together. And the answer suddenly seemed obvious - someone was going to have to make a sacrifice for us to have any chance of a normal family relationship.

I scrubbed my knuckle against Lacey's gray and brown-flecked jaw. "So she wants to talk to me."

"Yes, but," Phoebe continued as she slid past me to run her hand along Lacey's back, "she can't officially talk to you face to face until after July first since you're only a junior. Based on what I know she's looking for, I'd have to say there's going to be a spot open for you on the McDonough equestrian team."

I didn't look at Phoebe as I smoothed the brush along Lacey's neck again. "That's great."

Out of the corner of my eye I saw Phoebe turn toward me, resting her arm on Lacey's back. "Wow! That didn't sound very enthusiastic. Last night you were all about it. You okay?"

I shrugged and avoided looking directly at her. "Yeah. It's just, between this and what's going on with my father, I have a lot on my mind."

"Have you heard an update on him this morning?"

I nodded and smiled, a genuine smile this time, and looked at her. "Chase sent me a text. They're letting him come home today as long as he's not alone. So, his friend, Rashawn, is staying with him for a couple of days."

"That's great news!"

"Yeah, it is." I ducked under Lacey's neck to toss the brush into the grooming bucket. When I straightened and turned around, Phoebe peered at me from over Lacey's back.

"Phoebe," I said, "I want you to know that, whatever happens, I appreciate everything you've done for me, from teaching me to ride, to sharing Lacey with me, and supporting me with my dreams of competing at college."

She tipped her head. "*Whatever* happens? Is there something you're trying to tell me?"

Biting down on my lower lip, I considered sharing what had been going through my mind since last night, but I wasn't ready. "Well, you know," I hedged, "there are no guarantees on anything."

"True." She patted Lacey's neck. "I better get back into the house and pay some bills. Will you be here Tuesday to work?"

"Of course." I removed the cross tie from Lacey's halter and hooked on a braided lead rope while Phoebe started down the aisle. "You want me to put her out in the pasture?" I asked.

"Yep," she threw over her shoulder as she rounded the corner and out of sight.

Instead of leading Lacey out right away, I threw my arms around her neck and pressed my cheek against her warm, silky hair. Closing my eyes, I breathed in her horsey scent, one that often stayed on my skin and clothes for hours after if I didn't change and take a shower. Every goal and dream I'd had for the last four years, and my future, was wrapped up in this beautiful Appaloosa mare.

"Got it!"

I popped my head back to see Jamie coming down the aisle, holding her phone up.

"I'll text you this picture I just took," she said, stopping in front of Lacey and me, her fingers already flying across the screen's keyboard. "Shows the true love between the two of you. Lacey's head was down and her eyes were half closed."

A moment later, I heard the telltale ding of a text arriving.

"Can you stay and ride with me?" she asked as she shoved the phone in her back pocket.

"Can't. I actually was going to ask you for Charlotte Taylor's number at CharTay Kennels. Do you have any idea if she's around today?"

Jamie nodded. "I just came from there. She has a couple of training sessions."

She pulled the phone back out of her pocket and started pressing numbers on the face. "I'll send her number to your phone."

Again, the phone dinged with Charlotte Taylor's contact information. Anticipation and dread battled within me. Now I had the connection to move forward with my plan. I was fully aware that I was acting with my heart and not my head. Hopefully I wasn't setting myself up for the biggest mistake of my life.

As I drove to CharTay Kennels, I kept telling myself I could change my mind at any time. But, something in my heart told me I was making the right decision. When I'd called, Charlotte told me she'd be in the training room in the barn. As I climbed the steps to the second floor, I tried to imagine what the barn had been like when it was a dairy farm. At the top of the stairs, in the area that I assumed had once been used to store hay, it was fascinating to see how it had been transformed for the space Charlotte needed for her kennel.

Now, scattered throughout the giant, open area on the restored barn board floor were obstacles and ramps. Three free-standing doors, painted bright colors, looked like abstract art because they

led to nowhere and were placed in random places around the
room.

I moved to a wooden bench next to the wall and sat. A couple
sat in chairs adjacent to the bench. We exchanged smiles of
acknowledgement, then I turned toward the training in session.
Charlotte gave me a quick wave, then returned her attention to a
teenaged boy and the Golden Retriever with him.

"That's our son, Jeremy," the woman said. "Charlotte sold us
Tucker for Jeremy because he has anxiety issues."

"Oh," I said, surprised that these people were so open about
sharing private information.

"Charlotte trained Tucker to alert to high stress situations that
could cause Jeremy to have an anxiety attack. Charlotte is
amazing."

"And so is Tucker," the dad threw in.

We watched Charlotte conclude the session. Jeremy looked
calm and satisfied, and so did Tucker.

"I'll be right back," Charlotte offered as she followed them
down the stairs.

While I waited, I wandered around looking at the different
obstacles. I was surprised when I stopped in front of a dog crate
in the corner and discovered a dog in it. It looked like it was
some kind of brown and white mixed breed dog. When I
approached, it lifted its head, the brown eyes alert and warm. I
wasn't sure whether protocol allowed me to talk to it or not, so I
opted to merely smile.

"Hey, thanks for your patience," Charlotte said when she
returned. "Do you want to chat now, or do you want to watch me
work with Shadow a little bit?" She crossed the large expanse of
the room, looking at the crate I was standing near.

"That would be fun to watch you work with him," I said. "Go
ahead."

Charlotte opened the crate door, but Shadow didn't move.

"Shadow, here" she commanded, and the dog popped out. He
circled Charlotte a few times as they walked toward the middle
of the room.

"Shadow was trained to open doors, retrieve items and things
like that for her owner who was paralyzed in a swimming
accident," she said as the dog sidled up next to her, its backside

pushing into Charlotte's leg. "I didn't do the initial training, but I was hired to do some fine tuning of his skills. The family moved here from Indiana, and he hadn't quite mastered a few of the tasks. He's a brilliant dog, so it's easy to work with him."

"That's so awesome," I said. Because Shadow was wearing his service dog vest, I made sure not to pet him.

"Wait until you see some of his mad skills."

I laughed at Charlotte's terminology. I figured she was in her early forties, but something about her demeanor made her seem younger.

Charlotte ran Shadow through a few of the paces, having him retrieve a drink from the refrigerator, tear a paper towel off a roll and find a "lost" cell phone. After a few minutes of perfect execution, she stopped to give Shadow a break. She sat down on the floor and patted an area next to her leg to indicate to Shadow to lie down next to her.

"Have a seat," she said to me, pointing at the floor across from her. "Are you okay with sitting on the floor?"

"Sure. No problem." I sat with my legs crossed and my elbows resting on my knees. Her casualness made me feel more comfortable since I hardly knew her.

"So," Charlotte said, "you told me on the phone that you have some questions about Jem?"

I nodded.

"What kind of questions?"

There were a million streaming through my mind all at once, but for right now, I only needed to focus on the most immediate.

"When we came to the demonstration, you said that Jem was undergoing the same kind of training as Trooper, Rashawn's dog."

Charlotte tipped her chin down as if to say *get on with it*.

"Rashawn said that Trooper helps him with his PTSD. That his marriage and his life were saved because of his dog."

Charlotte frowned. "Yes, Rashawn truly believes that, and, of course, I concur, but what does that have to do with Jem?"

I shifted my attention toward Shadow. How did I ask my next question? Finally, I decided to blurt it out.

"How does someone get a dog like Trooper? Like Jem?"

Leaning back on her arms, Charlotte stretched her legs out in front of her. "It depends. Not everyone uses the same method that I do, but first I like to try and match the dog and the person to see if they're going to bond before I'll even consider putting them through the rigorous training. In Jem's case, because I haven't wanted her to bond with any trainers or foster owners, I've rotated her though four different homes since she left me."

"Has she stayed with any veterans with PTSD?"

"No. I feel that would be too confusing for the dog. Once a match is made, and we know they're going to bond, it's two weeks of very intense training and then continued training for months after that. If the pair haven't bonded, the handler gets frustrated, the dog gets frustrated, and the project fails. The dog is then considered washed out of the program."

My heart sank. I'd never considered that it doesn't always work. "Fails? What happens if it fails?"

Shrugging, Charlotte said, "Then I have to make the decision about whether the dog is right for the program, and whether to look for a new prospect for the person. Sometimes it's the dog that can't adjust, and sometimes it's the person. It's only happened once, but it's heartbreaking for everyone. Including me."

"That's sad," I acknowledged.

Charlotte nodded. "So why these questions? Do you know someone who is looking for a service dog?"

I nibbled on my lower lip for a moment before answering. Honesty was the best route to take.

"My biological father is an Iraq War veteran. He has PTSD."

"And he's looking for a dog?" Charlotte asked.

"Well, not exactly," I hedged. "I'm looking for a dog *for* him."

Charlotte's eyebrows lifted. "But he doesn't know it, right?"

I shook my head. "No. It's a long story, but I'll tell a short version. Yesterday he had an allergic reaction to bees, so he was in the hospital in Rochester. We haven't lived with him since I was four and my brother, Alex, was two. It's mostly because of the PTSD. Last night when we were with Rashawn and Trooper at the hospital, Rashawn was telling me that he's suggested that my father get a dog to help him. But Rashawn said he's stubborn."

"And you're thinking Jem is the right dog?"

"Maybe." I flexed my fingers against my legs, suddenly feeling nervous. "When Jamie has brought her places where my dad is, it always seems like Jem is tuned into him. And a few weeks ago, when my father had a flashback and was really upset, it was Trooper who seemed to bring him around. I think he should try it."

When Shadow lifted his ears and tipped his head at me, Charlotte reached over and laid her hand on the neck fur above the vest.

"This is really important to you, isn't it?" Charlotte said.

"It is. It may be the only way our family can really get back together again. He's worried about having flashbacks and doing something that could hurt us. He feels responsible for our mom dying in a car accident."

Charlotte grimaced. "Ooh, that's tough."

I nodded. "Maybe if I tell him Jem is available —" My voice trailed off, because there really wasn't anything to add to the end of that comment.

"Savannah, do you or your dad know how much professionally trained service dogs cost?"

It was my turn to shrug. "Maybe Rashawn told him, but I don't know. And I have no idea."

She studied me for a second. "Well, Trooper was almost nine thousand dollars."

My eyes flew open, and I sucked in a breath. I couldn't even talk to respond.

"Some dogs are a lot more than that, some dogs are less. There are a lot of factors that go into it."

I was afraid to ask, but I had to. "How much is Jem?"

"Seventy-five hundred."

When I gulped, I was sure it was so loud that Charlotte probably heard it. "Wow! It's a lot more than I thought."

"She's actually on the lower end right now. Many times people hold fundraisers or organizations sponsor them so that they can purchase the dog. But, of course, that all takes a lot of time. If your father has the financial resources himself, then that's a different story. He could get Jem right away."

"But, what if people buy the dog, and it doesn't work out?"

Charlotte smiled. "I'm a business person, but the animals' well-being comes first. The majority of the money would be refunded, and I would take the dog back."

Charlotte shifted so she could get up off the floor. Shadow stayed where he was since Charlotte hadn't released him to stand.

"If I can get my father to agree to try it, is Jem available?" For the moment I wouldn't bring up the financial part again. If he agreed, we'd cross that bridge later.

She shook out first one leg, then the other, like they had fallen asleep.

"I'll tell you what," she said, looking up at me, "if I see you and your father, or at the very least, your father, walk through the kennel door, then I'll know he's interested. But he has to come to Jem, I won't take Jem to him. He has to be invested in this process in order for it to work. Then we can talk. Deal?"

Hope surged through me. I smiled and thrust my hand forward for a handshake. "Deal!"

My imagination filled with images of Alex, Drew and me being a family again. Premature, but a girl had to have dreams.

I hoped trying for that dream was worth all that I was willing to sacrifice.

CHAPTER 18

A ticking clock and a potential bomb. And there was no way for me to control either one.

The idea to invite everyone to a picnic at Keuka Lake State Park seemed like a good idea, but now that Alex, Chase, Jamie, Kyle and I were waiting for everyone to arrive, second thoughts hammered in my brain. What if this was too soon?

I looked around the treed picnic area we'd picked out near the water and tried to imagine Drew, Angela, my parents, and Charlotte Taylor all sitting around these two picnic tables with us, eating hamburgers and hot dogs.

Focused on their food in an awkward silence.

I shook my head to clear the image. They had all agreed to be here. Together. One more step forward. Hopefully they would all chat cordially.

In the two weeks since Drew had been discharged from the hospital, it was like a switch had been flipped in our relationship. Not quite a family again, but getting closer to feeling like it. I wondered if his near-death experience had been the catalyst for his sudden willingness to consider different possibilities — including fostering Jem.

The one big unanswered question still loomed. Did he have a gun? I'd found no way to bring up that subject. But, at some point soon, the issue would have to be dealt with. If he no longer had one, then we were good. If he still had one, how difficult would it be to convince him to part with it?

Although we hadn't gone to his house because of Alex's fear of a gun, we had spent quality time together. We'd taken a hike on the Finger Lakes Trail, gone out to dinner at Seneca Farms, and spent more time at Rashawn's house, painting the deck that had been added almost two months before.

But, today's outing was the most important of all. So much was at stake.

"What time are your parents supposed to get here?" Jamie asked — probably because she saw me looking up at the parking lot for the tenth time in ten minutes.

I grabbed my end of the checkered plastic table cloth, and together we straightened it across the first picnic table. "Noon. I figured it was better to have them arrive after Drew has had a chance to see Jem for a little while." Smoothing my hand along the slippery edges, I looked up at her. "Charlotte's definitely bringing Jem with her?"

"Yep. She's looking at it as a great opportunity for Jem to swim and work off some energy."

"And she'll be here by 11:30?" I asked.

Jamie held a table clip in her hand and stared at me. "You better hope Charlotte doesn't see this as you getting her to bring Jem to Drew."

"It's not like that at all." I grabbed a couple of tablecloth hooks and smoothed my hand across the plastic one more time. "I just figured if Drew had the chance to be around Jem more, maybe he'd start to be interested. It's probably not going to happen any other way."

We clipped the hooks around the tablecloth and table on all four sides to prevent the plastic sheet from blowing away if a breeze hit. Then Jamie and I moved on to the second one. Atticus sat on the ground at one end, his attention totally focused on the lake.

I glanced toward the water. The sun glinted off the surface where barely a ripple disturbed the glassy reflection. We'd selected the picnic area closest to the water on purpose. Even though the temperature was supposed to be in the eighties, the water would still be cool. I suspected Jem and Atticus would be the only ones going in to swim.

Jamie patted the top of Atticus's golden head as she stepped around him. "You'd love to get in that water, wouldn't you, boy?"

Without moving his head, he flicked his eyes toward her in a quick acknowledgement, then looked back toward the lake. I couldn't wait to see what it would be like when Charlotte got here with Jem and both dogs could play.

"I thought the guys would be back with the ice by now," I said as I shook out the next plastic tablecloth.

Jamie grabbed the other end of it, and we laid it over the table.

"Our mistake was sending all three of them together," she answered.

As if talking about them had been the key, Chase pulled his car into the parking spot next to our van. He, Alex, and Kyle climbed from the car and retrieved six bags of ice from the trunk. They were laughing and swinging them at each other as they approached our picnic area.

"You guys look like a bunch of middle schoolers," Jamie yelled.

"I *am* a middle schooler for three more weeks," Alex cracked as he swung one bag of ice and let it fly toward me.

I managed to catch it in a full-on hug grip that left the bottom of my shirt spattered with moisture and my arms instantly cold. After juggling it for a second to get a good hold, I tossed it into the drink cooler.

"Great reflexes," Chase said, as he emptied the other bags of ice between the coolers.

"Any sign of your mom and Drew?" I asked.

"Nope." he closed the cooler lids and wiped his hands on his shorts.

Jamie pulled out her cell phone and checked the time. "Charlotte should be rolling in with Jem anytime."

"Good. I want to make sure there's time for Drew to interact with Jem before Mom and Dad get here." I planned out everyone's arrival times."

Alex hopped on one foot as he yanked at the sandal on the other foot."Anyone else want to check out the lake to see if it's warm enough to swim?"

We all looked at each other and shrugged simultaneously. Alex removed the second sandal and kicked both under the picnic table bench.

"Come on."

"Might as well." I took hold of Chase's hand, still cool and moist from smoothing out the ice, and tugged him toward the beach. "You can be my lifeguard."

"Well," he said, wiggling his eyebrows, "maybe I can practice a little resuscitation."

"Uggh!" Alex looked over his shoulder and groaned. "Really, guys?" He grabbed the soccer ball from the duffel bag of sports equipment Kyle had brought, tossed it toward the lake, then sprinted after it, dribbling toward the shore.

Chase bumped lightly against me as we walked. "You doing okay with this impending gathering of the forces?"

Shrugging, I let out a loud breath. "I'm not gonna lie. I'm really nervous."

He dropped my hand and put his arm around my shoulders, pulling me in close to him as we walked. "Have faith. What's the worst that could happen?"

I jerked my head up to look at him. "You and I both know the answer to that."

And it would probably keep me on edge for the entire afternoon.

We were playing fetch with Atticus on the beach when I looked toward the parking lot to see that Drew, Angela and Charlotte had arrived at the same time. Drew was already kneeling on the ground in front of Jem, ruffling the fur around her neck. Her nose was lifted toward him as they stared at each other. It looked like Jem was wearing her red and blue Service Dog In Training vest.

My throat swelled with emotion. I tapped Chase's forearm with the back of my hand. When he turned, I nodded toward the parking lot.

"Look at Drew and Jem. I'm going to take that as a positive sign."

"Awesome!" Chase responded.

"Hey," I called to Jamie, Alex, and Kyle, "I'm going back up to the picnic area. The others are starting to arrive."

"We'll be right up," Jamie called back.

Chase and I had covered only half the distance back to the picnic area when I saw Dad's Jeep pull into a parking space not far from Drew.

"You've gotta be kidding me. Mom and Dad are never early anywhere," I said, pulling my phone out of my pocket. I glanced at the time. They were a half hour early. "No, it wasn't supposed to happen this way."

"Well, it did, and they're all here. Did you have a Plan B?"

I shook my head and stared toward the cars. The sun's reflection on the windshield prevented me from seeing inside the Jeep, but I imagined Mom and Dad watching Drew.

The skin on the back of my neck prickled. Without looking, I stabbed the air in search of Chase's hand and clasped it with a death grip. Forcing this interaction between Mom and Drew was either my best idea, or the worst ever.

"Relax," Chase whispered. "Whatever happens now is out of your control."

"I know. That's the problem." I pressed my free hand against my churning stomach. It was like a movie scene unfolding in front of us. We were the audience, on edge, wondering what was going to happen next.

Chase stopped when we reached the picnic tables, but I let go of his hand and started to go around them. I'd barely taken a few steps when he reached out and took hold of my hand again, stopping me.

"What are you doing?" he asked.

I whirled toward him. "Averting a disaster."

He scowled. "No. You can't solve all problems, Savannah."

"I'm not looking to solve a problem." I shook free of his hand. "I forced this. Maybe I was wrong."

"Maybe you were right," he shot back.

When I turned back toward the parking lot, Charlotte and Angela were coming toward us, walking side by side, each carrying a few grocery bags in their hands.

Drew continued to kneel, and Jem side-stepped next to him. He draped his arm over her shoulder, pulling her next to his leg, then turned his attention toward the Jeep. He had to know it was Mom and Dad.

"Why aren't they getting out of the car?" My breaths were shallow, making my voice sound tight.

The closer Charlotte and Angela got to us, the more they inadvertently blocked my view of Drew. I ducked my head back and forth to try to see beyond them as Charlotte lifted a bag-laden hand to waggle her fingers at us.

"Hey, guys. Perfect day for a picnic. Thanks for the invitation."

I pulled out of Chase's grip and stepped to the side, but Angela moved in front of me, extending one bag toward me. "This salad will need to go in a cooler, if you wouldn't mind."

How could she be so calm and matter-of-fact with the big unknown going on behind her?

I snagged it from her hand and without even looking in his direction, passed it to Chase. "Can you take care of this, please?"

My attention was on the Jeep and Drew and Jem.

Finally, the driver's side door of the Jeep opened, and Dad emerged.

At the same time Drew stood and turned toward him. His body was rigid, his military background manifesting itself in his stance. From this distance he looked ready for battle. With his right hand he held Jem's leash and laid his palm against her ear. His left hand hung next to his hip, and he slowly flexed it open and closed. At the same time, Jem sidled even tighter against his leg. Was she sensing anxiety? Was he anxious?

Dad threw his hand up to acknowledge Drew. But I wasn't worried about him.

Out of the corner of my eye, I saw the passenger door open. My shoulders tensed. Mom climbed out of the Jeep with her head down and her eyes on the pavement in front of her. Even though she'd come to the hospital the night Drew almost died, she hadn't seen him then, and still hadn't in twelve years.

She closed her door, then moved to the back and retrieved what looked like a cake pan from the passenger seat, prolonging my agony. Despite the movement and conversation around me about where to put food and drinks and what games would be set up, I couldn't pull my attention away from the scene in the parking lot. She closed the door, but instead of coming around the front of the Jeep, she moved behind it and out of sight.

Dad took folding lawn chairs from the back seat, then stepped to the rear of the Jeep where Mom had gone. It looked like he was talking, but then he turned away from her and crossed the lawn to where Drew and Jem stood. I couldn't hear their exchange, but after a few seconds Drew grabbed hold of the straps on a couple of the canvas carrying cases for the folding chairs that Dad brought, and the two of them turned and started toward us. Jem trotted on the other side of Drew, seeming content to respond to his commands.

But Mom didn't reappear from behind the Jeep. I wondered if she would even come down to the picnic.

I closed my eyes and took a deep breath. Mistake. Big mistake. The word bounced around in my head.

The fine gravel under their feet crunched as they got closer to our picnic area. I opened my eyes, hoping that beyond them I would see Mom following. But she wasn't.

"You already got the charcoal going, I see," Drew said to Chase as they approached.

"Yes, sir. I wanted it to be ready for us to start cooking at noon," Chase responded.

By the surprised expression on Dad's face, I guessed he hadn't expected Chase to respond so formally to Drew. He shot a glance at me, arching his eyebrows. I shook my head, warning him not to comment on it. It wasn't uncommon for Chase to answer Drew that way, and it was done out of respect. That wasn't my concern at the moment though.

When Dad and Drew split, I went to Dad, reaching for one of the chairs he carried.

"Dad, what's Mom doing? Why isn't she coming down?"

He turned his back to the others so they couldn't hear his response. "This is hard for her, Savannah. She needs a few minutes."

My lungs tightened. Needed a few minutes for what? To figure out how to skewer him for something that happened twelve years before?

Behind us, I heard Charlotte say, "Jem likes you, Drew. She looks pretty comfortable."

"She's a nice dog," he responded.

Alex, Jamie and Kyle returned from the beach, chatting about a Yankees and Red Sox game like they'd been there, even thought they'd only watched it on television.

Snippets of everyday conversation. Mundane.

All I could do was wait. The ball was in Mom's court now.

I joined the others in busying ourselves laying out the food and utensils. It was better than staring toward the Jeep and worrying. Twinges of pain in my stomach emphasized how I felt.

"I haven't been here in so long," Dad said as he pulled ketchup, mustard and relish from a bag. "We used to come to the lake several times a summer when we were kids."

"We did, too," Charlotte added.

Alex grabbed a handful of barbecue potato chips from the open bag on the table as he scooted past. "Hey, Chase," he said, "Kyle and I are going to get the Corn Hole game out of the car. Can I have your keys?"

Chase reached into his shorts pocket, pulled out the key ring and tossed it across the table to Alex. "Don't forget the bean bags are in the box behind the driver's seat."

It was in the midst of all of this that I looked again and saw that Mom was coming across the grass. As he and Kyle passed her, Alex stopped to say something, but she continued to walk, almost like she wasn't hearing him. He shrugged and continued on.

I glanced at Drew. Although he and Charlotte were talking about different commands she'd taught Jem, Drew's facial expression told me there was a part of his brain that was registering Mom getting closer. His attention darted between her and Charlotte. All of a sudden he straightened and handed the end of Jem's leash to Charlotte.

"Can you take her?"

"Sure." Although she looked bewildered, she took the leash.

His abrupt movement and the edge in the tone of his voice caught my attention. I froze.

He pivoted, taking long strides up the path toward the parking lot. My breath caught in my throat.

Was he leaving?

From our angle it looked like he was headed for the parking lot, but then I realized Mom was his target. He looked like a man on a mission.

When she saw him approaching, she jerked to a halt. She was still far enough away that I couldn't read the expression on her face, but I could see her arms stiffen. Then I realized her reaction wasn't fear or concern. She was ready to meet him head on. My throat hurt when I tried to swallow against the lump there.

"Oh, no!" I whispered.

Fearful of a confrontation, I lunged around the table to intervene, but Dad's reflexes were fast. He grabbed my arm, almost making me whirl toward him. It was like he and Chase were my sentries today, keeping me from intervening when I sensed opportunities for confrontation.

"Leave them alone," he warned. "This has been a long time coming."

"But what if —"

He cut me off. "Give them a chance to work this out, Savannah. The time may be right for forgiveness."

Dad stretched his arm across my shoulders and tucked me against his side. Chase stepped in next to me on the other side, and Angela and Charlotte broke the awkward silence by turning away from the scene and discussing whether or not to set the table or leave the plates and plastic silverware stacked.

Drew stopped a few feet in front of Mom. I couldn't tell if either of them was talking. It was more like they were staring at each other.

I tried to relieve the heavy sensation in my chest by taking deep breaths. *"Do something. Say something,"* I silently commanded. I'd lost control of this situation that I'd created. If anyone was hurt in any way, I'd never forgive myself.

A breeze had picked up. It moved the leaves on the branch above them enough so that the sun shone straight onto Mom's face. Her face crinkled, and Drew moved toward her, wrapping his arms around her. The cake pan nearly slipped off her hip as she returned his embrace with her free arm.

Tears sprang to my eyes and my body sagged between Dad and Chase. I was sure things wouldn't be perfect, but at least it felt like one emotional bomb had finally been diffused.

Mom sat at the far end of one picnic table, and Drew sat at the far end of the other one. Even though they didn't interact with one another, there was no tension during the meal.

"Anyone want that last hot dog?" Alex asked, his hand hovering above it on the paper plate.

When no one objected, he snatched it, smothered it with ketchup, then took a huge bite off one end. Mom got up from the table bench and started stacking the used paper plates and plastic silverware.

"Why don't all of you go down and enjoy the water," she suggested. "I'll set out dessert while you're gone."

Alex poised the second half of the hot dog near his lips. "How about dessert now?" Then he shoved the entire half in his mouth, the mass of food puffing his cheeks out as he tried to chew.

Mom swatted his shoulder. "Alexander Andrew, you're going to choke," she scolded. Her eyes flew open wide when she realized what she'd said. Andrew. Our father's full name, and Alex had been named after him. She flicked a glance toward Drew, and so did I.

There was a slight crook to the corners of his mouth. Her slip of the tongue had pleased him.

"I won't choke," Alex responded with a full mouth while licking ketchup off the ends of his fingers. "That's an old wives' tale."

Snapping out of her momentary stupor, Mom lightly whacked him again. "Ugh! Teenagers."

Her light tone conveyed the image that everything was fine, but her rigid body screamed *still trying to come to terms with all of the uncertainty about Drew's role in our lives.*

"You love me, and you know it," he shot back as he ducked away from her and jumped up from the bench. "I'm hitting the lake."

He tossed his sandals next to the cooler, then turned back toward us. "Come on, you guys. The day's gettin' old. I'll take the dog toys, and maybe Atticus and Jem will chase tennis balls or a Frisbee in the water."

"I'll help you with dessert, Nicole," Angela offered. To the rest of us she said, "Alex has a good idea. Go down and have some fun."

Mom stopped moving and stared at her for a moment. The two of them had had minimal interaction. "Thanks," she said, a bit of hesitation in her voice.

Dad stood. "I'll hang back here, make sure the fire is put out completely and take the stuff we're done with to the car."

"Want my help?" Drew asked.

"Nah, I'm good," Dad said. "You can go and make sure no one drowns." It was meant as a joke, but the truth hit a little too close to home. Dad dropped his chin and shook his head. "Now that was the stupidest thing I've said today." He added, "Get those dogs down to the water to play."

"Let's go," Alex prodded as he grabbed a small bucket with dog toys that Charlotte had brought. Jamie, Chase, Kyle and I moved in unison, getting up from the table and finding our towels in case we went into the water, also.

"Yep, no sense wasting a good lake," Drew said, swinging his legs across the table bench so he could stand up. He hooked a thumb toward Jem, who laid sprawled out a few feet away where she was tied, but looked at Charlotte. "You taking her down?"

"No, you take her. I'll stay here with Nicole and Angela." Charlotte retrieved a leash from next to the table and handed it to him. "Have fun."

Hope swelled in me, and I couldn't contain a smile as another piece of the puzzle for getting our family back together slipped into place.

And I had a plan for this puzzle to become a completed picture soon.

Because I had to detour to the restroom on the way to the lake, everyone else was already either in the water or at the edge when I got down there. They had chosen an area at the very end of the public beach up closer to the life guards so the dogs could go into the water without disturbing the handful of people who were braving the chilly water.

When Chase saw me approaching, he met me part way and took hold of my hand.

"This picnic was a great idea, Savannah. Everybody's having fun, and I think some walls have been broken down."

I smiled up at him as we walked side by side to the water. "I know. I hardly slept last night, but now I guess all that worry was for nothing."

"This all could have gone either way," he said.

Jamie and Kyle stood with their feet in the water while Atticus pawed at the pebbles below the surface. Occasionally the dog dipped his nose below the surface and pushed at the little piles his pawing had created.

"Hey!" Alex called from the water. "Someone toss me the Frisbee."

"How about I throw it out for Jem to retrieve?" Drew suggested. He commanded Jem to sit and stay, then skimmed the Frisbee across the water. Jem's tail brushed a pattern into the coarse sand while she stared at the Frisbee bobbing on the surface. She darted a glance up toward Drew, a plea in her eyes. Her backside wriggled as if she could barely contain herself in that one spot, then, finally, with a swing of his hand toward the water, he commanded her.

"Jem, retrieve."

Sand flew behind every paw as she dug in and covered the few feet to the water's edge where she jumped in and began paddling as soon as she was in deep enough. Her attention was beaded on the Frisbee, and within seconds she reached it and chomped it between her teeth before paddling one hundred and eighty degrees in the water to bring it back to Drew.

She bounded from the lake, stopped, and shook, then trotted back to him. Her tail fanned the air, and she lifted her chin as if trying to hand the Frisbee to him. He laughed and took it.

"Good girl, Jem" He dropped the disc before kneeling so he could ruff up the wet fur on her neck. "Nice job."

Their eyes met, and it was clear there was a connection. I heard Jamie send Atticus out after a ball and was amazed that Jem didn't break her concentration. At that moment, her whole world was Drew. And he looked like he was absorbed into hers. Hope zipped along my nerves. Maybe, just maybe, he was being won over.

We spent more than half an hour with the dogs in and out of the water after tennis balls, the Frisbee, and a floating rubber bone. Even Alex got in on the fetching games, racing the dogs to see who could reach the thrown toy first. He only won once.

But it was the laughter and joking among us that mattered most to me. Even if we didn't feel like one yet, in a way, we sounded like one. Even the banter between Alex and our father as we made our way back to the picnic tables sounded more familial. Tiny steps of progress on a long road, but I'd take them.

It also gave me the courage to ask Drew something that had been rolling around in my brain for a few weeks. Now, finally, seemed like the right time. All I had to do was scoot up next to him as he walked.

"I need to talk to my father before we get back with everyone else," I said, dropping Chase's hand.

He gave me a puzzled look. "Okay."

It was still an odd feeling for me to refer, out loud, to Drew as my father, and I guessed it sounded strange to him, too.

I turned to Jamie, Kyle and Atticus. "I don't mean to be rude."

Jamie waved off my comment. "You're not. Come on, Atty," she said, lightly tugging on his leash. "Let's get you a treat."

Pivoting back in Drew's direction, I waited until Alex finished telling him something, then sidled up next to them.

"Excuse me," I said, taking a slight step in front of Drew.

He stopped and turned toward me, probably startled by the formality of my interruption.

"Can I talk to you for a second?"

Drew glanced at Alex, then back at me. Alex stopped and waited, too.

I gave Alex a pointed look. "Privately, please."

"Come on, Alex," Chase said, coming up next to him and lightly shoving his shoulder. "We know when we're not wanted." Chase winked at me and encouraged Alex to walk away. He was the most considerate guy I'd ever known, and it made me appreciate him even more.

As they moved away from us. Drew wrapped Jem's leash around one hand and reached down to lay his other hand on top of her head.

"So, what's up?" he asked.

I took a deep breath to bolster my confidence, hoping my idea wouldn't be rejected. "I know you used to ride horses, so I wanted to invite you to something that's kind of important to me."

His eyebrows shot up, but he waited for me to explain.

"Next weekend our stable is holding the family trail ride. It's Saturday and Sunday, and we have a stopping point on the trail Saturday night where we camp out for the night. I was hoping you would go on the ride with me."

He tipped his head and smirked. "I have a problem with that."

My heart sank. Here came the rejection I feared.

Even though I really didn't want to hear an excuse, I asked anyway. "What's the problem?"

Shrugging he said, "I don't have a horse."

I brightened. "I already worked it out with Phoebe. She'll let you use her quarter horse, Buster. Even if you haven't ridden in a while, Buster's a good horse." The more I tried to convince him, the faster I talked. "Phoebe said you can come over this week and ride him to see if he's a good fit. She has lots of saddles to choose from. He's not the quietest horse she has, but he's the right size for you, and I think his temperament would work."

Suddenly I stopped and shook my head. Streaks of heat shot up my neck. "I'm sorry. I'm babbling."

Drew smirked, but the twinkle in his eyes told me he wasn't laughing at me. "You're quite a salesperson."

My eyes flew open wide. "Does that mean you'll do it?"

"Well. let me try the horse first. If he works out, then I'll commit."

I grabbed his forearm. "Really? You'll really go?"

"You bet."

My spirits soared, and I threw my hands to the top of my head as if I had to hold my excitement in. "I can't believe you'll do this. It's going to be awesome."

He glanced toward everyone mingling around the tables. "What about Max?" he said, referring to Dad. "I don't want to step on his toes."

"You won't. He doesn't ride. He always meets us at camp that night and then spends the night."

"And Nikki?"

"Mom doesn't ride, and she definitely doesn't camp in the woods. It'll be okay."

Drew chuckled and turned to move toward the rest of the group. "Okay, then. Bring on the saddle sores and bowed legs."

"Do you have time to go to the barn when we leave here?"

He glanced at me. "Tenacity suits you."

I laughed. "Thanks, I think."

"Inherited it from your mother." His eyes softened. "And, yes, it's a compliment."

I gulped, feeling proud. "Compliment accepted."

My steps couldn't have been any lighter as we joined the rest. I was on top of the world.

The desserts, small paper plates and more plastic silverware were spread out on the tables. We were within feet of the picnic area when Jem stopped and shook one last time, sending water all over us.

"Quick, protect the desserts!" I yelled, grabbing Chase and Jamie to plaster them to my side so we could create a human shield between the dogs and the table. Laughter filled the air, a continuation of the easy, comfortable mood that had developed naturally as we hung out by the water with the dogs.

Alex barged into our human wall between Chase and me. "Outta my way. No one gets between me and dessert."

At first Chase and I squished closer together to form a stronger barrier, but then without warning, I jumped back, creating an opening between us that Alex stumbled through. He caught himself with his hands against the edge of a table.

Mom's hand shot out in the automatic protective mom response that kept him from completely falling. "Alex, no sane person gets between you and food. Period."

When we sat, our seating arrangement differed from earlier. It no longer looked like anyone was taking sides. Alex stepped over the attached bench but didn't sit right away as he perused the sweet choices. Moist-looking, fudgy brownies, some kind of cookie bar made with Rice Krispies, lemon bars, and something in a cake carrier, but we couldn't see the contents with the plastic top still covering it.

"What are these?" Alex asked, his hand hovering above the crisped rice bars.

"Scotcharoos," Jamie said. "They're made with Rice Krispies and peanut butter. The frosting is made of melted chocolate and butterscotch chips. It's a required dessert at all fire department functions."

"I can attest to that," Drew concurred. "It's always the first dessert gone."

"Why did we bother with lunch?" Dad asked as he snagged a Scotcharoo from the plate. "I'll test these to make sure they're okay to consume."

Holding the square up to admire it, he then sank his teeth in, closed his eyes and made noises to indicate his pleasure as he chewed. After he swallowed the first bite, he opened his eyes and saw all of us staring at him.

"Safe," he declared, raising the remaining part of the cookie toward the sky. "Dig in."

Our hands and arms crossed and weaved like the game of Twister as we reached for the different cookies. At the same time, Mom removed the cover from the cake carrier to reveal three layers of chocolate cake with a caramel-colored frosting full of coconut and pecans. I'd never seen Mom make this dessert.

"What kind of cake is that?" Alex asked in between bites of brownie.

"German chocolate," she answered.

Out of the corner of my eye, I saw Drew jerk around in her direction. And what surprised me was that Mom looked directly at him.

"If I remember correctly," she said, "it's Drew's birthday next week."

There was a long moment of silence when he didn't respond, but Angela did. "Yes, it's Thursday."

"So what's so special about a German chocolate cake?" Alex asked, as usual oblivious to a dramatic moment.

Mom's eyes were still locked on Drew's. "It used to be Drew's favorite. I made it for his homecoming party when he was discharged from the Marine Corps."

He cleared his throat and looked up toward the tops of the trees for a moment. No one moved, not even Alex, this time. No one said anything. It was only seconds, but it felt a lot longer.

Finally, I heard Drew drag in a deep breath and let it out slowly before clearing his throat again.

"And that's the last time I had it. Thank you, Nikki." His voice was low and strained. "I haven't had it in years."

At least twelve or thirteen years was my guess. The shock of Mom's thoughtfulness caught us all off guard. No outward gesture could have said more than the peace offering this special cake symbolized.

Dad spoke up in a jovial tone. "I told her not to put candles on it or you'd have to get your fire extinguisher to put out the fire."

It was the right comment to make us all laugh. Not that it was that funny, but it was an interruption that we needed.

I turned to Drew. Had I ever had this opportunity or was I too young to realize? "Happy almost birthday. I hope it's the best ever."

He scrubbed his knuckles across his chin and smiled. For a moment I thought I caught a glimpse of mistiness in his eyes. "I think there's a good chance of that," he said quietly. Then he added in a brighter tone, "So let's eat cake."

I continued to stare at him as the moment registered in my brain as yet another positive turning point.

In Drew's honor, we all tried a piece of the cake. Even Alex, the fussiest eater in the world, gave in to one bite. By the quick way he chewed and then chased it with a big gulp of Gatorade, I knew he didn't like it. He slanted a glance at me as if he thought I would make a snarky comment, but the day was going too well for me to rattle any chains. There was no way I'd do or say anything to spoil this moment.

It wasn't until I lifted the last forkful of my slice of cake that I jumped into the conversations happening around me. Before that, I'd been content to be a *watcher*.

"So, Alex, can you ride home with Mom and Dad? Drew and I are going to the barn."

That question and statement brought the side conversations to a screeching halt, and all heads turned in my direction.

I shrugged, pretending the comment wasn't out of the blue. "He said he'd go on the family weekend trail ride with me. He needs to get to know his horse."

Dad nodded. Angela stared at Drew, but no one else reacted.

"Dad," I said, turning to him, "This doesn't change your plans. I still want you to come to the overnight. I hope you will."

He smiled, looking relieved. "Of course, honey. I wouldn't miss it."

"Awesome!"

I moved my knee against Chase's leg under the table while sliding the last piece of my cake into my mouth. He knew that I was going to ask Drew. He also knew this was a major victory for me.

Charlotte slid off her end of the bench. "I'm sorry to leave early, but I have a training session a little later that I have to get ready for. What can I do to help before I leave?"

"We're good," Mom said. "There's not much left to do."

"Thanks so much for the invitation," Charlotte said as she picked up the plastic bowl she'd brought fruit salad in. "It was a lot of fun." She started toward Jem.

At the same time, Drew spoke up. "Wait, I'll take Jem for you." He maneuvered himself off the bench and went to the dog, taking her off the tie out and snapping the leash on her collar.

I nudged Chase with my elbow, and when he looked at me, I raised my eyebrows and offered a hopeful look. Maybe this was it.

While the others continued eating dessert, I watched Charlotte, Drew and Jem walk toward the parking lot, my mind buzzing. Would Drew ever accept Charlotte's offer for him to foster Jem for a few weeks? She'd been nice enough to agree to my plan. Now Drew needed to do his part.

"Want anything else?" Chase asked as the plate of brownies passed in front of me.

"Um, no, thanks." Right now, with the little knot forming in my stomach, I couldn't eat another bite of anything. Even a brownie.

The idle chatter at the table was white noise. Once they reached the parking lot, Charlotte took Jem's leash and led her to the back door of her car.

The knot in my stomach morphed into a rock.

I turned toward Chase, grabbed his hand under the table and squeezed. "I was sure Drew was going with Charlotte to tell her that he wanted to take Jem home. They were so good together today."

Chase smiled and leaned next to my ear, pressing a quick kiss there before Mom and Dad noticed. "Relax. Not everything is going to happen on your timeline."

"I know," I whispered, but the words almost choked me. Chase didn't know about the text message I received from Phoebe this morning that made me all too aware of my lack of control over some very important things. The people interested in Lacey were pressuring her for a decision. Even though she wanted to be fair to me, she also couldn't lose almost eight thousand dollars.

Tick! Tick! Tick!

The way everything was falling into place, I couldn't imagine anything going wrong now. Unless I ran out of time.

CHAPTER 19

"Whoa, Savannah! *He's* your father?"

I whipped my head toward Phoebe as she sidled up next to me along the wooden fence lining the outdoor ring. This was the first she was seeing Drew as he took Buster, Phoebe's bay Quarter Horse, through his gaits.

I let my mouth drop open for dramatic effect, but a grin took over. "Phoebe, you're married!"

She smiled and nodded toward Drew. "I'm referring to the way he rides. Your father's no novice on a horse."

Dust kicked up behind Buster as Drew took him through figure eights in the center of the ring.

Pride bubbled in my core. "Yeah, I had no idea he rode *this* well." It was cool to have a father who shared my interest in horseback riding.

"He's good." She lifted her right hand to the side of her face to shade her eyes from the setting sun. "Did he commit to coming on the family trail ride next weekend?" Phoebe asked.

I'm sure my face lit up when I nodded. "He said as long as he clicked with Buster, he'd go." I looked back toward the horse loping along the side rail. "It looks like he'll be going."

Drew slowed Buster to a jog when he saw Phoebe standing with me, then stopped in front of us. Buster tossed his head, not happy to stop moving.

"Whoa, boy," Drew said, settling himself more into the seat of the saddle. Yeah, he knew what he was doing on a horse, for sure.

Phoebe stepped on the lowest fence rail and leaned across, extending her hand up toward my father. "Hi, Drew. I'm Phoebe. It's so nice to finally meet you."

Drew nodded, then stretched to meet her hand. "Likewise."

She stepped back off the rail. "So what do you think of Buster? Will he work for you on the trail ride? We'd love to have you join us."

"Looks like he will." Drew leaned over and patted Buster's neck. "I haven't ridden in a couple of years, so I wanted to make sure of what I was getting into."

"You look great on him," I said. "No one would ever know it's been that long."

He smiled. "Thanks, kid. And now, before I succumb to an unmanly blush, I'm going to ride off into the sunset."

Drew saluted, then wheeled Buster toward the center of the ring. In two steps he had him in a comfortable lope and moving toward the far end.

I stared at his retreating back, trying to process what he'd said. Had he called me "kid" in a warm, fatherly way? I couldn't imagine him using some sweet endearment, but the way he said this one word sounded warm. Or was I reading too much into it?

In the midst of my musing, Phoebe tapped me on the arm. When I looked at her, she wagged her eyebrows and fanned her face with her hand.

"It's too bad I don't know any single women to introduce him to," she whispered, then turned toward the barn, continuing to fan herself as she walked away from me.

I burst out laughing. "Phoebe! Come on! You're embarrassing me. Besides, I think he and Chase's mom may have a future together."

"Good for her. If she's lucky, he's as good a guy as Ross is."

Ross, her husband, didn't ride with us. His job was to take the supplies for the campers and horses to the site. He always spent the night at camp, bringing along a harmonica and guitar to entertain us cowboy-style.

I heard the soft rhythmic sound of Buster's feet on the hardened outside area of the ring as Drew brought him closer. I turned back toward them.

"Nice horse," Drew said. He glanced toward the sky. The sun was still above the trees, but definitely on its downward trajectory. "Do you think Phoebe would mind if we went for a short ride in the woods so I can see what he's like on the trail?"

"She wouldn't mind at all." I headed for the gate so I could let them out. "I can have Lacey saddled fast."

I waited for them to exit, then re-latched the gate. My thoughts buzzed with wanting to share what was on my mind. My biggest fear was that I would do or say something that would make my father back away from Alex and me. But I decided I wanted him to know how I really felt. I hurried to catch up to them, then I took hold of Buster's reins and stopped him.

Drew looked startled, but I needed to share my feelings before I chickened out, and I needed to see his face to see his initial reaction.

"I want you to know how happy I am," I blurted. "I feel happier than I have in a long time."

He inhaled deeply, lifting his shoulders up with the breath and letting them drop slowly as he exhaled. A stab of regret pierced my chest. Why hadn't I kept my thoughts to myself, even though they were positive?

I took my hand off the reins, feeling foolish. When I started to drop my chin, he spoke.

"And I want you to know how happy I've felt all day, Savannah."

My head shot up to meet his gaze. "Really?"

"Yes, really. And," he added, "I think what I'm about to ask you is going to make you even happier."

I furrowed my brow. "Go ahead."

"I wondered if you would go with me to CharTay Kennels after we're done riding."

"Does this mean what I think it does?"

He smiled. "If you're thinking that I made arrangements with Charlotte to pick up Jem tonight, then, yes."

My excitement got the best of me, and without thinking, I grabbed hold of his pant leg and shook it. "Oh my gosh! This is amazing."

"It's temporary, because Charlotte doesn't want the dog to bond with Jamie. I've decided to try it, because I can help get her prepared for a handler with PTSD."

I clamped my lips closed, fighting the urge to point out that his struggles for the last dozen or more years were a result of combat-related PTSD. He could use a service dog himself. I glanced at my hands holding onto his pant leg, and embarrassed, yanked them away.

"Maybe she'd be a good fit for you."

He shook his head. "I don't have that kind of cash available. I couldn't afford her. But maybe I'll get another dog, someday."

My hopes crept toward the positive again. I wrangled with the interpretation of what he'd just said. This is what I needed to know. It was what had been weighing heavily on my mind since the first time I saw how a trained dog changed Rashawn's life. How Drew had reacted to Trooper. A dog trained specifically to assist him was what he needed if Alex and I were ever going to be able to spend more than a few hours with him. It wasn't that he didn't want a trained service dog. He couldn't afford one.

But I'd been saving my money for over two years. Maybe I could..

I looked back and forth between Lacey standing at the edge of the pasture and my father. Phoebe had told me I was pretty much guaranteed a scholarship at McDonough College to cover Lacey's board there, so all I had to do was buy her, and everything else for her would be covered while I was in college.

I could still be on the equestrian team, even without Lacey. But could another horse be as good of a partner for me?

The thoughts swirling through my mind made me crazy.

I stepped away from my father and Buster. "I have to get Lacey's halter then I can be ready fast."

Drew nodded. "I'll ride on the driveway while we wait."

"Great!" I said, turning to jog toward the barn. My eyes suddenly stung, and moisture gathered, clouding my vision. Despite the short distance, my lungs protested. Nerves. It had to be raw nerves.

When I rounded the corner to enter the barn, I stopped and bent over, trying to catch my breath. "Breathe and live in the moment," I whispered to myself.

When I felt like I could breathe again, I straightened and continued to the tack area to get Lacey's halter. "You'll figure this out, Savannah," I choked out.

Then my burst of laughter echoed through the empty barn. Now I was talking to myself. Yep, proof that considering all of the choices ahead of me was making me crazy.

It didn't take long to saddle Lacey, but every step of tacking her — putting on her saddle, tightening the girth, checking buckles, stirrups and straps to make sure all was safe, bridling — was a reminder of the possibility that our days as a team were numbered.

I wrapped my arms around her neck and pressed my cheek next to her mane, breathing in the comforting horse scent. God, how I loved this horse.

After a moment, I patted her shoulder then took hold of the rein.

"All right, girl, let's get going."

Drew and Buster waited at the end of the path that led to the trail in the woods. I mounted Lacey then trotted to them.

"Thanks for your patience," I said to my father.

He lifted a hand in a dismissive motion. "I'm in no hurry."

When Lacey and I came up next to them, he reined Buster around so we could walk side by side down the path toward the woods. We started out in silence, letting the canopy of green trees swallow us as we moved farther into the woods. Being with him brought back the memory of the day that Chase walked with me and gave me his phone number.

That was before I knew about the demons that had chased my father since he came home from the war. Despite our rough start, now I felt closer to him than I ever had before. We shared the love of horseback riding. Maybe the interest was hereditary.

The stillness was broken only by the crunching of leaves and snapping of tiny, dried branches under the horses' feet. Other than birds flitting between trees and a couple of chipmunks scurrying for cover, it felt like we were the only living beings on Earth.

Maybe that's what emboldened me. So many questions had been swirling in my head for weeks. Out here, riding in our own little oasis, nothing felt off-limits. I ran my tongue along my lower lip, mentally assessing the potential damage to our relationship if my curiosity crossed some imaginary personal line.

But we were alone. I was willing to take the risk.

"Can I ask you a couple of questions that have been on my mind for a while?" I called from behind him.

His back stiffened slightly. and he turned his head to glance out of the corner of his eye in my direction. "Go ahead."

I cleared the little lump from my throat. Which one should I ask first? I decided on the one that seemed less volatile. I'd work my way up to the most important question. I rested my hand holding the reins on the saddle horn like I needed to hang on for the answers.

"How long have you known Angela and Chase? Chase has pictures of us together when we were little kids. Alex and I are in them."

Still half-turned toward me, he twisted his lips and squinted like he was thinking. "About thirteen years, I guess."

"So you met them after I was born? Like, you didn't know his mother before that?"

He gave me a crooked smile. "That would be about right."

I didn't know if that smile indicated he had figured out what I was attempting to deduce by my question, but the relief that washed over me made every fiber in my body feel lighter. Although Chase didn't call Drew *Dad,* ever since that first time I'd seen him getting in Drew's truck to go to his lacrosse game, there was a little tug of uncertainty that played with my conscience every time we were together.

With that concern finally erased over the chance that Chase and I could have been related, I dug a little deeper in my quest to understand more about the time when we had been a family and how all of these pieces of the puzzle of my past, and future, fit together.

"Was it before or after Chase's father was killed?"

The smile dropped and his expression hardened. Tentacles of dread gripped my stomach. My gut said change the subject. My heart begged me to forge ahead until I got the answers. I hurried on before he had a chance to answer.

"I'm trying to understand that part of our lives. There's a big chunk of time from my past that only you know about. Some of this could have an effect on my future. Our future."

He didn't flinch. And, at first, he didn't respond.

"Please. This is important to me. Chase has asked me to go out on a real date this week, but before I say yes, I need to understand anything that could affect a relationship with him."

Drew lifted his chin, looking up through the narrow opening of trees that revealed the sky turning pale.

"I met them after his father died. I escorted his father's body home from Iraq. After the funeral, your mother and I talked about it and vowed we'd take care of them like they were family. They had no one else on this side of the country. It was the right thing to do."

"Angela's in love with you," I blurted out. "How do you feel about her?"

What I wanted to say was, *If Chase and I get serious, is this going to end up weird for us?*

"I have an obligation to her." His voice was low. Pained. "And to Chase."

"That doesn't answer my question. How do you feel about *her*?"

He eased Buster's reins back, halted him, and turned toward me. "It's complicated."

I shrugged as I moved Lacey up next to him and Buster.

"Isn't she worth working through the complications? Have you ever noticed the way she looks at you? She'd walk across hot coals if you asked her to."

He tipped his head and gave me a crooked smile. "You've watched too many romance movies."

I laughed. "Maybe I have, but it's made me more attuned when I see two people in love. I think you should ask her to marry you."

"Why does this matter to you?" he asked.

I nudged Lacey to start walking forward again. He did the same with Buster.

"Because it matters to Chase. He wants to know when he goes to college that his mom isn't alone. And it's clear that he has so much respect for you."

"And you're falling in love with Chase," he said matter-of-factly. "And your first question was because you wanted to make sure he wasn't actually your half-brother, right?"

My first instinct was to argue, but there was no point. Every time Chase and I were together, our feelings for each other strengthened. But that wasn't what I wanted to talk about.

"I'll admit there was a little bit of me that worried about that, but he's not, and you're deflecting," I countered.

"Yes. But I'm also right about your feelings for Chase."

"Maybe. And I suppose that's your way of telling me you're not taking the conversation any further?"

"Pretty much." He rubbed the palm of his right hand along the leg of his jeans. Sweaty? Was I making him nervous?

I studied him for a minute. Okay. I'd opened the door. I'd walk through it another time. That question was merely a warm-up for the more important one anyway.

"One more kind of personal question?" I asked.

He gave me a wary scowl. "Like that first one wasn't personal?"

"That one was kind of rhetorical, actually."

Buster snorted. Drew reached down and patted him. "My sentiments exactly, buddy. I think we've been ambushed."

His choice of words sent a little chill down my spine. He was joking, but my next question couldn't have been more serious.

"So," I said, dragging out the word, "Alex and I would like to spend more time with you."

"We've been spending more time together."

"Spend more time with you at your house." I hesitated, then amended my comment, "*Our* house."

I could tell by the look on his face that he understood what I meant. Even though we hadn't lived there in years, his house *was* our house. Our bedrooms hadn't even been changed. Somewhere deep inside, I was sure he'd always wanted us to come back home.

He stared at me. "It takes time."

"It's going to take something else, too."

He quirked an eyebrow at me. "What's that?"

I'd come this far, I figured I had nothing to lose by being direct.

"You have to get rid of any guns you have."

His jaw tightened.

I gulped against the saliva that flooded my mouth, praying that that one demand hadn't just unraveled the relationship we'd been slowly knitting together. But, for Alex, and really, for me, too, a gun in his house was a roadblock to moving forward.

"It's gone." Although it was only two words, they were thick with emotion. His Adam's apple bobbed before he added, "I got rid of it twelve years ago."

At a loss for words, I drew in a deep breath and let the relief wash over me. We were up one more rung on the ladder of hope. I wouldn't give up until we reached the top, because the top was Alex and me finding our way back home.

For a few minutes the ride was silent, but slowly we eased back into conversation when I started filling Drew in on what to expect on the trail ride. My questions hadn't scared him off. In fact, once he started talking again, it was as if that difficult topic had never been discussed. I took my cue from him. That discussion was behind us.

After we got back and turned the horses out to pasture, I followed Drew and his truck to CharTay Kennel to pick up Jem. We drove separately since we had to go in opposite directions.

I was so giddy that I couldn't keep still as I drove. Relief about the gun. Excitement that he was willing to give Jem a try. Nervousness about what it would mean if the opportunity rose for her to become his dog permanently. Maybe he wasn't planning on it being long-term, but if Jem made a difference for him, then my decision was made.

I gripped the steering wheel with one hand while I tapped out the rhythm to the song on the radio with my other. Except, I did it with more energy than the song generated. Even my left leg bounced with pent-up energy, something that never happened.

Today had been a pivotal day.

When we pulled up, Charlotte sat on her porch steps, with Jem lying next to her on the top one. The driveway gravel crunched under our tires, making Jem lift her head and ears. She shifted her body so her side was pressed against Charlotte's leg — I assumed a natural protective instinct. If all went well, her loyalty and protectiveness would shift to Drew. And, maybe then, we could start the next chapter in our lives — reunited family chapter.

Charlotte waited for us to park and get out of our vehicles before she signaled Jem to get up.

"How was your ride at the barn?" she asked as we approached.

"Great!" Drew answered.

"We found out he was understating his riding skill," I said.

Charlotte held a palm up to Jem and walked off the porch, but Jem remained in place. "Well, then maybe this is going to be a surprising day all the way around," she said. Looking directly at Drew she added, "As I said at the park, taking Jem is a commitment to more than feeding and walking her. Over the next few months, you and I will work on the basics that would be specific to someone with PTSD."

He straightened and widened his stance. Defensive reaction? "Understood. I've completely cleared my schedule for the first two weeks."

Charlotte nodded, then turned to Jem, motioning her to come off the steps and stand next to her. The dog did as commanded and stood with tail wagging and tongue lolling out of her mouth. It was clear that she was listening to Charlotte, but it was also obvious that part of her attention was on Drew, almost as if she were assessing him.

"I'm going to have Jem go with you, but I'm going to follow you to your house. Before I fully release her to you, I want to see what her living conditions will be like."

"She has to be okay with cats," Drew said.

"You have a lot of cats?" Charlotte asked.

"Ferals. I started a program with some local veterans to build houses for feral cats. We also work in conjunction with a rescue group to trap, spay and neuter."

A smile lifted Charlotte's cheeks. "Really?" She pushed her hand through tendrils of red hair that bounced across her forehead. "That's commendable."

"Maybe," Drew responded. "But, more than that, it's therapy for the vets. Something positive that we can do to help make lives better — those lives happen to be cats."

Charlotte clipped a leash onto Jem's collar. "Well, Jem couldn't care less about cats. So, game on." She held the end of the leash out to Drew. "Let's do this." Charlotte started to walk away, then pivoted. "She should always sit in the back seat."

"Okay. Let's go, Jem." Drew turned toward his truck, and Jem didn't hesitate to follow. When he opened the back door to let her into the cab, she leaped up and in as if she'd done it before. He settled her in, then turned to me. "Thanks for everything today, kid."

There it was again. Kid. There was definitely warmth in that. I gave him a thumbs up. "Maybe you can text me pictures so I can see how the two of you are doing?"

He returned the thumbs up. "Will do." He climbed in the cab and closed the door. He twisted toward the back to check on Jem, then straightened and started the truck. I signaled to him to roll down his window.

"What's up?" he asked.

"I don't know what Chase has planned for Friday because he's calling it a *mystery date*, but maybe we can stop over to your house."

For a second he hesitated, then a tentative smile lifted his lips

"Sounds good." He reached for the shift lever. "I'll have mint chocolate chip ice cream and hot fudge sauce from Seneca Farms waiting."

Nodding, I took a few steps back toward my car so he could pull away. A warm glow spread through my body as I waved goodbye. The offering of the ice cream was a little thing, but to me, it proved he cared.

"And, Savannah?" he called through the window.

"Yeah?" I wondered if that quickly, he had changed his mind.

"Let's see if we can work it out so Alex can come for ice cream, too."

I nodded, stunned by how this relationship was changing.

I thought of Lacey. Of the McDonough College Equestrian Team. The dreams I'd nurtured and worked toward. And a tiny ache gripped my heart.

Those dreams were before I realized there was a chance I could bring my family back together.

As Drew drove off with Jem, I had to face the truth. Sometimes the right decisions were the most difficult to make.

CHAPTER 20

My heart fluttered when my phone dinged with a message from Chase. I figured he was sending an update on what he deemed would be our mystery date tonight. But when I clicked on the text, what he'd sent was far from that.

Instead, a photo of Jem flying through the air with Drew a bit blurry in the background popped onto my iPhone screen. There was Jem, golden body with front paws and legs extended in front of her like she was flying like Superman. Her eyes were big, bright and sparkling. She was in doggie heaven.

My fingers flew across the tiny keyboard.

fun...back at state park?

Yeah, came Chase's response. *Mom and I kayaking. Drew on shore throwing ball for Jem*

Chase in a kayak explained the perfect head-on shot of Jem launching from the dock. I could picture the scenario now. When we were all by the water before our picnic over the weekend, I noticed Drew staring at a kid whose dog was running and leaping off the end of the dock a bit farther down the beach, retrieving a Frisbee the kid had thrown. For several minutes Drew had seemingly blocked out that there was anyone else around except that dog and the boy. And his smile was almost wistful.

Drew said he invited Alex on Saturday Chase texted. *We can pick him up on the way back to the house*

OK I answered. *Thanks.*

I'd wondered how to get Alex to Drew's for ice cream without asking Mom and Dad to drive him out, which still felt awkward. I didn't know what Chase had planned for our date, but I was relieved to know Alex wouldn't miss this opportunity to be with our father at our old house.

A series of texted photos followed. Drew sitting on the grass above the beach, his arm across Jem's shoulder with the dog tucked against his side. Drew squatting at the edge of the water, his hand under the surface and Jem next to him, staring intently at whatever Drew was doing. Still shots of Jem taken in quick succession as she bounded down the dock preparing to leap into the water.

I tapped the screen so I could zoom in on Drew's face in one of the crisper shots. I hadn't seen or talked with him since he picked up Jem. When I saw Jamie at the stable a few days later, she told me that Drew and Jem were doing great with the training Charlotte required. And, as I requested, Drew had sent me a couple of text photos from his house of Jem curled up in a dog bed on the floor or stretched out on his front porch, but I'd had nothing of them together.

These pictures told the story. The tension lines in my father's face were gone. The corners of his mouth tipped up a little more. I swallowed against the growing lump in my throat. In truth, I wasn't sure if this was making my decision harder or easier.

I swiped at a tear that trickled from my eye. This wasn't about me. This was about a possible future for our family.

"Have you figured out where we're going for the first part of our date?" Chase asked after he'd been driving us for more than half an hour. We'd been talking, but not about his plan for this afternoon.

I scanned the wooded hillside, looking for clues. "Are we going hiking or having a picnic in the woods?"

"Nope," he said, a satisfied smile lighting up his features. "Since you still don't know, close your eyes and cover them with your hands." He clicked on the signal light to turn left off the windy road we'd been ascending.

I shifted in my seat to look at him. "What?"

He tipped his head and gave me a quick look. "Come on. I want to keep the mystery going a little longer." He returned his attention to the road, then quickly added, "And look down toward your lap so I know you can't see anything."

"I only see trees and houses here and there, anyway," I retorted.

He gave me another sidewise glance, and I grinned before closing my eyes, covering them, then tipping my face toward my lap.

"There. Satisfied?" I said, sounding like a petulant child.

"Yup," he replied. The tone of his response made it clear that he was having fun.

I stifled a giggle. If it weren't for the fact that I totally trusted him, the mystery date thing would have made me uneasy. Surprises weren't my thing.

We rode for a couple of minutes in silence. I wondered how long I'd have to keep my eyes covered.

"Drew invited us to stop over for ice cream when we get back," I said, breaking the silence . "Did you know that?"

"Yeah. We'll be back in time."

Chase slowed the car, and I heard the signal light come on again.

"Can I uncover my eyes yet?"

"Nope."

Less than a minute later my body leaned in the seat as he apparently pulled into a parking space.

"You're lucky I don't get car sick anymore," I said. "If you'd asked me to do this when I was ten, I would have been throwing up all over the floor."

He laughed as he cut the engine. "Thanks for telling me now."

I heard fabric on fabric as he moved in his seat.

"Don't uncover your eyes yet. Obviously, this is phase one of our date. If you're afraid of heights, tell me now, and we'll bypass this part and move to phase two."

I laughed, giddy about his fun nature and desire to keep details of the date a secret. "There are multiple phases to our date?"

"Just two, not counting ice cream sundaes with Drew and Mom later."

I startled and sat up straighter when his fingers came to rest on the back of my neck. Little currents of energy heated my skin where he touched me. "I don't want this to be an ordinary date," he said, "but I also don't want you uncomfortable in any way."

The urge to uncover my eyes was strong. Was he going to kiss me? If he was, I wanted to see his eyes as he got closer.

"Well, it's definitely not starting out ordinary. When can I open my eyes?"

"After you tell me if you're afraid of heights.

My curiosity was definitely heightened. "Ordinarily, no. But since I don't really know what you're referencing right now, I guess a little more information would help me answer."

He grasped my hands and lowered them. "Okay, go ahead and open your eyes."

It took a minute for my eyes to adjust to the light again, but I looked ahead toward a canopy of trees. Then, I saw the sign for the aerial adventures.

"Oh my gosh! Is this one of those ropes challenge courses? Are we in Bristol?"

"Yes, we're in Bristol. And, it's kind of a ropes challenge course. It also has zip lining. I've never been here, but I thought it could be something fun and exciting." Then, he added quickly, "Does this change your answer about being afraid of heights?"

"Hmm," I said, tapping my fingers against my lips. "I race around a ring on a half ton animal, and you think I'd be afraid of heights?"

He laughed and squeezed my shoulder. "Point made. Let's go."

Chase hurried from the car, and before I had climbed from my seat, he was already at my door, holding his palm toward me. I'd never met more of a gentleman. The thought flashed through my mind that maybe my father's influence had contributed to this.

I accepted his hand, and we walked with our fingers clasped on the way to the building to buy our tickets. This felt natural and comfortable. It made my heart sing.

A family with three teenage boys exited the ticket building as we entered. The boys were poking and nudging each other, making me wonder if they would mess around once we got on the zip lines. Chase bought our tickets, we signed the release forms, and then we proceeded to the staging area.

We were each outfitted with a pair of leather gloves, helmets, a carabiner and a snug harness that guaranteed we wouldn't slip out. Once the rigging was secured on me, I slapped my gloved hands together, the leather making a hollow sound.

"This is so exciting," I said, energy bubbling inside me.

"Yeah." Chase's response was unenthusiastic, his lips drawn in a tight line. His attention was on the lines overhead. There was a group of four, two guys and two girls who looked like they were in their mid-twenties, already starting out. One of the girls looked hesitant and the others took off before her. Finally, with the help of one of the park workers, she was confident enough to make the leap to start sliding along the line with no footing below her. As soon as she was off the platform, her scream pierced the air.

I couldn't miss the way Chase's glance darted from the platform to the line that got lost in the trees. He swallowed so hard that I heard it from a couple of feet away. I stepped closer and slid my arm under his and across his back, patting his side in a reassuring way.

"Hey, are you sure *you're* okay with this?" I asked.

He gnawed at the inside of his cheek as he studied what we could see of the course. After a moment, he exhaled a loud breath, put his arm around me and nodded.

"Yeah, let's do this." His voice wasn't strong, but he jutted his chin up a bit to prove his bravado.

Considering this was his idea, I was surprised that he was having second thoughts, but I decided not to point that out. There was no way that I'd embarrass him.

Our guide, Bridgette, must have picked up on Chase's hesitancy. "Have you ever done anything like this before?" she asked as she checked both of our harnesses one more time.

"I did the ropes course at Keuka College during camp one year," Chase said, and then looking up again, added, "but I've never done zip lining."

"That's okay. If you've done a ropes course, you're already one step ahead of a lot of people who come to do this."

Bridgette turned to me. "How about you?"

I shrugged. "Nope, but I'm excited to try." I hoped my confidence would boost Chase's.

"Well, I saw you watching the four who just left," Bridgette said. "They're regulars, so that's why they started off on something more challenging. I'll show you the options, and then you pick your comfort level, okay?"

Chase and I looked at each other and nodded. "Sounds good," I said.

We followed Bridgette past the two courses that were clearly for the younger kids, or at least for the less adventurous visitors. She explained each of the levels as we walked and eventually stopped at one where the platform wasn't too high up.

Bridgette turned to us. "First, I'm going to give you an orientation before you go onto the full course. I want you to have an idea of how it will feel when you're zip lining on the higher courses."

Within minutes of the orientation, I could see the muscles in Chase's shoulders and neck relax. By the time Bridgette finished, Chase's smile was genuine — matching mine.

"This is the central station," she explained. "Everything starts here."

It only took her a minute to snap the cables on both of us.

"I'll travel with you, leading the way," she explained. She double checked each hook, then declared us ready.

We followed her up the heavy wooden ladder to the platform, awkwardly maneuvering around the cables. Another worker greeted us there.

Once we were in place, I looked out across the zip line path cut through the forest. The cable stretched high above the ground, and I could only see part of the ride down because a good length of it was obscured by the canopy of trees.

"Ready?" Chase asked me. He rolled his shoulders forward and blew out a loud breath before stretching his arms out in front of him and shaking out his hands.

I smiled and nodded. "Looks like I'm more ready than you are, though. Are you okay with this?"

His return smile was weak. "I'm good." He turned to Bridgette. "Let's get going before I have any more time to conjure up images of the worst case scenarios."

Bridgette and I burst out laughing.

"You're going to be perfectly safe," she said, checking our harnesses one more time now that we were on the platform. "Who's going first?"

"Me," I volunteered.

She guided me to the edge of the platform. "Okay, remember what I taught you down below, and have a blast. Just do what I do." The other worker checked Bridgette's harnesses one more time, then Bridgette stepped off the edge.

The cable whined as she whisked toward the next station.

I grabbed hold of the bar attached to the cable over my head. An adrenaline rush of anticipation shot through my veins. Every inch of my body was jittery. With a quick nod to her and Chase, I took the leap that sent me whizzing along the cable. A tiny squeal of delight escaped my lips as the wind buffeted my cheeks. For the first few seconds, I was tense, but I forced myself to relax and take in my surroundings for the brief time that I'd be suspended above the earth.

The friction of the pulley riding atop the cable created a high-pitched whirring sound that masked any other sounds below and reminded me that I was zipping through air at a speed way faster than even Lacey could run. Looking straight out, all I could see were waves of trees of varying heights, their green, late spring leaves covering acres and acres of the side of the mountain. In the far distance, I could see a stand of evergreens whose tops pointed toward the sky. I wondered what kind of wildlife was hidden among the foliage. Halfway along the cable, I looked down to see a deer race across the narrow clearing below and bound into the cover of the dense brush.

As I approached the platform at the other end, I lifted my legs and feet so it looked like I was sitting on air. Bridgette had explained that each section of the course would get progressively higher above the ground and be at a steeper angle to increase the speed. I couldn't wait.

With the platform a few feet away, as we'd been informed, the speed of my descent was controlled by the park worker, a guy in his twenties, who awaited my arrival. When I touched my feet to the platform, my landing was smooth.

I threw my hands in the air for a double high five with him. "That. Was. Awesome!"

Less than a minute later, Chase came in behind me. As soon as his feet were planted on the platform, he fist pumped the air and turned his face toward the sky, letting out the biggest whoop I'd ever heard.

The freedom of flying through the air was exhilarating, and seeing that he was having fun, too, made the experience even more enjoyable for me. I threw my arms around his waist and squeezed myself against him.

"This is the best date ever!" I was embarrassed by the little squeal at the end of my sentence, but I couldn't contain the thrill coursing through my veins.

He hugged me back, then pressed a quick kiss to my cheek. "Then, mission accomplished for phase one."

I stepped back and tugged on his harness. "Yes, mission accomplished. This is definitely no ordinary date."

Looking into his eyes, I felt a quickening of my heartbeat that had nothing to do with ziplining. I'd found my perfect guy.

"That was amazing, Chase!"

When we climbed into his car in the parking lot, I was still on a natural high from soaring through the air along the ziplines. It reminded me of my middle school musical when I played Peter Pan and had to be flown around the stage with a pulley system. Only this was way better, because the zipline rigging didn't cause me to fly into a bunk bed on stage.

Chase turned toward me, and his grin filled his face. "I think *you're* amazing."

He leaned across the seat and gave me a quick kiss on the lips, but when he drew back, he was still close enough that his breath fanned along my cheek. "I'm not embarrassed to say when we first started, I was having second thoughts about doing this, but thanks to your reassurance and confidence, it boosted mine. It was great."

Goose bumps jumped to my arms. Was he talking about the zip-lining or our relationship? Either would have fit at this moment.

I had little time to ponder. His lips met mine again, and my eyes drifted closed. I breathed in his scent — fresh and clean from being immersed in the outdoors. This time we held the kiss for longer. He trailed his hand up my left arm until his cool fingers came to rest against the back of my neck. With a little pressure to move me closer, he slanted his head to deepen the kiss.

My whole body tingled. I'd kissed boys before, but never had it felt like this. His warm lips melted against mine, like we were made for each other. I was a princess. He was my prince. Life was good.

A loud rap on the back window startled us apart. Chase threw his arm across the back of the seat as if protecting me.

We twisted in our seats to see the culprit, a young twenty-something guy with a group of three others who had been behind us on the ropes course.

"Get a room!" the guy yelled, then wheeled around. He and his friends broke into raucous laughter as they headed across the parking lot.

Heat shot across my cheeks, and I dipped my head in case I started blushing.

"Geez, sorry about that, Savannah," Chase said.

I lifted only my eyes to look at him. "It's okay. They're just being guys."

"They're being jerks."

I shrugged. "It's a blip on the radar of life. As my parents often say, there are bigger fish to fry."

He smiled. "Ah, my English teacher would be impressed by your use of metaphors."

I laughed. "Gosh, you must have had an incredible English teacher if that's what comes to mind at a time like this."

"Sixth grade English class. You don't forget the best."

He settled his hand on my jaw and stroked my lower lip with his thumb.

"You know what I like most about you, Savannah?"

"Is it my brute strength?"

He chuckled. "Well, yeah, besides that." He moved his thumb under my chin to lift my face so our gazes met. "I like that you're beautiful on the outside, but you're even more beautiful on the inside. I don't know how your heart fits inside your body."

I chuckled. "That line is definitely a new one." The softness in his expression told me how deeply he believed what he'd said, so I reverted to being serious. "Thanks, Chase. I think you're pretty terrific, too."

"Thanks. I'm humbled, and," he rubbed the backs of my hands with his fingers, "it makes the next question that much easier."

I tipped my head and arched my brows. "And that would be?"

"Would you officially be my girlfriend?"

My heart thumped extra hard against my chest, and my stomach somersaulted. This time I made the move. I leaned forward, pressed a kiss to his lips and said, "Absolutely."

He held his hand up, extending his little finger. "Okay, then let's pinky swear on it."

I couldn't help but laugh as I planted my palm in the middle of his chest and shoved him slightly back. "What? You goof! What's that about?"

"Well, isn't that what girls do when they make promises?"

"I never have, but I'm easy to get along with." I hooked my pinky with his and lifted his hand up and down. "I pinky swear to be your girlfriend, Chase Craig Warner."

His eyes widened. "Ooh, now it's serious if you're using my middle name. You've been listening to my mother yell at me. My father would be proud."

The mention of his father jarred me for a moment, even though I knew his middle name was after his father.

"You're right," I said. "Your father would be extremely proud of the man you've become. I know I'm proud to be your girlfriend."

He smiled and shifted back toward the steering wheel. "Perfect segue into phase two of our date. He put on his seatbelt, then turned the key in the ignition.

For a moment I stared at him, wondering if I'd crossed some uncomfortable line by bringing up his father. His expression gave no hint, so I decided to save any further mention of his father for another day.

I followed suit by buckling my seatbelt. "And is this part of the date also a mystery?"

"Nope." He put the car in reverse. "We're going to Grimes Glen in Naples where we'll enjoy the picnic I brought for us right next to a waterfall. It's the perfect setting to inaugurate us being an official couple."

My happiness soared, making me feel lighter than I had in weeks. With Chase by my side, even the difficult decision that loomed around me like a black shadow felt less painful. I looked out my window and up toward Heaven. *Thank you*, I mouthed.

God. My mother. Chase's father. I wanted to thank anyone who might have had a hand in helping my dreams come true. Now I wished for guidance to do what was right.

There were definitely trade-offs to my dreams. First, I wanted to see for myself that Jem was making a difference for my father. And if she really was, then I'd text Charlotte Taylor later.

CHAPTER 21

"I have the perfect spot for our picnic," Chase announced as we rounded a bend that he said led to the first waterfall at Grimes Glen. He'd brought old sneakers for both of us to change into since a good portion of the walk to get to the falls was through the creek bed. The pair he'd brought me were a bit big, but I pulled the laces as tight as possible.

We each carried a backpack with the picnic supplies Chase had packed, and he carried his guitar in a case.

"To serenade you," he had said with a laugh when he'd removed it from the car's trunk.

I'd never had a guy sing to me before, but the idea sounded very romantic. Chase was full of surprises, and I suspected being his girlfriend would be amazing.

I heard the splashing of the water cascading over the falls before I saw it, so I knew we had to be close. Birds flitted between trees, chirping a warning about intruders, and the occasional squirrel dashed along the shore and up trees. It was like a mirror of the calm that was slowly filling my life.

Chase led the way. Because the terrain was rougher, he took my hand to help me. It made me hope that we'd be crossing a lot of difficult areas.

"Do you come here often?" I asked as he helped me over a small dead tree trunk in the water.

"A few times a year, either with Mom and Drew or some of my friends."

I glanced around. "Is it always this quiet? I mean, we've only passed three other people."

"Since it's close to dinner time, probably everyone else left." He stretched his neck to look past some trees. "Here we are."

I moved up next to him, and after a few feet, we had a clear view of the waterfalls.

"Wow!" I stared at the hundreds of shelves of shale that created the high waterfall. A man and his black lab walked along a flat area on a lower level. "Drew should bring Jem here."

"Yeah, that would be cool." Chase led us to a spot still a bit downstream from the waterfall where there was an area of small, gravelly stones with large pieces of flat stone washed up on shore. A large, barkless tree lay on the bank of the creek.

He let go of my hand. "You okay with setting up our picnic here?"

"Looks great," I said, sliding the backpack off my shoulder. "It's a beautiful spot."

After leaning his guitar against the tree, he took my backpack.

"I don't have fancy food," he said as he pulled what looked like a medium green tablecloth out of my backpack. "A couple of subs, some chips, grapes, and chocolate chip cookies."

"That sounds great to me. What kind of subs?"

"One's ham and cheese, and the other is turkey."

"Perfect," I said, taking the tablecloth from him so I could spread it out on the grassy patch. "And after all that fresh air, I'm starving."

Within minutes we had the food out, and I sat cross-legged on the cloth next to Chase.

"So, how long have you played guitar?"

He swallowed the bite of ham sub in his mouth while he closed one eye and looked up like he was calculating. "Let's see, I was about ten, so seven years."

"That's really cool. What kind of music do you play?"

He tipped his head and gave me a sideways look. "What kind of music do you like?"

"Everything," I said.

He laughed and leaned over to give me a quick kiss. "Well, then that's what I play."

We finished our picnic while sharing stories about friends, classes at school and favorite movies and books. I loved that Chase was so easy to talk with and be around. It comforted me to know, with the decisions I was considering, that I would have him by my side to help me through. There was no doubt there would probably be rough days ahead. As kind and thoughtful as he was, I'd be well supported.

Chase got up from the blanket and took his guitar from the case. He sat on the log next to the water and took a minute to tune the strings before he asked, "So, what's your first song request?"

Facing him from my seated position on the tablecloth, I reached for the grapes while I considered my options.

"Hmm." I tapped my finger against my lips as I thought. "Do you know *Sweet Home Alabama*?"

"Ha!" he said, immediately strumming. "Who doesn't? Can't guarantee that I'll get all the words right, but maybe if you sing along, I'll do okay."

"I'll chime in on the chorus," I responded. I stretched my legs out and leaned back, popping grapes into my mouth as Chase's fingers flew across the strings. He hunched toward the guitar, closed his eyes, and set his jaw as he concentrated on picking out the opening.

From the first chord, he had me. My eyes widened, and my jaw dropped.

"Oh my gosh, Chase! You're amazing." His rendition sounded like Lynyrd Skynyrd's.

He tipped his chin toward me, peeked out of one eye for a couple of seconds and smiled, his concentration fixed, before he was back into it, his head slightly bobbing on the downbeats. Once he started singing, he opened his eyes to look at me. And my heart swelled with the adoration I saw in his eyes.

As promised, I sang along with the chorus. On each line we raised our voices higher and I swayed to the beat. Chase made me feel more comfortable than I ever had with another guy. By the time he strummed the last note I was sure every creature in the woods had scattered because we were so loud.

Chase straightened on the log and rested his forearm on the top of the guitar.

"You are so talented," I said.

"Thanks. I practice a lot."

I grabbed another couple of grapes from the bag I'd all but forgotten while we were singing and tossed them in my mouth, savoring the sweetness. When I looked up, he sat with his mouth wide open.

"What?"

He shot a look toward the bag of grapes. "I thought maybe you'd share. Aren't grapes a food of the Greek gods, or something?"

"And you think you're Dionysus?" I asked, referring to the son of Zeus who was the god of the vine and harvest.

"Sure. I know my mythology," he countered, before opening his mouth wide again.

I giggled and grabbed a grape, tossing it toward his mouth. He dipped his head to catch it.

"Nice job," he said after he'd chewed and swallowed it. "You should play basketball or softball."

I moved up onto my knees so I was kneeling in front of him. "As a matter of fact, I'm a starting point guard on the basketball team. But, I'm not going to push my luck." I took two more grapes from the bag and held them in front of him. "Open up. You can have a couple of more before the next song."

"Your generosity is astounding," he joked before opening his mouth.

This time I stretched on my knees and set the grapes in his mouth one at a time. His eyes locked on mine as he ate them, and the softness melted my heart.

He bent forward over the top of the guitar until his face was inches from mine. "If I'm Dionysus, then you're Aphrodite, because I think I'm falling in love."

My heart pounded.

"I'll catch you," I promised, my voice tight from the air trapped in my lungs.

"Deal," he whispered as he slanted his lips across mine and sealed it with a kiss.

"Alex! We're going for ice cream. Why do you have those with you?" I looked between Chase in the driver's seat and Alex in the back seat, wondering if I'd missed some detail about our visit with our father.

Alex tossed his backpack and a sleeping bag to the other side of the back seat of Chase's car, then climbed in himself.

"Maybe once we're there he'll invite us to stay overnight, too," he said as he slammed shut the back door on Chase's car.

I shook my head and sighed. "Gosh! What are you, eight years old? I wouldn't count on it. Just inviting us over is a big step."

"He's going on the overnight trail ride next weekend," he argued.

Chase glanced in his rearview mirror as he pulled away from the house. "The trail ride's neutral territory, man. I have to agree with Savannah. I don't think Drew's ready for you staying there."

Once we convinced Alex that things might not go the way he was thinking, he and Chase chatted about guy things while my mind drifted back over the day. Ziplining was thrilling, and the picnic by the waterfall was worthy of a plot in a romantic movie. With those positive vibes powering me, I was eager to see if Drew and Jem were bonding.

A haze of euphoria had settled over me by the time we arrived at Drew's house. I unbuckled my seatbelt and turned toward Alex, giving him a stern look.

"You're leaving that stuff in the car, right?"

"Yeah," he answered with a hint of annoyance. He reached for the door handle and shoved his shoulder against the side panel to open it.

Chase and I walked hand-in-hand up the sidewalk.

"This is a whole lot better than the last time we were here," Alex said from behind us.

"That's for sure," I said, my mind flashing back to Drew's anger when he caught us in his house.

When Chase clicked open the wooden gate, one of the feral cats Drew was taking care of skittered off under a bush so fast that I only caught a glimpse of an orange-ringed tail disappearing into the dense shrubbery.

I glanced toward one of the feral cat houses Drew and a couple of other veterans had built under a big tree in the corner of the yard. The fur of a white cat contrasted with the black roof. It flicked its tail in slow motion while it stared at something up in the tree.

"Does my father name these cats?" I asked. Referring to him as *my father* rolled off my tongue so smoothly that Chase didn't even react. But the two words bounced around in my mind like my head was a pinball machine. Would there ever come a time when my brain wouldn't stumble over that reference?

"Yeah, if it's a cat that's really feral and will probably be hanging around for a while."

So he was willing to have some sort of bond with an animal. That was another encouraging sign.

As soon as we reached the top step, the front door swung open. Drew stepped to the opening in front of the screen, with Jem inches from his side. His right hand rested on the top of her furry, golden head.

"Hey, perfect timing," he said, stepping back. "Angela just finished warming up the hot fudge sauce she made. Come in."

He pushed open the screen door and Chase grabbed the frame from behind me.

There was no mistaking Drew's cheerful demeanor. It was as if his edginess had been softened. I shifted my eyes toward Jem as she and Drew walked back toward the kitchen, wondering if her presence was responsible.

Chase let go of my hand and indicated for Alex and me to enter ahead of him.

"So, are hot fudge sundaes a regular thing with all of you?" I asked.

"It's not unusual to do this at our house," he said quietly as we passed, "but this is the first time here at Drew's. Even for us. You're gonna love my mother's hot fudge." Chase didn't miss a beat, but I picked up on what he was trying to tell me. Drew was letting people back into his world.

"Well, I'm excited to be back here," I said.

"Me, too," Alex added.

Drew was ahead of us, wending his way between the coffee table and couch. I couldn't help noticing how his fingers stretched so the tips remained touching Jem at all times. And, by the way his broad shoulders rounded slightly, I got the sense that he was more relaxed than I'd ever seen him.

I tried to act casual, like it was no big deal that I was going inside the house. The truth was, knowing I'd spent four years here, that my life started here with a different family — my real family — was freaking me out a little bit. Unlike the last time I was here, this time Drew was inviting me in, not kicking me out. I wasn't sure how to act, what to say, or where to look. By the tense set of Alex's shoulders, I figured he was feeling the same way.

"We'll make the sundaes in the kitchen, but we'll take them out on the porch" Drew said, popping his head out from around the kitchen door sill.

The sweet aroma of warm chocolate hit me as soon as we started across the room, but that wasn't what my mind focused on. I couldn't resist glancing down the hall toward my old bedroom. An image of my mother carrying a white basket of laundry went through my mind. For a second, I even thought I heard her calling my name.

I stifled a shudder. My imagination was getting the best of me. There was already proof that not all of my memories from my early childhood were lost. No doubt, there would be memory triggers all over the house and neighborhood once I spent more time here. That was if Drew allowed Alex and me to spend more time here. At least this was a start.

I took a deep breath to slow my racing mind as we entered the kitchen. When we entered the kitchen, Angela was taking two containers of ice cream out of the freezer. Mint chocolate chip and fudge swirl. Spirals of aromatic heat drifted up from the hot fudge topping in the saucepan on the counter. Next to that, Angela set a bowl filled with what looked like a cloud of homemade whipped cream.

"The sundae dishes are up on the top shelf of this cupboard," Drew said, stepping up next to Angela. "I'll grab those if you can get the spoons out of the drawer next to the dishwasher."

They worked side by side, elbows brushing against each other as they set the dishes and spoons on the island. Comfortable with each other. I wondered why Drew wouldn't admit that they belonged together as a couple, not just friends. I couldn't imagine what could be so big, after all these years of being a part of Angela and Chase's lives, that it would continue to create a roadblock.

Angela buried a serving scoop in each flavor of ice cream. "Help yourself," she said, interrupting my silent musings.

Again, ever the gentlemen, Chase and Drew took a step back from the kitchen island to indicate that Angela and I should start. At first Alex remained next to the island, but when he noticed Drew and Alex had moved back to allow Angela and me to go first, he joined them.

"Ladies first," Chase said.

Drew signaled for Jem to go to an oval braided rug by the back door. She followed his command without hesitation, circling on top of the rug until she was satisfied with the positioning of her body, which was purposely toward Drew. Comfortable that he wasn't too far away, she rested her muzzle on her outstretched front legs with him in her direct line of sight.

I picked up the scoop and dug into the mint chocolate chip ice cream. "It looks like Jem's settled in with you," I observed while I served myself.

Drew looked at Jem, clearly with a degree of admiration. "Well, we have five training sessions with Charlotte under our belts. They're pretty intense, but Jem's smart and adaptable. Charlotte said all indications are that she'll make an excellent service dog."

"You know what Rashawn said about Trooper. That dog changed his life and even saved him." I moved along the side of the island to spoon the hot fudge onto my ice cream. Angela mirrored me on the opposite side, creating her sundae.

When Drew didn't respond, I picked up my sundae dish and turned to look at him. He was staring at Jem.

"Charlotte said Jem has the potential to do the same," I continued as I added a large dollop of the whipped cream.

Drew lifted his chin and smiled. "So I've heard. A few times." He surprised me with a wink. "Someone's going to be lucky to have her."

The three guys stepped to the island to create their own sundaes. I stood off to the side, waiting.

I used my spoon to move more of the hot fudge to the top of the ice cream mound. "I bet you'd miss her if she left."

Drew focused on putting three scoops of the mint chocolate chip ice cream into his bowl, so his response was a distracted, "Probably."

Because the whole day had left me feeling optimistic, that response was enough for me. Tonight had the potential to be the turning point that I'd been hoping for in my quest to realize the goal of reuniting our little family. For the rest of the visit, I'd watch the interaction between Drew and Jem.

When I followed the others to the porch, I noticed the muscles in my neck tightening with the weight of my choices. Phoebe was getting pressure from the other family who wanted to buy Lacey, and Charlotte didn't want to leave Jem with Drew for long for fear that they would bond. Even though no one except me knew it, I was caught in the middle. I was the hinge to opening and closing the doors of choices.

Alex sat on the top step of the front porch while the rest of us settled into the chairs lined up in front of the railing. Jem, her head up and alert, was lying next to Drew.

For the first couple of minutes we were quiet, except for the occasional murmur of pleasure over the spoonfuls of ice cream and hot fudge. Chase had not exaggerated. Angela's hot fudge sauce was an amazing chocolate, velvety topping.

"So, Savannah," Angela said after a few bites, "you've been on this overnight trail ride before?"

Nodding, I savored the melding of the ice cream and warm fudge as it slid down my throat before I answered.

"This is my third year. It's really a blast. As much as I enjoy the ride, my favorite part is at the campsite. We make a temporary corral for the horses. We have a huge bonfire in a pit that we use for cooking, and then after dinner we sit around and tell stories, play cards, or sing songs. Whatever people feel like doing." I glanced at Drew. "This will be the first time I've had a family member on the ride with me. Dad and Mom never —"

I stopped abruptly, feeling awkward using the term "dad" for my uncle who'd adopted me when my real dad was sitting near me. But Uncle Max *had* been my dad for twelve years. Even if he wasn't my biological father, he was the man who'd been there when my father wasn't.

Angela came to my rescue, probably understanding my temporary confusion and easing me past it.

"Your dad and mom never..." she prompted.

"Um, they don't ride horses. And my mom doesn't camp. So —" I hesitated one more time before forging ahead — "so my dad meets us at the campsite and spends the night. He's going to do the same this year. Everyone likes it because he brings his guitar. Makes it feel like a cowboy camp out."

I was imagining the scene around the campfire when my mind added Drew to the picture. And in my mind, the two dads were sitting next to each other. Had we gotten to that point yet? I turned toward Drew.

"I hope you don't mind if he's there."

He swallowed and shook his head. "Not at all. He should be there."

Dad had also seemed okay with Drew going on the ride. I wondered if either of them would feel differently once they were forced to spend hours together at the camp. I hoped not. I hoped we'd made enough progress in the last few weeks that instead this would be more opportunity to get reacquainted.

Suddenly a realization hit, and I turned to Drew again. "You won't be able to take Jem on the trail ride. What are you going to do with her?"

He shrugged. "I'm trying to work that out. I'd like her to spend the night at the campsite, but I have to figure out how to get her there."

Happiness danced inside me. Whether he wanted to admit it or not, it sounded like he was bonding with Jem.

"I'll take care of her."

All heads jerked toward Alex, surprised by his announcement.

"I'll ask Mom and Dad if you can leave Jem with us during the day," he explained, "then Dad and I will bring her to the campsite that night, and bring her back home with us the next day. I thought it would be cool to camp out that night, too."

I stared at Alex. He'd never shown interest in joining us at the campsite. Had he been thinking about this or was the offer to take Jem an extemporaneous decision?

Drew rested his sundae dish on his knee. "That's thoughtful of you, Alex, but —"

"Really, I want to do it. I'll check with them and see if they'd mind."

Drew studied Alex for a moment before saying, "Well, okay."

"Wish I didn't have lacrosse camp next weekend," Chase said, shifting the direction of the conversation. "I'm not much of a cowboy, but this sounds like fun."

"Next year," I said.

And as soon as the comment crossed my lips, a spark of pain shot through my chest. Would there be a *next year*?

Before Chase had time to respond, a loud, metallic bang from nearby made all of us jump. But Drew was the only one who came to his feet, letting go of his ice cream dish that smashed into pieces on the gray porch floor. Jem launched to Drew's side, nudging his leg and hand.

My heart lurched as I was watched his reaction to the crashing sound. His knees were slightly bent in a defensive position, and his head swiveled back and forth as he scanned the surrounding area. He held his hands out stiff toward us, as if indicating for us to stay still and quiet. I froze, waiting to see how Angela and Chase would react since I guessed they'd had experience with these responses. Angela didn't move, but Chase jumped up and placed himself between us and my father.

"Drew," he said, his voice low and steady, "there's no problem. It was one of the cats knocking over a trash can. That's all."

There was no acknowledgement from Drew that he'd heard him. When he didn't respond, Jem persisted, her nudging turning into forceful pushing until he reacted to her.

He straightened, allowing his hands to drop straight down, with one of them coming to rest on Jem's head. Slowly he dropped his eyes and stroked the fur around her ears. Her nose lifted in the air, and her brown eyes were fixed on his face. Without a sound, she was grounding him. Charlotte had told me about this service dog task, and now I was seeing it firsthand. With a simple nudge, Jem had brought Drew back to the present.

Angela stood and stepped close enough so she could rest a hand on his forearm. "You okay?" Her voice was soft, comforting.

He shifted his attention away from Jem and looked at the spill on the floor — hot fudge and green ice cream littered among pieces of white glass. "Yea, but I need to clean up this mess. I don't want her stepping in glass."

His voice was tight, like the tenseness inside his body hadn't released yet.

"I'll grab paper towels." Angela pivoted and disappeared into the house.

"I'll get a pail of water so the sweet doesn't draw bees," Chase offered as he followed his mother inside.

And then it was only the three of us on the porch.

Alex shifted on the stair so he had a clear view of everything, and his confusion showed in his eyes.

I was glad for him to see that this was what we were up against with our father's PTSD. While we were making incredible progress compared to the first time we saw him, there was still so much for our father to work through. Even if Jem did become his permanent service dog, it would be a long road to travel before our family relationship could become what we hoped for.

I didn't know what to do, so I did nothing but watch. It was clear that Jem was already tuned into Drew. Since I couldn't see in my father's head, I didn't know if the noise had caused a quick flashback to the war or not, but his reaction indicated that. Jem had done her job.

And that's what I had come here tonight to see. I needed proof that what I planned to do was the right thing. Now I had it. If this was the effect Jem had on Drew in just a week, I could only imagine her long-term impact.

A lump formed in my throat. In a perfect world, I could have it all. I could have Chase. I could have my horse. My family would be reunited.

But, my reality was anything but perfect. I couldn't deny the fact that I'd have to sacrifice some of my dreams if I wanted others to come true.

While Angela and Chase scurried to clean up the ice cream and fudge, I set my sundae bowl on the railing and stepped to the bottom of the stairs. I slipped my phone from my pocket and clicked on a new text message for Charlotte Taylor. My fingers were ice cold. It wasn't like this was a sudden decision. In fact, I was sleep-deprived because I'd spent so many nights tossing and turning — my mind bogged down with the pros and cons of the outcome of whatever decision I would make.

"Stay right next to me so you don't cut your paw on that glass," Drew said.

I glanced up one more time at Drew who was again sitting in his chair with Jem flush to his knees, his hand buried in her fur.

My eyes misted over as I pulled my attention away from them and looked back at the keyboard on my phone. Usually my fingers flew across the letters when I texted, but this time my mind whirled, and that slowed down my cold fingers. In the message box, I typed the words to Charlotte that would change the course of not only my future, but hopefully my father's and Alex's, too.

I'll bring you the $7500 for Jem on Monday

She must have had her cell phone on her, because her response was immediate.

U sure?

I responded quickly.

Yes

She and I had talked several times during the week. She knew this was something I was serious about if it came to this decision. Cramming my phone back into my pocket, I tried to picture going to the barn and Lacey not being there. Just the thought made my breath catch in my throat. If it was meant to be, some day I would find another dream horse as perfect for me as she was.

Before there was a chance that anyone might see, I used the back of my hand to wipe away the tears that had slipped from my eyes. As hard as it was, this was the right thing to do, and I had to do it before I had a change of heart.

CHAPTER 22

My face was smeared with tears, and I was sure my cheeks were a red, hot mess. I laid my hand against the bank check for Charlotte in my pants pocket. Doing the right thing didn't make it any less heartbreaking.

I opened the gate to go into the pasture where Lacey grazed up on a knoll with the others. When she saw me, her head flew up and her ears pricked forward. At first, she only stared, but then she started to walk toward me. And the walk turned into a jog, then a full-out gallop. The other horses picked up their heads, and munching on grass, watched her race toward me.

This felt like betrayal. I was her human. Her partner. And I was giving her up.

An ache settled in my chest, and I fought the urge to sob. The effort to tamp down my emotions hampered my ability to take in a full breath. I bent at the waist, my hands on my knees. Maybe I'd never be able to fully breathe again.

"Easy, Lace," I choked out as the dust flew up behind her hooves.

I straightened and stood my ground as she made a wide arc around me before coming to an abrupt halt at my side. She tossed her head and blew out a noisy breath that sprayed me.

"Eww, Lacey," I groaned, stepping next to her so I could wipe my sleeve against her silky hair.

She brought her head around to nudge my hands, looking for a treat.

Rubbing the side of her face, I said, "Sorry, girl. I didn't grab any."

She dipped her head and pushed my shoulder, forcing a laugh from me. "Take that, huh?"

I leaned my head against her neck, closed my eyes and breathed in her warm, horsey scent. I tried to convince myself that I'd get over this. Phoebe had other horses. There'd be another one I could take to competitions. Like, Misty. She was fast and knew her job. I'd ridden her dozens of times over the years. She was a good horse.

My shoulders slumped. But none could compare to the bond that I had with Lacey.

"Hey! What are you doing here in the middle of the school day?"

Phoebe. I rubbed my soaked face against each shoulder and turned toward her.

"Hey!" She said again when she saw I was crying, the tone of her voice and alarmed expression different from the first "hey". Scooting through the gate, she took extra long strides to reach me faster. She took hold of my shoulders and looked me right in the eyes. "What's going on?"

My throat was too tight for any words to come out, so I just shook my head.

She narrowed her eyes. "Is it boy trouble?"

"Ha! I wish," I all but blubbered. "It's Lacey."

I'd confided in her about my dilemma regarding buying Lacey for myself versus buying Jem for my father. To her credit, she'd stayed neutral, offering advice, but not trying to sway me in either direction. In some ways, I wished she had.

A sob bubbled up and came out almost like a snort when I collapsed into her arms. She laid her hands against my back and squeezed me.

"You made your decision, didn't you?"

My forehead rubbed against her shirt when I nodded. One of her hands moved up to the back of my head, and she pressed my face harder against her shoulder.

"Oh, honey, I don't know what to say." Now her voice was tight. I didn't move because I didn't want to know if she was crying, too, although, I suspected she was.

We stood that way for more than a minute until I felt I was under control again. A couple of times Lacey tapped my arm or back with her soft nose, but I couldn't move.

Finally, I took a bolstering breath and stepped back, wiping my face with the back of my hand. I opened my mouth to say something, but stopped, averted my eyes to the ground, and shook my head. Lacey moved up behind me and laid her head across my shoulder, so I put my hand up on her muzzle.

"You crazy horse," I said, then leaned my head against her face.

Phoebe and I laughed - more to cover our pain than because we thought it was funny.

"I know Lacey's been very special to you," she began, "and the two of you have done amazing things, but, Savannah, this decision is the most unselfish act I've ever witnessed. It shows you're mature way beyond your years." She reached out and scrubbed her knuckles across Lacey's forehead before continuing. "It breaks my heart to see you two separated, but she'll still have a great home. She'll still be loved. And I'm sure Tessa will let you visit her whenever you want."

I nodded, considering what she said. Tessa. Although she was three years younger than I was, she'd been competing for as long as I had. I'd seen her ride at competitions. She'd always been great with her own horse. In fact, I was shocked when her parents approached Phoebe about buying Lacey because that meant Tessa had to give up the horse she'd ridden with successful results for four years. But, they thought that Tessa should be challenged with a faster, stronger horse.

"When will you let them know Lacey's available?" I asked.

Phoebe shrugged. "After next weekend. I want you to have her for the trail ride."

"Hmph," I said, rolling my eyes as fresh tears threatened. "Our swan song?"

My mom loved that term, but it had never seemed negative to me. Until now.

"I think it will be good for you," Phoebe said. "And, I'm still going to reiterate that I don't think it's a good idea to keep this from your parents. Seventy-five hundred dollars is a lot of money."

"And, I earned it all myself," I countered, "so it's my decision how to use it."

Phoebe pressed her lips together and tipped her head, but she said nothing more.

"I'm taking the check to Charlotte right now. I have to be back at school for sixth period, so I only have forty-five minutes." I nibbled at my lower lip. "I plan on telling them Sunday night after we get back from the trail ride."

Phoebe shrugged. "This is your gig, but if you want me there for moral support —"

"Thanks." I gave her a hug, then turned to throw my arms around Lacey's neck and press my cheek against her hair. "I'll see you tomorrow when I come to work, Lace."

Walking away was one of the hardest things I'd ever done. It hurt to know our days together were numbered.

"Okay, you have poop patrol for the next nine hours," Drew announced as he handed Jem's leash and a wad of biodegradable doggie bags to Alex. "Have fun."

Alex took the leash and lifted the bags to stare at them. "I charge extra for this," he joked.

"Good luck collecting," Drew tossed back. "And I'm not referring to the little presents Jem will leave you."

I stood a few feet away next to the ring at the stable holding Lacey's and Buster's lead lines, and the expression on Alex's face was priceless. He was loving this banter.

I'd come right after breakfast to pull both of the horses from the pasture so I could feed them, groom them, and have them ready for the trail ride.

"While you two are enjoying this lovely conversation, I'll take Lacey and Buster in and start saddling."

"I'll be right in," Drew said before turning back to Alex and Dad with instructions for Jem and confirming meeting up with us at the campsite. Between the rhythmic clicking of the horses' shoes on the hard-packed dirt driveway and the discussions between the dozen or so other riders who were also getting ready, Drew's voice faded away.

He came into the barn, a cowboy hat perched on his head, as I finished tightening Lacey's girth.

"Nice hat," I said.

Giving me a two finger salute off the brim, he said, "Need to look the part of a cowboy."

"Hope you don't fall off and hit your head, because that cowboy hat's not going to protect your noggin." I was surprised Phoebe wasn't requiring everyone to wear a helmet on the ride since it was a rule at the stable.

"You're right." Taking the pad from the rack by the tack room, he changed the subject. "I'll saddle Buster." He smoothed his hand along the horse's back before setting the pad on him.

"Alex is excited about taking care of Jem for you," I said with a last tug on the cinch strap. I stepped around to take Lacey's bridle from the hook on the wall. "After having Jem around all the time for the last two weeks, it'll probably seem weird to be without her, won't it? Chase said you even take her to work with you."

"I do. Charlotte wants her with me as much as possible." He placed the saddle on Buster's back like it weighed nothing. "I like having her around. She has a calming effect."

Those were the words I needed to hear. A weight that had been on my shoulders since giving Charlotte the payment for Jem on Monday lifted a bit. Knowing she'd be gone soon, I'd ridden Lacey every day this week. And every ride left me questioning my decision, but after I left each night, I'd convinced myself that it would take time, but I'd get over the pain. Hearing my father acknowledge that Jem was having a positive effect, reinforced it.

"Fifteen minute heads up until we hit the trail," Phoebe called from the big double doors.

"I have our saddle bags in the van," I told Drew. "I packed drinks, snacks and lunch for both of us. I'll take Lacey, grab the bags, and meet you outside."

He gave me a quick thumbs up. "It's a plan."

The other riders were already congregating in the driveway, making their last minute adjustments to gear and tack. A few minutes later, Drew and I joined them.

"Savannah, I need you to put these in the saddle bag," he said, handing me two clear plastic tubes with blue at one end and orange at the other.

He must have noticed my frown, because he added, "My EpiPens. Hopefully they won't be needed, but it's very possible we might find bees. I'm giving it to you in case I'm not able to administer it myself."

Even though I was pretty sure I knew what he was implying, I asked, "You want me to give you a shot?"

"Yeah. It's not difficult."

My heart quickened. "I don't know what to do."

"I'll give you a lesson, and if you forget, the instructions are on it."

I'd given horses shots before, but never a human. But the way Drew explained it, I knew in an emergency, I could do it. I took the tubes and put them in a secure place in the saddle bag. I didn't want to take the chance that they would fall out.

Phoebe rode up on her black Morgan, Cali. The horse pranced in place for a moment, eager to start the trail ride.

"Easy, Cal." She patted the horse's neck, and after a few more side steps, Cali stood still.

"I want to give some last minute instructions and safety reminders," Phoebe announced. Because most of us had participated in this trail ride before, it didn't take long to share the information.

"And when we return from the ride tomorrow," Phoebe said, looking past the riders and toward the few family members who were gathered to give us a send-off, "we'll have our trail's end party. Everyone's invited. Bring your families. Bring your friends. Bring your friends' friends. But the most important thing is to bring something to share for the snack table. I'll leave you all to decide who's bringing what. Thank you, everyone. We're hitting the trail."

With Phoebe in the lead, one by one we formed a single file caravan to make our way to the trailhead to begin the twenty mile trek to the campsite.

The ride was a mixture of wooded trails and open fields. When we got to a point where we could ride in pairs rather than single file, Drew brought Buster up next to Lacey and me.

While we continued walking, he stood in the stirrups and stretched his lanky legs. "I bet after this ride, I'm going to discover muscles I never knew I had."

I chuckled. "No doubt. But I'm glad you came along and are willing to suffer later."

The corner of his mouth lifted in a crooked grin. "Suffer, huh? You make this ride sound so appealing."

I shrugged. "Keepin' it real, that's all."

He laughed, and that set the stage for a morning of sharing stories.

He told me about working on a ranch out west with one of his roommates during summer breaks from college and riding camels in the desert in the Middle East during his deployment in the Marine Corps. The way he described both experiences, they sounded like fun vacations rather than hard work and life-threatening situations.

I told him how I had collected horse statues so I could create my own imaginary stable. How Dad loved to bring me back statues after his business trips. About the time Dad had challenged me to a game of pool, and when I won, he bought me a special black glass horse statue that I'd always eyed at the store.

"When I turned eleven, I was convinced I'd wake up on my birthday and Mom and Dad would surprise me with a horse," I explained. "Of course, I have no idea where I thought we were going to keep it since we live in the middle of town. And, I didn't get it anyway, but it never stopped me from dreaming of owning my own horse one day."

As soon as the words were out of my mouth, a stab of pain ripped through me. The realization of that dream had been within reach. I closed my eyes and took a few slow, deep breaths to keep my emotions from surging. It was better to steer the conversation away from talking about horses. After wracking my brain for safe topics, I decided talking about school activities over the years would work.

After awhile I realized I was doing the majority of the talking.

"You must be sick of listening to me," I said. "You're not saying much."

Drew glanced at me, then pushed his cowboy hat back to scratch his forehead at the hairline. "No," he said, his voice barely audible, "I'm not saying much because I'm realizing how much I've missed." He settled the hat back in place just above his eyebrows and swallowed so hard that his Adam's apple pushed far out against his skin. His voice cracked when he added, "And what I'll never get back."

He darted a glance at me, but then looked away toward the tops of the trees, working his jaw muscle hard.

"Should I stop talking?" I asked, wondering if his reaction was sadness or anger.

He cleared his throat and looked back at me. "Absolutely not. Don't leave anything out."

We rode for a few minutes listening to everyone else's chatter, but eventually I relaxed again and while I shared memories, he asked questions.

I noticed when I attempted to ask questions about him, he skirted around many of them.

"I've had some dark years," was his response when I pressed. When he went silent and turned his head to look away from me, I picked up on his cue.

So, I didn't ask any more questions. For now. I hoped the time would come soon when he'd open up to me, too.

After our stop for lunch, we rode another two hours until we came to a pond. Here we stopped, and anyone who wanted to take their horse into the water could remove the saddles and ride bareback into the shallow end.

I dismounted from Lacey and started removing her saddle.

"You going in?" I asked Drew.

He flicked the brim of his cowboy hat back a few inches before he folded his hands over the saddle horn and sat back in the seat. "Uh, no. I'll pass."

"Buster's gone into a pond before, so you don't have to wor—" I broke off mid-sentence, wishing I could click my fingers and start this conversation over again. How insensitive could I be?

"I'm sorry," I said. "Pond. Bees."

"Anaphylactic shock," he added with a grimace. "Yeah, been there, done that. I'd like to take those EpiPens home with me."

I nodded and smiled. "Stay away from the pond."

Since there were four others who also didn't want to take their horses into the pond, Drew had company while he waited in the meadow a safe distance away. From my vantage point in the water I could see Buster munching grass, perfectly content to not be in the water.

We gave the horses a break in the meadow for half an hour before we continued the ride toward our camp in the woods. The Finger Lakes Trail was well marked and easy to follow. In a few places we had to take slight detours around low-hanging branches or fallen tree trunks we couldn't jump over. Through the woods we had to ride single file, so personal conversations were more difficult to hold. But, whenever we were in the open fields and trails, I always made sure that Drew and I rode side by side so we could easily talk with a feeling of semi-privacy.

He felt like he'd missed out on so much of my life, but the feeling was mutual. There was so much about him that I didn't know and wanted to. I took full advantage of having his undivided attention.

By the time we reached camp just before dinner time, everyone was dusty, tired and hungry. The dense woods hid the tiny, rustic cabin that had seen better days, but it was secure enough that the supplies for eating, cooking and sleeping were stored inside for the weekend. The smell of smoke drifted through the woods in our direction, so we knew those who were meeting us here, including Dad and Alex, had arrived and, as instructed, started the fire so it would be ready for cooking.

A little outhouse thirty feet from the cabin was popular as soon as we arrived.

"Let's divide and conquer," Phoebe instructed as she dismounted. "Half of you hold the horses while the other half of us set up our rope corral."

"How 'bout you hold Buster, and I'll help set up the corral?" Drew suggested as he dismounted.

"Sure." I climbed off Lacey and took hold of her and Buster's reins.

It took less than ten minutes for the corral group to use the long lengths of rope to wrap around trees and create a large fenced area where the horses would spend the night. We removed the horses' tack and set the bridles and saddles on a tarp that Dad had stretched out on the ground between the trees. A couple of large tubs had been set up and filled with water that the non-riders had brought. After brushing the horses, we tossed hay that had been delivered at the same time as the other supplies into the corral and left them to rest for the night.

Alex and Jem met us as soon as we left the corral. Jem's ears were up, her tail wagging as we approached.

"Go ahead and let her go," Drew said, squatting and holding his hand out to motion her toward him.

As soon as Alex dropped the leash, Jem raced toward Drew, nearly body slamming him when she got there. He teetered to hold his ground and laughed, lifting his chin to avoid her licks.

"I'm glad to see you, too." He wrapped his arms around her and pulled her against him, using his knuckles to ruffle the fur behind her ears.

"She sure is happy to see you," I said. "And it looks like the feeling is mutual."

"It is." He gave her side a final pat then stood. "This cowboy wants some grub. What's the chow routine around here?"

Alex pointed toward the campfire. "Dad and I and a couple of other parents have been cooking chili, hot dogs, salt potatoes and chicken."

Drawing on my memory, I added, "If it's like last year, there will also be raw vegetables and dip,and apples. Of course, cookies for dessert."

Drew looked shocked. "There's a campfire and no s'mores?"

"Later, when it's dark and we're all hanging round the campfire. That's when we pull those out."

He lifted his hat and wiped his brow. "Whew! That's the only reason I agreed to come on this ride."

"Thanks," I said, feigning disappointment. "And here I thought you wanted to spend time with your daughter."

It wasn't my attempt at levity that caught us all off guard, but rather the fact that I'd casually referred to myself as *your daughter*. For a few seconds none of us reacted. It was Drew who took the lead.

"Nailed it," he said, then shrugged. "I was going for subtle."

"Yeah, me, too," I joked.

"I noticed," he said, then stepped up and put his arm around my shoulder. "Let's get some grub, cowgirl. Come on, Alex," he said, putting his other arm across Alex's shoulder. "Heel, Jem."

With another awkward moment behind us, we joined the others who were putting food out on the three picnic tables near the cabin.

The sun was still up high enough after supper, that the light filtering through the trees made the woods look magical. I sat on the side of the picnic table closest to the fire and relaxed. While there were three or four conversations going on around me, my mind drifted to thoughts of Chase, memories of our first official date, wondering what he was doing, and wishing he were here.

"Hey, Savannah."

I jumped when Alex tapped me on the shoulder from behind.

"Sheesh!" I squeaked. "Don't sneak up on me like that."

He glanced around the circle of people and shrugged. "Sorry. Didn't know you were off in Lala Land. You said you'd show me those waterfalls you saw last year. Wanna go now before it gets dark?"

I stood from the table and looked around. "Sure. I promised a couple of the younger girls I'd show them, too." They were by the corral with the horses. "Olivia. Heather," I called to them. They turned toward me. "Alex and I are going to the waterfalls. Want to come?"

"Yeah," they answered in unison and joined us.

Dad shifted in his position at another table. "Does your phone have signal in case you have a problem?" he asked.

"Dad," I said, giving him the best annoyed look I could, "you're such a worrywart." I pulled my phone from my pocket and checked the signal strength, then turned to face it toward him, even though at that distance it wasn't possible for him to see. "Four bars, but nothing's going to happen."

Out of the corner of my eye, as I tucked my phone back into my pocket, I noticed Drew studying Dad during our exchange. Was he also concerned about us going deeper into the woods? Or was he intrigued by Dad's paternal concern? I'd never know, but it did have the wheels turning in my head.

"Expect the unexpected," Dad added.

Alex rolled his eyes, which was a major no-no when Mom was around, but Dad only laughed. "Someday you'll look back on my words of wisdom and start repeating them yourself to your kids. Watch and see."

That made several of the adults laugh.

"Come on, let's go," I said to Olivia, Heather and Alex.

They followed me behind the cabin to the path that led to the waterfalls. It was longer than I remembered, and at one point so steep and rocky that I was concerned that Dad's worry wasn't unfounded after all. We carefully picked our way down toward the creek, using tree trunks and saplings to keep us from losing our footing and rolling down the fifteen or so feet. At the bottom of the hill, there was a five foot drop-off, then the creek.

We stood at the edge and looked over. Because it had been a wet spring, the creek was wider and deeper than it had been the year before. There was a small area of dry rock bed along our side of the creek. On the other side, the water ran right up against the wall of rock.

"Do we have to go in the water?" Heather asked, her eyebrows furrowed. "I don't want to get my boots wet in case they won't have time to dry overnight."

"We should be able to stay out of the water. Alex, hold my hand so I can look over," I said. He took hold of my wrist, and I stepped closer to the edge and bent over as far as I dared. "I think if we stay up against the rocks on this side," I said, pointing to the natural wall we stood on, "then we'll be good."

I moved back away from the edge, and Alex released my arm, and swapped places with me, except he peered over the edge without me holding him.

"Come on, let's go for it," he said, dropping to his knees, ready to climb over the side.

"What about you two," I asked Heather and Olivia. "If you're game, we'll follow the creek bed back toward the campsite so we don't have to try to get back up here."

"You're sure we'll be able to get back out?" Olivia asked.

"Yeah," I said. Then I heard the thud of Alex landing on the pieces of broken shale on the bank below.

"Come on," he urged. "It's cool down here."

I looked both ways up and down the creek bed. I was pretty sure the falls were to our left. "I'm not concerned, but if you want to go back, that's okay."

Heather looked at the woods we'd come through. "Geez, I'd get lost if I tried to find my way back. I'm sticking with you guys."

Olivia shrugged. "Well, I can't go back alone, so I guess I'm in." Her expression told me she wasn't convinced she was making the right decision.

"We'll be fine," I reassured her.

I helped her and Heather over the side, and Alex kept them from falling into the water. Once we were down in the creek bed, my confidence waned, but I didn't want them to know it. I wasn't positive I'd brought us to the right spot.

"Let's go up this way, because I'm pretty sure the falls are up here."

I led the way, relieved when in a few hundred feet upstream the mini waterfalls came into view.

"Whoa, these are cool," Olivia said.

"Not like the falls at Grimes Glen," I said, "but still beautiful. Come on. Turn around and I'll take a selfie of us with the falls in the background."

We posed for the photo, then spent a few minutes exploring. When I finally looked up toward the sky through the bit of opening above the trees, I could see the sun was starting to set.

"It's going to get dark soon. Let's head back," I said.

Again, I led the way along the creek, keeping one hand on the rock wall to my right. In some spots we had to jump from rock to rock to stay out of the water, but there were only a couple of places where our feet got a little wet.

"Savannah," Heather called. "Is there some place up here where the bank is low enough that we can climb out so we don't have to follow the creek bed anymore? I feel like we must be closer to camp."

Once again I tried to use the sky to get my bearings, but it was nothing but a mass of trees.

"We're close, Heather," I called over my shoulder. I was starting to be able to see up the hill beyond the steep banks.

We'd gone another fifty feet when we came to an spot where the edge looked low enough that we could help each other out. Beyond this area, the sides were steep and unforgiving again.

"Here we go," I called back to them. I stopped and waited for them to catch up. Alex brought up the rear. "Alex, why don't you give me a leg up, and then we'll help Heather and Olivia. The three of us girls should be able to help you up the side after that."

"Okay." He jumped out onto a couple of rocks in the stream so he could get around them. Once he was next to me, he laced his hands to create a step. I put my hands on his shoulder and lifted my leg to put my foot in his palms.

At the top of the bank, I reached out to grab onto a small tree that grew along the edge.

"I need a little more lift," I told Alex, and he hoisted me a few inches higher. I focused on the tree, reaching out until I was able to grab onto it. My head and chest were above the edge. I was ready to pull myself up the rest of the way, but when I took my eyes off the tree and scanned the surroundings, I froze, my breath caught in my throat.

A coyote stood a few feet away, its eyes laser-focused on me.

My heart slammed against my chest. Back! I needed to back away!

I kicked my foot out of Alex's hands, then dropped back down, knocking him off his feet. I heard the splash as he landed in the water with me partly on top of him.

"Savannah, what the hell?" he sputtered, yanking his leg out from under me.

I scrambled to my feet. "Get up!" I hissed, trying not to yell. "There's a coyote right there."

One of the other girls squeaked, but I whipped around to shush them with a finger across my lips. "Shhh! Listen to me." I looked back toward the top where I could barely see the tips of the coyote's ears. "Let's cross to the other side of the stream. Put the water between us. Maybe if we stand still over there, it'll go away."

The hair on the back of my neck and arms was electrified, but I tried to keep calm. Alex and Heather wasted no time in splashing across the thigh deep water, but Olivia was rooted to the ground in fear.

"Come on, cross the creek," I ordered, grabbing hold of her arm and yanking her. She stumbled into the water, losing her balance and falling. I whirled to look up toward the bank at the coyote. It had crept a closer so now even its eyes were visible. "Get up!" I pulled Olivia to her feet and helped her wade across. Because she was smaller, the water was closer to her waist. When we reached the other side, she collapsed against the wall of the stream bank, barely standing, her eyes wide, and tears filling them.

"We have to stay calm," I whispered. I looked up and down the creek bed again. The side behind us was still too high to climb. I knew at some point the bank would be lower if we kept going toward camp, but my gut told me to move away from the coyote. Then a horrible thought popped into my mind, and a shudder shot through me. What if there was more than one coyote?

"We need to backtrack," I said, keeping my voice even, and sounding more confident than I felt. "Alex, keep along this wall, and walk back where we came from."

So unusual for Alex, he didn't argue, but instead followed my instructions. I kept my eyes on what I could see of the top of the coyote's head. To my horror, it moved along with us.

"Alex, stop!" I said in a stage whisper so as not to alarm the animal. "It's following us."

"We're trapped?" Olivia cried. "It's going to get us? It has rabies."

I grabbed hold of her arm and squeezed. "No. Olivia, you have to stay calm, and talk quieter."

"But —"

I silenced her with my fingers against her mouth. "It doesn't have rabies."

I didn't know that for sure, but in my quick face-to-face look, it had appeared healthy.

Alex leaned in front of Olivia and Heather to whisper to me. "Maybe if we make a lot of noise or throw rocks at it, it will run away."

I shook my head. "We can't chance making it angry."

"We can't just stand here," he retorted. "We have to do *something*."

"I'm going to call for help."

I slipped my phone from my back pocket, and with my hands shaking, dialed Dad's number. When he answered, I could hear laughter and voices in the background.

"Hey, kiddo," he said, no hint of concern in his voice, "what's up?"

"Dad," I said quietly, "we're in the creek bed. There's a coyote on the bank. We can't get away because it follows us when we move."

"What? A coyote?" His voice was so loud that I saw Alex react. "Are you alright? Are you hurt? How do we find you?"

His reaction must have quieted everyone around the campfire, because suddenly the laughter stopped and his rapid-fire questions hammered into my brain.

"We're not hurt. The coyote's on the bank above us. Maybe fifteen feet away. I don't know. It's close. We put the water in the creek between us."

"Tell me how to find you," he repeated, the tone of his voice raising with his panic.

I pushed my fingers against my forehead, trying to picture where I had planned on us coming out farther up in the stream. He wouldn't know where to go. He didn't know these woods. But Phoebe and a couple of others did. My mind reeled as I tried to think of the fastest way for them to get to us. It would take too long if they took the same route we had taken toward the falls. Where we were now was much closer to the campsite. They needed to approach from the other side.

"Phoebe will know. Tell her we're in the creek bed a little ways below the small cave. She'll know where that is."

I listened as he called to Phoebe. Now I heard voices in the background again as concern swept through everyone at camp.

"Yes, she knows where you are," he said. "Don't hang up. We're coming to get you."

Dad, who was normally very calm, was almost panting. I could only imagine his fear.

I swallowed hard and looked at the other three. Heather looked like she was in shock. Alex stared toward the coyote, apparently also able to see it now. Next to me, Olivia sniffled and shook. For the moment, as long as she did that quietly, I'd leave her alone.

Even though Dad had me on the phone, he was talking to the others with him. He was breathing hard, and I could hear them breaking past leaves and brush as they ran through the woods. I hoped that the coyote would run when it heard them approaching.

"They're coming," I said. "And as long as we don't move, the coyote's not moving."

"How long will it be?" Olivia whined.

"Just a few minutes, maybe. Not long." In my head I pictured them moving through the woods. What if they ran into the coyote because they didn't know where it was? What if it turned and attacked them? I fought the whirring of horrible scenarios in my mind, concentrated on breathing slowly, and not losing sight of the coyote.

Waiting was excruciating. Ten minutes? Fifteen? Finally, I heard noises in the distance. Phoebe was giving instructions somewhere farther down the creek. The coyote turned its head to stare in that direction. I tensed.

"Dad! Dad, can you hear me?" I said into the phone.

"Yes," he said, out of breath.

"The coyote hears you. You must be close."

I took my eyes off the coyote and turned my attention in the same direction he was staring. At first I didn't see anything, but then, out of the corner of my eye, I saw the coyote move. I looked back quickly. It had taken a step closer to the edge of the bank. Toward us!

A lump jumped to my throat. I turned to the other three and said, "Get ready to run if I tell you."

Olivia pushed against me, her arm pressed to mine.

I looked down the creek bed and saw movement. I squinted, trying to make out what it was. A person. It was a person. Then, I caught a glimpse of the bright orange shirt Phoebe wore on the ride. And someone else next to her.

Then suddenly there was some sort of commotion in their direction. There were several voices, but I couldn't make out clearly what they were saying. Were they giving us instructions? Trying to scare the coyote?

"Dad. What's happening?" I whispered loudly into the phone.

At the same time, the coyote slowly pivoted in that direction. It was no longer focused on us, but I worried that it would go after them.

My heart squeezed. "Dad! It's looking at you."

"Okay," he responded. "We see it."

There was another flurry of activity and raised voices coming from their direction. I leaned forward. I could see what looked like three or four people in the distance, but with the trees and brush in the way, I couldn't tell who else was there.

"Savannah," Dad said, "we see you. Can you move toward us but stay in the water?"

Even though he couldn't details at that distance, I shook my head. "No, we tried that, and the coyote moved with us. The bank is lower the closer it gets to you, so it would be able to jump down here easier." I looked back up at it. "It's creeping closer to us again."

"We have no way of —"

Dad was interrupted by a woman's shrill voice that I heard both over the phone and from this distance.

"Drew, what are you doing?"

The sound of running feet crushing dry leaves and sticks on the bank on our side of the creek startled me. Another coyote? A person? I took a step into the creek so I could crane my neck to see the top of the bank on our side.

In the instant I flicked my attention back toward the group to figure out what was happening, I saw Drew, and so did Alex.

"He's got a gun!" Alex yelled.

"Get down and cover your heads!" Drew ordered from above us.

The coyote startled.

As commanded, the four of us squatted into the water, throwing our arms over our heads.

Simultaneously, the blast of a gunshot echoed through the woods.

CHAPTER 23

Were we all alive? I let my arms slide off my head, and I slowly looked around. Olivia and Heather were still huddled under their arms, but Alex had also turned. His face was powder white, his body shaking.

From above, I heard Drew's tight voice. "Is everyone okay? No one's hurt, right?"

I looked up. He was lying on the ground, the upper part of his body hanging over so he could see us. Loose dirt trickled down from the edge, barely missing my head.

"I - I think we're okay," I answered. "Just wet from the water in the creek."

"Alex!" Drew said. "Alex, are you okay?"

Alex's head turned toward us in slow, jerky movements. Like a robot. His expression blank. Shock? Was he in shock?

"Alex, say something." He stared. "Are you okay?"

His nod was barely perceptible. "Yeah."

Then Drew pulled back from the edge of the bank so we couldn't see him anymore.

Alex shifted his attention to the bank opposite us. "I can't see the coyote."

Taking my arms away from the girls, I looked in that direction. "I don't either." The water in my boots sloshed when I stood on my toes to scan the bank in both directions. "I wonder where it is."

"Do you think it's dead?" he asked. "Where's Drew? Did he kill it?"

I glanced up at the bank to where Drew had been, but he was still gone.

One of the girls whimpered, probably Olivia. I turned my attention to the girls and put my arms around them.

"We're all fine," I said. "We're safe."

Olivia and Heather turned around, too. Tears teetered on Olivia's eyelids, but otherwise, they both looked calmer than I expected.

"Savannah! Alex!" Dad called. And when I looked downstream, he, Phoebe, Ross, and Mrs. Wyllis, Olivia's mom, were jogging toward us the best they could around trees and tree stumps lining the bank.

"Where's the coyote?" I yelled.

They slowed down when they got close to us, but they still had to weave in and out of skinny trees to get to the bank across from us.

"Gone," Dad said. "Drew was close enough that when he shot into the air, it scared it away."

"He didn't kill it?" Alex asked.

Phoebe shook her head. "No. That would be a last resort. It looked healthy." She brushed her bangs off her face. "There are a couple of places in these woods where the coyotes have dens. We think the coyote may be protecting pups."

As much as the coyote had scared us, I was relieved that it hadn't been hurt or killed, especially if it had babies.

"Where's the gun? Was that Drew's gun?" Alex asked.

"No, that's Ross's gun," Phoebe explained. "We bring it to camp, because in the past we've had bears come close during the night. We've never had to use it, but, for safety reasons, we also don't broadcast that we have it."

"Why did *Drew* have it?" Alex asked.

I knew his anxiety about his friend's accidental shooting was the motivation for perseverating about the gun.

"Drew grabbed it from Ross," Dad interjected. "It's okay, Alex. Ross has it, now. As soon as we get you guys out of here, he's going to take it back and lock it in the case, again. He and Phoebe are the only ones who can get it out."

I'm sure Dad was wondering if this incident could set Alex back. He'd had several counseling sessions after his friend's death. Would this ramp up his fear again? I hoped now that Alex was older that he'd be able to process and deal with it better.

I glanced to where we'd seen Drew with the gun. "Where did Drew go?"

The four adults looked down toward where we still huddled across the creek.

"Drew seemed upset," Phoebe said. "He left. Ross is watching to make sure the coyote doesn't come back."

"Left?" My question was covered by Mrs. Wyllis's voice.

"Olivia," Mrs. Wyllis said, and she sidled up behind Dad, "honey, are you okay? Are you all okay?"

Our relieved chorus of, "Yes" couldn't have been more succinct. It was like we were one voice.

"I'm scared. I want to get back to camp," Heather said, surprising me. She'd been quiet throughout the ordeal, following directions and doing exactly what she was asked, so I hadn't known her level of fear. Even now, she was very controlled.

"Getting back to camp is a great idea," Phoebe said.

"Come on," Dad said as he knelt on the edge and extended his hand toward us. "Send up the girls, first. Let's get out of here."

Alex, Olivia and Heather waded toward the other side, but I took a step, then stopped, whirling in a circle in the water.

"Savannah, what's wrong?" Dad asked.

"My phone. I dropped it when Drew shot the gun."

I turned around again, searching the gray rocks under the ripples of water. At first I didn't see it, but then, when I took another step, there it was. Straight down. Under my boot and a foot or more of water, the lime green case looking wavy in the moving stream.

"No!"

I fished it out and frantically shook it to get the excess water off. When I turned it over to look at the front, my heart sank. It was dark. The phone could be replaced. The contacts I could re-enter, but what I couldn't get back if the phone was ruined was all of my pictures of Lacey. Some I'd posted on social media, but many I'd kept to myself. My shoulders dropped as I released a big sigh. Why hadn't I saved them somewhere else? What next?

With Dad helping, we didn't even have to go to the area of the bank downstream where it was lower. He had no trouble hoisting us up as we used the steep bank to walk ourselves out. I glanced around, wondering if the coyote was nearby, but I didn't see it. I wanted to get back to camp and make sure that Alex and Drew were going to be okay.

"Do you know where the coyote went?" I asked, not interested in another encounter.

"It ran deeper into the woods," Phoebe answered. "It could be keeping an eye on us from a distance, but as long as it sees we're moving away from its den, it won't consider us a threat anymore."

Phoebe led the way, and Dad and Alex brought up the rear. I heard them talking, and it seemed like Alex's initial shocked reaction was wearing off. Dad had that calming effect. That's what made him such a good high school counselor.

When we got closer, the others in camp saw us and erupted in a cheer. I scanned the group and then the camp. Drew wasn't anywhere that I could see.

The other campers surrounded us, insisting we had to tell the details of our harrowing ordeal. Most of them took places again around the campfire, but I was worried and couldn't sit still.

"Has anyone seen Drew?" I asked.

My question was met by the murmurs of "no" and shaking heads.

"Where's Jem?"

Phoebe turned and pointed toward a small tree closer to the corral. "When we heard there was a coyote, Drew tied her over there next to his rolled up sleeping bag so Jem wouldn't follow."

"But he needs her. We have to find him." I looked from Phoebe to Dad to Alex. "Where would he go?" I pulled my cell phone from my pocket, my mind whirling. "This fell in the water, so it's dead. I don't have his number memorized."

"I'll call him," Alex offered, and he dialed the number. We stared at him, waiting, until he shook his head and hit the end button. "Not answering."

I turned toward the woods. "We didn't pass him when we came that way." I turned around and pointed in the opposite direction. "So, he must be over in that direction."

I started walking in that direction, but Dad took hold of my arm to stop me. "You stay here," he said. "I'll go find him."

"I want to go, too. I can take Jem to him." I was embarrassed when I realized I sounded like a little kid.

Dad let go of my arm and gave me a compassionate look. "I appreciate your concern, Savannah, but, no. He was really upset when he handed off the gun and walked away. I'll go find him. You wait here with Alex." He held up his phone. "I'll send Alex a text when I find him." He kissed me on the forehead and looked into my eyes with the fatherly love he'd given me for the last twelve years. "It'll be okay, sweetheart."

Dad went over to Phoebe and a couple of the other adults who stood near the fire wrapping Olivia and Heather in blankets to dry them. He pulled Phoebe aside and spoke with her for a minute before continuing farther into the woods.

"I'm going to take these wet clothes off," Alex said.

"Okay." I barely registered what he had said because I was so distracted.

He walked away, and I watched until he'd grabbed his duffel bag and disappeared into the little cabin. It was such a helpless feeling to wait. It also gave my mind too much free rein. I licked my upper lip, my nerves on edge, my thoughts scattered and frantic.

Balling my hands into fists, I silently cursed the circumstances. What if this incident undid all of the progress Drew had made since we had met him? The progress in the two weeks he'd had Jem had given me hope that we'd be able to spend more time with him at his house sooner.

I glanced again at Dad's retreating back, not wanting to lose sight of him and the direction he was going. Everyone else was already back to what I assume they were doing before our excitement with the coyote. No one paid attention to me.

Jem stared into the woods, her brown eyes alert, her body rigid.

Standing here, doing nothing, was killing me. And opportunity was knocking.

Feeling like a thief in the night, I crept toward Jem, trying not to look suspicious or make noise. When I reached her, I knelt on one knee in front of her, stroking her head and neck.

"What do you say, girl?" I whispered. "I think Drew needs you."

I glanced over my shoulder at the others. They were all busy making s'mores or swapping stories, totally oblivious to me, so I untied Jem's leash from the tree.

"Jem, heel," I said, patting my leg. At first she tried to pull in the direction Dad had gone, but I didn't want to be that obvious. We'd make it look like we were walking in a different direction, then I'd make an arc to get back on the path behind Dad. I hoped he'd lead us right to Drew.

With the snapping of sticks and crackling of leaves under our feet, I knew I'd have to move slower once I had Dad in sight again so he wouldn't hear us behind him. I didn't want to take the chance that he'd send us back. We couldn't go back. I was sure Jem would make a difference with Drew.

It didn't take long before we were deep enough in the woods so that I didn't have to worry about people from camp seeing us. I stopped and listened, watching Jem for any clues, too.

"Hey, Drew. You out here?" I heard Dad calling in the distance, so I knew which way to go.

It was like playing cat and mouse. I wasn't good at being sneaky, and my guilty conscience jangled my nerves. I swore every snap of a twig echoed through the woods. Eventually I spotted Dad not too far away, so I pulled back on Jem's leash to slow her down. I picked my way around the trees, keeping a safe distance. One time Dad turned in our direction, so I dropped to a crouch and held Jem against me, hoping Dad wouldn't spot us. I held my breath as if that would keep us from being seen.

He continued forward for a couple of minutes before I heard him say, "Drew, it's me, Max. I came out to check on you."

Dad had found him. I froze, assessing the situation. Should I take Jem to Drew or wait and see how he responded to Dad? Turning my head, I listened to see if they were talking, but we were out of range. We had to move in a little closer.

We approached one slow step at a time. Take a step. Stop and squat. Crouch and take a step. Stop and crouch. I continued this pattern until we were able to get behind the base of a large, uprooted tree, where I took up a discreet position, pulling Jem in close to me again. Her ears were perked, and her attention focused in Drew's direction because she heard him talking.

I peeked over the roots, hoping to hear better. Dad stood several feet from Drew, who paced one way, then pivoted and paced the other. His shoulders were squared off, tense-looking. Like the soldiers at the tomb of the Unknown Soldier in Arlington Cemetery, he looked regimented in his movements.

I heard the end of Drew's sentence, "...what I wanted to do."

"No one got hurt," Dad responded. "You did what you *had* to do."

Drew whirled toward him, and even from this distance, I saw anger radiating from his face.

"Don't say that!" he yelled, throwing his hands in the air. Drew swore, then pivoted away and shouted into the woods. "Those words have haunted me for thirteen years."

My heartbeat kicked up, and the muscles in my neck tightened. I'd never heard him swear. Why was he so angry? Why was he shouting?

"Drew," Dad said, his voice even, "I'm sorry. I wanted you to know the kids are fine and back at —"

As if he hadn't heard Dad speaking, Drew wheeled toward him again, his anger palpable. "Do you know today was the first time I've shot a gun since Iraq?" Drew said, pointing off in the direction of where we'd been earlier. He laced his fingers and pressed them against the back of his head like he had to manually hold his thoughts in. "You don't know what it did to me."

Now my whole body tensed. Jem tugged against the leash, wanting to go to Drew, but I was afraid to let her go because she would alert him that I was nearby.

"No, I don't know what it did to you," Dad said, his voice calm, demonstrating why he was such a good counselor, "but if you want to tell me, I'm listening."

Little bolts of pain shot through my knees from the awkward squatting position. I wanted to stand and straighten my body so my knees wouldn't hurt and my lungs would no longer feel squished.

Drew took a couple of steps closer to Dad. He wouldn't hurt Dad, would he?

"Yeah, I'll tell you. The colonel said to me, 'Son, you did what you had to do' after I'd just shot and killed my best friend."

A little gasp escaped before I could stifle it. I ducked my head back behind the tree root, hoping I hadn't given myself away. Drew had been in the Marine Corps. In a war. He was trained to kill. But his best friend? I tried to wrap my head around a scenario where that would be his only option.

"The colonel telling me that *I did what I had to do* didn't make it any better," he growled.

I took a calming breath, then, tucked against the tree, I leaned toward the end of the roots so I could again see what was happening. Jem shifted with me, and I held onto her to keep from losing my balance.

Drew looked into the woods for a few seconds and swore again before looking at Dad. "You know, Max, while I'm spilling my guts, I might as well go all out. Killing my best friend wasn't the worst. To add to that hell, I had to come home and face his family. They didn't know what I'd done. But I knew."

His pacing resumed. "Friendly fire, they were told. Your husband, your father, was killed by *friendly* fire." Suddenly he shook his fist toward the sky. "No, he was shot and killed by his *friend*."

Dad took a couple of steps back while Drew was turned away from him. I didn't blame him. Was he as nervous as I was? "Why *did* you shoot him?"

Drew dropped his chin and his shoulders slumped.

"Because he went off the deep end," he said, his voice suddenly calm. "It was kill him or let him blow up twenty plus other guys in the platoon. He was ready to pull the pin and hurl a grenade." He shook his head. "But I stopped him."

My chest ached for the pain I heard in Drew's voice. No wonder he had nightmares and flashbacks. I pressed my head against Jem's cheek. She had a big job ahead of her.

"Drew, have you talked with anyone about this?" Dad asked.

He nodded. "Yeah. A long time ago. I moved on. Tried to atone for what I'd done." Scrubbing his hand across his face, he said, "But by shooting that gun today, every minute detail of that night in Iraq flashed back into my mind. The guilt over what I'd stolen from that family punched me in the gut again."

"I'm no psychologist," Dad said, "but did you ever think about finding out where the family is and see how they're doing? Maybe that would give you peace of mind."

Drew squeezed his hands together and grimaced. "I know exactly how they're doing."

"You've been in touch with them?"

He nodded and forced a fake laugh. "I guess you can say that."

"I'm not following," Dad responded.

I wasn't either. Drew was talking in riddles. But now, he went silent, staring up through the trees toward the patches of blue sky.

Jem shifted again, trying to get to him, but I held her tight. Every sound in the forest was magnified. The flapping of a bird's wings. The scuttling of a chipmunk. The whisper of the breeze through the leaves. Even my beating heart.

Dad broke the silence. "So, does the guy's family know the truth now?"

Finally, Drew cleared his throat and shook his head. "No."

"Drew, if they've moved on, then maybe it's okay for you to put it behind you. You can't change the past, and look at your future. Your daughter and son are back in your life. That's gotta make you happy."

"It makes me scared."

"Why?"

"Because I'm afraid the truth will come out."

"I know it's a cliché," Dad said, "but maybe the truth will set you free."

"And then I risk losing everything that matters to me again. Everything."

Now Dad took a step closer again. "Is it really that bad?"

"Oh, yeah," Drew said.

Dad started to glance around, so I ducked behind the root.

"Look, Drew, it's only you and me out here. Get it off your chest so you can move on. You have two kids who would give anything for a closer relationship with you. Give up the ghosts."

"Another cliché," Drew quipped. He sucked in a big breath and let it out slowly. "That guy I killed," he continued, his voice gravelly, "was Chase's father."

A scream erupted in my throat, but I slammed my hand over my mouth to stop it.

Now it was Dad's turn to swear, also a rarity, but that was nothing compared to the shock that exploded inside me as I processed whether I'd heard Drew right. Bile rose in my throat, and I dropped into a sitting position with my head between my knees as I tried to keep my dinner down.

My father had killed *my boyfriend's* father.

A wave of heat raced through my body, chased away by a coldness that seeped to my core. In an instant my entire body shivered uncontrollably.

This was a nightmare. Surely I'd wake up and find myself in my sleeping bag.

Jem pulled at the leash again, and I didn't have the will to fight her. As soon as I opened my fingers and let the flat nylon slip through, she darted around the uprooted tree, and I was sure, straight toward Drew.

"Jem?" I heard the confusion in Drew's voice. "Where did you come from?"

The tags on her collar jangled, and I imagined her pushing against Drew, desperate to do her job and calm him. Keeping myself low so I wouldn't be detected, I shifted to look between the dried roots. As I'd suspected, Drew was kneeling with his arms wrapped around Jem, and she was tucked as tight against his body as she could get.

"Savannah? Alex?" Dad called. "Are you here?"

I sat back against the trunk again and wrapped my arms around my bent legs, pulling my knees tight to my chest. There should have been tears, but my mind was numb.

I heard the movement of feet on the leaves and sticks. It was unclear who was moving or in what direction. But within a few seconds, the question was answered when Dad leaned over the fallen tree I was hiding behind.

"Savannah! What are you doing here?"

I couldn't face anyone. I couldn't talk. Right now I had no words to describe the volcano of emotions building in my body.

Without answering, I scrambled to my feet and let the adrenaline propel me back toward camp.

"Savannah! Come back," Dad called behind me.

I ignored him and sprinted through the woods until I finally saw the campsite come into view. I stopped, bent over with my hands on my knees and gasped for air, my mind spinning. How could a day that had started out so great end in such a horrific mess?

I took a few minutes to collect myself enough so that I felt I could walk back into camp without arousing suspicion. I acted like I'd only been wandering in the woods as I walked the camp outskirts to go directly to the makeshift corral. Right now I needed to see Lacey.

Her back was to me, and her head down, as she munched hay. I gave a quick whistle and her head popped up. At first she looked ahead because she didn't know where the sound had come from, but when I repeated it, she swung around in my direction. Her ears swiveled forward and she picked her way through the other horses to come greet me.

"Hey, girl," I said when she stuck her head over the rope fence. She stretched her nose, probably looking for a treat.

I slid my fingers along the length of her face, staring into her brown eyes. I'd given her up because I thought it was the right thing to do for the best chance of bringing our family back together. But now I wondered if it had all been a waste. Despite my best effort to hold in my emotions, they worked their way up, anyway. My throat started clogging, then my nose stuffed up, and the tears came.

Drew's admission rolled around in my head, making my stomach clench. I'd already given up my horse for him. Would I now lose Chase, too?

CHAPTER 24

"I'd understand if you don't want anything to do with me again."

I whirled away from Lacey to face Drew, surprised to hear him behind me. Jem was at his side, pressed close to his leg. How long had I been standing here hugging Lacey? Wishing I could snap my fingers and change everything.

Narrowing my eyes, I straightened to take a more challenging stance. "I'm not a quitter."

Dad stopped several feet off to Drew's side, leaving a respectful distance between us. His furrowed brow told me how worried he was.

Drew looked toward Dad, then at the other campers before returning his attention to me. "I'm not a quitter, either, but I never planned on you knowing these details about what happened with Chase's father. I had no idea you were there."

A twinge of guilt for sneaking up on him and Dad in the woods zipped through me, but I tamped it. "Dad said you were upset. I thought you might need Jem."

He nodded. "I did. Thank you." As if to reinforce his statement, he laid his hand on Jem's neck and pushed his fingers in her fur. "My concern isn't for me, Savannah. I don't want this secret to come between you and Chase."

I stiffened. "This is bigger than that. I'm scared about how this will affect him, but —"

Drew's eyes widened as he cut me off. "He doesn't need to know. What purpose would it serve to tell him?"

"What purpose does it serve to *not* tell him? He and Angela deserve to know the truth."

"They're happy now," he retorted. "Why would I ruin that?"

"Number one," I said, holding up one finger, "because they deserve to know what really happened." My voice's volume rose on each word, prompting him to glance over his shoulder and give me the signal to talk quieter. "And, number two," I continued, holding up a second finger and lowering my voice, "because you're living a lie and forcing them to do the same without their knowledge, and a lie can never have a happy ending."

He narrowed his eyes and studied me as he contemplated what I'd said. Finally, he shook his head and said, "I can't tell them."

Lifting my chin, I said, "Fine. Then I will."

I was as shocked as he looked by my response. There'd been no thought behind it. *Would* I tell them? *Could* I tell them? My chest tightened. I wouldn't be able to face Chase again with a secret like that.

"You don't have the right —" he continued, but this time I cut *him* off.

"Oh, yes, I do. This affects me as much as it affects you."

"You can go back to the way things were before you found me," he said.

"No, no I can't. And, I don't want to. You have no idea what I've sacrificed in order to bring our family back together. There's no going back. I've taken a risk. Now you have to do the same."

"Sacrifice? Risk? I don't know what you're talking about," he said.

I pointed at Jem. "I bought her for you to help with the PTSD. It was a risk I took, because I didn't know if it would work. But I can already see a difference in you."

Out of the corner of my eye I saw Dad take a long stride closer to us. "Where did you get that kind of money?" he asked.

I swallowed hard, preparing myself for the reaction to my confession. "It's the money I've saved to buy Lacey."

"What?" Dad and Drew responded in unison, each moving even closer to me.

"Why would you do that?" Dad asked. "Buying Lacey has been your dream."

"But Alex and me being able to spend more time with him," I said, looking at Drew, "is a dream Alex and I both have. Jem can help with that. College, the equestrian team, they're four years. Reuniting our family is for life."

Drew glanced at Jem then back at me. "No. I can't accept this. Her. As much as I love this dog, you love that horse more. I can't take that dream from you." Jem sidled closer to Drew's leg.

I culled all of the bravery I could from inside and stood straighter. "It's done. Phoebe has another buyer for Lacey, so I can't change anything now." Even though I didn't believe what I was about to say, it came out anyway in a tumble of thoughts.

"Besides, there are other horses. It doesn't have to be her. I had the money to buy Jem, the timing was right, and she has already changed you and made your life better in just two weeks. And now maybe you'll be comfortable letting Alex and me stay at your house."

I stopped and took a second to consider what I'd said, then amended it. "No, *our* house. We want to stay with you sometimes. Really be a family, even if it's only for weekends. The only way to make that happen was to get a service dog that could help you deal with your PTSD. You couldn't afford one. I could. The end."

Drew shook his head. "No, you're wrong." He pushed his hands against his scalp and squeezed, making his biceps tighten. "I could buy her. I could have applied for a service dog to be donated to me."

"Then why didn't you?" I asked.

"The truth?"

"Yeah, the truth," I challenged.

"Because I'm stubborn. Because I'm a jerk. Because I deserve the pain I feel every day from the guilt over what I stole from Angela and Chase."

I thought of the account of the shooting incident he'd given Dad. There was a big piece to the whole picture that he was missing. "What happened was hard for one family, but what if you hadn't stopped Chase's father? What if he had thrown that grenade? More than twenty families could have lost a loved one. Instead, because you made that tough decision, only one family did. And look what you've done for them to help them through it."

The muscles in his neck twitched, and Jem looked up at him, nudging his palm with her nose until he responded. She must have sensed whatever turmoil was eating him up inside.

"Let Alex and me help. Do you like having us back in your life?"

He walked toward me and took me by the shoulders. "I do, Savannah. God, more than you know."

I stared up into his eyes. His pain went way beyond the depths visible to me.

"Then quit being stubborn. You don't deserve to live like this. None of us do. The ball's in your court. You have Jem. Chase told me you tried counseling once. Go again. But, no one can move on until you tell Angela and Chase the truth. And like I said before, if you don't, I will. I'm not living with that kind of secret."

"We may lose them," he said, his voice strained.

The reality struck me, and my lower lip trembled. I extended my arms for a hug. "I hope not," I said, fighting tears, "but, if we do, we'll still have each other. We're family first and forever."

Drew accepted my hug, wrapping his arms tight around me. Dad stepped in behind me to lay his arm across my shoulders, too. I was surrounded by love - fatherly love. For now, I'd rely on that strength to help me through the rough days ahead when I'd have to say goodbye to Lacey, and maybe Chase, too.

When we rejoined the group by the campfire, Alex tried to wheedle information from me because he'd seen Dad, Drew and me talking, but the only part I shared was about me using the money I'd saved to buy Jem for our father. That was shocking enough to satisfy him. The rest he didn't need to know until after Drew told Chase and Angela.

I'm not sure how, but Drew and I managed to keep it together so we could finish the overnight at the campsite and the trail ride home without too much awkwardness. Our conversations weren't as free-flowing as they had been on the first day, because uncertainty about what the future held kept both of us preoccupied much of the time.

As soon as we came out of the woods where we had entered the trail yesterday, the horses knew we were close to home and picked up their pace. I glanced at Drew riding to my right. His jaw looked clenched. No doubt he was feeling the same anxiety I was. Chase and Angela were supposed to be at the trail's end party. It was going to be difficult to act like nothing was different.

Drew stood up in his stirrups to stretch. "I'm going to be one hurtin' puppy tomorrow. I'm not as young as I used to be."

"You did great," I said, then added, "and I'm really glad you came on the ride. I was glad to spend time with you."

He settled back into his saddle and lifted his cowboy hat to scratch his head. "You got more than you bargained for, kid. I'm afraid I wasn't much company for anyone last night."

I shrugged. "You were there. That made Alex happy."

"He invited me to his eighth grade graduation next week," Drew said.

Shifting in my saddle so I could look at him, I asked, "Are you going?"

He wrapped his hands over the saddle horn and stretched his arms. "I have to see how things play out."

It wasn't necessary for him to explain what *things* he was talking about. For the moment, our lives were all hanging in a precarious balance, with no way of knowing which way things would tip.

As we approached the stable, I could see two canopy tents had been set up on Phoebe's lawn between her house and the practice ring. People were setting out food. My stomach rumbled when I thought of what might be there. I didn't know what anyone else was bringing, but my mouth watered when I thought of the Mexican nacho dip and chips Mom said she was bringing. We hadn't eaten since our stop at noon for lunch, so four hours later, we were all ready.

When I spotted Chase, I waved, and the hunger pangs twisted into knots.

"Hey!" he called, as he came up the driveway to meet me. He looked so happy.

So naïve.

"Hey to you," I called, trying to sound casual. I stopped Lacey and dismounted.

When he reached me, he laid his palm on my cheek and gave me a kiss. "Welcome back."

Every inch of me tingled at his touch. Oh how I prayed I wouldn't lose him.

He looked over Lacey's neck at Drew who had dismounted Buster and was leading him to the barn. "Hey, Drew. Thanks for taking good care of my girl."

Drew gave him a quick smile and salute from the brim of his hat but didn't linger.

"You want to come in the barn while I unsaddle her?" I asked.

"Sure."

Taking hold of my free hand, Chase walked next to me.

"Alex told me about your excitement in the woods last night." He squeezed my hand. "Glad you're okay."

I smiled. "Thanks."

He leaned a little in front of me to look into my eyes. "You don't have much to say. You tired?"

"Exhausted," I said. Mentally and physically, but I'd let him believe it was only physical.

Angela and Alex appeared at the entrance to the barn with Jem on a leash next to Alex. Jem held her head high and her tail wagged when she spotted Drew approaching.

Drew stopped Buster and squatted. "Come 'ere, Jem."

The dog jumped into a sprint, her tongue hanging out, her face looking like she was smiling. As soon as she got in front of him, Drew pointed his finger to the ground and she stopped and sat. Her tail brushed the ground, sending up little puffs of dust. He leaned his forehead against hers, then took her leash and walked her with him.

"I can't believe how fast those two bonded," Chase said. "I don't think Drew will be able to give her up."

I whipped toward Chase. "Give her up? Why would he give her up?"

"I'm talking about when she goes to the veteran she's being trained for."

Nodding, I said, "Oh, right." I hesitated for a moment, then said, "Want to know a secret?"

He leaned into me a little as we walked. "Um, okay."

"I bought Jem for Drew."

Chase stopped abruptly, using my hand to turn me toward him. "Seriously? But Rashawn said those dogs cost a lot of money."

"They do. Come on," I said, tugging on his hand to continue taking Lacey into the barn, "I'll explain while I'm unsaddling her".

I took Lacey to a far area of the barn where I could talk to Chase without anyone else overhearing. By the time I'd finished telling him, his shocked expression mirrored that of Dad's and Drew's the night before.

"For now, please don't say anything to anyone about it," I said. "I can't handle people feeling sorry for me. I made the decision, and yeah, in some ways it's eating me up inside, but I couldn't be selfish. Not to sound dramatic, but I had to choose between a horse and my family. I chose my family. I did what I had to do."

The irony of those words hit me. Drew was right. Saying them didn't make the pain any less.

I threw my arms around Chase's waist and pressed against him, laying my cheek against his shoulder. "I haven't said this before, but I've felt it." I leaned back and looked into his eyes. "I do love you, Chase. No matter what happens, I want you to know that."

A skeptical expression crossed his face. "I love you, too, but you're making me a little nervous. What do you mean 'no matter what happens'?"

I forced a smile and patted his chest with one hand. "Oh, I'm only being a girl," I said. "You know, I get a little tired and the drama kicks in."

He furrowed his brow and nodded, and I was sure he wasn't convinced that was all there was to it, but he didn't say any more. Before Drew left today, I intended to remind him that he had only two choices: either he told Chase and Angela what happened in Iraq all those years ago or I would.

And I was giving him a deadline. One week.

The waiting game was on. With Chase and me studying for finals and New York State Regents exams, it meant there was no opportunity to see each other all week, but we texted and talked a few times a day. Every time my cell phone rang or dinged with a text, my heart jumped to my throat. And every time, I wondered if this was *the* call.

By Friday afternoon, when I'd still heard nothing from Drew, and it was clear Chase still knew nothing, I was tempted to text Drew and remind him that the deadline was Sunday. Almost as if Chase could read my mind from afar, my phone rang and his name showed up on the caller I.D. I tossed my book bag onto the chair in front of my desk and sat on the edge of my bed. Oh, man, was this it? One deep breath, in case this was it, then I pressed the button to accept the call.

"Hello," I answered warily.

"Hey, Savannah!"

My whole body relaxed, and I slumped a bit in relief. I wanted him to know the truth, but I didn't want things to change between us. And I was sure they would.

"Are you studied out?" I asked.

"My brain's going to explode," he said, laughing. "But, hey, I'm graduating and after next Thursday, I won't have to take another Regents the rest of my life."

"Lucky." It was another reminder that he'd be going off to college in the fall.

"I think we both need a break, and I really miss you," he said. "How about going to a movie tomorrow night?"

I closed my eyes and sucked in my upper lip. I imagined his kiss. His arms wrapped around me while he whispered in my ear. His fingers combing through my hair. The warmth of his breath on my temple as we looked up at the stars. Torture. Every thought was pure torture, knowing this would probably be our last date.

"You know," I said, nodding even though he couldn't see it, "that would be great. I have to work at the stable until early afternoon, but anytime after that is fine."

"I'll pick you up at four," he said. "We'll grab something to eat first. Sound like a plan?"

"It sounds great."

We were silent for a few moments. I scrubbed the toe of my sandal against the braided rug in front of my bed, trying to decide whether or not to ask my next question. But curiosity was killing me.

"Chase, have you seen Drew this week?"

"Yeah."

I sat up straighter on the edge of the bed. "Really? What did he say?"

There was a moment of hesitation on Chase's end before he said, "What did he *say*? I don't know. Um, something about checking the propane tank for the grill, I think." His tone told me he was confused. "I didn't really pay attention, but it was kind of weird because he came in and sat in the kitchen for a few minutes while Mom was making dinner and acted kind of awkward. Why, is something going on?"

I mentally kicked myself. I should have known asking a question like that would arouse his suspicion.

"I haven't heard from him all week. I wanted to make sure he was okay."

"Yeah, I guess. I mean, we usually see him a lot more than this, but maybe he's been busy with the training with Jem, or maybe he's been busy at work or at the firehouse. I don't know."

I massaged the back of my neck with my free hand to relieve some of the tension that pulled across my shoulders. "Yeah, that's probably it. I probably should go and see if Mom needs help with dinner. So, I'll see you tomorrow."

"Can't wait," Chase said.

"Me, too. 'Night."

I pressed *end* and cradled my phone in my hands like it was my last connection to Chase. My entire body felt heavy with dread, and the weight pulled my shoulders in.

Would Chase and I even have a tomorrow?

My agony was short-lived. Mentally exhausted from worrying and studying, I headed to bed less than an hour after dinner. I tried watching a sitcom with Mom, Dad and Alex, but the silly humor only irritated me.

I was in the middle of brushing my teeth when my phone dinged with a text. I spit out the toothpaste and snatched the phone from the edge of the sink while I wiped toothpaste from my lips with my free hand. It was from Drew.

It's done

A shiver shot up my spine. I swiped my finger across the face of the phone to see if there was more to his message, but that was it.

My fingers hovered over the letters on the pop up keyboard, dozens of questions battering my brain. It wasn't a question of what those two words meant, it was that I didn't even know where to start or what to write. How did Angela and Chase take the news? Would Chase reach out to me? How was *he*?

I stabbed my finger against the home button. The heck with texting. I pulled up my contact list, typed in the first two letters of Drew's name and his number popped up. There was no hesitation. I pressed it so the phone would automatically dial. I waited while it rang. Once. Twice. Three times. It kept ringing, but he didn't answer.

"Damn you!" I growled as I rinsed the toothbrush and jammed it into the holder, frustration making every move forceful.

After more than a dozen rings, his voicemail greeting came on. I listened to his message, his assurance that if a message was left, he'd return it as soon as possible, and wondered if he really would.

My mind spun with the different options for my message. What could I possibly say that would convince him to call me back? When I heard the beep at the end of the message, I opened my mouth to speak, then clamped my lips shut and hit the END button on my phone.

I leaned against the edge of the sink and looked into the mirror. My eyes were bloodshot. My forehead was creased with worry. My body was shaking.

Was it possible that in this one night every one of my dreams had been destroyed?

CHAPTER 25

I had no idea silence could be so deafening.

Seven days. Almost 168 hours, 10,080 minutes, 604,800 seconds. Each of those days, hours, minutes and seconds had been the longest of my life. Except for one text from Chase, there'd been absolute silence from everyone since Drew told Angela and Chase that he was responsible for Angela being a widow and Chase, fatherless.

There'd also been no movie date with Chase last Saturday as planned. The one message I had received from him said:

Need time. Can we postpone our date?

And since then, there had been no phone calls, no more texts, no e-mails. Nothing.

And now another Saturday was well underway. As hard as I tried to keep my chin up, to believe that everything would work out, I still felt lost and alone. At least here at the stable, the routine and the animals helped ground me.

I looked out across the pastures at the grazing horses. As was typical, Lacey was in the middle of six of them. She looked content with her buddies, but if plans stayed on track, she was due to leave next Saturday. Only one more week with her..

The one positive was that Jamie told me she'd seen Drew and Jem at the kennel for their training sessions with Charlotte. It was the only thing that kept my hopes from sinking. Despite his claims that he couldn't accept Jem as a gift from me, Drew wasn't giving up on her. But was he giving up on Alex and me?

"Hey, you must be a million miles away." Phoebe's voice startled me as she came up next to the fence. "Gosh, I was beginning to wonder if I was only imagining that I was talking."

I shrugged. "Sorry. Yeah, I'm pretty distracted."

"Hear from anyone?" she asked. I'd confided in her when I'd come to work Sunday because she knew something was wrong. It had helped to tell her everything and have her to talk to when I'd been at work this week.

I shook my head. "Nope. Nothing. Nada. Zilch."

She brushed a stray lock of hair away from her face. "It's a pretty heavy thing for everyone to take in."

"Yeah." I put my booted foot up on the bottom railing of the wooden fence and leaned on the next railing up to continue staring out at the horses.

"How did Alex take it?" she asked.

"Better than I thought, especially considering his history with guns. He gets that Drew had no choice." I sighed and looked at Phoebe. "He's just as anxious as I am to know where we fit in his life, now, though. Everything was going so perfectly. Even though I hated giving up Lacey, I knew I held the key to helping our family get together again. I'd come to terms with that. I had the best boyfriend. Mom and Dad were okay with the relationship Alex and I were rebuilding with our father. And then, BAM!" I slammed my fist into my hand for emphasis. "I feel like I've lost everything."

Phoebe turned to lean her shoulder against the fence so she could see me straight on. "The sale for Lacey isn't finalized. We're still negotiating."

I shook my head. "No, I appreciate it, Phoebe, but it took me over three years to save up the money I had. I made my decision. Drew needed Jem now. I wasn't willing to wait to see if he'd be approved for a dog to be donated to him." My throat tightened, so I stopped to give it a second. For the hundredth time this week, I wanted to cry, but somehow I kept it in check. "Really, I'll be fine. It's just hard right now."

Her eyes glistened. If she lost it, so would I.

"You're an amazing young woman, Savannah. I've always had respect for you, but you never cease to amaze me. The world is definitely a better place with you in it."

My eyes welled up. "Thank you."

She stepped away from the fence and threw her arms around me. "Have faith, kiddo. I truly believe everything happens for a reason. If it's meant to be, it will be."

I laughed and sniffled as I stepped back. "Any other clichés you want to throw out?"

"I am on a roll, but that'll do for today. I'd hate to use them all up at one time. Besides, I have to get back inside to make some calls. I just happened to look out my office window and saw you standing here looking like you didn't have a friend in the world. Thought I'd come out and let you know that's not the case."

"Thanks, I appreciate it." I turned to walk toward the barn and Phoebe headed toward her house. Over my shoulder I yelled, "I have two more stalls to muck out, then I think I'll take Lacey for a ride since she still technically belongs to the stable. Is that okay?"

Phoebe threw her hand up. "Until those papers are signed and she's walked up onto a trailer, she's all yours to do what you want. Take advantage of the extra time with her."

While I continued to the barn, I pulled my cell phone out of my pocket and glanced at it in case I had missed something. I swiped my finger across the black screen and entered my code. No missed calls. No text messages. The pit in my stomach tightened a tiny bit more. I prayed this wasn't my new reality.

While I cleaned the stalls, I tried to distract myself by reviewing facts in my head for my history and government Regents exam. Since I was the only one in the barn, I talked out loud to myself. Which president's platform was to preserve the wilderness? Theodore Roosevelt. What was the Trail of Tears? Who succeeded FDR?

Once I concentrated, my mind blanked out everything else. It was so successful that I continued reviewing during my ride on Lacey, too. Despite the fact that I was reviewing for a major exam, I was more relaxed than I'd been in a week.

By the time I got back to the barn, my growling stomach distracted me more than the history and government questions. Since we hadn't ridden hard, I unsaddled Lacey next to the pasture, gave her a couple of treats I'd stashed in my pocket, then let her out. One of the other horses whinnied, and Lacey took off at a gallop, throwing up dust from her back feet. She'd been with these pasture mates since before I started riding here. It saddened me to think of them being separated.

I retrieved her saddle and bridle from where I'd set them on the fence railing and carried them back to the barn. The stirrup banged against my shin, and by the time I got to the tack room, my arms quivered from the weight. I slid the saddle onto the rack and hung the bridle on the hook next to it.

I started to walk away, but horse smell coming from the warm saddle pad made me turn around. Smoothing my hand across the suede seat of the saddle, I reminisced about the history Lacey and I shared. The saddle was mine, it wouldn't go with her, but I wondered if it would be as comfortable on another horse? How long would it take me to work another horse up to the level Lacey and I had reached?

My musings were interrupted by a familiar voice.

"I figured I'd find you here."

I wheeled around to face Chase. His athletic frame filled the doorway as he stood with his hands shoved into his jeans pockets, his expression serious.

"Hi." My heart hammered against my chest, making my voice breathy. As badly as I wanted to run and throw my arms around him, I waited, hoping he hadn't come to say goodbye. Instead, I asked, "How are you?"

"I'm okay."

"How's your mom?"

"Amazing."

His response caught me off-guard. "What?"

"Yeah, she's amazing." Chase moved inside the tack room and sat on the wooden plank bench against the wall. He leaned back and stretched his legs out, crossing them at the ankles as if he were settling in for a relaxed chat. He patted the spot next to him. "Come and sit with me."

"Okay." I sat, but apparently not close enough, because Chase reached to take my hand so I'd slide closer. And then he continued to hold it, staring at my fingers.

After a week of no communication, it felt good to be close to him, again.

He rubbed his thumb across the back of my hand before looking up at me.

"Thanks for giving me time to sort things out this week. Drew's confession was a bombshell." He gave a little laugh. "No pun intended." He shifted his crossed feet. "It took a few days for my mom and me to work through the shock, but like I said, she's amazing."

"In what way?"

"I think she handled it better than Drew did. Maybe it's because it's been twelve years, and she's had time to work through the grief before learning the truth, but she didn't blame Drew."

"She wasn't upset?"

"Oh, she had a few rough days, but she told me she'd always suspected there was more to the story than what she'd been told. Because of that, as sad as it made her, she said it also gave her relief and closure."

"And what about you? Does it make you angry?"

He shook his head and laid his cheek against my hair. "No, and that's what bothered me at first. I felt like I should be totally pissed off at Drew. Even hate him. And I told my mother that." He paused for a few seconds. "But the truth is, Drew is the only father figure I've really ever known. I don't know if it had anything to do with the issues my father was dealing with in relation to the war, but even when he was home, I don't remember him having anything to do with me. At least, nothing positive. I remember him yelling a lot. Being mad all of the time. When he'd lose it, I would grab my stuffed bear and hide under my bed." He shrugged. "I was there a lot when he was home."

Sadness and fear for the little boy he'd been filled me. "Did he hurt you?"

"No. He'd never hurt us. He'd storm out of the house. I think to go and drink his anger away. I don't know. That's just what I came up with when I got older and thought about those days, because he'd come back home and go right to bed. And Mom would make sure we didn't make noise."

He stopped again, like he had drifted off into the memory. And I stared at the racks of saddles, lost in my own thoughts as I waited for him to come back to me.

When he spoke again, his voice was raspy. "I think Drew saved my mother and me. If anyone should be angry, it's you and Alex."

Surprised, I leaned back to look at him. "Us? Why?"

"Because his survivor's guilt caused him to choose us over you."

I shook my head. "I'll admit, at first I was jealous of you and the time you had with him that we didn't. But, we can't change the past. We can only look to our future." I pulled in a deep breath and let it out slowly. "Except, we've heard nothing from Drew since he told you, so I don't know if we even have a future."

Chase leaned forward to put his elbows on his knees, and turned to look at me.

"I think he'll come around, Savannah. Mom and I saw him two nights ago. He was so sure that us knowing what really happened would make us hate him, that he wasn't prepared for us to understand and accept. He didn't know how to handle it."

"I want him to know that we don't hold anything against him, either."

"Tell him."

"I would, if he'd give me a chance."

He sat straighter again. "He's still training with Jem."

His abrupt change in topic surprised me. "I know. Jamie told me."

"I think it's a sign that he's thinking about his future and making changes. I believe those changes include you and Alex."

"I hope you're right." I used my knee to nudge him. "So, where do *we* stand, Chase? You and me — as a couple? What's *our* future?"

He put his arm around me and tucked me against his shoulder again. I felt safe there.

"Well, since I'm off to college in the fall, I think we enjoy the summer and see where things stand at the end of August." He kissed me just above my ear. "Does that sound like a plan?"

Twisting to lay my arm across his abdomen and nestle my head under his chin, I nodded. "I like it."

"Good, because I owe you a date. So, even though there's a week left of school, I think we pretend our summer starts now.

The movie we were supposed to see last Saturday is still at the theater. Want to try again?"

"Absolutely."

He pressed his lips to my head, and I felt his body relax. "Okay. But, for the moment, I want to sit here and hold you in this romantic setting."

I giggled as I looked around the tack room at the saddles on racks, bridles, halters and lead ropes hanging on hooks and the other horse paraphernalia that made this small room smell like horses.

"Yeah, very romantic," I said.

"It doesn't matter where we are," he said, his voice barely above a whisper, "if we're together, it's romantic."

Contentment settled over me like a warm, fuzzy blanket. Maybe it would only be a summer love, but we'd make the most of it. One thing was for certain, I knew in Chase I'd have a friend for life. I could live with that.

The previews before the movie had just started when I felt my phone vibrate in my pocket. I handed the small bag of popcorn to Chase.

"Somebody's calling," I whispered as I stretched out in the seat so I could pull the phone out. "Everybody knows I'm at the movies. I want to make sure it's not an emergency."

I bent over and angled myself so the light from the phone wouldn't disturb anyone around us. When I saw the caller ID, my fingers tightened on the phone.

"I have to take this," I said turning to Chase. "It's Drew."

Before he could respond, I got up, remaining bent over to avoid blocking other people's view of the screen, and hurriedly shuffled my way past the others in our row. "Sorry," I said over and over, panicking that the phone would stop ringing before I got outside the theater.

As soon as I made it partway down the exit hallway, I pressed the accept button on my phone.

"Hello?" Between my rapid heartbeat and hurrying, I was out of breath.

"Hi, Savannah. I'm sorry if I'm interrupting something," Drew said.

"No, no, that's fine," I responded. "Excuse me," I said as I passed the usher who scowled at me as I pushed through the door to the lobby.

"I apologize if I caught you at a bad time," Drew said. "I won't keep you."

I found a quiet spot near a large pillar and ducked behind it for a bit of privacy. "I'm so happy to hear from you."

There was a moment of silence, then he said, "Yeah, I'm sorry. I just didn't — There was a lot on — Oh, hell!" he sputtered.

I didn't want him to get frustrated and hang up. I was beginning to fear that our relationship had been set way back by his admission last week, so the relief coursing through me now because he was reaching out made my knees weak.

"It's okay," I said. "You don't have to explain anything. I'm just glad you're calling."

A group of five girls approached, laughing and talking loud. I turned my back to them to try to block the noise out.

"Where are you?" he asked.

"At the movies with Chase. But, that's okay. I came out into the lobby."

"Sorry. I won't keep you. I wanted to invite you and Alex to come to my house tomorrow."

"Really?" The question came out before I had a chance to filter my thought.

"Yeah, really. Are you free right after lunch?"

I ran my tongue across my lower lip, thinking fast. I was supposed to meet Jamie at the stable for a trail ride, but she'd understand my need to back out, or at the very least, change the time.

"Yeah, yeah, that's good," I said. "Have you asked Alex, yet?"

"No, I started with you.."

"Okay. Is one o'clock good?" I asked.

"That's fine. And, Savannah, I want —" I actually heard him swallow hard on his end — "I want your aunt and unc—" another hesitation then — "Max and Nicole to come, too."

"Um, okay." My mind whirled with this unexpected twist. "Are you going to call them?"

"Yes. As soon as I hang up."

My face flushed. I used my free hand to fan myself. For some reason, the prospect of all of us at his house made me nervous. Whatever he wanted, it had to be important if he was taking such a drastic step.

"Go back to your movie," he said. "I'll see you around one tomorrow."

I nodded, even though he couldn't see me. "Okay. See you then." My voice sounded robotic.

He hung up before I did. After staring at the phone for a few seconds, I slid it into my pocket and leaned back against the pillar, staring off into space. I couldn't even imagine what he was planning.

CHAPTER 26

Welcome home!

I had just reached the top step of Drew's porch when I spotted the sign taped to his front door. It was simple — the two words written in blue marker on a piece of plain printer paper. I stopped so abruptly that Alex ran into the back of me, knocking me off balance.

"Hey! What gives?" he sputtered, as he grabbed for the porch railing.

Behind us, Mom gasped, and I turned in time to see her throw her hand over her mouth. Her eyes were big, round orbs.

Dad put his arm across her shoulder and pulled her close. "Don't read into it. Let's hear him out," he said, probably hoping I wouldn't hear, but I did.

At the same time, the front door opened, swinging the sign out of view.

"Hi," Drew said. "I'm glad you all could come today." Jem stepped up next to him, her tail wagging. Drew pushed open the screen door and stretched to hold it while Alex and I walked past him. When Dad took hold of it from the outside, Drew moved inside with us while Dad guided Mom in.

"You want the inside door closed?" Dad asked as he glanced at the *Welcome Home* sign.

Drew shook his head. "No, that's fine. Let the fresh air in." He walked toward the living room. "Please, come in here."

We followed. I wanted to look at Mom and Dad, to see their reaction to being in this house for the first time in twelve years — at least, I assumed they hadn't been here since our mother died — but Drew started talking and it seemed rude to look away.

There was a pitcher of what looked like lemonade and five glasses on the coffee table in front of the couch.

"Sit, please," Drew said, indicating the chairs and couch.

Alex took a chair, while I took one end of the sofa, and Mom and Dad sat with me.

Drew sat in a chair across from us, and Jem took up position against his legs. "You're welcome to lemonade," he said, pointing to the coffee table.

When no one else moved, I slid forward so I could pour myself a glass. I set it on a coaster then looked at everyone else.

"Anyone else want any?"

"Not right now," Dad said, then turned to Mom. "Nic?"

She shook her head, barely moving because her body was so rigid.

"Alex?" I asked.

He held up a hand to indicate he was declining.

I set the pitcher down and picked up my glass. The moment couldn't have felt more awkward.

Drew rubbed his palms across his jeans, drawing in a long, deep breath as he straightened his shoulders. Jem nudged his wrist, and he laid his hand on the back of her neck.

"I'm nervous as hell right now," he said with a tight smile. He scrubbed his free hand across his chin."I wanted you all here because I want you all to hear the same thing at once."

No one responded, but we all had our attention focused on him.

"I'm going to be direct. That's what the counselor told me to do."

I gripped my glass of lemonade and sat up straighter, and he must have noticed.

"Yeah, Savannah, a counselor. I went back to the V.A. Having Jem, working with Charlotte to train Jem, has opened my eyes. I don't have to beat myself up over what happened. I don't have to live in this dark hole. There's help for me."

He quirked his eyebrows and added, "There's always been help. The problem is, I had convinced myself that I was beyond it. I'm not going to let PTSD control my life. I don't want to live in the past anymore. I want my life back. All of it. The part I denied myself for the last twelve years."

Mom lowered her chin and sniffled. Her fingers shook in her lap.

Drew continued. "This is all going to take time for me, but I figure if we move forward in baby steps, as the counselor said — " he gave me another quick look and smiled — "then we have a chance of getting back to where we belong with each other. To being a family. If that's still what you want."

My heart fluttered, and I shot a glance toward Alex, who was now sitting closer to the edge of his seat. His gaze met mine, and the sparkle in his eyes said it all. We'd been on a crazy roller coaster ride since the day three months before when I'd found Drew's picture on the internet.

"Nothing has changed," I said.

"Then, I have a proposal to make." Drew stood up, and so did Jem. "Follow me."

I set my lemonade on the coffee table, then we all followed him. He led us down the hallway toward our old bedrooms.

We stopped in front of Alex's first. We hadn't been in it since the night Drew caught us snooping. Drew turned to us.

"Nicole and Max, first, I want you to know how much I appreciate the love and home you've given Savannah and Alex for all these years. You've done a helluva job raising them. You're fantastic parents."

Dad nodded and laid his hand on Mom's back. Mom's lower lip trembled and tears teetered on her eyelids.

"Thank you," she said, her voice choked.

"I'm not taking anything away from you, but I hope you can trust me enough so that we can share."

Drew stepped back and opened Alex's door, and indicated for him to go in.

"Whoa!" Alex said, turning in a circle to scan the room that had been completely remodeled from a toddler's bedroom to one that could easily be decorated for a teenaged boy. A double bed had replaced the crib against the wall, but the rest of the room was like a blank slate with the walls a colonial blue.

Mom and Dad peeked in, but didn't enter.

"And, Savannah," Drew said, "let's go to your room."

We walked the few feet down the hall to my room. As he did with Alex, Drew swung the door open and encouraged me to enter. Unlike the last time I was in here, most of the things from my childhood were gone. All that remained were two stuffed animals - my well-loved Winnie the Pooh and the worn black and white cat - both angled against the pillow on the new bed.

"I want you to make the room yours, Savannah," he said, stepping in to join me. "To be honest, it will be a while before I'm comfortable with you and Alex spending nights here, but I want to get to that point. And, when I do, I want this to feel like home to you."

I crossed the carpet to sit on the bed, smoothing my hands across the thick white comforter. "What did you do with everything that was in here?"

"Angela helped me box it all. I didn't throw out anything. It's all in storage in case you ever want to go through it."

"Wow! This wasn't what I was expecting."

"What were you expecting?"

I laughed. "Actually, I had no expectations."

I stood and went to him in the doorway.

"Thank you." I slipped my hands around his waist and hugged him. "Thank you for giving us a chance. This is a dream come true."

It took a moment, but finally he reciprocated. His arms wrapped around me, and he let his chin settle against the top of my head. I felt the soft gulp of air that squeezed around his Adam's apple. "That's a father's job," he said in a husky voice, "to make their little girls' dreams come true."

I squeezed my arms tighter around his waist. "And what's your dream?"

He cleared his throat. "I don't want to take anything away from Max, but maybe someday you'll call *me* Dad again."

My breath caught in my lungs. Right now, that felt like a leap. I had a *dad* who'd been there for me through good and bad for the last twelve years.

Not today, but, maybe someday.

Three Regents, three final exams and a final paper for Current Events class. Because of the hectic schedule, I'd been able to talk to Chase and Drew on the phone, but there was no time to see either one of them. It also meant I could only work at the stable Tuesday afternoon this week, so when Phoebe called Thursday night, my heart sank.

I snatched the paper for the Current Events class and shoved it into a folder. The last thing in the world I wanted to do was answer that call. I pressed the button, mentally preparing myself for bad news.

"Hey, Phoebe," I said, sounding more cheery than I felt.

"Hi, Savannah. Sorry to bother you, but I'm wondering if you want to come in and work Saturday morning. Megan just called, and she can't be here."

I closed my eyes and let out a slow breath, thankful that was why she was calling.

"Sure, I can do that."

"And," Phoebe continued, "it looks like Lacey's sale is going through this weekend."

My stomach lurched, and I fought the bile rising up. I sank into the mattress on my bed, the strength to hold the phone to my ear suddenly sapped.

"Saturday?" I asked.

"I think so."

My face flushed, and I wiped at the tears that threatened. "Okay," I squeaked out.

"She'll have a good home, Savannah," Phoebe offered as consolation. "You know I wouldn't allow anything else."

"Yeah." The word barely came out of my mouth.

"Drew called and asked if he could come and ride Buster Saturday morning."

"Are you going to let him?"

"Sure. Maybe you'll want to take Lacey out for a ride, too."

One last ride. I didn't know if my heart would be able to take it.

My face scrunched with emotion begging to be released, but I wouldn't lose it with Phoebe on the phone.

"I'll decide Saturday. I've gotta go. Bye."

I felt rude ending the call so abruptly, but I couldn't talk. There was nothing more to say. I rolled over onto my bed and let the tears flow. Dozens of ribbons and trophies that I'd won with

Lacey over the last four years hung on my wall or sat on the shelf above my bed. Would I be able to deal with those reminders of my shattered dreams day in and day out?

No. They had to come down. Now.

I wiped my arm across my wet face and climbed from the bed. One by one, I took the memories off the wall. For each ribbon that I took down, there was another little stab of pain in my heart. I'd done what I had to do, I reminded myself as I stacked them in an empty plastic bin from my closet.

When I'd taken them all down and tucked them away, I lay back on my bed and stared at the walls. Empty. Just like my college equestrian team dream.

A rumble of thunder woke me from sleep. I yanked the blanket over my head and groaned when the thunder was followed by a downpour. Appropriate weather for my mood. Saturday. My first official day of summer. The day my heart would officially break.

I pulled the covers down far enough so I could look at my clock. As much as I'd rather cocoon myself in these blankets and pretend this wasn't happening, I knew I had to get up and face reality.

It didn't take long for a quick shower and an English muffin with peanut butter that I forced down before I was out the door. I dashed through the rain to get to the van. As soon as I had the door shut, my phone dinged with a text message from Chase.

Thinking of u will see u at the barn

thanks I responded, then pressed the phone to my chest. His support would help get me through.

The heavens opened up with thunder and streak lightning all the way to the stable, but like a faucet had been turned off, the storm subsided as soon as I pulled into the driveway. When I entered the barn, I was met by nickering, pawing, and snorting.

"Hold your horses," I called, then actually smiled at the ridiculousness of the comment considering my audience.

I made up all of the bowls of food, measuring grain, adding supplements to those who needed them, all the while aware of Lacey staring at me, patient and trusting.

I'd told myself I was done crying. Instead, I'd enjoy the time left with her.

When the horses finished eating, I led them out one by one to the pasture, leaving Buster and Lacey in their stalls. Lacey stared after the others, leaning into her stall door with the expectation of joining them. She nickered at her friends as she flicked her ears back and forth. My throat constricted, but I willed myself to stay strong.

"Not this time, girl," I said. I tossed her a flake of hay, and that was enough to distract her while I mucked stalls. Then I threw a flake into Buster's stall, too, since I didn't know if Drew was still planning to come and ride.

Grabbing the pitchfork and wheelbarrow, I turned on the dust-covered radio as I passed by it and let the country music reverberate from the walls. If I was lucky, it would be loud enough to drown out all of my thoughts, too.

I had just finished cleaning the last stall and was pushing the wheelbarrow to dump it outside when Drew and Chase came through the door. As was the norm, Jem was next to Drew, her service-dog-in-training vest on.

"Hey! I'll be right back," I called as I disappeared out the back door. By the time I came back in, raindrops rolled down my face and my shoulders of my t-shirt were soaked.

"I didn't know it was raining again," I said. "At least there's no lightning." I returned the wheelbarrow to its corner, turned down the volume on the radio, then met Chase and Drew at Lacey's stall.

Drew was stretched over the door, petting her. Jem sat next to him, her nose straight up in the air, taking in all of the barn smells.

"Is it okay to pet Jem?" I asked.

"Sure," Drew responded.

I kneeled to be at her level. "Hey, there, Jem." I ruffled the fur at the back of her neck, and she arched a bit in pleasure.

"Guess the rain's putting a damper on the plans to ride," he said.

I nodded toward the other end of the barn. "You can always ride in the indoor ring, if you want."

"Will you ride with me?"

I shrugged as I stood. "Maybe. I have to find out from Phoebe what time Lacey's being picked up." I'm sure my lack of enthusiasm was obvious.

Chase reached for my hand and pulled me toward him. He gave me a kiss, then asked, "How're you doing?" before he wrapped me in a hug.

I melted against him, boosted by his strength.

"I'm okay."

He'd have to be my rock this summer, the one to help me get through this. "Sorry that my shirt sleeves are wet." But, his shirt was wet, too.

We stood that way for a minute until I realized how awkward it probably was for Drew. I stepped back and, holding Chase's hands, I looked up into his eyes.

"Thanks for being here," I said. "It means a lot to me."

Then, I turned to Drew. "And, you, too." I felt bad that it sounded like an afterthought.

"I wouldn't want to be anywhere else," he said.

My cell phone rang in my pocket. I pulled it out and looked at the screen.

"Excuse me, it's Phoebe. Let me find out what she wants, and I'll see if there's time for us to ride." In that split second I decided I did want to spend some time on the horses with my father.

"Hey, Phoebe. What's up?"

"Can you tell Chase that his car lights are still on, please?"

I turned toward him. "Phoebe says your car lights are on."

"Oh, right." He started to back away from us. "I'll go take care of that. Be right back." He pivoted and jogged out into the rain.

"Wow! I thought all car lights go off automatically these days."

Drew smiled, a sheepish look on his face. "Most do. His do."

I frowned, confused. "Then what —"

Drew looked past me. "I set Phoebe up to that. I wanted a few minutes to talk with you alone."

Heat rushed up my neck. "What? Why?" It was bad enough that I was losing Lacey; his serious tone scared me.

He reached in his back pocket and pulled out a stack of envelopes, all different sizes, shapes and colors. He stared at them and I saw his jaw twitch like he was nervous.

"What are those?" I asked.

He drew in a deep breath. "They're cards that were never delivered."

I squinted at him, trying to make sense of this scene. "Who are they for?"

He extended them toward me, his hand shaking. "They're for you."

For a moment I stared at them. There had to have been more than a dozen cards. Finally, I took them and turned them over in my hands. My name was written in neat print on the top of the first one.

"Um, do I open them now?"

"Yeah, but can we sit down? I, uh —" He glanced around, then said, "How about on those bales of straw? My knees don't want to hold me up right now."

I glanced at his legs as if I was going to see some weakness or something. Everything seemed fine, but I noticed Jem was more tuned-in to him, as if she sensed anxiety.

"Sure. Are you okay?" I followed him, and we each took a bale. I looked for any signs of a bigger problem, but nothing showed in his body language.

"Yeah, I'd just feel better sitting." Jem wedged herself between his knees and rested her chin against his chest.

I laid the stack of cards next to me, and picked up the first one — a big, square, lavender envelope.

"Does the order matter?" I asked.

"In the grand scheme of things, no. But, it will make the most sense if you pick them up in the order I gave them to you."

He leaned over and folded his arms around Jem's chest. She licked under his chin, then looked back at me, like she knew this was all about what I was doing at the moment.

The envelope was sealed, so I slid the tip of my finger under the small opening at the corner and carefully slid it along the edge of the flap to break the seal. There was barely any resistance from the glue. I lifted it and removed the card, turning it over so I could see it.

The picture caught my attention first. Dora the Explorer holding five balloons. Then the wording on front.

For a girl who's five!

I glanced up at Drew. His lips were drawn tight as he watched me. I returned my attention to the card, opening it to read the inside.

Wishes for a special girl
that adventure comes your way
but there's nothing more exciting
than celebrating your birthday.

Then, written in the same handwriting as on the envelope, the card was signed.

Happy birthday to my sunshine!
Love, Daddy

I stared at the last two lines, then closed my eyes and swallowed the lump in my throat when a hazy memory from long ago came into my mind. I was a little girl in my pajamas, cuddled up on my father's lap in a rocking chair, and I could hear his voice singing the song "You Are My Sunshine" to me.

A feeling of warmth, security, and love washed over me, just like it had when I was little. I remembered. Hot tears pressed against the inside of my eyelids and leaked out.

I opened my eyes and wiped the tears away with the back of my hand, but I couldn't look up at my father. Instead, I laid the first card down and picked up the next one.

Happy birthday six year old!

When I finished that, I opened the next one.

Seven wishes for a girl who's 7

The pattern was clear as I worked my way through the cards. Farther down in the stack there was a card that started with the line:

To a special daughter on her birthday.

The messages tugged at my heart as I imagined him picking them out in a store, taking them home and signing them, then tucking them away, one year on top of the next. Some weren't marked with ages, but Drew had dated every card in the upper right hand corner inside. The last one I opened was for my fifteenth birthday. It read:

For a daughter who's loved so much

I picked the whole bunch up and held them in my hands, believing that the love from inside was traveling up my fingers and through my body. I didn't bother to hide the tears, now. When I looked up at Drew, his eyes were rimmed with red, too.

I sniffled and wiped at my runny nose with the back of my arm, disgusted that I didn't have a tissue. I smiled and forced a little laugh.

"You missed my sixteenth, too, you know."

He nodded. "I know. So we'll consider this an almost seventeen party."

I cocked my head. "Party?"

"Yeah." He pointed behind me. "Take a look."

I twisted on the bale, then jumped to my feet when Phoebe, Chase, Angela, Mom, Dad and Alex stepped into the aisle just past the first set of stalls. They each held mylar birthday balloons.

"What's going on?" I turned back toward Drew. "What is this?"

He came up next to me and put his arm around me.

"It's time to make up for missed birthdays," he said.

I glanced down the aisle at Alex. "But, you've missed Alex's birthdays, too."

"Yeah, I have. But Alex and I talked, and he agreed since you're older, yours comes first."

"Surprise!" they yelled in unison, causing Lacey and Buster to step to their stall doors to check out the commotion.

I laughed, not sure how to react. "I have to admit, I've never been more surprised. Ever."

Phoebe led the others down the aisle toward us. "Well, there's one more surprise for you." Her smile couldn't have been any wider. "I didn't want to tell you before, but Tessa is passing on buying Lacey. Her father said she couldn't keep two horses, and she wasn't ready to give up the one she has. So —"

She cut off her sentence with a big smile. I knew what she was implying, but, that dream was gone. I didn't really want Drew to hear me, so I stepped closer to her and lowered my voice.

"It doesn't matter. I won't be able to earn enough money again to buy her before I go to college."

Drew reached into his back pocket and took out a thick envelope and handed it to me. "Here, This is to replace the money you spent to buy Jem for me."

I held up my hands and stepped back, unwilling to accept the envelope. "No! I'm not taking that. You *need* Jem."

"You're right. I do need Jem. But you and Lacey belong together, too" he countered.

I put my hands behind my back. "No, I'm not taking it."

He smiled and gave me a hug. "That's okay. I knew you wouldn't." When he released me, he stepped back and shrugged. "And, I'm glad you wouldn't accept the money, because it actually isn't mine, anyway."

"Then why do you have it?"

"I was holding it for Phoebe." Drew extended the envelope to Phoebe."It just so happens that *I* bought a horse today," he said. He took me by the shoulders and turned me toward Lacey's stall. "*That* one."

I whirled toward him, my jaw dropping open. "What?"

"She's yours, Savannah. Consider Lacey as your gift for twelve years worth of birthdays."

I opened my mouth to argue, but he stopped me.

"And, you can't say no. She's paid for."

"This is crazy!" I said, throwing my arms around him.

"No, you want to know what's crazy?" he said. He chuckled and looked down the aisle. "I also bought Buster for me."

"No way!"

"Yeah, I did. You've worked hard to bring our family back together, Savannah. Now I'm going to do my part to really get to know you and Alex again."

I glanced at Alex. His smile told me how happy he was for me, but this didn't seem fair.

"What about Alex's birthdays?" I asked again. "This isn't fair to him."

"Oh, don't worry, I have a plan." He turned and looked at Mom and Dad. "But that's a surprise for later."

Drew knelt next to Jem and laid his hand on her head and looked up at me. "Savannah, I didn't thank you for the sacrifice you made so I'd have Jem. You deserve the credit for where we all are today. You held to your promise."

I tipped my head, wracking my brain. "What promise?"

"You never gave up on me or our family."

If it was possible for a heart to swell instantaneously, then that would explain what I felt. I joined Drew next to Jem and put my arm across his back.

"That's because I won't give up on a dream without a fight, either."

I looked up at everyone else and beckoned to them.

"Come on. Group hug."

Alex and Chase moved first, then I saw Mom take hold of Dad's and Angela's hands and bring them into our little circle. "Come on, Phoebe," I said. "You, too."

She joined us as we encircled Drew and Jem. We locked arms around each other. I heard sniffling, and saw Mom and Angela exchange understanding looks. My heart filled with love and pride. We'd all sacrificed and stepped out of our comfort zones to make this moment happen.

Jem licked Drew's ear as we tightened our circle. And in that moment, Jem taught me a lesson. Conveying love, loyalty and trust required no words.

I stared at everyone gathered here for me, wanting to burn this moment into my memory. When Lacey distracted me by pawing the floor, I looked in her direction, but my attention was drawn to the huge open door to the outside.

I gasped and my eyes widened when I saw the end of the most vibrant, shimmering rainbow I'd ever experienced.

"Oh my gosh, look!" I said, pointing toward it.

Our huddle fell apart as we hurried to the barn's entrance.

Pulling my phone from my pocket, I waved everyone in closer again. "Okay, squeeze in. Selfie time with the rainbow."

I had to kneel and point the camera up so I could fit Jem in the frame, as well.

"Too bad we can't get Lacey and Buster in this, too," Phoebe joked as they jostled into position behind me. "They're family, too, right?"

The ensuing laughs resulted in the happiest selfie photos ever. I snapped a few, then scrolled through them.

"Wow! Look!" I held up the best one. "I captured the pot of gold."

Happiness bubbled inside me. As I moved the phone from person to person, they leaned in and squinted at the picture. Their confused expressions told me that they didn't understand.

"We almost missed it." I bent to lift Jem's chin. Her eyebrows waggled as her brown eyes searched my face. My eyes welled with tears, and I struggled against the catch in my breath before I spoke.

"Don't you see? It's right here." I planted a kiss on top of Jem's soft head, hoping I'd be forgiven for breaking service dog etiquette and touching her without permission. "*She's* our pot of gold. She helped bring us all together. We have family. We're rich."

Then, I realized I'd forgotten my manners. I stepped toward Lacey, pulling the "Perfect Together" token from my pocket. I moved in front of her so she could rest her head on my shoulder and held up the token.

"Thank you, Chase, for this token. I truly believe it has multiple meanings." Then, I turned my attention to Drew.

"And, thank you, Drew —" I stopped and smiled — "No, thank you, *Dad*," I amended, granting his wish, "for your part in so many dreams coming true. What more could I ask for than this big family celebrating with me today?"

I looked at the people I loved most in the world. Although the outcome may not have been exactly as I imagined, I realized it took something from every one of them, and from me, to prove that people should never give up on their dreams. They can come true.

AUTHOR'S NOTE

Each of my books features dogs who have been trained as service dogs. In Finding Atticus, Atticus was a therapy dog used at nursing homes. In Over the Edge, Scout is the service dog for a seven-year old with autism. In this novel, the service dog is for a veteran with Post Traumatic Stress Disorder.

Because in my heart I'll always be a teacher, these novels are an opportunity to not only entertain audiences but to educate, as well. My hope is that readers' curiosity will be piqued and that they will take the time to learn more about some of the issues dealt with in the books. In the opening pages, I have listed a few organizations that help veterans get matched with a specially trained dog that will help improve the veterans' quality of life. I also included a link to a website that has many stories in the veterans' own words in which they explain their daily struggles. I hope readers will go and learn more.

A final group I'd like to mention is Purple Heart Homes based in Statesville, North Carolina. With their permission, the name of their organization was used in *Before I Knew* as the organization that helped a local veteran in my fictional town of Keuka Shores who had been badly wounded and needed renovations to his home.

This organization was founded by two Purple Heart recipients from the war in Iraq. John Gallina and Dale Beatty saw a need among the veteran population returning home from wars that had left many of them with life-altering injuries. The goal of Purple Heart Homes is to reach out to veterans who may need a "hand up" in order to carry on with life independently. They have several programs to meet veterans' needs. Please take a few minutes to check out this wonderful organization. There are many ways you can contribute to this group and make a difference in veterans' lives. After all, they risked all so that we can continue to live in freedom.

https://www.purplehearthomesusa.org/

Purple Heart Homes
1551 Salisbury Rd.
PO Box 5535
Statesville, NC 28687
704-838-4044
855-PURPLE-9

www.ingramcontent.com/pod-product-compliance
Lightning Source LLC
Chambersburg PA
CBHW071205250626
47159CB00001B/213